Praise for the novels of
Jasmine Haynes

"Super sexy . . . I love, love, loved it!" —Bella Andre, author of *Love Me*

"Deliciously erotic."

—Susan Johnson, *New York Times* bestselling author

"An erotic, emotional adventure of discovery you don't want to miss."

—Lora Leigh, #1 *New York Times* bestselling author

"So incredibly hot that I'm trying to find the right words to describe it without having to be edited for content . . . extremely stimulating from the first page to the last! Of course, that means that I loved it! . . . One of the hottest, sexiest erotic books I have read so far."

—*Romance Reader at Heart*

"Sexy." —*Sensual Romance Reviews*

"Delightfully torrid." —*Midwest Book Review*

"Bursting with sensuality and eroticism." —*In the Library Reviews*

"The passion is intense, hot, and purely erotic . . . recommended for any reader who likes their stories realistic, hot, captivating, and very, very well written." —*Road to Romance*

"Not your typical romance. This one's going to remain one of my favorites." —*The Romance Studio*

"Jasmine Haynes keeps the plot moving and the love scenes very hot." —*Just Erotic Romance Reviews*

"A wonderful novel . . . Try this one—you won't be sorry."

—*The Best Reviews*

"More than a fast-paced erotic romance, this is a story of family, filled with memorable characters who will keep you engaged in the plot and the great sex. A good read to warm a winter's night."

—*Romantic Times*

Berkley Books by Jasmine Haynes

WHAT HAPPENS AFTER DARK

PAST MIDNIGHT

MINE UNTIL MORNING

HERS FOR THE EVENING

YOURS FOR THE NIGHT

FAIR GAME

LACED WITH DESIRE

(with Jaci Burton, Joey W. Hill, and Denise Rossetti)

UNLACED

(with Jaci Burton, Joey W. Hill, and Denise Rossetti)

SHOW AND TELL

THE FORTUNE HUNTER

OPEN INVITATION

TWIN PEAKS

(with Susan Johnson)

SOMEBODY'S LOVER

WHAT HAPPENS AFTER DARK

Jasmine Haynes

HEAT
New York

THE BERKLEY PUBLISHING GROUP
Published by the Penguin Group
Penguin Group (USA) Inc.
375 Hudson Street, New York, New York 10014, USA
Penguin Group (Canada), 90 Eglinton Avenue East, Suite 700, Toronto, Ontario M4P 2Y3, Canada
(a division of Pearson Penguin Canada Inc.)
Penguin Books Ltd., 80 Strand, London WC2R 0RL, England
Penguin Group Ireland, 25 St. Stephen's Green, Dublin 2, Ireland (a division of Penguin Books Ltd.)
Penguin Group (Australia), 250 Camberwell Road, Camberwell, Victoria 3124, Australia
(a division of Pearson Australia Group Pty. Ltd.)
Penguin Books India Pvt. Ltd., 11 Community Centre, Panchsheel Park, New Delhi—110 017, India
Penguin Group (NZ), 67 Apollo Drive, Rosedale, Auckland 0632, New Zealand
(a division of Pearson New Zealand Ltd.)
Penguin Books (South Africa) (Pty.) Ltd., 24 Sturdee Avenue, Rosebank, Johannesburg 2196,
South Africa

Penguin Books Ltd., Registered Offices: 80 Strand, London WC2R 0RL, England

This book is an original publication of The Berkley Publishing Group.

This is a work of fiction. Names, characters, places, and incidents either are the product of the author's imagination or are used fictitiously, and any resemblance to actual persons, living or dead, business establishments, events, or locales is entirely coincidental. The publisher does not have any control over and does not assume any responsibility for author or third-party websites or their content.

PRINTING HISTORY
Heat trade paperback edition / November 2011

Library of Congress Cataloging-in-Publication Data

Haynes, Jasmine.
    What happens after dark / Jasmine Haynes.—Heat trade paperback ed.
        p. cm.
    ISBN 978-0-425-24412-8
    I. Title.
PS3608.A936W47   2011
813'.6—dc22

                                                    2011011591

PRINTED IN THE UNITED STATES OF AMERICA

10 9 8 7 6 5 4 3 2 1

To my mom,
because she's a wonderful lady.
Love you, Mom!

ACKNOWLEDGMENTS

Thanks to my special network of friends who support me, brainstorm with me, and encourage me: Bella Andre, Shelley Bates, Jenny Andersen, Jackie Yau, Ellen Higuchi, Kathy Coatney, Pamela Fryer, Rosemary Gunn, and Laurel Jacobson. And of course, thank you to my agent, Lucienne Diver, and my editor, Wendy McCurdy.

PROLOGUE

HE TIPPED HIS HEAD BACK, SAVORING THE FEEL OF HER MOUTH ON him. Christ. She knew every nerve that excited him. Dropping his chin, he opened his eyes to drink in the sight of her down on her knees on the plush navy carpet, her silky black hair cascading down the slope of her back. With red fingernails, red lips, and alabaster skin, she was more beautiful than any model gracing the cover of a fashion magazine.

He groaned as she hit a sweet spot with her tongue. His legs trembled, his tension rising, need pulling at him.

For six months, she'd been his to command. Since the night he'd won her away from Derek, her bruiser boyfriend, in a downtown club. She wasn't made for the club scene, and he'd taken her from Derek as if she were the war prize in hand-to-hand combat, which technically she was, since he'd decked the guy to rescue her.

And what a prize she was. Squeezing his cock, she tantalized him, drove him mad. He thought his head would explode. Shoving his fingers through her hair, he pushed her back. "Not yet," he murmured.

She gazed up at him with eyes the shade of sapphires. "Did I do something wrong, Master?" Her voice was soft, sweet, like the gentle babble of a distant brook.

She insisted on calling him Master as if he were her dom and she his submissive. He'd never gone in for the dominance and submission lifestyle, but after he found her in that San Francisco sex club, he'd read a bit on the Internet. There were aspects of it he enjoyed immensely—tying her down, blindfolding her, a good spanking, toys, forcing her to push her sexual limits—but other elements, humiliation, degradation, making her cry, giving her to another man as if she were chattel—which was what he'd caught Derek doing—that stuff, not so much. She liked to be dominated, but she needed to feel special. She needed approval. She withered when she was ignored.

He couldn't have ignored her if he'd tried. Even when she wasn't within sight, he fantasized about her. Hot fantasies where she was handcuffed, spread out on his bed, and begging him to crawl between her legs. Yeah, he liked the dominant role. "I told you not to make me come yet," he said sternly.

"You should punish me for that," she whispered. "Because I'm such a slut, and I'm bad."

That was another thing she liked, the name-calling. Bitch, slut, even worse. At first he'd used the names because they made her wild. But they made him burn hotter, too. Being with her had taught him how sexy a little dirty talk could be. And then there was the punishment thing . . .

"Get on the bed, whore," he ordered, and his erection surged, his blood pumping faster.

She bit her bottom lip, drew in a breath, her nostrils flaring with her excitement. Then she rose gracefully, her movements steady. He'd closed the blinds against the cold January night, and the soft lighting of his bedroom illuminated her slender body, the elegant curves of her back and bottom. Her limbs were long and lithe, her breasts small, the areoles dusky pink buttons. She was a tall woman at five nine, and barefoot, she was only a couple of inches shorter than him. He'd never been worried about his height; Derek had been taller and bigger than he was, but he'd still won the girl.

She climbed onto the big bed on all fours, her ass heart-shaped.

"On your back," he instructed. "Spread your legs and arms."

She laid down, her pussy glistening. The rich burgundy of the bedspread made her skin glow. "I know I've been bad, Master. You need to punish me and call me the names I deserve."

For her to feel that way, he'd assumed she'd had bad relationships in the past that had marked her with some deep-seated insecurities. Derek the horse's ass certainly wasn't the first. He also couldn't deny his desire for a little tender lovemaking and more intimacy. He wanted to know more about her, exchange more than sex, reach a deeper level. But there was power in dominating her, too. They both excelled at dirty, nasty games. He'd bought the fur-lined handcuffs; then he'd bought the four-poster bed to attach them to. The scarves in the top drawer of his dresser—which could be used as either blindfolds or bindings—hid a variety of toys he'd used on her.

He hoped to God one of his daughters didn't start rooting around in there during their frequent trips home from college.

"Scarves or handcuffs?" He could gauge her mood by the kind of restraints she asked for. "Which do you deserve, you dirty little bitch?"

Her lips parted; her eyes darkened. "Handcuffs," she whispered.

She wanted things a little rougher. Something must have happened at work today. Not that she ever told him much about her life outside the bounds of their relationship. She was secretive even when he questioned her. Her evasiveness was one of the things he'd had yet to break her of, but he would, eventually. Tonight, she'd been tense when she arrived. In fact, she'd been unusually stressed for weeks, and he'd learned that the worse her day had been, the higher degree of domination she required.

"Wider, slut," he demanded as he took one delicate ankle in his hand. She stretched for him, her scent rising, swirling around him. He was hard for her, ravenous, but the night would end quickly after he came. He wanted to stretch it out.

She'd never spent the night. They didn't cuddle afterward. He didn't know precisely where she lived or the name of the company she worked for, only that she was thirty-five, unmarried, no children, made her living as an accountant, and she was promiscuous. He'd gathered that the fact he'd been her only lover over the past six months was unusual.

He took it as a testament to how good he was at giving her what she needed.

She needed the trappings of submission, but what she loved best was making him climax with her mouth and swallowing his come. She relished every groan, every cry of pleasure he gave. If he didn't make her come before he did, she wouldn't come at all. As if she didn't require the orgasm to be satisfied.

But in this moment, he craved *her* climax, *her* pleasure, to feel her body tremble for him.

Rounding the bed, he restrained her other ankle. Then he went to work on her wrists, anchoring them to the bedposts. He didn't ask her if it was too tight; she would merely tell him that she would take whatever he chose to dish out.

"What are you going to do to me, Master?" Her voice quavered, but it wasn't fear; it was need. When she was restrained, he could force her to let go.

"Would you like me to fuck you?" he murmured, climbing

onto the bed, leaning close to draw in the scent of her. She made his head spin.

"I'm your whore. You can do whatever you need, Master."

Need? Christ. He needed so much, all the things she withheld, *herself*. Her thoughts, her feelings, her fears, her joys, her past. Yes, all those things; but for now, he would take this, savor it, until she gave him more.

He grabbed her chin, held her, forced eye contact. "I want to hear you scream my name when you come."

She blinked rapidly a moment, and he knew that wasn't what she wanted to hear. She wanted *his* orgasm. But she was his slave, and she answered the way she had to. "I will."

He lowered his lips to hers, though he didn't kiss her. "I'm going to lick you, my sweet little slut. That's how I want you to come," he whispered against her mouth.

She tensed. He'd never gone down on her when she wasn't restrained. He'd never made her come with his mouth, tongue, or fingers when she wasn't immobilized and unable to fight him. He loved it that way, too, because in those moments, she was *his*, she let herself go. As if somehow the restraints actually set her free.

"But don't you need to come?" Her tone rose slightly at the end as if it were a question, yet she cajoled, her voice like a siren in the night.

God yes, he needed to come inside her, or her mouth. Or by her hand. She could work him up in any way she tried. But he wanted her climax, which was tantamount to her capitulation.

"I'm going to lick you, and you're going to scream." He covered her, flesh to flesh, held her gaze, her eyes wide, pupils dilated, her nipples pebbled against his chest. "Right?"

She gave in. "Yes, Master," she whispered on nothing more than a puff of air.

Then he crawled down her body, tasting her skin as he dragged his tongue over her breasts, her belly, down to the finely trimmed mound of her sex.

"You have the sweetest scent." He breathed her in, then put his tongue to her a moment. "And the sweetest taste." He loved her pussy; she was gorgeous, full, pink, her clit burgeoning.

He swiped his tongue across her, back and forth, swirling her taste in his mouth. God. How he loved this. She writhed against her bonds, and her soft sounds of delicious distress filled the room. He fit first one, then two fingers inside her, and played her G-spot and her clit in tandem.

She panted. Moaned. Music to his ears. Then her legs started to shake, her cries rose, she called out his name, and her body jerked. He kept at her, rode the tide of her orgasm, until she fell limp against the comforter, her dark hair splayed across his pillows.

Her taste lingered on his lips as he shimmied up her body to lay beside her. "Was it good?"

"Master, it was heaven." She swallowed, closed her eyes.

He wasn't looking for affirmation. There was just something too . . . fast. As if she'd wanted to appease him.

"But you didn't come," she added.

He gave her a long, measured look, something inside him shifting. "You didn't come either, did you?"

She swallowed again. Like a nervous habit she'd suddenly acquired. "I did."

"Don't lie to your master." He clenched his teeth against the epithet that rose to his lips. He could call her *whore*, *slut*, *bitch*, almost anything as he was seducing her, but the words lost their sexiness in the aftermath.

She filled herself with a great gulp of air, her chest rising, her skin tinged with pink, though not as if she'd just surrendered to a luscious orgasm. More like . . . nerves.

"I'm very displeased that you didn't come." He used language she understood and responded to.

Yet this time she evaded him. "I'll suck you," she whispered. Straining against the handcuffs, she tugged her wrists as if she needed to touch him. "I'll make you come."

A coldness spread through him. "How often do you fake it?"

"I don't," she whispered, looking at his nose, his cheek, his mouth, anything to avoid meeting his eyes.

But he felt her lie in the stiffening of her limbs. He wondered how many times she'd faked an orgasm, how many times he'd been so wrapped up in her, in what she made him feel, that he hadn't realized how good an actress she was.

Fuck. He was forty-five years old, too old to get rankled, yet the fake cut him. He wanted into her life. He wanted her to know about him, his daughters, his work, even his failed marriage. And he wanted to know everything about her. There were times his gut roiled against her secrets, the way she held him emotionally at bay. But *this* was what they had. She phoned, came to his house, had him call her names, tie her down or cuff her, blindfold her, spank her. When she was at his mercy, he could do anything he wanted. The sex between them was fantastic, but he wanted something more authentic from her, more real, more than just bits and pieces of her life. He wanted a whole night without her rushing away. He'd wanted all that for months, but he hadn't pushed. He'd bided his time. Only to find out she'd actually faked some of her orgasms. Damn her.

"Fuck me," she whispered, and he recognized the deliberate seduction in it. She never said what she wanted, never asked for anything, but she could follow orders. Jesus, she could follow orders and blow his mind. This, asking for it, was different, unlike her. "I'll make you feel good," she added.

Sinking inside her body, he'd feel better than good. When he was buried deep, she took him to another plane of existence. No other woman had done that, not even his ex-wife when he'd still believed her to be the woman of his dreams.

He was being manipulated. She was avoiding what he really wanted from her. He climbed from the bed, stood beside it, gazing down at the perfection of her body in her supine position, losing himself in the shimmer of her brilliant blue eyes. He knew he'd fuck her. Because he wanted her, badly. He had from the moment he first laid eyes on her.

But the game would have to change, the rules revised. He wanted more than sex; he wanted everything. And he would have it. Even if he had to order her to give it to him.

After all, he was the master.

1

BREE MASON HAD SPENT HER ENTIRE ADULTHOOD—MAYBE EVEN longer—learning to handle men. Last night, she'd handled *him* all wrong. She wasn't sure how she'd managed to screw things up. She'd quivered and cried out his name, bucked against his mouth, made all the right sounds, all the right moves. It was so much easier to fake it and give herself the orgasm later if she needed the relief. Where *she* was the one doing it. Where there was no guilt about a man touching her or making her feel good. She didn't really like men making her come unless it was part of her punishment. But this time Luke Raven had known she was faking. How?

He was the only man who'd ever wanted tenderness. He liked to make her come just for the sake of pleasure. Sometimes, she thought he was trying to look inside her soul. She was terrified he'd despise what he saw if she ever let him.

"Hey, Bree, can you come into my office a minute?"

Bree almost flipped out of her skin at the voice. As if she were an apparition that had suddenly materialized, her boss, Erin DeKnight, stood in the office doorway, her finger crooked. Bree's stomach rolled over on principle. Bree always assumed the worst; it was her nature. If you expected it, sometimes you could circumvent it, do some damage control. The last time Erin had called her into her office with that tone of voice, she'd ripped Bree a new one. Of course, that had been Bree's fault. When you act all weird and secretive, it eventually bites you in the ass.

So she jumped up to follow and do damage control if it was required.

Erin was forty, five years older than Bree, but still slender with vibrant red hair. She was smart and assertive, and ran DeKnight Gauges like she was captaining a ship. Erin never seemed to doubt herself, and she never deferred to Dominic just because he was her husband and a man. They shared the company, fondly called DKG by its employees, splitting responsibilities. Erin managed day-to-day operations, including the assembly of the ultrasonic testing gauges they produced, while Dominic, the engineer in the family, did all the design work on the products and most of the marketing. In the six years Bree had worked for them, she hadn't noticed a lot of toe-stepping between them. Of course, after losing their son Jay a little over a year ago, things had been hard for them both; it had been hard on everyone at DKG. But in the last few weeks, something was different about Erin. Where before no one mentioned him, the pain too great for her to bear, pictures of Jay had started showing up in Erin's office again. When she'd brought her WORLD'S BEST MOM mug into work again, it was a complete shock, yet it was almost like an invitation to start remembering Jay again.

Erin closed her door on the roundhouse, which was the central area housing the conference table, shared office equipment, and coffee nook. If you were pouring yourself a cup, you could hear everything that was said in any office that ringed the roundhouse, and sometimes even pick up stuff out in the factory on one side or from the engineering hallway on the other end. When she closed her door, Erin had something to say that she didn't want to be overheard.

Sitting down in the chair opposite, Bree clasped her hands tightly.

Erin pulled on her blazer before she sat behind her desk. "Damn, it's cold today."

Rain spat against the office window. January was usually a nice month in the San Francisco Bay Area; sometimes you could even wear short sleeves. The rains came back in February. But this year was proving to be wetter than the last few. Bree curled her fingers together to warm them.

Erin slid a piece of paper across the desk. "This came in the morning mail, and I just got off the phone with Marbury."

Denton Marbury was their CPA and tax accountant. While Bree managed DKG's in-house accounting, she didn't do any of the various governmental filings except for sales tax reporting, which was fairly easy. Leaning in, she pulled the letter closer with one finger. Close enough to see *Internal Revenue Service* across the top. Her heart dropped to her stomach where she could feel it beating, making her ill with the incessant throb.

"They're going to audit us," Erin said. "I faxed that over to Marbury."

Even if you haven't done anything wrong, your pulse automatically races when you see *IRS*.

"You don't have to worry, Bree. Marbury says he'll handle it, but he needs you to collect all the data they've asked for. He says he'll email me a complete list of documentation he'll need once he's gone over the letter thoroughly."

Denton Marbury. *Ugh.* Of course, he wouldn't email the list to Bree. No, he'd go through Erin first. It was then Bree realized she hadn't said a word. She stuffed down her pissy attitude.

"That's fine. When are the auditors coming?" She tried to sound unconcerned rather than bone-deep terrified.

"The audit isn't until the middle of February, but Marbury needs the backup in two weeks so he can review it first."

"Two *weeks*?" Bree almost squeaked. It was Friday, day five of year-end closing. There was all the reporting to do, verifying the new standard costs, including the standards roll reserve to be amortized over the year, analyzing the work order variances since they'd brought the transducer production in-house, a ton of stuff, plus she had to get started on the 1099s for all their noncorporate vendors, which were due at the end of January. The really irritating thing was that she damn well knew Marbury wouldn't look at anything she gave him until the morning of the audit. He was just that way. He was a big man with a big voice that emanated from deep in his belly until it actually felt like it boomed, and he made her feel . . . less than. She had this terrible urge to cringe whenever she saw him, something she hated herself for. The saving grace was that she never actually let him see her cringe.

"It's a lot to ask," Erin said. "Especially with your dad. Do you want me to get Marbury to call them and postpone?"

"No," Bree said quickly. She could do this. She was organized. She had everything at her fingertips. She didn't want to be considered *less than*. "I'll look over the stuff they want and if there's any issues, I'll let you know." She glanced at the list briefly. "It all looks pretty routine." She clutched the paper to her chest.

"Bree."

Bree swallowed. She knew what was coming. "I'm fine," she said, trying to forestall Erin's words.

"I know you are," Erin said kindly. "How's your dad?"

Bree pursed her lips and hated the expression it gave her. "As well as can be expected." She didn't say he was fine; he was far from it.

"Dominic and I are so sorry about this."

This. Her father's cancer. His *sickness*. "Thank you," Bree said.

"If you want time off, let me know. We'll accommodate anything you need."

"I appreciate that." Her fingers felt numb, like they did whenever she had to talk about *this*.

They'd discussed it before New Year's. Okay, they'd talked about her father after that huge *disturbance* regarding the fact that someone outside the company had hacked proprietary information.

"I know you don't want to think about it," Erin said, "but when the time comes, whatever you decide, you've got our full support." That was another recent change in Erin; she'd become so much better at dealing with sympathy and grief.

"I really appreciate that, Erin." Since the *disturbance*, as Bree thought of it, Erin had gone overboard to apologize for even *thinking* Bree was somehow involved with their sales numbers getting out. See, there was that acting-weird-and-secretive thing at work. She couldn't blame Erin for being suspicious. But they'd gotten over that, and what Erin didn't have a clue about was how much her acceptance had meant to Bree. Erin had validated Bree's feelings about her father's illness; she'd understood the fears. Erin understood all about burying your head in the sand and trying to pretend nothing had happened, or was happening, that everything was absolutely *fine*.

Erin sat back, putting her hands up as if in surrender. "I'm not going to belabor the point. I know you can handle it all, but if you ever feel you can't, just tell me. And this audit is no big deal. Marbury will take the brunt of it. He's assured me."

Right. Marbury had assured *Erin*, but how he treated Bree was a different matter. Whatever. She'd handle it. And what she couldn't handle, she'd fake.

She was good at faking. Isn't that what Luke had said? Thinking of him made her warm, soothed the savage little beast inside her, which was odd considering how they'd parted last night.

Bree rose. "Okay, I've got it. And I'll have the inventory variances analyzed by the end of the day." There were a few parts whose valuations had significantly changed in the standard cost roll for the new year. She needed to make sense of it; could be that the routings were incorrect or the bills of material had errors.

Back in her office, she reviewed the list of audit requirements. It wasn't so bad. The biggest issue was the overhead rates used for valuing their inventory. It would require some explanation, but she'd made good notes in the allocations file, and she'd been using the same methodology since they'd gone onto the new system a couple of years ago. She'd done a demo for Marbury, too.

Her father thought she should be further ahead in her career, at least a controller, but she wasn't a manager, not even a supervisor. No, she was little more than a full-charge bookkeeper. Except that she knew *everything* about DKG. The DeKnights *needed* her. And she was doing well for herself. She even owned her own small condo over in Newark. She was independent. She was *happy*.

But she didn't like change.

Her desk phone rang. "Bree Mason here. How can I help you?"

The voice on the other end was barely more than a whisper. "I just can't do it anymore, Brianna. Please."

Bree's insides clenched. Only her mother called her Brianna, and only when she was really upset. "Why didn't you call me on my cell phone, Mom?"

"Because you wouldn't have answered."

All right, she fully admitted she was a shitty daughter. "I've answered every day." But only once a day because she couldn't handle any more than that.

"I can't take care of him on my own, Brianna." Tears bubbled in her mother's voice.

"He needs to go into hospice, Mom."

"He wants to die here."

Bree concentrated on her breathing. "He'll get better care in hospice."

"This is his home."

Her parents had lived in the same house in Saratoga since before Bree was born. They'd paid forty thousand; it was long since paid off and worth a small fortune, even after the housing dump. Her parents should sell it and get something smaller and more manageable.

Her father refused. He always refused.

"You have to put your foot down, Mom, and tell him you can't do it."

"I could if you came home and helped me."

That was it. They wanted her to come home. They wanted her back. Her father had been diagnosed with lung cancer fifteen months ago. He'd had radiation treatments. They'd arrested things for a while. Until two months ago, just after Thanksgiving, when the doctors found the cancer had moved to his kidneys. Now, it was only a matter of time.

Please don't make me do it, Daddy.

She could not go home to that full time. It was hard enough going over there for the usual Sunday dinner, a habit her mother had pushed her into since Bree had first gotten her own apartment after college. Last Sunday, she was sure her father'd had a stroke. His face had simply collapsed as she fed him his mashed peaches, as if every muscle had ceased to function. He'd looked like a clown, an upside-down smile painted on his face. Then it was gone. He'd finished eating as if nothing had happened. Finally, her heart had started beating again.

She simply could not do that day in and day out.

On the phone, her mother started crying. Bree stopped breathing. Her eyes ached. She sniffed.

"Please, Brianna, help me. I don't know what to do."

Bree thought about what Erin had said just before New Year's, when Bree confessed about her father's illness, his imminent *death*. Erin said she wasn't a terrible person because she didn't want to go, didn't want to face it, didn't want to see it. Erin thought it was a natural reaction for some people.

And maybe it was. But Bree knew she was a terrible person for hearing her mother's cries and refusing her.

Don't make me. Please don't make me.

She was thirty-five years old and praying to God as if she were a little child. God wasn't going to save her. He wasn't suddenly going to offer her another alternative. And in the end, she didn't know how much longer she could live with herself if she didn't go.

"All right, Mom," she finally said, "I'll come. I'll be there tomorrow morning." Saturday. After she'd packed a few things and watered her plants. She couldn't let her plants die.

After the disconnecting click of the phone, Bree held the receiver to her chest, breathing, just breathing. She could do this. She could be strong. She could be like Erin.

But if she had to do it, then she needed something to get her through. She didn't usually ask for two nights in a row from him, but she needed him so badly.

Rising from her desk, she closed her office door with a soft snick. Back in her chair, she hit his speed dial and when Luke answered, she whispered the magic words, "Do you want me tonight, Master?"

2

HELL, YES, LUKE WANTED HER. HE WANTED TO REACH THROUGH the phone lines and touch her, lay claim to her. He sat in the spacious second-floor office of the Silicon Valley company for which he was CEO and dictated to her. "On my terms," he said.

"It's always your terms, Master. I'll do whatever you want."

He'd thought about what he wanted. He'd thought about what she needed. "You must be punished."

"Yes, Master." Excitement lowered her voice to a breathy whisper.

"You will not scream and you will not struggle, slut." The kick start of heat and desire swelled in him.

He could almost feel the quiver of her body as her voice shuddered across the airwaves. "No, Master, I won't struggle."

He would make her beg for release. He would spank her, then he'd put his mouth to her and make her come. He would force the climax out of her.

"What time shall I be there, Master?"

"We're not going to my house. We're going to do this in yours." He heard her sharp intake of breath and felt the pause like a black hole that had suddenly opened up in front of him. "Or we're not doing it at all."

"Please don't make me." Her whisper had lost all the animation of her excitement.

She might not want it, but she needed it. He needed it. "It's time. There's no other way. I'll be there at eight."

"It has to be earlier," she said quickly, ending abruptly as if suddenly realizing she was usurping his authority.

Good. All the more time with her. "Then I will see you at seven."

"I don't have a headboard or anything you can attach handcuffs to," she told him.

"We won't need them. Because you're going to accept everything without fighting me."

She hesitated, then finally said, "Yes, I'll do everything."

Not *Yes, Master*. He wondered at the difference and whether it boded ill or good. Not that it mattered. He'd already decided the way things would be done.

"You need to email me your address." He didn't know exactly where she lived. But now he would own that secret along with everything else.

"Yes." She said it so softly, he almost mistook it for her breath.

He pondered a long moment after she hung up. Despite the dominance play between them, he gave her an extraordinary amount of control. He never called her; he always let her call him when she needed him. He never pressured, never pushed, always gave her freedom. That was the problem; he gave her too much freedom. It was time to take off the kid gloves. He would enter her home, he would punish her, he would make her come. Then he would hold her in his arms, and there would be no rushing out of the bed. He would stay until the morning.

Before he could give rein to fantasies of the evening ahead, he had work issues to manage. He punched in an extension number on his desk phone.

"Yeah, Luke?" Beeman's answer came only seconds later.

"I need preliminary numbers for the board meeting on Wednesday."

Beeman sighed. "Luke, you know that's impossible." No *Yes, Master* from him. As CFO, Beeman said everything was impossible, then it looked like he was a miracle worker when he came across with what Luke asked for.

"We're talking prelim, Beeman. They know it's subject to change."

"I don't have an answer from the auditors on that reserve question yet."

"Put it in a footnote, worst case, best case."

"And there's something wrong with the currency conversions."

They'd built a manufacturing plant over in Germany two years ago, and while the product shipped out of the German facility, the billing was done in the United States. It had given accounting nothing but headaches. The Germans didn't like being told what to do. He understood the issues; they didn't change the facts. All he said was, "Beeman."

"Shit. All right. Prelims by Wednesday."

"Tuesday night, Beeman. I will review them before the board meeting." He never went into a meeting blind.

His CFO growled assent.

"Thank you, Beeman." He was actually a good guy, did his job extremely well. A CEO was only as good as the people he had supporting him, and Luke had assembled an exemplary team.

His cell rang again. A phone, be it cell or landline, had become almost another part of his anatomy. His heart skipped a beat anticipating that it was Bree again.

But it wasn't her number when he picked up the phone. "Hey," he said.

"Dad?" His eldest, Keira. She was a sophomore at Cal Poly down in San Luis Obispo.

"Who else is going to answer my phone, sweetheart?"

"Your secretary."

"She doesn't answer my cell phone."

Keira sighed and he could actually hear her roll her eyes. "I just called to tell you I broke up with Billie."

"I'm sorry, sweetie," he offered. Keira started dating Billie at the beginning of the fall quarter. Luke hadn't met him.

"It's a good thing." But she punctuated her words with another sigh.

"I'm glad you're handling it well."

"He started pulling all this dominant crap."

For a moment, Luke bristled. No one took advantage of his little girl, but one thing he'd taught both his daughters was to stick up for themselves. Keira went on. "He actually told me that he didn't want me seeing Stephie anymore because she was a bad influence."

Luke held his tongue.

"Does he think I'm lame enough to start smoking dope just because my friend does? Like I'm some weakling?"

Keira had been friends with Stephie since middle school. In high school, when Stephie fell in with a bad crowd and started smoking marijuana, Keira stuck by her, hoping to get her back on the straight and narrow. His daughter had always had a good head on her shoulders. She was strong, knew her own mind, and what she wanted. He truly believed that if it weren't for Keira, Stephie would have started using hard drugs, gotten hooked. God only knows what her life would have been like now.

"I'm proud of you for sticking by your friends, sweetheart. There're plenty of other fish in the sea."

"God, Dad, that is *such* a cliché."

He laughed. "I'm a walking cliché. When are you and Kyla coming home for a visit?" Of course, they'd only been back at school for a week since the winter break ended, but he missed them.

"We're hoping in a couple of weeks. After we settle into the new quarter."

"Okay, honey, let me know for sure. I'll tell your mom."

She blew him a kiss before she hung up.

He liked the short phone calls and text messages from both his girls. Keira was twenty, and Kyla a year younger, a freshman, also at Cal Poly; their sound-alike names had been Beth's idea. But really, that's all they'd gotten from their mother. They were far too much like him, both of them. That's what Beth said to him, that she felt eclipsed around the three of them, like she wasn't there, just a mere shadow.

He had a lot of regrets, one of them being that he hadn't even noticed Beth slipping away until that day five years ago when she told him she'd die if she stayed with him. He'd believed he'd been doing everything for her, a faithful husband and a good provider, the big house, any material thing she could want. Something in him had died that day, too. He'd buried the pain if not the guilt, but he couldn't stop being proud of how strong his daughters were. He wouldn't have it any other way. Though he would always be there to beat the crap out of any guys who broke their hearts.

Of all the things he'd done in his life, that was the thing he was most proud of, raising daughters who didn't need him. He'd been so intent on teaching his girls the lesson, though, he'd completely overlooked his wife's needs until it was too late.

Yet for all the strength he'd instilled in his daughters and his wife's grievances, he'd chosen a woman who craved his domination. It was a completely different situation. And hell yes, he was looking forward to the intimacies he'd force on Bree in her own home tonight.

LUKE WAS COMING TO HER CONDO. THE PLACE WAS CLEAN, HER dishes done, her bed made, no dirty clothes tossed on the carpet, no ring around the bathtub. Usually when Bree knew she was going to see him, the anticipation made her giddy. Now she was terrified. She wanted things separate. She wanted dominance in a controlled environment. She wanted to be able to leave when she needed to, if things suddenly got more than she could handle. Like the other night, when he realized she'd only pretended to climax.

Bree took a deep breath. "Calm down," she whispered. Then she went into the bathroom for her cosmetics bag and toiletries and continued packing for the stay at her parents in Saratoga, half an hour and a lifetime away. She'd loaded blouses, slacks, and work blazers into her hanging carrier. Her suitcase lay open on the bed, half filled with panties, bras, socks, jeans, T-shirts, nightshirts, her unfinished needlepoint, and her three favorite DVDs, the Disney version of *Beauty and the Beast*, the twelve-part *Jane Eyre* with Timothy Dalton, and *Pitch Black*. Okay, it was a sci-fi horror flick, but there was something about the pilot's redemption at the end that Bree had to watch over and over. Redemption was a theme in all her favorites. If things got totally crazy at her parents', she could plug in one of those DVDs and melt into it as if she were taking a hallucinogen. Alice down the rabbit hole.

She hadn't told Erin about the move to her parents. She wanted to go through the schedule with her mother over the weekend. Since her commute would be much shorter than it was from her condo in Newark—her parents' house was only ten minutes from

DKG—she could come in later and leave earlier. She could work from her parents' as well, if she had to. It would be okay. She'd be fine.

She couldn't count the number of times she'd repeated that mantra to herself since talking with her mother this morning. But when she really thought about it, being in that house again, she felt so sick she couldn't even eat.

God only knew how she would manage to see Luke. That's why she needed tonight so badly, because it could be the last time for a long time.

Even if she was nervous now, she had to have the kick being with him gave her. He was like a drug; when she felt bad, he forced her to feel other things. He'd saved her from Derek. She'd been in over her head with Derek. She'd met him online, and things had seemed great for a few weeks. Then he began taking her to the clubs. He'd made her give hand jobs to other guys while he watched. It wasn't so bad; she liked that it turned him on. Anything was okay as long as it turned him on. But things started to get out of control. He'd wanted her to give blow jobs, to fuck strangers, more than one. He even wanted to start charging for her services. That might all have been okay, except that he no longer made her feel special. The whole relationship became about making him look like a big man. She was just this *thing* he could order around and give away. He barely touched her; his eye was always wandering. When she balked, he'd said he'd have to beat her. Then suddenly, there was Luke. He took her away. He made her feel precious. For six months, he'd given her everything she needed. All she had to do was hit his speed dial on her phone.

Bree threw the last few things into her suitcase and zipped it. It wasn't as if she'd be so far away she couldn't drop by to pick up stuff when she needed. Plus she'd have to come by to water her plants. Hauling the bag off the bed onto the carpet, she stood for a moment. She couldn't leave it down in the front hall; Luke was bound to ask. She didn't want to explain. That was the thing about Luke, she wanted everything she did with him to be separate. There was her real life, and there was what she did with him. God, if anyone ever knew about her secret life, about the men, about all the things she'd done.

She rolled the suitcase over to the closet, shoved the remaining clothes aside and made space for it. Then she hung the carrier beside it. As an afterthought, she went to the bathroom, grabbed three condoms out of the package she kept under the sink, and shoved them into a pocket in her purse. She probably wouldn't get a chance to see Luke after tonight, not for a while. But she'd still be prepared for anything.

Okay, the room was neat. She straightened the blue comforter, then, glancing around one last time, she backed out. Her condo was two floors; two bedrooms and a bathroom upstairs, kitchen, dining area, living room, and half bath downstairs. In the kitchen, she'd opened a bottle of merlot to let it breathe. She preferred white, but Luke liked red.

When the doorbell rang, her heart began racing again, half excitement, half fear that she'd revealed a big piece of her *other* life to him. Though the time she spent with him was more real to her than anything else. She didn't think he truly understood that.

He was dressed all in black, from a turtleneck to jeans to tennis shoes, a cat burglar like Cary Grant in *To Catch a Thief*. His short hair was black, too, his dark raven looks in keeping with his last name. His eyes, though, were light brown, amber almost. She liked that he was only a couple of inches taller than her. He was powerfully built, with thick muscles uncommon to the usual executive type's physique. If he'd been over six feet, his size would have been too overwhelming.

"Nice place," he said. Flowerpots ringed her tiny front porch. The rain had stopped, and her wind chimes tinkled gently in the night wind. Of course there were also the noisy neighbors on one side, and the pack of children shrieking as they played out in the parking lot.

It had nowhere near the grandeur of his place in Atherton. But it was hers. And the bank's. "Come in." She held the door wide, thinking of the innocent giving the vampire permission to enter.

Except that she'd lost her innocence long ago.

3

THE FRONT DOOR OPENED STRAIGHT INTO THE LIVING ROOM, with the stairs up to the second floor along the wall adjoining the condo next door. Another wall separated the kitchen from the main room, and a small bathroom, just a toilet and sink, filled the space under the tall end of the stairs. She had no one above her, and being an end unit, Bree got noise only from the one side. Luke prowled the living room, looking at everything. The institutional blue gray carpet was new when she moved in two years ago, the white paint job as well. She had the requisite couch and loveseat, though she didn't entertain, and a fairly new flat screen TV.

Luke leaned close to inspect her needlepoint over the sofa, a historical horse-and-carriage scene outside a manor house. "Your work?"

Bree actually blushed. "Yes." Needlepoint soothed her.

"I never would have imagined you sewing."

Why? Because being a promiscuous slut and needlework didn't go together? She didn't say that. Instead she pointed to the others on the walls. "I've been doing it since I was a kid." It had always been a relaxing hobby. Some might have called it monotonous, but she loved how it was always so easy to make it perfect, each stitch the same, the finished parts growing beneath her fingers.

"I'm impressed." He smiled, wandering backward through the living room until he entered the dining area.

She had a table-and-chair set from IKEA. She'd had only her parents over to dinner, once, when she first moved in. For the most part, she ate dinner on the sofa in front of the TV.

"I've got some wine." She held a hand aloft, indicating the kitchen. They'd had sex, done so many dirty things together, and yet she felt as tongue-tied and nervous as a first date.

He laughed. "I forgot. The man's supposed to bring a bottle of something. How remiss of me." Then he leaned in and sniffed her hair. "Christ, you smell good. And I love the tight leggings."

She was barefoot, but still, her lips were almost on the same level as his. Some men didn't like that she was tall; it made them feel inferior. It had never bothered Luke. She gazed at his mouth, wanting his kiss, but she never initiated. Instead, she brushed a hand down her white Lycra top to the waistband of the leggings resting at her hips. "I know you like this shirt." She'd dressed for him. He loved the fact that all he had to do was tug on the Lycra to expose her breasts. She wasn't big, but she had tight nipples that peaked against the material, tempting him, she hoped.

He didn't take the bait, turning to the kitchen instead. "Nice," he said, and he could have been talking about her clothing or her cabinets as he drew his hand across the wood surfaces. He opened one, then another.

"What are you doing?" She didn't know why it made her nervous; she didn't have anything to hide, at least not in her cabinets.

"I want to see what's in your cupboards. Wow, you actually

cook." He turned the spice carousel; she had everything from nutmeg and cardamom to cayenne and Italian spices. On the shelf above sat her bottles of soy sauce, sesame oil, red wine vinegar, cooking sherry, and more.

"I like to make stir fry," she offered.

"Needlepoint and cooking." He quirked a Spock-like eyebrow. "I'm learning so much about you."

"Maybe you need to check the fridge, too," she said dryly.

He did just that. "You like vanilla yogurt. A lot. And milk." Bent down to look inside, he turned his head back up to her. "Two *gallons*? Do you have kids you didn't tell me about?"

Her skin felt hot. "It's cheaper if you buy two gallons at once. I like to make my mocha in the morning." She had a routine. Every morning, she made her own mocha for the drive to work; Starbucks every day was a thousand dollars a year. Besides, she liked routines. They were soothing, just like needlepoint and cooking. If you had a routine, you were in control.

"Thrifty but with expensive tastes, I like it." He opened the lettuce drawer, maybe to see if she had rotting vegetables inside.

She stepped back. "Why are you doing this?" He made her feel claustrophobic in her own home.

He straightened, closed the fridge, the soft *pfft* of the door filling the kitchen. "Doing what?"

"Looking in everything. Checking me out."

He cupped her chin, his touch sending a shiver through her. "You've never let me into your house before. I want to discover everything I can."

He was always asking her questions, but if she didn't answer, he hadn't seemed to care. She'd liked it that way. "It's just that I'm a very private person."

He closed the brief space between them, coming chest to chest, and it was all she could do not to back up. He might have been only a couple of inches taller, yet right now she felt as if he were a giant above her.

"I've fucked you, licked you, spanked you," he murmured softly as he if were whispering love words. "I've tied you up, blindfolded you, and forced you to take my cock and my come down your throat. I think that strips away any privacy between us, don't you?"

His censure made her tremble inside.

He tugged the Lycra shirt down until her nipples popped free. "We have a new rule from now on." He stroked the beads into hard nubs. "When I ask, you will answer." He stared at her hard. "And you will tell me the truth." With her nipples between thumb and forefinger of each hand, he pinched, and sensation streaked down between her legs. "Right?"

She gasped, her knees weak. "Yes."

"Yes, what?"

"Yes, Master." She'd always chosen to call him Master, but he'd never insisted. He'd played her games of dominance and submission, but they were always *her* games.

Suddenly everything was different. He'd turned the tables on her. And God help her, she was going to love it.

"SHOW ME THE UPSTAIRS." AS SHE'D STARED AT HIM WIDE-EYED and spellbound, Luke had gone through every cupboard in her kitchen, asked her favorite meals, her favorite foods. He'd finished the glass of wine and felt the mellowness of it in his knees. Now he wanted her, to fuck her, to hold her, to do anything he wanted.

She was an enigma, and the needlepoint and cooking had taken him totally off guard, as did the number of plants. He'd never seen her as domestic; she was too sexual for that, though for the life of him he couldn't say why the two should be mutually exclusive. He decided that the next time, she would cook for him. Yet he still hadn't learned enough about her. There were more mysteries to uncover.

He followed the siren sway of her slender hips up the stairs. There were two bedrooms, one large, one small. He was surprised to see a sewing machine in the guest bedroom which, as evidenced by the bookcases, desk, and computer, she used as a home office. He wanted to get into her computer. What would he learn there?

"Your room," he said, pushing her ahead of him. A pale blue comforter covered the bed, pillows in shams piled at the head of it. A bureau stood beneath the curtained window and a tallboy on the other wall. On the opposite side of the bed lay the mirrored closet doors.

He could watch everything he did to her in those mirrors.

"I was expecting stuffed animals on the bed." To go with the needlepoints of kittens and puppies on the walls.

She laughed. It was the first time she'd laughed all evening. She didn't like being invaded, and to her, he'd invaded her space with every cupboard and closet door he'd opened.

"They're all on the top of the bookcase in the spare bedroom," she told him.

He padded down the short hall, past the bathroom in the middle, and entered the other bedroom again. Sure enough, cats, bunnies, teddy bears, fish, and puppies covered the top of the bookcase with bright colors and soft fur. The book titles ranged from horror to mystery to romance to classics. But what did it all tell him about her?

Not much except that she was real. With hobbies and reading tastes and a softer side that she'd never shown him.

She'd actually been nothing more than a sex object to him,

everything between them based solely on sex. She came to his house; they did nasty things; she went home. She never stayed the night. Occasionally he'd taken her out for a meal, but mostly to show her off in a sexy outfit. They'd never watched TV together; he didn't know what kind of movies she liked.

He knew only that she needed to be directed, that she wanted to feel forced to do what he asked, yet while sometimes she cried and begged him to stop, she loved it when he punished her. That continued to make him wonder about her past relationships. There had to be something there to explain it. Nevertheless, he would gladly give her what she needed.

Then he would give her more than she'd ever asked for.

"You've been withholding things from me, Bree."

"What do you mean?" She'd followed him halfway down the hall, but as he turned from the spare room and advanced on her, she backed up. She'd tugged her shirt back over her small perfect breasts, but her nipples were still diamond-tipped beneath the Lycra.

"You've never cooked for me."

She gaped. "You want me to make you dinner *now*?"

"Not now. Instead, I'm going to punish you for never offering. A good submissive must tend to all her master's needs, including food, and you haven't done so."

"But I've—"

He was close enough to put his fingers to her lips and cut her off. "A master requires more than sexual sustenance, and you have denied me your full range of skills."

Her eyes were wide and brilliantly blue. A pulse beat fast at her throat. Her breath puffed over his fingers.

He lowered his voice to a whisper. "Take off your leggings and panties."

Without a word, she stripped down, and threw the leggings to the hall carpet. Her pussy was trimmed, the musky scent of her arousal rising to him, wrapping around his mind. His cock flexed in his jeans.

"Go into the bedroom, kneel on the floor at the end of the bed and face the wall." Then he added, "Slut," for good measure.

She didn't hesitate, turning, the taut lines of her ass beckoning him.

This is what she loved, orders. *Do this, do that.* No thinking, no questions. His blood pumped faster imagining all that he would do to her tonight.

He entered the bedroom to find her on her knees, her body already prone across the bed, her arms outstretched, her ass in the air.

"You love a good spanking, don't you, slut?"

"No, Master. It hurts."

He went down beside her on the carpet. "You like the way it feels when it's smarting."

"No."

"Don't lie. I just told you the rule was for you to always answer my questions with the truth."

"Yes, but—"

He slapped her ass with a cupped hand, cutting off her words as she yelped.

He stroked the reddened flesh, dipped down, and found her pussy wet against his palm. "If you don't like it, tell me to stop."

She didn't say a thing. Which was the same as begging for more.

He wouldn't let her get away with simple acquiescence. "Tell me what you want, Bree."

"I want to take my punishment so that you'll forgive me. I want you to call me the names I deserve to be called."

He rubbed her bottom in rhythmic circles. "That's not good

enough, Bree." He refused to use the words she wanted until she begged. "Tell me exactly how you want it."

She turned her head to look at him, her eyes pleading. "I want what you want."

"You think I like to hurt you?"

She rolled her lips together, smudging her lipstick slightly. "Well, not *like* but, you know, um, that I deserve to be punished. I deserve to be called a slut and a whore and a bitch."

Deserve. She wasn't going to admit that she got off on it.

He smacked her again, harder, but still with a cupped hand that did no real damage. She closed her eyes, moaned.

"Did you like that?"

She gazed at him.

"If you don't like it, I won't do it again."

She breathed deeply, then her lips tightened as if she were refusing to speak.

He didn't slap her bottom again. Instead, he trailed the smooth line of her ass until his fingers slipped in the moisture between her legs. "You like it. You're wet. You need more."

She swallowed, but didn't say a word.

His cock throbbed, and his jeans were suddenly too tight. "Say it," he murmured. "You can only have what you want if you say it." He leaned close to whisper against her silky hair. "I order you to say it." Though he stroked up and down her cleft, he never entered, never touched her clit, yet she drenched him with her desire.

Christ, they both wanted it. Goddammit, she needed to say it. He wasn't doing this alone. She was going to admit she wanted it.

Then finally, her lips moved, her words were soundless. "Please spank me. Please tell me I'm your dirty slut."

4

SHE DIDN'T WANT TO BEG. SHE DIDN'T WANT TO *NEED* THIS WAY. She wanted him to just do it.

Bree wasn't a true submissive. She was always in control, giving only enough to get what she wanted. But as Luke's hand descended one more time on her ass, she couldn't help giving in. "Please," she whispered. "I need it."

When he slipped down to her pussy, sliding against her, caressing, she felt herself go mindless with that need. The moan that slipped from her lips didn't even sound like her. She never wanted to think about all the reasons she needed it this way, hot and hard and painful and dirty. It was just the *only* way.

"Your butt cheeks are warm, you dirty girl," he murmured, caressing her. His fingers grazed her rear hole, then he swatted her once more.

It stung but in such a delicious way, the pain zipping to her clitoris and making it throb. *Do it again,* she wanted to beg. *Please, please, make me feel.* Her very skin seemed to quiver beneath his touch.

She clenched her fingers in the comforter as he punished and soothed, slid across her pussy, this time reaching down to glide deeper between her legs, over her clit. She ached. The punishment was all tied up with the pleasure. She couldn't have one without the other.

"Do you want to come?"

"No." Not yet. She preferred to ride the edge. And he wasn't spanking hard enough; he hadn't hurt her enough. With someone else making you come, there was all the guilt and the bad feelings associated with it. Unless there was the hurt first. She only deserved the pleasure if she took the pain. Derek had known what she needed; Derek had been a sadist. Luke was too good to her.

But tonight, he took her again and again with the slap of his hand until every nerve ending tingled and spasmed and the bedspread abraded her nipples with each move of her body. Still, her ass didn't hurt enough yet.

"Look at us," he said, putting his hand under her chin and turning her head to the closet mirror.

He was dark, and with her naked bottom and the white top, she was light in contrast, despite her black hair spread across the light blue spread. Her ass gleamed red. He buried his hand between her legs, and the woman in the mirror groaned. The sight was decadent, naughty, tantalizing.

He spanked her bottom again as she watched, sensation rippling through her flesh. "Come," he demanded, delving deep between her legs to her clit. She shuddered for him.

She bucked and rode his hand, moaned, groaned, then cried out.

He swatted her. "Liar. You didn't come." Then he leaned down and whispered in her ear. "Dirty little cunt."

She quivered. He rarely used that word, but he wanted her to come. He wanted her climax to be real, unlike the other night. So many men had never cared if she faked her orgasms. But not Luke. Why did he have to care one way or the other?

"Harder, Master. I deserve a harder spanking."

"I will spank you until you come. I won't stop until you scream my name and mean it."

He smacked harder, then caressed, a steady rhythm that was driving her mad. Abusing her ass, then sliding along her pussy to stroke her clit. She was wet and quaking, teetering on the edge, gasping, crying. God, it was so horribly good.

He slapped her hard. "Take that, you filthy slut."

Her bottom burned. She wanted to cry out her need. "I'm a whore. I deserve it harder, Master, more."

"Whore." He swatted her again, slid between her legs, abused her clit, stuffed his fingers inside her. It was on the edge of brutal. And so perfect.

Oh God, oh God.

His hand on her, time after time, until she was screaming for him, until the pain shot down her legs. In a blinding flash, she simply imploded, her legs clamping around his hand, her breath puffing, her mind whirling. Then she was gone.

HAVING SEEN BREE IN THE MIRROR, LUKE DIDN'T BELIEVE SHE'D ever truly come for him before, or if she had, it was nothing to rival this. It was the way she said his name, almost on the backs of her tears, sobbing. He didn't know how he could have missed it all those months. He was an idiot.

He closed his eyes remembering her in the throes of that orgasm. Christ, she was gorgeous. The spanking wasn't his usual mild fare; his hand smarted and his heart was only just coming down off the high. Yet even as he wanted to be pissed that she'd withheld so much from him—that he hadn't even *known* the extent of it—it was all too fucking good to let the anger seep in. He'd finally breached some sort of barrier. He was in her house; he'd made her come cataclysmically.

Now, propped beside her so he could see them both in the mirror, he stroked the hair back from her face. "You've done well," he said. "You've taken your punishment and now you deserve your reward."

She opened her eyes and met his gaze in the reflection. A normal woman would have said that the orgasm was the reward. But not Bree. "You want me to make you come?"

She was so quick to give him pleasure, so uncaring of her own. "No. You're going to make me dinner."

She rolled to face him. Without the mirror distancing them, he saw the gleam in the blue depths of her eyes. "I make a mean mu shu chicken."

"And dessert."

She smiled like a glowing child eager to please. "Hot chocolate pudding. My mother used to make it."

Used to? He didn't know whether her parents were living or dead. He didn't know a damn thing about her, except that she was eager to suck him off, make him come, cook him dinner, prepare a favorite dessert. It was all about him.

He'd been fighting that all along. Now he understood how to use it to his advantage.

SHE WOKE IN THE DARK TO FIND HIM WRAPPED AROUND HER. SHE felt overheated, constrained, tied down. And not in the good way she liked when he handcuffed her to his bed. She hadn't expected him to spend the night, but he'd insisted. He'd actually wanted to *cuddle*, for God's sake. "*You will fall asleep in my arms. I want to feel it.*" Rather than melt the ice around her heart, it terrified her. She'd never spent the night with him in his bed. He'd never asked her to. She didn't want to. He was mixing her up by stepping into places she hadn't expected him to go.

Yet he'd loved her mu shu chicken. It was simple, easy, and she used tortillas instead of the thin Chinese pancakes, but the food was delicious. Hot chocolate pudding didn't go with the mu shu at all, but he'd liked that, too.

She'd been breathless with his praise. She'd felt as if she'd performed some sort of miracle. Then he'd made her suck him to climax in the darkness of her bedroom. He said she was the best he'd ever had. Those words were what she lived for. *I'm the best. I'm special.*

Now, lying in her bed, his chest to her back, he shifted, his arm tightening around her. She couldn't move without waking him.

Men, they said whatever you wanted to hear. Until they were tired of you. Until you weren't special anymore. Then they stopped complimenting, stopped saying you were the best. You spent all your time trying to figure out how to fix it, how to anticipate their needs, how to make sure they forgave whatever sin you'd committed that had alienated them. Of course, it didn't work. After that, there was only the punishment with none of the pleasure. Because suddenly you were nothing to them. Nothing. The way Derek had made her feel in the end.

But not Luke. She'd never been with a man this long. They weren't in a relationship, but still, she'd never had a man keep coming back for six months. Of course she knew the fact no one else ever stuck around meant there was something wrong with her; she just didn't know how to fix that.

His breath ruffled the hair at her ear. Through the thin curtains, the light pink of sunrise pushed back against the bedroom's shadows.

She'd never thought of telling him she cooked. Because she lived alone, most people thought she didn't cook for herself. Even her mother asked her if she ate ramen out of a cup for dinner.

She wondered at the other things she could do for Luke, things that would make her special to him.

His hand suddenly slid up her abdomen to cup her breast. A thumb flicked her nipple. Then he pinched her. Bree sighed. She didn't have incredibly sensitive nipples. But when he pinched hard enough, she could feel it all the way down to her belly.

Maybe he'd like her to get breast enhancements. She had a bit of money in the bank, and she didn't think it cost as much as it used to. "Do you wish my breasts were bigger?"

He was silent a long moment, his hand unmoving on her, then finally he ran his fingers in a circle around her breast. "You're perfect."

Like her cocksucking and her cooking.

"Don't change yourself. I want a real woman." He slipped down to palm her pussy. He'd made her sleep naked, and she was already wet. His morning woody throbbed at the base of her spine. "I want everything to be real.

She knew he meant her orgasms. "What do you want me to do to you this morning?" she whispered, her gaze on the sun rising outside the window.

"Spread your legs and masturbate for me. I want to watch."

Masturbation was dirty and naughty, and Luke loved watching. He made her feel beautiful and precious when he watched her.

They shifted almost synchronously in the bed as Luke threw back the covers. His cock, turgid, cast a long shadow. He stroked himself as she spread her legs and tunneled down to her pussy, finding her clit and circling.

"I can see how wet you are."

"It's too dark," she murmured, her body already starting to move against her fingers, an unconscious matching of rhythms. She could come easily this way for him, without guilt, because he wasn't touching her.

"There's enough light. I love the way you masturbate. Close your eyes and pretend I'm not here."

She obeyed, feeling the shift on the mattress as he propped himself on an elbow. Then she slid a finger straight into her channel, gathering her moisture and moving back to her clit. "I'm such a dirty slut," she said, willing him to pick up on her needs.

"You're a filthy slut, and I have a fantasy that will show just how much of a slut you are," he whispered as if he were part of a dream. "I will take you to a club, lay you down on a clean bed, and have you masturbate for strangers. So they'll all see what a slut you are."

She felt something cut loose inside her with his words, his desire. She was suddenly a thousand feet higher on the precipice, her breath puffing through her lips.

"You want to do it because you're a dirty bitch. I need to see how hard my filthy slut will make them. I want them to salivate for a taste of your pretty, naughty cunt, knowing that you're mine and they can never have you."

The names he called her were like endearments, and she moaned to the vision he created. All those men craving her, touching themselves because they wanted her so badly. She thrashed her head on the pillow, his words surrounding her like a chant.

"They will beg me to let them fuck my little whore. I want to know how much they'll pay me to let them have you. Then I'll slam them down, tell them you're mine and they can never have you, not at any price. My slut isn't for sale. She belongs to me alone."

How did he do that, make her crazy? From anxious upon waking up with him in her bed to mindless with desire. He knew that she needed to be desired and special.

"They'll try to fight me for you. But I'll beat them back. Can you hear them, my sweet little whore?" he whispered his seduction.

She could. In that state, above herself, just a body, just sensation, wholly sexual, she could hear men clamoring for her.

"Fuck her, they beg. Let us see you fuck the bitch. And I'll fuck you harder than I ever have while they watch."

She was wet, her clit hard beneath her fingers, her heart racing in her chest. His fantasy, his story, his words went on and on. Her own touch made her fly higher with him, until she reached a pinnacle far above herself. She cried out, plunging into orgasm as if he'd actually entered her in front of a hundred men who desired her, who would pay a million dollars for just one night with her.

When she came back to herself, the room was almost light and tears streaked her temples.

Luke lay beside her, idly stroking his cock. "That was fucking hot," he murmured, holding her with the magnetic pull of his gaze. "I want to do it."

5

CHRIST. WATCHING HER MAKE HERSELF COME HAD BEEN A RELI-
gious experience. He'd loved it almost as much as he loved the
way she sucked him. Afterward, Luke had taken her into the
bathroom, shoved her down in the tub as the showerhead shot
water hard against her, hair streaming down her back, and forced
her to suck his cock until he lost himself in the feel of her mouth.

She'd made him breakfast, French toast with powdered sugar
and maple syrup, and now they sat at her kitchen table. "We're
going to spend the day together," he said blithely. Step one, getting in her house, step two, forcing her to give him more time.

Her head snapped up as if he'd zapped her with a cattle prod.
"I can't."

Such a quick denial. It hit him as if she'd denied everything
they'd done in the last twelve hours. "I'm not asking you to play
out the fantasy I made up while you were masturbating," he said
dryly, although the idea did appeal to him. "I'm merely ordering
you to spend the day with me."

He wasn't a prude by any means. He'd had two lovers before
his wife Beth, and though he'd never cheated while he was married, he'd done a lot in the five years since the divorce. A couple
of years ago, he'd met a woman who loved it kinky, and she

was totally into the club scene. She'd introduced him to it, and for a while he'd been like a kid in a toy store, trying everything. By the time he'd found Bree, his lady friend had moved on, and he was starting to lose his taste for clubs. The sex lacked any sort of emotional connection. But if he went back with Bree now . . .

Against the backdrop of her black hair, Bree's skin was pale, almost ethereal in the morning light. "I'll do that scenario if you want me to."

It sounded as if she'd be happier granting his fantasy, masturbating for a bunch of horny men, than frittering away her day off with him. Then he almost laughed out loud. He sounded like a teenager who'd been tossed aside for the football hunk. Or a wife who had to deal with Sunday sporting events. He was becoming a bit of a pantywaist.

He guessed he'd been silent so long, she felt forced to add, "I have to see my parents."

So her parents weren't dead. The information felt almost like a victory. She'd revealed something of her own accord.

He grabbed on to the trophy and said, "I'll grant you that. We'll have our day together another time."

She didn't smile, didn't acknowledge, but reiterated what she'd said earlier. "I will do that if you want."

"What?" He'd make her repeat it, to state her intentions.

She watched him, streamers of sunlight falling across the table between them and reflecting back up to beam on her face. "Masturbate for you. In front of strangers."

The fantasy set something ablaze inside him, and he'd certainly been hard as a rock while he'd watched her and made up the story. He imagined showing her off, but at the same time holding all the cards. It would be like laying claim to her. And having her accept that claim. It would be as good as having her fall asleep in his arms last night. A first. But this was still the strangest relationship he'd ever had.

"We're not normal, you and I, are we." He didn't ask it as question.

Yet she answered. "No. We're not."

"Most men would hate for another man to see their woman." He found the idea exciting, and his cock was hard again. He wanted her to lay in his arms, to make love with him, spend the night, yet he wouldn't give up the other things they did, the cuffs, blindfolding her, slapping her ass. Most men wouldn't like that either, but he wasn't most men. She wasn't most women. They sure as hell weren't normal, but they were fucking good together.

"You want it, don't you?" she said, fork aloft, the French toast going cold on her plate.

"I want Dickhead to see you're mine." Derek, the dickhead bruiser. But really it was every man out there who'd had her, every man who'd touched her and screwed her over.

"I'd like that," she whispered.

He felt the tightness of need in his chest. If any man had tried to exercise such power over one of his daughters, he'd have beaten the guy to a bloody pulp. But for Bree, for him, this was right. This was some strange step forward for them. "Someday," he said. It was a promise of so many things to come.

She put her fork down and gave up all pretense of finishing her breakfast. "I don't know how often I'll be able to take care of your needs over the next few weeks."

She'd let him into her house, into her bed, allowed him to spend the night, and now she was backing off again? As if saying she'd do things for him at a sex club was like a bone she'd thrown him before she slammed him down. "Here I was thinking we were mutually meeting each other's needs." He heard the acid in his tone.

She stared at her plate, her lips pursed, her hair falling forward to cast a shadow over one side of her face. "I have to move in with my parents over in Saratoga."

He was an ass for the relief he felt that she wasn't going beyond his reach. "Is something wrong? Are you having financial problems?" Without question, he would help.

She shook her head, breathed deeply and exhaled, not with a sigh but as if the air fortified her. "My father's ill."

Her words sent a chill across his skin. He was always misinterpreting her, but then he knew so little about her that he couldn't make accurate assessments. "I'm sorry to hear that."

"He's dying." She spoke to her plate.

Luke wanted to touch her, hold her hand, give her his warmth, yet in that moment, she was further away than ever. Still, she'd told him, and that meant a measure of closeness. "I'm a phone call away when you need me," he told her.

For the first time, she looked up at him, her gaze stark, pained. "I don't want to go, Luke."

Something trembled inside him. He rose, rounded the table, hunkered down by the side of her chair and put his hand on her thigh. "No one wants to face losing their parents." He had lost his. He understood.

The next breath Bree took was shaky. "Do you think I'm an awful person?"

"No," he murmured soothingly. "I don't." He suddenly had a glimmer of why she'd called him yesterday. She needed him; he was her panacea, and that touched him deeply. "I'm here, baby."

She rolled her lips between her teeth, held them a long moment. "What if I call you up in the middle of the night for phone sex?"

"That will be fucking hot." He had the sense to realize that the phone sex would be less about sex and more about comfort.

"What if I say I need to see you and suck you and nothing else?"

He smiled. "That won't be a problem." Though true, he'd made it a problem in the past, wanting more. "Suck me anytime."

She laughed, choked it off. "I just don't feel right about anything."

He soothed her with a hand down her arm. "That's normal."

She snorted, a touch of derision mixed with pain. "I am so not normal."

He wanted to pull her down into his arms and tell her he didn't care about *normal*. He didn't know what stopped him except that she had never wanted coddling from him. He felt like an ass for pushing so hard for what *he* wanted when she was going through such a painful time. But then she hadn't given him a clue. "Screw normal," he offered. "We just decided we're great at not being normal."

"Sex with you makes me feel better," she said, her gaze once again on the table in front of her.

She was trying to explain herself to him. She'd never done that before. She could be seductive and manipulative even as she was submissive. He always had to read between the lines. Now, she was trying to communicate how she felt. They never called what they did *making love*, but she was acknowledging the importance of what he gave her.

"Sex makes me feel better, too," he said, as if somehow he was validating her. It was the oddest conversation, saying little, yet holding so much meaning. *This* was intimacy. "We'll do quickies at lunch, too."

She laughed, sniffed. "I should have thought of that."

"Yes, definitely. You'll suck me in my office." There were all sorts of possibilities he hadn't considered before.

"We could get caught." She smiled, put her hand on top of his as it rested on her thigh.

He felt her mood rising. "I have a lock on my door."

She squeezed his hand. "It would be kinkier to do it with the door unlocked."

Kinkier. And riskier. Yeah. Perfect. She was giving him so much more than she'd ever offered before. *More* than sex. Finally, here was something he could actually *do* for her; offer his shoulder, his strength, his comfort. And a little cocksucking, too.

BREE FELT LIKE SHE'D ENTERED A DUNGEON. EVERYTHING WAS SO dark. Her parents' house had been built in the late sixties. It was a T-shape, with living room, dining room, breakfast nook and kitchen facing the street, and the bedrooms and den along the center part of the T. Though her mother kept the house meticulously clean, dark paneling still covered its walls and the faux-brick kitchen linoleum went too well with the root beer appliances. Bree hated this house, hated its reminders. When would they break down and update, for God's sake? At least if it was modernized, it wouldn't carry such a punch every time she walked in the door.

It was only the memory of Luke's hand on her thigh this morning that kept her from screaming. He didn't think less of her, didn't think she was terrible or even selfish. His words made what she had to do the tiniest bit easier.

Lunchtime had come and gone. Now her father was taking a nap. The hospice coordinator had arrived an hour ago; her father hadn't been well enough to attend the meeting. They weren't putting him in a facility, but at least he'd agreed to allowing hospice in to help. The middle-aged woman gave Bree and her mom pamphlets on the stages of dying and the support services they offered. They'd arrange for an aide to come in twice a day starting tomorrow, Sunday, to help with her father's personal care. When the time came, they could order a hospital bed—there was enough space for it by the window in her parents' bedroom—and any other homecare items they needed. A bed pan, IV, catheter, a tray of drugs by his bedside. Morphine for the pain.

Bree couldn't take it in. Her father was actually dying.

Once the visit was over, Bree had made her mother a cup of tea. They sat at the table in the breakfast nook. Outside, the sky had grown dark with impending rain, but inside, the heater was pumping stuffy, hot air into the small eating area.

"Here's what we can do, Mom. Since my commute won't be as long, I can go into work about nine-thirty, which means we can get Father fed and everything before I go. Then I'll leave work early, say about two-thirty." Bree would tell Erin on Monday, but she already knew Erin and Dominic would support whatever was necessary. "You can have one of the respite care volunteers come in for a little while during the day, too." The volunteer could help with meals or just let her mother get out of the house for a bit. "Plus I can work from here if I need to."

Her mother wrapped her hands around the mug. "Thank you. I couldn't do this without you," she answered, her voice listless.

She wasn't old, only sixty-five, yet the last few months had added years to her face. She'd stopped dyeing her hair, and it was now a harsh gray, not even a strand of her original black left. Bree had gotten her height from her mother, but now she was taller. Back stooped, shoulders slumped, her mom seemed to have lost a couple of inches, and the once vibrant blue of her eyes had been washed out of her gaze.

Bree leaned forward to cover her mother's hands with her own. Sitting across the table reminded her of this morning with

Luke, only then he'd been the one offering the comfort, she the one in need. "I'm sorry it took me so long, Mom."

"I understand, dear."

They'd never been close. Sometimes Bree wondered what it would be like when her father was gone. Would their relationship finally have a chance to improve?

"I know you don't want to be here, Brianna. But I'm grateful that you're doing it for me."

Brianna. Her full name. Yes, her mom was in distress. God, the screws of guilt. Bree sat back, holding her own mug so her mother wouldn't see the tension in her hands. "It's difficult."

"You won't leave me alone at night, will you? I don't want to be all alone in the dark if . . ." Her mom bit her lip. "You know, if something happens."

Yeah, Bree knew. Her mother didn't want to be alone when he died. For just a moment, she was pissed as hell that her father had refused to go into a hospice care facility. It would have been so much easier on everyone, him included, especially her mom, but he had said no. He could be such a selfish bastard.

"I won't leave you alone at night." God, what if she needed Luke? What if she had to see him or go crazy? Did the volunteers come in when you needed to see your master?

"I love you, Bree."

She wanted to say the words, too, but her brain wouldn't form them and her lips couldn't say them. "We'll get through this, Mom."

They lapsed into their own thoughts. The house was so quiet. Usually her father was calling for this, that, or the other. He'd always been a big presence. Though not a tall man, he'd been stocky and thickly built. Older than her mother by five years, he'd made his living as a car mechanic. He'd had his own shop until a few years ago when his customer base dropped off. He'd blamed the failure on the new-fangled electronics on cars, but he wasn't a man who easily changed his ways. That's when he'd gone downhill, when he didn't have his work anymore. The cancer seemed like a byproduct of his disappointment in what life had left him with. The only good thing to be said was that he'd made sure there was enough in savings for her mother to live decently once he was gone.

"Did you hear that?" her mother said, jumping to her feet, knocking her mug over, and rushing out of the breakfast nook. A milky tea stain spilled across the lacy tablecloth, but she hadn't even noticed in her haste.

That's how Bree had grown up, exactly like her mother, jumping whenever her father demanded something.

She wondered if she and her mom would still be jumping long after the bastard was dead.

6

BREE LAID A FEW NAPKINS OVER THE MESS, SOPPING UP THE WORST, then followed her mother down the hall. She hadn't heard a thing, but her mom was hypersensitive. She passed the den, then her old room, the bathroom she'd used, and the spare room her mom kept for sewing. Her parents' bedroom was at the end of the hall.

Pretty lace curtains covered the big window facing the large back garden, where the grass was green and overgrown with the recent rains. Her dollhouse stood in the corner by the back fence, though it wasn't really a *doll*house. As a child, she'd been able to stand fully upright in it. Her father had built it for her eighth birthday. Its shingles were pink, lemon yellow scallops edging the roof and window like a gingerbread house. The bottom of the yellow siding was painted with a border of pink and red flowers, the colors still bright as if it had been touched up in the recent past. As if her father had been out there taking care of it.

Bree clenched her hands into fists and turned away from the sight. The sky had turned cloudy, casting shadows across the bedroom's worn beige carpet. The room's air was stale with bad breath, medicines, and the scent of a body that hadn't been washed well.

A small wheeled canister of oxygen sat beside the bed, but her father hadn't been using it while he was napping. He didn't need the oxygen all the time, only when he'd exerted himself with too much activity, like now, as her mother struggled to pull him up from the queen-size mattress, straining with two hands on his arm.

"I gotta pee," he said in a longtime smoker's gravel, phlegm bubbling in his throat as he breathed heavily.

"I'll help you, dear," her mom was saying, but he batted her aside, muttering curses. "He's not himself," she told Bree.

Not *himself*? The lung cancer was starving his brain of oxygen, and his mind was definitely going. Last weekend when she was leaving, he'd asked her where she lived. But this, the belligerence, was *exactly* like him.

Bree went to his other side, grabbing his arm, and together, she and her mom pulled him to his feet.

"Goddamn, see what I have to put up with," he groused, steadying himself with his hand on Bree's forearm.

See what her *mother* had to put up with. The oxygen deprivation was like Alzheimer's, bringing out his mean streak. What was already there got exaggerated.

"The mattress is too low," she told her mom. "We need to have hospice bring in the hospital bed so it's easier to get him in and out of it."

"I don't need no fucking hospital bed."

Bree ignored him. "Come on, you have to walk. We can't carry you." She tugged gently on his arm, and with her mom steadying him on the other side, they shuffled over the carpet.

He stumbled on the rug leading into the master bathroom, and Bree almost lost her grip on him.

"Goddamn," he said again. "I'm gonna piss myself if you don't get me there."

Her mother *tsked*. "You're doing beautifully, dear, just a few more steps."

Dear. Bree felt an irrational anger at her mother's tone, as if she were talking to a petulant child, not a man who had so often treated her like dirt.

The bathroom was small, but the tub was huge, taking up a good portion, and Bree ended up sidling him closer to the toilet, her mother having to step back.

"You have to unzip him, dear."

Why do I have to do it?

Bree wondered how her mother had managed to dress him this morning, every morning. She hadn't realized how weak he'd grown. Just last weekend, he'd still been walking under his own steam. But there was no time for guilt or blame. Or anything else. Letting him lean slightly against her body to keep him steady, she unzipped his pants, feeling queasy with the chore.

"You have to take it out, Father."

He fumbled, and there it was. Like a worm. Swallowing back the bile that had suddenly risen in her throat, she closed her eyes to let him do his business.

"Bree" her mother shrieked, "he's getting it all over."

He was peeing on the bathmat, the seat, the tank, even the little row of flowered plates her mother had hung above the toilet. It was everywhere.

"Bree, you have to *hold* it."

Please don't make me, Daddy.

She wanted to scream at her mother. But she grabbed his shriveled penis, forced it down, held on until there were only dribbles into the toilet water.

She was going to be sick all over the floor.

"Help me zip him up, Bree." Her mother was now close

enough to shove him back in his pants, and Bree held the bottom of the zipper as her mom tugged up the tab.

"I'll clean up the mess," her mom said.

Then her father turned, as if suddenly he was going to move under his own power. And his foot caught. On her mother's shoe, the bath rug, who knew? He started to go down, and Bree grabbed, pulled, but he was like a dead weight, and her mother was shouting, stumbling back herself, knocking her hip on the countertop. *Jesus, Jesus.* Bree couldn't hold him; she just could not hold on, and they went down in a tangle of limbs, his knees cracking on the floor, Bree's back slamming into the edge of the porcelain bathtub.

Her mother was crying. "Oh my God, oh my God."

He was half on her legs, and Bree couldn't move him. Was he dead? Had she killed him, letting his neck snap when he went down? *God, oh God.* She wanted to lay there and die, never get up, let it be over. *Please, please, God, I can't do this.*

Then she heard him curse. "Goddamn bitches."

And she would not let him beat her.

"He's okay, Mom, we're okay. We just need to get him up." Once he was back in the bed, she would never let him up again.

She pushed his legs off hers, got to her hands and knees.

It took fifteen minutes, her T-shirt was drenched with sweat, and her father's breathing was labored, but they got him back into the bed.

"Have some water, dear." Her mother bent over him, putting a straw into his mouth. He sucked like a child with a sippy cup. When he was done, she fit the oxygen tubing into his nostrils and turned on the canister. "You rest." She patted his arm.

What about me? Bree wanted to shout at her mother. *What about how I feel?*

Her heart still pounding from the ordeal, the terror of that moment in the bathroom, she followed as her mother tiptoed out of the room.

She was so good to him, so patient. Bree didn't know how she did it. Sometimes, she almost hated her mother for always doing everything he said. For always taking his side. For always making excuses for him.

But she couldn't expect her mother to change now. That was the past; it was all over. Now, she was the one to blame for leaving her mom all alone with him. Her mother was simply coping the way she'd always coped, and Bree was the shitty daughter.

"I'm sorry," Bree said in the kitchen. "I didn't realize how bad it had gotten." She hadn't wanted to believe when her mother kept calling to say he was going down fast.

Her mom patted her arm just as she'd patted Bree's father in the bedroom. "It's all right, dear. This whole thing has been very fast. You're right, we need the hospital bed."

"And a bedpan. Even between us, we can't get him to the bathroom."

"What about a walker?" her mom suggested.

"I don't know, the carpet could catch on it." If he fell . . . Bree hated to think about it happening when she wasn't there to help. "We're safer if he doesn't get up at all."

Her mother squeezed her arm, sniffed away the last of her fright. "I don't know what I would have done when he fell if you hadn't been here."

"I'm so sorry." Her eyes ached, but Bree didn't cry. "I'll clean up the bathroom while you call hospice to order the bed."

He was already asleep again when she went back in there. She pulled the curtains against the afternoon light, shutting out the sight of the dollhouse, too. Then she stood at his side a moment. His cheeks sunken, his eyes like big dark pools in his gaunt face. With the *shoosh* of oxygen, his breathing seemed a bit easier after the exertion in the bathroom. He'd been so strong, such a force. When he spoke, his voice had been thunder. When he slammed a fist down on the table, the house shook. When he told you to do something, you did it, right that minute.

He was a shrunken version of the man he'd once been. She wasn't sure he even frightened her anymore.

She was more frightened of how she'd feel when he was gone if she let her mother do this all alone. It was the guilt. She'd only avoided it this long by ignoring it. After he was gone, she'd never get rid of the guilt.

There it was, staring her in the face. The old man was dying. She couldn't ignore it, and she wasn't such a bad person that she'd leave her mother to handle this by herself.

For a long moment, she simply hung her head, and breathed in the stale scent of him. Then she went into the bathroom to clean up the mess her father had made.

IT WAS BARELY TEN O'CLOCK, BUT SHE WAS EXHAUSTED. LYING IN her old bed in her old room with the rain pattering on the roof, Bree was slightly woozy from the wine she and her mother had drunk. After finally getting her father fed, into his pajamas, his pills taken, her mom using an old piece of Tupperware as a makeshift bedpan, and all the other tasks Bree had never known could be so hard, they were drained. He'd fought every step of the way. When Bree had tried to get him to take his pain pills, he'd groused and spat them out. When her mother tried to take off his pants, he'd called her a whore. The language had turned her cheeks crimson, but she just kept on doing things for him. Like she always had.

Bree wondered how her mother could still sleep beside him, smelling his decay, hearing that throaty rattle.

Well, tomorrow, she wouldn't have to. The hospital bed would come first thing in the morning. Along with a portable potty. Jesus, the indignities.

She wanted to go home to her own bed, her own house.

In the darkness, her cell phone suddenly broke the quiet. She grabbed it, her pulse racing. Not that it would wake her parents since they were two doors down. But who the hell was calling her at . . .

Luke. God, it was Luke. He never called her. Yet he must have known how badly she needed him, so badly she could feel her heart pounding against the wall of her chest.

"Hello?" She was sure her voice cracked.

"Are you alone?"

"Yes," she murmured.

"Touch yourself for me and pretend I'm there with you."

"I can't. My parents are down the hall."

"Do what I say. Just don't scream when you come."

"Luke." What was she supposed to say? *My father's dying down the hall so I can't play right now*? She didn't want to talk about it. When she'd made the suggestion to him this morning— God, this morning, almost a lifetime ago—she hadn't really thought of the enormity of it.

"Do it. You need this, baby." He rarely called her pet names, probably because she liked him to call her the bad names, but this one warmed her inside. "You've had a hard day, haven't you." His voice melted her.

It wasn't a question, and she made a guttural noise of despair he obviously heard.

"Let me make you feel better," he murmured.

For a moment, he brought her close to tears. Sure it was kinky, but there was a sweetness to it, a caring in his voice. She so needed that soft, deep, gentle tone that soothed yet turned her liquid inside.

"No one will hear," he cajoled. She felt the rumble of his voice along her nerve endings.

They'd had phone sex a few times when he was traveling. He'd email when he arrived at his hotel and tell her when to call. Usually late. She liked it deep in the night.

She needed it now, even with her parents just down the hall and her father on his deathbed. She needed sex, not talk. She needed Luke to transport her to a place where none of this was happening. She needed *this*, his voice giving her relief and mindless release.

7

LUKE WANTED TO ASK HOW HER FATHER WAS DOING, HOW *SHE* WAS doing, how she was handling it all, offer his comfort. He didn't know details; she'd merely said her dad was dying. Yet that could mean anything from slow and degenerative to something virulent, though it had to be serious if her parents wanted her at home. But she didn't need questions right now.

Bree had always needed a different kind of comfort from him. She'd revealed it at the condo; sex made her feel better. "You're the sexiest woman I've ever known, so precious. The way you touch yourself, the sounds you make. Make them for me now."

She moaned softly, and he envisioned her naked on his bed, legs spread for him, just as she'd been last night. Before he called her, he'd turned off the lights, pushed up the heater to ward off the night's chill, tossed his clothes on a chair, then lay across the bed with his Bluetooth on. He stacked his hands beneath his head and drank in every sigh that caressed his ear.

"Tell me how wet you are," he instructed. He wanted her words as well as her sounds.

"I'm so creamy, Master." She gasped.

Master. She needed more than phone sex tonight. She needed to feel bad, nasty. He wouldn't deny her. "You're such a dirty bitch. When I listen to you, you make me need to stroke my cock."

She moaned deeply. He imagined she'd pushed her fingers inside.

"You drive me mad, just the sound of your sluttiness." He took his cock in his hand. He was already hard and pulsing. "That's what you do to me. It's all your fault, filthy slut." He gave her the words she needed, and his cock throbbed in his fist.

"Oh, Master, I'll do anything for you."

In this state, he had no doubt she would. On the phone, she usually came hard, as if the distance released more of her inhibitions. "Tell me what you'll do for me. Get kinky. The kinkier the better." He'd learned more about her fantasies that way.

"I would go down on my knees and suck another man for you if that's what you wanted." She groaned. He knew it was what she wanted, almost as if it were a token of her fealty.

"I'd love to hold you against my body, your ass to my cock, then lift your skirt and let another man see your pretty pussy."

"Would you let him touch me?" Her breath puffed so close to his ear, he could almost feel her heat.

"I'd let him stand within an inch of you and put his hand between your legs."

"Oh." She let out a deep moan. "I can feel him fingering my clit, Master."

"You love it, don't you, you dirty whore."

"Yes. Because you're holding me, keeping me safe. I love feeling you at my back while he touches me. Oh, oh God." She panted.

"I tip your head back and kiss you while he's fingerfucking you. I can feel the ripples of pleasure straight through your body into mine." Christ, he was so hard he almost couldn't speak. He got off on the fantasy of giving her away, being totally in charge of her body, owning her. But the words were important, his only tie to her over the phone. "I want him to lick you, get down on his knees and worship your pretty, slutty little pussy."

"Yes, Master, make me do anything, Master." She made soft cries that reached up inside and took possession of him.

"Master, Master, Master," she chanted softly, obviously with enough thought left to keep her voice quiet.

Yet he wanted her out of control and screaming, willing to do anything for her master. "I want to fuck you while he's licking you." He let himself be caught up in the fantasy, too, imagined unzipping his pants and shoving inside her while the other man licked her clit.

For a moment, there was nothing but the sound of her sighs and moans, her soft chants, then the huff of her orgasm filtering through her voice, and he climaxed across his abdomen.

"Jesus," she swore.

"Christ," he punctuated. Then he laughed. "Baby, you never cease to amaze me."

Her only answer was the puff of her breath as she calmed.

"Do you feel better?" He had to know he'd done the right thing for her.

"I feel sleepy." Her voice had the dreamy quality of satiation and exhaustion.

"That's good."

"I was thinking too hard. Now I don't have to think anymore."

Wasn't that exactly what he'd hoped for, that his words would help her step off the merry-go-round of life and death so she could rest.

"Sleep, baby. I'll talk to you tomorrow." He waited a beat; there was no sound but her breathing and he thought she'd already dropped off. He was just about to hit End.

"Luke?"

"Yeah, baby?"

"Thank you. That helped." She sighed, then there was the silence of dead air.

He cleaned up in the bathroom, then stretched out on the bed once more. His body now sated, he felt a sense of power. He'd anticipated her and given her what she needed. He enjoyed the element of kink to it, got off on calling her a slut and imagining other men touching her. As long as he was in control, the one calling the shots, allowing only so much, then cutting the other guy off at the knees.

His cell rang, and in the dark, his heart raced. She needed him for more. Perfect. "I'm here," he said softly, waiting for her voice.

"Dad?"

Shit. He threw the covers over himself as if Keira could see, his sense of satisfaction disappearing in a flash like he'd been caught at something. And fuck if he hadn't. It was kind of laughable. What if he'd opened the conversation with something dirty? Je*sus.* "What's up, kiddo?"

"I miss Billie. Even if he is a butthead," she said softly.

"Sweetie, you'll be okay. You're strong." And Billie was a dickhead if he couldn't accept Keira the way she was, perfect. He'd spent his entire fatherhood teaching her and Kyla not to take shit from anyone, to stand up for themselves. He was so damn proud of them both.

He hung on the phone with Keira for the five-minute call. Until she blew him a good-bye kiss and told him he was wonderful for making her feel better.

He'd been a great dad, but in his quest to give his daughters what they needed, he'd also ended up being a poor husband. He'd ignored Beth's needs, never even figuring out what they were. As he laid the phone on his bedside table, it came to him that Bree was his second chance at getting it right. Sure, he enjoyed all the kinky stuff, the naughty punishments she craved, the dirty words, but now was his opportunity to take care of her, too. No way was he fucking that up.

"DO YOU HAVE A MINUTE?"

Erin started. Bree stood in her door. She was always so quiet that, despite the fact the desk faced the door, Erin hadn't even noticed the shadow of Bree's movement. It was unnerving the way the girl moved so silently. Like a wraith.

She shook off the thought. "Sure, come in."

Bree closed the door. Unusual. Erin feared this meant Bree's father hadn't improved over the weekend.

"I need to adjust my work hours," Bree said as she sat in the chair opposite.

She was striking, with long black hair and unblemished skin. At her height, she could have been a model. Today, she'd dressed in jeans, a white shirt, black vest, and a black jacket, a combination that came off as completely sophisticated on her. They didn't have a dress code at DKG, except that one needed to at least look presentable, but Bree wasn't generally the jeans type. Sometimes she dressed as if she were the auditor she'd started out as before she couldn't take the lack of routine that came with moving from assignment to assignment.

Erin had always felt there was more to Bree's work history than that. She *needed* routine. Erin was sure that characteristic added to Bree's unsettled emotions about her father's illness.

"Take all the time you need, Bree. Set your own schedule."

Bree dropped her head slightly, her hair falling forward to obscure her face. "I was thinking that if I could come in by ten, do my stuff, then try to leave again at two-thirty." She tucked her hair behind her ear and glanced up as if pressed to make eye contact. "I can work from my parents' house, too."

"Are you going to stay with them?"

"Yes. My mother can't do it alone." She clasped her hands, holding them so tightly they turned white. "We had a hospital bed brought in yesterday. The man was very nice. He set it up and helped my father into it. And the hospice aides have already started coming in to help him—" She stopped, her lips parted, and her dark eyes glazed as if she were seeing all the indignities her father had to endure at the hands of strangers no matter how well intentioned they were.

"I'm sure it's very difficult for you and your mom. But you're doing a good thing, Bree, as hard as it is." Erin knew Bree hadn't been able to face it. No one can really *face* it. Erin understood all about losing someone. There were still moments when she saw something that reminded her of Jay, like his favorite Pop-Tarts at the grocery store, when she felt like her legs would collapse under her. But then she'd force herself to move down the aisle, to keep going. Somehow it was getting easier to talk to Bree about grief, to do what was necessary, to say the right things.

"My mom's great," Bree went on quickly. "She's stoic. And my dad, you know, he's such a special guy and it's really hard for her to see him like this. But he's been very careful over the years to make sure she's taken care of."

"That's good. I'm sure he's very proud of all you've accomplished, too."

Bree started tapping the heels of her shoes on the carpet. "Oh yeah. He's a mechanic, he had his own shop, and he was really proud when I graduated from college. Yes, that's really why this has been so hard, facing that he'll be gone and all, and he's such a special man. I just don't know what it'll be like for my mom. But I'll be there to help in any way I can."

It wasn't that Bree's tone was false. It wasn't even how quickly she spoke or that her heels kept beating out a rhythm on the carpet and her knuckles were white. It was that Bree simply didn't talk. She said what was necessary. She smiled at appropriate times. She laughed when you'd expect her to. But she wasn't effusive. Erin didn't think she even dated. She never talked about any boyfriends. She was completely private, and this was the most she'd said about her mom and dad. Ever. It was as if she had to explain away the indecision she'd felt over the last couple of weeks, as if she believed Erin would think awful things about her.

Well, hell, Erin was the one who had to explain away how badly *she'd* treated Bree. Back before year-end, she'd known something was wrong, but Bree was so tight-lipped. And Erin, well, she'd completely misinterpreted and because of the whole patent infringement problem they were having at the time, she'd said things she didn't mean. That's when Bree confessed that her father was dying.

It had been like a brick to the head.

Erin hadn't offered enough empathy then, but she was damn well going to offer Bree anything she could now. "You don't need to come in at all. We'll manage."

Bree gasped. "It's year-end reporting time. There's so much to do. And the IRS audit."

"Just send Marbury your spreadsheets. He can handle it. That's what we pay him for."

Bree gave a rapid left-right look as if she was searching for answers in her peripheral vision. "I'll explain whatever he can't understand."

"And show Rachel how to enter the cash receipts and match up the vendor invoices." Erin tapped her head with two fingers. Stupid. "I don't know why I didn't think of that before."

Bree flexed her fingers and rolled her lips between her teeth as if she were trapping everything inside.

"It's all right, Bree, let us help you."

Erin counted the seconds that Bree stared at the stapler on her desk. Ten. It seemed a very long time. "I appreciate it." Then finally she looked at Erin. "But I need to come in for a little while every day. Please let me."

Duh, Erin should have understood right away. Bree didn't need the work. She *needed* a break from home for a few hours. Things had been so different for Erin. She'd lost Jay in the blink of an eye. She didn't know how she'd have felt or what she'd have done if she'd known it was coming. And he was just a little boy. Bree's father was at the end of his life. The emotions were poles apart. She would never think of Jay without the ache of loss, but over the past couple of months, Dominic had helped her remember the joy of her son, too. And she'd *needed* that joy.

What Bree was dealing with wasn't the same. "You come in whenever you want," Erin said softly. "And you leave when you need to. At a moment's notice."

Bree's eyes glimmered with something, not quite tears, but a shimmer of emotion. "I'll get everything done, I promise."

"I know you will. You're the best accountant I've ever had. I have complete faith in you." Erin felt a twinge in her gut about that one moment when she *hadn't* shown complete faith. But that had been more about herself, her own emotions at the time, and not really about Bree at all.

"Thank you, Erin."

For once, Erin felt like she'd said the right thing. Bree was so quick to find fault with herself. She needed to be told she was okay. Sometimes Erin simply forgot that.

8

BREE'S HEAD ACHED WITH AN INCESSANT POUNDING AT HER TEMples. It was Monday morning and last night, she and her mother had once again eased the tribulations of the day with a couple of glasses of wine. She should have drunk more water before she went to sleep. Or taken an aspirin. Instead, Luke had called her. She'd come. It had been mind-numbing, exactly what she needed. It could only have been better if he'd been standing at the foot of her bed watching. She'd appreciated that he didn't ask questions, that he told her eloquently and explicitly how good she was, how special. *Precious*.

But that was last night, and this was today. She'd forced herself to talk with Erin, and Erin was fine about her shortened hours. The rain had stopped, and the sun had begun heating the office through the window that overlooked the parking lot. The leaves of her philodendron seemed almost iridescent in the sunlight. She'd coaxed it from a six-inch pot to a massive growth of greenery that hung down in vines from the top of the bookshelf. Somehow taking care of that plant soothed her in dark moments. She couldn't quite believe she'd made it blossom into this lushly gorgeous foliage that practically took over the office. It was the one thing she seemed to have done right.

"How's your mom doing?" Rachel asked. They were seated at Bree's desk, Rachel in front of the computer. As Erin had dictated, Bree was teaching Rachel the ins-and-outs of invoice matching and cash receipts.

Rachel was DKG's receptionist, pretty, blonde, four inches shorter than Bree, two cup sizes bigger, divorced, and a single mother of two teenage boys. Except that her husband had dual custody. Did that mean she *wasn't* a single mom since the kids' dad got them every other week? Bree wasn't sure how that worked.

"My mother is stoic," Bree said.

Which didn't necessarily mean her mom was okay, but Rachel took it that way. "I'm sure she's glad you're there to help."

Bree dipped her head, letting her hair fall across her face. She'd just had virtually the same conversation with Erin, and dammit, she'd come across as a diarrhea mouth. What was all that about her dad being so proud of her? The words just seemed to tumble out. All right, she'd wanted Erin to forget all the other things she'd said before about not wanting to go home to take care of her father. Because that sounded so bad, like she was an ingrate.

Erin had been supportive, suggesting Rachel help out. Yet the moment Erin offered, Bree had wanted to shout; no, no, no, she needed those routine tasks herself. They relaxed her, they were easy, and she felt like she'd accomplished something.

She had to admit, though, it would help for now. There was shipping, receiving, cash receipts, and purchase order documentation in the system. Bree could double-check Rachel's work from her parents' home. Rachel was smart, eager to learn something different and take on new responsibilities.

Except that Bree didn't like asking for anything from anyone because then she'd feel beholden to them with few ways to ever pay them back.

She had to stop thinking about that. Erin had made the decision, and here they were. The problem was that Rachel always wanted to make sure everyone was okay. She liked to talk, though she didn't spread rumors or gossip. If you told her something in confidence, it didn't go any further. She'd known Bree's father was ill before Bree even told Erin. It had happened during one of those moments of stress when Bree hadn't been able to hold back, when she'd lost control for a very short tick of time. Rachel was there to see the chink, and that seemed to make her feel she had a license to talk. And that Bree would want to talk back.

Bree *could* have talked, if she was a different type of person. She'd given a few details to Erin, but she could have gone further and told Rachel about the big, kind man who'd brought the hospital bed yesterday morning, his gentle, soothing Southern accenth that sounded like a melody. How he'd set the bed up right in front of the window because he wanted her father to feel the sun on his body during the day. How easy it had seemed for him to carry her father to it, and how meekly her father had accepted. Bree had watched from the far side of the bedroom so she didn't have see out the window. When the man was done, Bree had followed him back out to his truck like a puppy wagging its tail, dying for attention, unwilling to let him go, needing that contact, even from a stranger, someone who had *helped*. She'd almost cried when he drove away and she was alone again with her mother and her dying father.

But Bree wouldn't tell Rachel all that. Instead she said, "Yes, at least my mom's not alone anymore."

"Except for right now, and here I am pestering you with questions when you should be showing me stuff so you can get back home."

Bree felt a little blip of guilt in her belly. "I didn't mean it that way." The truth was she didn't want to rush things because then she'd have to go back too soon.

"I know you didn't." Rachel pointed at her chest. "*I* did. So you were telling me about the POs."

Bree pushed back from the desk and rose to tap the top drawer of the filing cabinet. "Purchase orders, receiving documents, and supplier invoices all go in here. You match the purchase order with the receiver, then with the invoice when you get it. I also put a copy of the check it's paid on in the vendor file as well. You follow the same procedure with receivables." She tapped the next drawer down. "Customer order matched to shipper matched to invoice, then a copy of the check they pay us on." She sat again.

"It sounds pretty simple."

"It is. You'll be fine. Let's do a few matchings in the system so you get the hang of it." Bree pushed a vendor invoice in front of Rachel who was already seated at the keyboard. "Open the accounts payable module, and I'll show you how to see the open receivers. You can search by vendor or purchase order."

Together they went through first the vendor invoices, then customer invoices and cash receipts for both wire transfers and checks. Rachel filed everything, then filled out the deposit slip for the physical checks that had to go to the bank. Rachel usually did the bank runs anyway.

"Wow," she said, sitting back and smiling. "I didn't make too many mistakes."

"It's a piece of cake once you get used to the system." It was all mindless work that Bree liked to do late in the afternoon when she was tired. "It's only a problem when a customer or vendor doesn't reference the PO or the part number or they don't put what invoices they're paying on a check, crap like that."

"And you do all this stuff yourself?"

Bree gave her a look. "Yeah."

"But you're an accountant. This is all clerical."

"I'm just a bookkeeper really." It wasn't like DKG had money to throw around. Erin did grunt work, too; they all did.

"But you have a *degree* in accounting." Rachel wasn't letting up, staring at Bree wide-eyed. "You shouldn't be wasting your time on clerical duties."

She made it sound like Bree devalued herself. Or was Rachel buttering her up?

Rachel's eyes suddenly lit with enthusiasm. "I bet Erin has tons of important stuff she needs you to do instead of inputting invoices. I do all *her* filing. And Yvonne's, too." Yvonne Colbert was their inside sales manager. "Sometimes Erin has me input purchase orders, too. Let me talk to her and see if I can take over some of this stuff for you on a regular basis."

For a moment, Bree felt a stab of terror, as if giving away even her simplest tasks made her less valuable, less needed. Yet she could hear her father's voice. *"I spent all that money on a college education just so you could be a peon at some two-bit company run by a couple of flakes who don't know they're asses from a hole in the ground? You don't have a hope in hell of ever making a hundred K."*

Bree swallowed with difficulty. Erin and Dominic weren't flakes. They'd built DKG from nothing; now their gross revenue was over five million. But Bree's father was right; she hadn't done much with her career. She wasn't a controller. She wasn't even a supervisor. She was a peon.

Something must have shown on her face because Rachel jumped in. "Only if you want me to help out, Bree. I just remember that sometimes you stay late or come in on the weekends."

Or she worked from home. She was salaried and didn't get

paid for extra hours. Not that Erin made her do a lot of overtime. But with the IRS audit coming up, she didn't know how she'd get everything done.

"Besides," Rachel went on as if she were making a sales pitch, "I can add accounts payable and accounts receivable experience to my resume. You'd be doing me a favor." Rachel was so eager about everything; she got an idea and she ran with it, like she was fearless. Bree always had to think, weigh the consequences, make sure she wasn't making a mistake. Except about sex. But then a person was never careful when it came to addictions.

"Then you'd be overloaded," Bree said, cutting off that last thought. Maybe handing off the matching to Rachel was a good idea. There was other stuff that needed doing, like reviewing the fixed assets, especially with the IRS looking at everything. The tax books were complicated, different from regular reporting with all the asset classes, lives, conventions, and depreciation methods like MACRS and AMT.

"On occasion, I have to ask Erin to search for things for me to do," Rachel continued the pitch. "Besides, I get paid for overtime if she authorizes it."

Rachel wanted the experience. What would be wrong with that? It wasn't like Bree would be taking advantage. She was always so worried about paying people back for what they did for her; well, here was a way to give something back to Rachel.

What if Rachel did a better job—and at cheaper pay—and Erin didn't need Bree anymore? The thought hit her like a low blow. God, she had to stop thinking like that all the time. She wasn't completely useless. She had value. *I'm good enough, I'm good enough.* It was a mantra she had to keep repeating to herself, and she still didn't always believe it. But Erin wouldn't fire her. Bree would make herself indispensable with other stuff, like taking care of the IRS with Marbury and not having to get Erin involved at all. Then, finally, everything would get back to normal when her father was dead.

Jesus. That was harsh. She swallowed, and even her saliva hurt going down.

"So what do you think, Bree? Is it a good idea?" Rachel asked.

Stop thinking bad thoughts, stop thinking.

"Yeah," she finally said. "We'll talk to Erin together."

Rachel smiled as if a beam of sunlight had lit her face. "Thanks. You won't regret it." With that, she turned the situation around as if Bree had truly done her the favor.

HALF AN HOUR LATER, BREE STARED AT THE PHONE LIKE IT WAS a snake ready to jump on her. Not that snakes could jump, but she'd had nightmares in which they did.

Rachel had taken all the matching back to her desk, and when she was done, Bree would check it. She was sure there wouldn't be anything wrong.

Now she had to call Marbury. No more excuses. His receptionist answered and put Bree through. It was pathetic the way her heart pounded in her chest. Marbury was *just* their accountant; that was all. He couldn't hurt her or anything.

"Marbury here." His voice boomed deeply and forced her to hold the receiver away from her ear.

The sound made her grit her teeth. "Hi, Mr. Marbury, it's Bree Mason."

"Bree," he singsonged loudly. "Erin told me she got my list. Having problems with it already?" He laughed. It wasn't a nice sound.

"No. I wanted to tell you I'm emailing the files. All the information you need is in the spreadsheets." She held her breath. He'd find something wrong with the idea, she was sure.

"Well, now, Bree, that means we're going to have to print everything out over here and that's going to cost some extra time to have Clarice do it." Clarice was his receptionist. She never looked all that busy when Bree stopped by to drop something off. "And time is money," he added.

"Erin says she's not worried about that. It'll save us the time." *Us.* The all-important client. Marbury always acted as if *he* were the customer. At least he did when he talked to Bree, though not so much with Erin.

"I'm sure there are pages we don't need to see, Bree. We'd be wasting all that *time*," he emphasized. "Why don't you print out what you think we need and drop it by. I'm sure that would be easier for everyone concerned, don't you?" He said it with what she thought of as *the idiot* inflection. As if she was too stupid to know it and needed a reminder. "And cheaper," he added as the kicker.

She gritted her teeth. Dammit. His office was actually on the way to her parents. It was smarter to print out the appropriate pages because, double damn, he was right, he didn't need everything in the files. Bree should have suggested that to Erin. But yet again, Denton Marbury had pointed out her failings.

9

BREE SPENT ANOTHER HALF HOUR PRINTING WHAT MARBURY
would need. By then it was a quarter to two, and she took off
since she'd told her mom she would leave work by two-thirty
anyway.

She was there in five minutes. Marbury's office sat atop a row
of small shops that included a dry cleaner, an insurance company,
a hair salon, and a Chinese restaurant. The scent of cooking oil
and spices followed her up the stairs. Her stomach growled;
she'd forgotten lunch. She didn't tell people that sometimes she
forgot to eat. In a world where just about everyone was dieting,
the few times she'd said anything about forgetting a meal, people
looked at her like she was an alien. Then they got hostile, as if
she were holier than thou and trying to make them feel bad. But
where some people turned to food when they were stressed, she
was the opposite; food made her sick. That was another thing she
didn't tell people.

The outer office consisted of Clarice seated at a very big desk
with her computer monitor, keyboard, and phone all within
reach, and a host of office machines lining the walls, including a
combination printer with scanner, fax, and copier, a color printer

for presentations, and of course a coffeemaker and large refrigerator. Denton Marbury was a large man.

The high-speed printer was spitting out documents while Clarice talked on the phone's headset and tapped on the keyboard. She'd fashioned her honey blonde hair into a ponytail on the crown of her head. At close to fifty, she seemed a bit old for ponytails, but she'd once confided to Bree that a tight ponytail was cheaper for stretching out the wrinkles than cosmetic surgery. And it seemed to work for her.

She held up a finger to keep Bree for a moment, her polish the most amazing neon orange that actually seemed to glow. Marbury was closeted in his office. Whenever Bree had an appointment with him, he always made her wait, sometimes only a few minutes, but always long enough to show his superiority.

But with his office door closed, escape might very well be hers. Bree merely waggled the manila envelope of documents, mouthed "I'll leave them," then slid the package onto the edge of Clarice's desk.

She almost made it out the door.

"Bree." The deafening voice raised her hackles. Even when Denton Marbury was trying to whisper, he boomed. The sound matched his body. He was six-foot-three and wide like an ex–football player who'd stopped pumping iron long ago. Because he was tall, she didn't think of him as fat; she wasn't even sure he was, there was just so much meat to him. He wore a light brown shirt, brown tie, and brown pants, and all the unrelenting brown seemed to amplify the bulge of his belly.

Okay, if she had an appointment, he kept her waiting. But if she was trying to sneak in, he had some unnatural radar to catch her. He always had to get his pound of flesh, so to speak. "Mr. Marbury, I have to run. Erin needs me right back."

"Why, I just talked to Erin and she said your father's ill and you're working half days." He smiled. He had the square jaw, fleshy lips, and perpetual five o'clock shadow of the Fred Flint-stone cartoon character. He held up his watch. "My understanding was you were on your way home." He didn't offer sympathy or condolences. Not that she'd have known what to say if he had.

She certainly shouldn't have lied, though. She shouldn't have offered an excuse at all. But he always made her feel as if she owed him something. "I have to run another errand for Erin, then I'm on my way home."

"What do you have to do for her?"

Most people would never even ask the question. If you were making an excuse, they'd let you get away with it. Because really, what skin off their nose was it? It wasn't his business anyway. But Denton Marbury *always* pushed her. He was a total asshole, and if she wasn't so pathetic, she'd tell him so.

"Denton, Roger says he needs to talk to you."

Marbury didn't bother to glance at Clarice as he snapped out, "Tell him I'm busy."

Clarice was silent a beat, then clucked her tongue. "He heard that, and he says that if you're too busy to talk to him, he's too busy to write you a check."

Bree wondered why *she* couldn't think of something pithy and brilliant like that to tell him when he was bullying her.

Marbury growled. "Fine. I'll be there in a second." Then he turned back to Bree. "We need to schedule a time to go over the documents."

Bree wanted to say that they were self-explanatory. At least for anyone who knew accounting *and* did DKG's taxes, but with certain people, it was just better to avoid confrontations. "Fine," she told him. "I'll look at my calendar when I get to work tomorrow."

"Be sure to call me," he said. Not *okay, give me a call when it's convenient* or *that'll be good.* No, he had to say it like she was a bimbo who would forget or simply ignore him.

Wouldn't she just *love* to ignore him. "I will." But gosh, with all the stress she was under, she was sure she'd promptly forget.

Behind him, Clarice shooed her away with a get-while-the-getting's-good hand gesture. Bree was well aware that Clarice had come to the rescue with that phone call.

Leaving, she felt like a frightened mouse scurrying away from the cat with the huge claws. She didn't know why she let Denton Marbury intimidate her. He wasn't even that smart or great at tax work. She'd had to call him lots of times about errors she found in the tax forms when she reviewed them. He always managed to make it sound as if her work papers were at fault. Not. But she could never tell Erin. She didn't want to be caught in the middle. Besides, it was humiliating to have to ask Erin to fight her battles.

As she climbed into her car, Bree realized her heart hadn't stopped racing. She felt almost dizzy, she was breathing so fast. After even a few minutes around Marbury, the thought of returning to her parents turned her stomach queasy.

Please don't make me do it.

She stared at her cell phone on the passenger seat. Almost as if her hand wasn't part of her, it reached for the phone. She couldn't see Luke tonight. She couldn't see him for all the nights it took for this to be over. But God, she *needed* him.

He answered on the first ring. As if he'd been waiting for her. As if it didn't matter that he had to interrupt a meeting or get rid of someone in his office or cut off another call; he'd do it for *her.* He was a busy CEO, but he always answered.

"What's wrong, baby?" he said after her hello. He could gauge her mood almost from her first word.

"Bad day," she whispered. Bad day, bad month, bad life. "But I can't see you tonight."

"Where are you now?"

"On my way back to my parents."

"Meet me for coffee."

"It's the middle of the day," she protested. He saw her only at night. As if they could do the things they did only after dark. As if he couldn't see her in the light.

"Yeah, it's the middle of the afternoon and time for a coffee break. Where's the nearest Starbucks?"

"There's a Peet's." It was in a strip mall two blocks from her parents' house.

"Tell me how to get there."

"But you can't just leave work."

"I'm the boss. I'm taking fifteen minutes to calm you down."

He always knew when she needed him. He always knew what to say and do. Today she wanted to touch his hand, let his voice wash over her, and bask in the beauty of his male features. Then she'd feel better. Then she could face going home to that death house. What an awful thought, but she couldn't help it.

Please, Daddy, don't make me.

In the end, though, she'd always done what she was supposed to.

"I DIDN'T MEAN FOR YOU TO DRIVE ALL THIS WAY." BREE PUSHED her hair behind her ear as they waited for their coffee drinks. Luke had to lean close to hear over the murmur of conversation and the whir of espresso machines and steam valves.

"It was five minutes." He touched her chin. "You're worth five minutes." And so much more.

Her cheeks brightened with color, though he wasn't sure

whether it was embarrassment or pleasure. Despite the shirt, blazer, and vest, she wasn't in strictly business attire because of the jeans, and her boot heels put her at perhaps an inch over him. Because he preferred it, around him she wore tight clothing, leggings, short skirts, Spandex tops, and sexy heels. He liked the fact that when he pulled her close, her nipples would touch his through their clothing.

"I can't be very long," she said.

"I understand." She'd called, she'd needed, he'd responded, canceling a meeting to see her. Pussy-whipped? No, more like obsessed. He didn't care about that either. He wanted her, to be there for her; that was all that mattered.

"White chocolate mocha for Luke," the barista called. Luke retrieved it, then snagged a small table in a corner just past the pastry case.

The mocha was for her. He had a cup of black coffee.

"Thank you," she said, scooping the whipped cream off the top with two stir sticks. When she sucked it down, she moaned with pleasure.

Luke relished the sound. For the duration of her father's illness, it was probably all he was going to get beyond the late night phone calls. That, too, was okay.

"Touch me," she murmured.

Christ. She blew a few of his brain cells with those two words. His chair was close enough that his knee pressed her leg, but instead of putting his hand on her thigh, he laced his fingers through hers on the tabletop. They would have made an odd picture, a man in his midforties holding hands with a woman ten years younger. Bree, with her delicate features, could pass for even younger, thirty or so.

They had never held hands like this, never gone out for coffee, never even had a date. They were all about sex, hot, kinky, delectable sex, but this held its own unique pleasures. "We've done everything backward," he said.

"What do you mean?"

"Fancy dinners and candlelight. Then the sex."

She sipped her mocha, licked whipped cream from her lip. Everything she did had a touch of sensuality to it, though he didn't think she recognized that. "I'm not a romantic," she said.

"Why?" She deserved romance in addition to whatever else she craved.

She blinked as if at first she didn't understand the question, then stared into space a long moment. "I don't believe in all that lovey-dovey stuff. It isn't real."

"I was in love with my wife," he said, not to hurt or dismiss Bree, but to make a point.

"You're divorced."

"True, but that's—"

She held up a hand in front of her face, blocking him out. "You don't need to tell me about your divorce."

Another intimacy she didn't want from him. He told her anyway. "My wife divorced me, not the other way round."

She pried her hand out of his. "Are you pining for her?"

"No. That's done." He paused a beat. "I pine for you."

She laughed, bright for a moment, but the look didn't last. "You're just teasing me."

"Not at all. I've decided we'll go on a few dates. There's a place up along Skyline, the best continental cuisine." He kissed his fingers.

"I'm uncomfortable letting a man pay for expensive meals like that."

But she was comfortable sucking his cock or letting him fuck her or spank her. "Do you think it's some sort of payment for sexual favors?"

"No."

He raised one eyebrow in question.

She toyed with her stir sticks.

Obviously her perceptions were a little skewed; fancy and romantic wasn't the way to go with her. But they did need to push the boundaries of their relationship, not just the limits of sexual inhibition. Especially now, when her father was ill. He wanted to give her something without stress. "We'll watch a video and eat popcorn." Of course, at his place on a couch they'd end up doing far more. He looked at it as killing two birds with one stone; a little intimacy and some hot kinky sex at the same time.

She bit the inside of her lip. Then let it go. "Why can't we have what we have? Why do we have to change it?" She'd been gazing steadily at her mocha, but now she raised her eyes to his through the lushness of her dark lashes. "Don't you like it anymore?"

He wanted sex with her, and he wanted more, to take her to the company barbecue, someday to come home to her. "It's time for us to change."

She took a deeper breath than normal, rolled her lips, swallowed. "I have to go," she said.

He grabbed her hand, made her stay put for another second. "What we do is good, Bree. But you need more. I intend to give it to you."

"I don't *want* more." She tipped her head and gave him a look. *Oh you poor deluded man.* "I've never had a boyfriend, Luke. I don't know how to have one. What we do is all I know how to do. I don't have anything more to give. But thank you for the mocha."

He wouldn't let her go with just a *thank-you.* "There are other pleasures to explore. A date. It isn't that difficult."

She didn't answer. Instead she leaned forward, kissed his cheek. "Thanks for coming over to make me feel better." She stood, purse in her hand.

The subtext was that he hadn't made her feel better despite his intention. He'd pushed, that's what he'd done. While it was necessary, maybe the timing wasn't perfect, but he'd already started down the path.

He rose before she could get away, commanding her with his closeness, his maleness, and his bigger body. It didn't matter about her high heels; he was master. "Bree," he said and didn't care if he was demanding. "Say yes."

He could see his distorted reflection in her eyes before she finally answered. "Yes."

"Yes what?" he murmured.

She moved only her lips. "Yes, Master." Then she left.

She'd do it because he'd ordered her to, but not of her own free will. With Bree, though, Luke wasn't sure that mattered. She was comfortable with commands.

He hadn't specified an evening for their date. He'd do that later. He'd done enough simply putting her on notice that it was coming. Now, however, he didn't like having her beyond his reach, not when things were falling apart in her life.

As he pushed through the coffee-shop door, he saw her head disappearing inside her car several spaces down. His Lexus was right at the front entrance, but by the time he'd pulled out and headed to the light, there were two cars between them. She turned left. He was supposed to go right.

There was no indecision about it; he followed her without missing a beat.

She accelerated faster than he did, but he could see her merge into the right lane ahead, then turn again. By the time he made the same right, she was two blocks down, turning left.

When he got to the street, he saw it was a cul-de-sac. She'd parked in a driveway and was climbing out of the car.

He didn't turn down the road, and she didn't see him.

It had taken her six months to tell him where she lived. He would have preferred that she offer him her parents' address, but he knew it would take another six months for that. He couldn't wait that long; he had to know where to come when she needed him.

10

HER PARENTS' HOUSE WAS SHADOWED, GRAY, COLORLESS, AND IT wasn't even dark yet, only four-thirty on Wednesday afternoon.

On the bright side, her work was getting done by someone else. She hadn't seen Luke since the coffee shop on Monday, but he'd called her both nights since then. They didn't have phone sex last night, just talked. It was strange yet soothing. She couldn't remember exactly what they said, and she thought she might actually have cried, but she couldn't say for sure. Sometimes she felt like she was in another world, disconnected. Luke's voice brought her back.

He'd tried to get her to meet him for coffee again, but she'd put him off. It wasn't that she didn't want to, but there was so much pressure in rushing to work and rushing home again. Besides he made her nervous. What else would he ask for? She was still amazed he wanted to *date* her. She hadn't dated since college. Dating had been bad, twisting her insides up. She'd given it up for simply having sex. With sex, she was more in control. With sex, it was just physical. She didn't have to give them anything. For a little while, a man desired her and she was special. That's all she'd wanted and needed for a long time. When a man stopped making her feel that way, he was replaceable.

Then suddenly, there was Luke, offering more, and after the initial rush of inexplicable fear—most women would have died and gone to heaven for a man like Luke to take her out for expensive dinners at fancy restaurants—Bree had started to think about it. Wanting something more than sex from a man always made you vulnerable. You got dependent on that *something*. Still, over the past two days, she'd fantasized about a real date. Finally, she'd started to want it.

Except that her father was dying in the hospital bed she'd consigned him to on Sunday.

"Brianna, would you give him the morphine? He won't take it from me." Her mother held the pill in the palm of her hand.

Bree shuddered as if it were a big, ugly spider. She'd been peeling potatoes for dinner. Her mom did most of the caretaking, running up and down the hall so many times she was wearing new holes in the tired old carpeting.

But there were things Bree couldn't avoid, like feeding him. Or getting him to take those damn pills.

"I'll try, Mom." She washed her hands, dried them, took the pill, and left her mother to finish the peeling.

In the bedroom, the bed was cranked up to a sitting position so her father could watch TV. She wasn't sure he understood the words anymore, but the flickering images were something he could fixate on.

She sidled around the bed, putting her back to the window and the dollhouse still visible in the quickly fading twilight. His flesh was sallow, and jaundice had set in. His veins were a patchwork of blue lines beneath his paper-thin skin. She had to cover his legs, which were no thicker than sticks; the sight of them frightened her. He was four days and a hundred years worse than he'd been at the beginning of the week when the hospice man had put him in the bed.

"Here's your pill, Father." She held it out along with the cup and its straw, not telling him it was the morphine he'd just refused from her mom.

He looked at her, blinked slowly, a crust along his upper eyelids. She'd clean that away once she got him to down the pill. The previous one would soon be wearing off, and when it did, he would start a pitiful moaning that sent chills along every nerve ending in her body.

"You're trying to kill me," he snapped, flinging his hand out. It fell back to the bed, missing her entirely.

"I just don't want you to be in pain. This will help."

"You want to kill me so you can have all my money."

She was patient. At least he wasn't calling her a stupid slut. She hated the word *stupid*. "I don't need your money, Father. Now take your pill."

"Bitch."

She'd been called far worse by him. The word sounded so much better in Luke's deep voice. She had to admit she deserved it, though, these past few days for sure. She'd refused to let her father get out of bed. She'd had the hospice aides put in the necessary tubes so they didn't have to help him go to the bathroom. He'd screamed at the indignity, but eventually he'd stopped trying to pull everything out, thank God.

"Daddy, please take your pill." She hadn't called him *daddy* since she was eight. The term only came into her head in bad moments. But if it worked now, she'd use it.

She was too close when he batted at her this time, and the pill went flying. The water splashed her face and dripped down onto the bedclothes.

"I want my fucking whiskey. Where's my whiskey? Nobody gives me my whiskey anymore."

She bent down to feel around on the carpet, but she couldn't find the pill. "I'll get you another one."

In the kitchen, she took another from the medicine bottle, then poured half a shot of whiskey.

Her mother gasped. "Brianna, you can't mix morphine and alcohol. It might kill him."

"Mom, he's been taking morphine for months now. A little bit of whiskey to wash it down isn't going to do a damn thing to him except get him to take the pill. Then he'll sleep."

She marched back into the bedroom. "Here's your whiskey. But you have to take your meds first."

He swallowed the pill with a sip of water like a child taking sweet cough syrup. Then she put the straw into the shot glass and let him suck down the whiskey.

He fell asleep so quickly, she thought she'd killed him. Grabbing his wrist, she felt for a pulse. She couldn't find it. Oh God, where the hell was it? Dear Lord, her mother was right, she'd murdered him. They'd put her in prison. Her blood rushed to her head, and she thought she was going to faint away in a panic. Then she felt a tiny pulse beat. Almost nonexistent, but then it always was.

Her head cleared. Of course she hadn't killed him. But even if she had, would it matter that he died tonight instead of tomorrow or the next day? On the other side of the bed, she closed the curtains on the now complete darkness outside. Then she left him alone.

Back in the kitchen, her mother was slicing the potatoes and putting them in the pan to boil. "Mashed tonight, don't you think?" she said, not mentioning the morphine or the whiskey.

"Sounds good." Bree opened the fridge, pulled out the wine bottle, and poured them both a glass.

"Cheers," her mom said. They clinked and drank. Her mom liked the sweeter stuff, and over the last few evenings, anything would do for Bree.

A quarter of an hour later, seated at the table in the breakfast nook, they ate baked chicken, mashed potatoes, and broccoli while her father slept.

"What movie do you want to watch?" her mom asked.

"*Beauty and the Beast.*"

"You're such a little girl," she said with a smile.

"Yeah." Bree would have suggested *Pitch Black*, but her mother wouldn't like all the gore.

The doorbell rang when they were doing the dishes, Bree washing the pans, her mom loading the dishwasher.

Bree glanced at her watch. "The aides are early." The hospice workers came in around seven to get her father washed and ready for bed. Not that he wasn't already in bed, but certain things had to be changed.

"I'll get it." Her mom's hands were dry while Bree's were covered in dishwater. She padded through the nook, the dining room, and into the front hall.

As Bree set the last pan in the drainer, a man's deep voice drifted back into the kitchen. So far, they'd had only one male aide, but that man's voice had been higher. This was a new one.

"Bree," her mom called.

She had the ungrateful wish that her mother would show them the way to her father's bedroom on her own. Yet she dried her hands and headed out to the hall.

"Hello, Bree."

Her heart stuttered to a full stop as Luke smiled at her.

What the hell are you doing here? She managed not to say it, but she felt like a viewer at a tennis match, her head bobbing back and forth between her mom and Luke.

"Your friend dropped by to see how you're doing." And oh, there was *so* much more absolute delight in her mother's voice than that understatement suggested.

"I'm fine," Bree said, her voice almost squeaky until she caught it. "Thanks for checking." A million questions ran through her mind. How did he know where her parents lived? Why was he here? What did he want? And oh God, what would he tell her mother about their relationship?

"Would you like a cup of coffee?" Dear Mom, ever so polite, always looking after her guests. Not that she'd had many. Her father hadn't liked to share her attention.

Please, please, please, let him say no.

Luke didn't hear her silent plea. "I'd love one, thanks."

"Bree, why don't you take Mr. Raven into the living room while I get the coffee?" Obviously, he'd introduced himself.

"Please, call me Luke," he said, his voice dripping with sweetness.

Her mother beamed and cut back through the dining room to the kitchen.

"What are you doing here?" she hissed at him as soon as they were in the living room on the other side of the front hall, far enough away so her mother wouldn't hear from the kitchen.

"You wouldn't meet me for coffee and last night you cried on the phone. I was worried, so I came." He didn't try to touch her, but she felt his body as if he were straining toward her.

"How did you find me?"

"I followed you on Monday," he said without a hint of remorse in his tone.

She gaped at him. "You're a stalker." The words were harsh, her voice hurtful.

"I'm your master," he said simply.

She glanced over her shoulder to make sure her mom wasn't

on the way back with the coffee. "My parents' house is off-limits."

He was silent for an excruciating count to ten. "Nothing is off limits where you're concerned. I take care of my submissive. And I was worried about you."

He was only using those words to control her. They weren't really master and slave. It was a game. It had always worked before. Until he wanted to turn the tables. Her skin felt stretched like a rubber band, ready to snap. Her ears were suddenly over-sensitive, listening for every noise from the kitchen, wondering how much sound traveled back to her mother.

Then her mom was carrying a tray across the dining room, and Bree ran to help her. Or maybe she was running away from him.

"Luke, please sit down," her mother said brightly.

Bree set the tray on the coffee table in front of the sofa as her mom indicated. The room had been used so rarely that the twenty-year-old couch was still pristine white and the roses on the pillows a deep red. The curtains were pulled even in the daytime to keep everything from fading. Her mother vacuumed and dusted once a week whether it was needed or not. The cleanliness and perpetual darkness was oppressive.

"It was so good of you to come over to see Bree." Her mother perched beside Luke on the sofa as Bree poured.

She gave Luke his black, then sat in the chair on the other side of her mother.

"It's my pleasure, Mrs. Mason."

"How did you and my daughter meet?" The smile on her mom's face was too wide to be real. Plus there was that hurt look she shot Bree. "I'm afraid she hasn't talked about you, Luke."

"Her company did work for my firm," he said vaguely, without giving any specifics on how long he'd known her. Or that he'd found her with Derek at a sex club.

"What do you for a living, Luke?" The question was none too subtle.

"I'm CEO for a company here in Silicon Valley."

"CEO?" Oh so innocent.

"Chief executive officer," Bree supplied. For God's sake, her mother *knew* what a CEO was. Next she'd be asking his annual salary and how much his stock options were worth.

"That must be a wonderful and important job."

God, her mother, gotta love her. At that point, Bree actually smiled as she looked at Luke. He'd let himself in for a matchmaking mama by coming here. He deserved what he got.

"I enjoy it. Bree and I hit it off. But your daughter's cagey, and I've been hard-pressed to pin her down for a date."

Bree almost rolled her eyes. Yeah, right, like she'd give him her parents' address and cry on his shoulder about her dad if they weren't even *dating*. "I told you that's not possible under the circumstances, Luke."

"Don't be silly, dear," her mom interrupted. "You can go out for a date. You probably need the time away."

What happened to the whole don't-leave-me-alone thing, which was how her mom had sucked her into coming back home? They weren't talking about her father; they were all studiously avoiding the issue. "I can't right now, Mom, you know that."

What if something happened? Honestly, she didn't want her mother alone for that.

"I'll be fine for a couple of hours, honey. I can ask one of the volunteers to come over and sit with me."

Dammit, she was taking away all of Bree's excuses.

"Bree's right, Mrs. Mason. I didn't mean that she needed to go out with me now. Just in the future." At least Luke was trying to save her.

Her mom reached for Bree's hand, squeezed. "No. Please. This weekend. I insist. Bree's done so much to help me already. She deserves a nice time out."

She was trapped, and she felt awkward, as if her mother was saying, *Hey, it's okay if you two go out while her father's dying in the back bedroom.* Bree had to close her eyes a moment, to breathe, to stuff it all back down.

Then, as if she'd said enough—or she'd heard a noise from the other end of the house—her mother jumped up. "I'll be back in a minute. You two decide where you want to go."

When they were alone, Luke looked at her. "I'm more than willing to wait to get what I want."

She couldn't say anything for a few seconds. She didn't know her own feelings. She'd never brought a man home. The kind of men she'd known in the last few years, her father would have killed her if she'd brought *them* home. Was Luke that much different? He'd found her in a sex club, for God's sake. He hadn't been *just* watching, either. He'd been there to play. She'd never asked him exactly what he'd done that night before he found her. She still didn't want to know.

"But you are different," she whispered almost without thinking. "I don't know why."

He didn't move from his spot on the couch. "I am different," he murmured, low, almost hypnotic. "We're different together, different from anything we've ever been to anyone else in our lives. I will make you a believer on Saturday."

She looked beyond him. To a place he held out to her like a gift. Or a mirage. She wanted to be special. She needed him to treat her that way. She wondered if he could do it without the sex. Could she? Because the only thing she had to offer men was that, her body, her sex. Without it, she didn't know what to say or do. But she knew what she wanted for one night.

"Treat me like a queen and I'll go with you."

"Done," he whispered.

11

IT WAS FRIDAY OF A HELLACIOUS WEEK. BREE DROPPED HER PURSE in the front hall. God, she wanted to go home to water her plants and to rest, even for a few hours. *Her* home, not *this* place. She hadn't been alone in six days. Sometimes she just needed time to herself. She wasn't one of those people who was afraid of being alone; she craved it.

Inevitably, her mother was at her father's bedside. "Hello, sweetheart," she said pleasantly.

Yet when Bree saw her father, she blanched. It felt like all the blood had rushed out of her head and she was dizzy.

He was pale and unmoving, his mouth open as he breathed—although it wasn't really a breath, more a gurgle—and the odor was foul. His eyes were half open yet unfocussed.

She had to sit down on the edge of her mother's bed before her legs gave out. "What the hell happened?"

"Hospice says he's lapsing into coma. It won't be long now."

"But yesterday he was talking." Bree hadn't seen him before she left for work this morning. Her mother had fed him and given him his pills.

Her mom shook her head. "It was just words, Bree, they didn't really make sense."

"This isn't possible." Okay, he'd stopped fighting her on the medication. He didn't ask for his whiskey. She'd crushed the pills and fed them to him with a spoon of mashed banana. Except that yesterday he hadn't wanted to eat. Or maybe she couldn't even say that. He simply hadn't opened his mouth. But he had looked at her. He had seen her. Hadn't he?

Why was she fighting it? It was better this way.

"The aides that came in this morning said it can happen very quickly," her mother said without much inflection. "Sometimes a person decides he's had enough. And he gives up."

Her father had *never* given up control. The one time he did, shutting down his business, he'd been forced to by the bank. He'd never lost his anger over the injustice of it.

But something had happened. Something had let loose in him this time.

That night, Bree didn't call Luke. She shut her phone off. He would ask. She couldn't talk. She couldn't think.

Things were even worse at five on Saturday evening when she was supposed to go out with Luke.

"I can't go." Bree stood in the doorway of her parents' bedroom. She hadn't started dressing, though Luke would be here in half an hour to pick her up. He'd suggested they go early to accommodate the hospice volunteer who would arrive soon to spend the evening with her mom and dad.

Seated beside her father's bed on a stool, her mother didn't turn. "You can't back out now. That isn't nice." She wiped something from the corner of his mouth. She was so tender.

Bree hadn't been able to find it in herself to show that level of tenderness. She couldn't even remain in the death room longer than it took to give him a pill. It had been the longest week of her life. This morning the aides had turned him to find ugly red bedsores developing. His eyes never seemed to close, but they never focused on anything either. His skin was turning a blue black along his back, butt, and legs where the blood had begun to pool as his circulation slowed. When he breathed, mucous rattled in this throat. Really, that was all he did: breathe. He hadn't taken solids in two days, the difference between the man who'd demanded his whiskey and this body lying in the bed inconceivable in just a few short days.

"It could happen any time," she told her mother.

"It won't happen while you're on your date. Your father promised." All the communicating must have been done through telepathy. Her mom sat in this room for hours at his bedside. She didn't touch him except to wipe away mucous or drool, and she didn't speak aloud to him. "You have to go. This one's a good one," she said, still not turning to Bree. "He can take care of you."

"I don't need anyone to take care of me."

"Every woman does. You have the babies, and the man goes to work."

She wasn't having babies either, but it was pointless to argue with her mother. One would never have believed she'd lived through the sexual revolution and women's liberation. She was a product of the fifties and the least liberated woman Bree had ever known.

She couldn't fight those ingrained beliefs. "It's just a first date. Luke might find out I'm not worth it."

"Don't be silly. Wear a pretty dress and do your hair and makeup. You're so lovely when you've got your makeup on."

As opposed to being ugly without it? Bree figured that had to be a time-honored tradition of mothers, the old you'd-be-so-pretty-if comment. "Mom."

Her mother swiveled on the stool, her face suddenly all hard lines. "You've never brought a man home before."

"I didn't bring him home. He just showed up."

Her mom rode right over her. "I won't have you screwing this one up, Bree."

Screwing it up? That was harsh. "Mom."

Her mother pointed. "Go. Get ready."

Maybe she should have fought harder. But she was a rotten daughter, and the truth was she didn't want to stay. She wanted out. Even if it was for only an evening. Especially with Luke. She didn't like it, but he'd become the lifeline she clung to when she wanted to scream *get me out of here*. "Fine, Mom. I'll go."

She was back in the doorway twenty-five minutes later, makeup applied, hair brushed. Luke liked it long, silky, and flowing free.

Her mother was still on the stool by the bed. "You're wearing jeans and high heels."

Bree looked down. Dark blue jeans, a fitted black blazer with belled sleeves and silver buttons down the front. "What's wrong with what I'm wearing?"

"Your heels are at least three inches. You'll be taller than him." Her mother had always worn flats so she wouldn't be taller than Bree's father. Bree had never known whether that was something he'd demanded in the beginning or her mother had decided on her own.

"Luke likes how tall I am, with or without heels." He'd once said that he loved being able to simply spread her legs, pull her panties aside, and fuck her right up against a wall. With the heels, she was the perfect height for it. But no, she wouldn't say that to her mother. She believed her mom thought she was a virgin because she didn't date.

Her mother harrumphed. "Jeans aren't fancy."

"Luke told me to dress casually."

"Jeans are casual, high heels are fancy. The two don't go

together. I don't understand it." Her mother rolled her eyes, very high school on her wrinkled face. "Young people these days," she groused, "always casual."

"He's not young, Mom. He's forty-five and has two daughters in college."

"Is he a widower?"

"He's divorced."

"How many times?"

"Just the one time." It would have been nice if she could say he'd been married two or three times, then watch him drop in her mother's estimation.

"Is he close to his daughters?"

"I don't know." *It doesn't come up in conversation while he's tying me up, spanking me, or fucking me.* Okay, she did know they were close, but how would her mother feel if she said *that*?

"If he's got two daughters, I'm sure he must want to try for a son."

"I have no idea, Mom." He wasn't having sons with Bree, that was for sure.

The doorbell rang. Thank God, saved by the proverbial bell. "Don't get up," Bree said, then jogged down the hall on her toes so she wouldn't ruin her heels.

It was Luke, raindrops dusting his hair and breathtaking in black jeans and a teal button-down shirt. She wanted to kiss him as if this were a real date.

He didn't say hello, just settled his gaze on her chest. "What are you wearing under the jacket?"

"A black bra." And no blouse.

He glanced over her shoulder to the hallway leading to the bedrooms. Finding it empty, he made a gap between the buttons and stroked the swell of her breast. "Nice."

As compliments went, it wasn't much, but Bree didn't get a lot of compliments, and accompanied by the fire in his amber eyes, this one made her flesh heat.

"Say good-bye to your mom before we leave."

She was glad he didn't ask how her father was doing. She didn't want to lie and say he was fine, but she didn't want to say he'd probably be dead by Monday. It was better to pretend none of it was real.

She stepped back to call down the hall. "I'm leaving, Mom. I've got my cell phone." She patted her purse as if her mother could see—she still had the condoms in there, too, just in case— then practically pushed Luke onto the porch. Light from the streetlamps shimmered in the raindrops on the car roof. "Are you taking me somewhere special to fuck me, Master?"

Luke laughed. He had a deep laugh that did funny things to her insides. She got hot and wet when he ordered her around, called her whore or slut, but his laugh did something different altogether. It warmed her somewhere around her heart.

"No fucking and no sucking. This is a non-sex date."

"We've never *not* had sex." It bothered her. Without sex, she wasn't sure how to behave. "Don't you want me anymore?" The moment the words were out, she wished them back.

He held her chin up with the tip of his finger. "I'd love to fuck you all night long, but as your master, I'm refusing to give you what you want all the time. We don't want the power to go to your head." He folded his hand around hers and walked with her in the light drizzle to his Lexus. "Be a good slave, get in the car, and shut up until we arrive at our destination. No questions. Your master wants to surprise you."

She felt a little thrill, sexual, physical, and emotional all rolled into one.

* * *

"YOU'RE TAKING ME BOWLING?" BREE GAVE HIM A LOOK. IT WAS SO womanlike. Incredulous, amused, and horrified.

Luke merely smiled. They sat in the car in front of the bowling alley, its neon lights flickering red, green, and blue through the rain across the windshield. It was falling harder now. "I haven't bowled in ages. So that's what I chose."

He'd discarded the fancy dinner idea because it was ordinary and she'd said she wasn't romantic. He'd considered a sports event, but baseball was long since over for the season, football was in playoffs, and hockey was too loud. With the chill and the rain, a bay cruise wasn't a hot prospect either, though he'd imagined taking her up to the top deck and bending her over the railing so he could slip inside her. In a movie theater, they couldn't talk. If he'd rented a DVD, he'd have fucked her because he couldn't keep his hands off her. The goal was to prove there was more to them than sex. That left only bowling.

Besides, he'd wanted to shock her.

"But I'm wearing high heels." She pointed down at her pumps, her voice rising.

She *was* shocked; he'd done well. "They give you bowling shoes."

She was silent a moment, then, "I don't know how to bowl."

"I'll teach you."

The rain pattering on the car roof was the only sound for a long time. "What if I'm not good at it?" she finally said.

"Then I'll win the game."

He thought the answer would satisfy her, but instead she said, "My father tried to teach me how to drive a stick shift when I was sixteen." Staring straight ahead at the flashing neon, she grabbed the door handle, stroking it with her fingers.

He marveled that she'd opened up to him. "That's good," he said when she didn't go on.

"It wasn't." Her hand flexed on the door, opened, closed, then fisted, her gaze unwaveringly ahead. "I have an automatic. I will always have an automatic."

"Not everyone gets the hang of a stick." But he felt a chill on the back of his neck. Something wasn't quite right with the story; there was more to it. He waited a beat, but she didn't add to what she'd said. "Bowling is fun whether you're good or bad at it. I bowled with my daughters, and they sucked. I love them anyway."

She turned and rain shadows drizzled down her face. "You took your daughters bowling?"

"Yeah." It was a long time ago, but they were good memories.

"And now you want to take me bowling?"

"Yeah."

She didn't smile; she didn't move. Neon prisms flashed on and off across her cheeks. "Okay."

He didn't have a clue whether that was good or bad, but he climbed out, unfolded the umbrella, and rounded the hood to her door. By the time they made it inside, rain sparkled on her blazer where he hadn't quite covered her. He got them shoes and had a lane assigned to them. Surprisingly the place was decently packed, a couple of bowling teams in jerseys, teens on group dates, families. The crash of the balls along the lanes, pins falling, laughter, the lights and bells of the pinball machines along the back wall, all mixed with the scent of wood-fired pizza; it took him back years, warm memories settling over him, just him and his girls. Beth had never come.

He suddenly understood the real reason he'd chosen this place for Bree. Because somewhere in his gut, he knew she'd never had this. It didn't take her questions about whether he'd be mad if she played badly or the brief insight about the stick shift. He simply knew that an outing like this was something she'd never experienced.

He could also touch her as he taught her the game. It was part of the play, especially when a man was on a date with a beautiful woman.

12

"I GOT THEM ALL." BREE JUMPED UP AND DOWN IN THE MIDDLE OF the lane. It was as if the ball had simply carried her a quarter of the way down. It had taken a couple of tries, first knocking down one side of the pins, then the other side, but she'd done it.

In the next lane, the kids cheered her. Two boys, two girls, sixteen or seventeen, double dating. She did a little happy dance back up the lane, then threw her arms around Luke and kissed his cheek. He laughed. God, he smelled good. Soap, not aftershave. Clean. And maybe that was the freshness of rain, too.

He grinned down at her. "And you said bowling was boring."

"It is when my ball keeps rolling into the gutter."

"My turn." With her still in his arms, he whirled on his heel and set her down by the chairs. "Watch a pro."

She stuck her tongue out at him. At first she was just going to pretend for him, because she was so good at faking. Somehow the pretending had ended, and she'd started having fun. Real fun. Unselfconscious fun. He never got mad when she blew it. He simply scrunched up behind her, wrapped his body around hers, and demonstrated how to do it right. Who'd have thought learning to bowl would be so sexy.

Luke picked up his ball, aimed, wriggled his ass temptingly, then strode to the lane and let the ball fly. And struck out. Or was that making a strike? She couldn't remember. Whatever. He got them all. She didn't understand exactly how the electronic scoring worked, but obviously he was way ahead.

"You cheated," she called out, just for the hell of it. "And I want pizza." The sausage and pepperoni smelled heavenly, almost as good as Luke.

He grinned, sidling up beside her, leaning close. "You're talking to your master, show some respect," he murmured, then cupped her nape and planted one on her mouth.

It was so good. She felt so normal. So special. She'd told him to treat her like a queen, and in the oddest way, he had. "Buy me some pizza, and I'll show you some respect."

"Don't cheat while I'm gone," he said, "Or you will be punished." Fishing out his wallet, he headed to pizza heaven.

"You're the cheater," she called after him, a delicious little thrill running through her at the thought of any punishment he might mete out later. Then she sashayed down to get a ball. He'd showed her the moves, the positions. Most of the time, she hit the gutter, but sometimes she actually hit the pins. And he didn't care either way. Maybe if they'd been playing on a team or against another couple, he would have hated losing, but since it was just them, he was fine.

Bree hadn't enjoyed herself this much since . . . Well, she'd never enjoyed herself this much. She'd never let herself go, never acted the idiot, jumping up and down. She'd never had plain old fun. She hated looking stupid. If anyone from work saw her antics, they'd actually have to do a double take to be sure it was her.

She lined herself up, held the ball the way Luke had shown her. Okay, okay, ready; she let it roll.

She didn't care what anyone else thought of her. Not tonight. Because Luke had given her something special. This was different than sex. Sex was a maze you had to negotiate to get what you needed. Sometimes you made a wrong turn and got screwed. Sometimes the prize at the center wasn't what you'd wanted or needed. Luke made bowling fun because he didn't expect anything. He didn't criticize; instead he laughed. She didn't have to be the one to make sure he was pleased. He seemed to do that all on his own.

The ball rolled and wobbled. And fell off into the gutter again. She stamped her foot. She'd been thinking too much.

Next door, the girl's ball flopped into the gutter right on the heels of Bree's, and the two balls rolled down to the bottom of the lanes together. The pretty petite blonde shrugged, laughed back at her friends, then looked at Bree and said, "I guess we're losers."

"Double losers," the two boys called, holding up thumbs and fingers against their foreheads in double *L*s.

The girl giggled and ran back to bump hips with her date.

Bree had never been like that girl. She had never laughed at herself.

Luke wrapped his arm around her waist and pulled her back hard and tight against him, surprising an *oomph* out of her.

"You scared me," she complained. But she liked the date. She liked pretending they were normal people. She'd never been normal, and it was nice, for once, to feel what it might have been like if she was.

"Pizza will be ready in fifteen minutes. You want to eat out here or back there?"

"Will we lose our lane?"

"Probably."

"Then let's eat out here." She didn't want to miss a moment. It was already seven, her clock was ticking, and pretty soon she'd turn back into Cinderella's ugly stepsister again. Okay, it wasn't quite the way the fairy tale went, but the point was that everything good eventually ended. She wanted this for now. She wanted Luke now. Not sex, just this, his laughter, his kisses, his touches.

"Who's winning?" she said bouncing on the toes of her bowling shoes. Bree had never bounced in her life. Now, for tonight, she couldn't stop.

Luke gave her a *duh* look.

They played, and she kept falling further behind his score, but she didn't care. When the pizza came, she ate three pieces until she thought she'd burst it was so good. She licked the sauce from her fingers.

"You've got it all over your mouth," Luke admonished and kissed it away. He stole her breath at the same time.

When she looked at her watch next, it was eight. She didn't want the night to end. She wanted to absorb how it felt to have fun, so she'd remember later. It was too soon to go back.

Then it was eight-thirty. Tick, tick, tick. The hospice volunteer wasn't staying all night.

Luke tipped her chin up. "We can take the long way home."

"We don't have to," she said as she gave up her bowling shoes and slipped back into her high heels.

Outside, it was still raining. Beneath his umbrella, they awkwardly ran to the car, Luke getting wetter than her. Once inside, he turned on the seat warmers, then slashed the wipers across the windshield.

"I changed my mind," she whispered. "I want the long way."

* * *

HE WANTED THE LONG WAY HOME, TOO.

Luke had never seen her like this. He couldn't have dreamed it was possible. She was a different woman in the bowling alley, childlike. Happy. That was a word he never would have applied to her.

But that woman was fading fast. He was sure she was thinking that soon she had to return to her father's house. He'd pulled into an empty lot at the county park, tuned the car radio to a jazz station, then they both moved to the backseat to watch the rain streaking the windshield. The jazz softly filled the car, blending with the rain's patter on the roof to create a symphony.

He wanted her. He'd intended a no-sex date, a way to change their pattern. But he wanted sex with the woman he'd met in the bowling alley.

"Kiss me." It sounded like an order, but if she could have seen into his heart, she'd have known he was begging.

She shifted in the seat next to him and bent to put her lips to his cock through his jeans.

He pulled her up. "Not there." Cupping her nape, he held her close, waiting, his breath stalled in his chest. His beating heart added to the symphony of rain and jazz.

They'd done all manner of kinky perversions, but kissing was rare. Sometimes, he'd have killed for it. Like now. Her lips were a luscious red, the color natural for her. She hadn't replaced her lipstick after the pizza.

"Kissing like teenagers in the backseat of your dad's Chevy," she murmured.

She'd read his mind. They were in tune. "Yeah. The perfect end to bowling night."

Her soft laugh burrowed beneath his skin. "All right," she said. "But I'm not going past first base."

Again, he marveled. She was so different tonight; a woman

without shadows. "We'll see how far I can get you to go after you kiss me."

"Oh, so like you're so good I'll change my mind?" she mocked.

"I'm a great kisser."

She turned things around on him. "Prove it."

He started slow, lightly tracing her lips with his tongue, then parting them, tasting, delving deeper. She smelled like baby powder and raindrops. The music wound around them, seduced him as much as her kiss did. The fall of her hair caressed his hand as he held her to him, the texture like fine threads of silk.

He knew what he wanted for the night, what he needed. Slipping his hand between her legs, he caressed the crease of her jeans. She was warm down there.

Bree pulled him back out. "No, no, no, that's a bad boy," she whispered against his lips.

"But I want it." He tried the same move, but she clamped her legs against him. Wrapping her hair around his hand, he pulled her head back. "Let me in."

Her eyes shone darkly. "Not tonight."

He wanted her to want his touch, to need the orgasm he could give her, the pleasure. "Don't make me force you."

She pursed her lips. He felt the *M* in Master coming, and as much as he enjoyed the kinky stuff, he didn't want to be her master tonight.

Instead he kissed her, taking her with his tongue, pushing her head back until she moaned into his mouth. The nipples of her small breasts were jewel-hard beneath her jacket. He rubbed his chest against her as he deepened the kiss. She tasted of spice and laughter, a heretofore unknown quality in her. She wrapped her arms around his neck and threw herself into the kiss, angling her head, threading her fingers through his hair to hold him. It was as if she ravished his mouth, licking, tasting, nipping his lips, then going deep. She'd never kissed him like that before. It drove him wild and yet the most tender of feelings blossomed inside him. The sweetness and purity of just a kiss, nothing more, yet the undeniably carnal nature of the taking turned him inside out.

He kissed her until he couldn't breathe, until his heart raced and his ears roared and her moans sounded as if they came from his own chest.

Then he pulled away, touched his fingers to her kiss-swollen lips. "Who taught you to kiss like that?" he murmured.

"You did."

He believed her.

"It's time to go," she said, leaning in to nip the flesh of his throat.

He didn't want her to leave. He knew the woman she was in the bowling alley, even the woman she'd become in the backseat of his car, would disappear. He may never find her again. But the dash clock flipped over to nine-forty-five, and ten o'clock was her witching hour.

"We will do this again," he said before he let her climb back into the front seat.

"A date?" she asked.

The laughter, the fun, the kiss. "Yes, a date."

"Some things you can have only once. If you try to duplicate perfection, it gets all screwed up and ruined," she said.

He'd always known she had a dim view of relationships, shadows from her past, but she was wrong about him, wrong about them together. And he would prove it. "We'll have other dates, Bree. A lot of them."

"Yes, Master," she answered softly before he could anticipate and stop her. He didn't want to turn it into an order or a demand.

But with those words, the night and the woman she'd been disappeared completely.

13

SHE HAD NEVER BEEN KISSED LIKE THAT, A KISS SIMPLY FOR A KISS'S sake. The melding of mouths, the touching of lips, and his taste mesmerizing her. Luke had always given her more than she'd ever had. He'd offered her a real honest-to-God date. A normal date, fun in a way she'd never known. And that perfect kiss.

He gave her a glimpse of the person she could have been.

Beneath the porch overhang, she watched him drive away. The night was over. The hospice volunteer's car was gone. She was fifteen minutes late getting home. The lights along the front of the house were off, which meant her mother was either in the den watching TV or sitting in the bedroom over her father's deathbed. Or maybe she'd already gone to sleep.

Bree unlocked the front door, and, once inside, quietly slid the deadbolt home. Locking Luke out, and locking herself in with her parents, with her past, with her fears.

She stopped a moment, hugging tonight's memory close. It had been so perfect, so unexpected. He hadn't fought when she wouldn't let him touch her. There was nothing to feel guilty about later. She'd been a good girl. Then he'd melted her very soul with his kiss.

No one *just* kissed her. The men she'd been with used it as punishment, or a reward, like a pat on the head. No one had kissed her just to kiss *her*. As if her taste were special. She couldn't have known how much she craved it until the moment Luke gave it to her. Just as she could never have imagined that bowling would be her dream date.

She almost laughed. Her mom would freak that it was pizza in a bowling alley instead of a five-course meal at an elegant restaurant.

Bree stood in the empty hallway, the sound of the rain running along the gutters and down the drain spouts. Except for that, the house was silent as a tomb. What an apt expression. It was a tomb. Her father was dying in this place, and she felt as if her mother's spirit might be dying with him.

Or maybe it only meant that soon her mother would be free.

She padded quietly down the hall that was the leg of the house's T. The den was empty. Her parents' room at the end was dark, too. She had the urge to simply walk into her own room and shut the door.

Instead, she pushed on to the end of the hall and her parents' doorway. It seemed to gape eerily. She forced herself to step over the threshold. Her father's hospital bed was silhouetted against the rainy sky. And against that silhouette stood her mother. One small lamp was on behind the head of the bed, shining on her father's face.

Bree could swear she heard voices, as if her father had come out of the semi-coma he'd been drifting in for the last thirty-six hours.

But no, as she moved closer, her feet silent on the carpet, it was only her mother's voice. Soft words, almost nonexistent, but there nonetheless.

Bree strained to hear them. As if they held the meaning of life, the meaning of death.

Until finally they coalesced beneath the rain's chatter. "Die, you old fuck, die."

She had never heard her mother use that word, not once in her entire life.

She couldn't speak, couldn't hear for a moment over the roar of blood in her ears as if it were a great waterfall. Yet the next thing she knew, she was by her mother's side, her father's emaciated, inert body in the bed before them. He didn't move, nothing but the incessant twitch of his eyes back and forth beneath his half-open lids.

Is that what her mother had been doing the past few days, sitting beside his bed willing him to die?

"If you felt that way, why didn't you ever leave him?"

Her mother didn't startle, didn't turn. "I was afraid," she said.

"So was I, Mom," Bree finally whispered into a quiet broken only by the rain and her father's torturous breaths.

Until her mother spoke again. "I thought whatever was out there was worse than staying with him."

"It wasn't worse," Bree said so softly she thought her mother wouldn't hear.

Yet she heard. "I did my best, Brianna."

Bree wanted to say she understood. But she didn't. She probably never would. They stood beside his bed, the man that been the most important thing in their lives for so long that neither of them knew how life would continue without him. He was all they'd ever known. Would you even recognize freedom if you'd never known it?

Finally, Bree took her mother's hand, laced their fingers. "Let's watch him die together."

Her mother squeezed. And hands clasped, they waited.

* * *

THEY WERE STILL WAITING AT EIGHT ON SUNDAY MORNING. BREE had wanted to run screaming into the sunrise, throwing herself into a blinding blaze of glory that blotted out everything else. But there was no escape. She'd taken her mother's hand, said they'd do it together, and now she couldn't let go.

When finally she couldn't stand on her feet anymore, she'd slept fully clothed on her mother's bed with only a blanket pulled over her. Her mom had taken her father's side of the bed, still touching Bree in the darkness deep in the middle of that endless night.

Upon waking, she'd gone to her bathroom to brush away the taste of a long night, but returned to her parents' room without changing or showering.

The doorbell broke through the gurgle of her father's breathing. He sounded like he was choking.

Please don't make me do this. No one listened.

"Get the door, Brianna," her mother said, once again ensconced on the stool by his bedside.

After the things her mom had said last night, Bree almost believed she sat there simply to make sure he was really dead when it finally happened.

The two aides she hadn't met before, one man, one woman, followed her back to the bedroom. Despite the fact that the sun was out after the rain, she felt as if she were leading them to a dungeon where she and her mother held her father captive, chained to a wall and spread out on a dirty straw mattress.

"This is Meredith and Geoffrey, Mom." They'd each given her a card when she let them in.

"How's Dad doing today?" Geoffrey said as he passed behind Bree's mom, trailing his hand across her back in comfort. Her mother still wore yesterday's housecoat.

How she'd changed; a few short weeks ago, she wouldn't

have been caught dead in a housecoat, not even by a delivery boy.

Her mom murmured something in reply that Bree didn't catch, and Geoffrey smiled. Tall with fair skin and a bald head, he was big, not fat but muscled. Though the aides were well-trained in how to move patients with the least amount of physical exertion, rolling them to one side, then the other to change the sheets beneath them, wash them, put on new pajamas, et cetera, a big man made the procedure run more smoothly. Meredith was a slight blonde with curly hair she'd tamed back into a bun. Having Geoffrey as her partner surely made things easier.

Leaning over the head of the bed, Geoffrey adjusted the oxygen tubes in her father's nostrils, then stroked his cheek in the gentlest of gestures. Meredith moved to the other side of the mattress, next to the window. Behind her, the sun shone on the roof of the dollhouse, glittering in the raindrops as it dried them. The miniature house looked so pretty with its scallops and flowers painted along the sides. So inviting, so innocent.

Bree suddenly hugged herself and looked at Geoffrey.

As he caressed her father's face, Meredith trailed a hand down his emaciated arm. They gave him a series of touches and caresses that were both a comfort and a test of his condition. Bree wondered idly if they'd have been so tender and caring if they'd known him before he was comatose. He didn't twitch, didn't move, didn't respond, not even a flutter of his eyelids that still hovered at half-mast.

"Ladies," Geoffrey said, his voice soft and gentle for such a big man. "You can see the mottled black and blue coloring along his bottom half. Dad has increased lividity. This means his circulatory system is shutting down."

Once again, her mother murmured a sound. Maybe she was saying nothing at all, just acknowledging Geoffrey's comments.

"If we move Dad," he went on, "we stand the chance of losing him. He's very close, and we could push him over by so much as turning him to wash him. How do you feel about that?"

Let him die. Do it now.

Her mom's back to her, Bree couldn't see her expression. But she said nothing, didn't even touch him. In the ensuing silence, Meredith pulled some prepackaged single-use cloths from her pocket and ripped one open. She soothed his brow, wiping gently, then his cheeks, his cracked lips.

"What would you like us to do, ladies? Meredith and I will wash him gently to prepare him, if you'd like to discuss it between you."

Bree couldn't find any voice with which to agree or even talk to her mother. Her heart beat in a staccato rhythm, and she heard her mother's words from last night.

Die, you old fuck, die.

She wanted it, Jesus, she wanted it. Just let it be done, let it be over, let him be gone.

"Turn him," her mother said, her voice a crack in the gentle, soothing atmosphere Geoffrey created with Meredith.

Wasn't that killing him, wasn't it murder? Or was it more mercy than he deserved?

Geoffrey closed his eyes and dipped his head in the briefest nod of agreement, then smiled. For him, it was an act of mercy. He must do it all the time, must know when the end is close, so close that a simple push could release the soul.

For a moment, Bree wished she was capable of that kind of delicate, caring emotion.

"Come close," Geoffrey whispered to her when she hung back. "You'll want to see. I believe it helps keep the loved ones in our hearts forever."

No, she didn't want to see, didn't want to remember or know.

Her father hadn't been in her heart for years. He'd been in her head, telling her what to do, how to do it, and how miserable her attempts at life were. But the hypnotic quality of Geoffrey's deep yet so very tender voice drew her near.

Please don't make me, Daddy.

Geoffrey's voice compelled her.

Closer, closer, she could now see the dark bruising along the underside of her father's arms and shoulders where the blood had settled.

How could a man die so quickly? Four days ago she'd fed him whiskey and morphine to shut him up. Now he was silent, still, even the twitching of his eyeballs back and forth had ceased. The bottom half of his irises—the only thing she could see other than the whites of his eyes—were milky. Like the corpses you see on TV.

By her side, she felt her mother's body pressed to hers. *Don't touch me.* Bree wanted to scream, to shout, to run.

When he was gone, who would she blame for the way she was?

"Meredith." That was all Geoffrey said as he lightly massaged her father's shoulders, then his neck, his fingers blunt and thick.

Meredith pulled the sheet aside. Her father's legs were nothing more than sticks protruding from the bottom of his hospital-style gown. His backside rested on a towel laid across the mattress. Meredith grasped one edge of the towel, pulling up, slowly turning his body.

"Watch his face with me, Bree." Geoffrey's words were little more than a voice in her head, and yet, as if he were a magician, she obeyed.

Her father's mouth hung grotesquely open, and his head seemed to move on its own, as if it were disconnected from his body, lolling backward on his neck. If her mother hadn't been holding fast to her sweaty hand, Bree might have touched him. Poked the waxen skin. Screamed at him.

Then Geoffrey cupped the back of his neck and held his head up, paper-thin flesh covering a skull.

There was a sound like a breath, with none of the gurgle that had rattled constantly with every rise and fall of his chest. Then a gentle whoosh of air like the wings of a butterfly right next to her cheek.

"There he goes," Geoffrey whispered.

Her heart contracted. A shimmering stream of breath slipped from her father's lips and rose gently, lightly, airily to the ceiling. He had never been a light and airy man. He had never been gentle. Yet his essence, if that's what it was, was all of those things.

"I see him," her mother murmured with the softness of awe. They watched the ceiling as if . . . well, as if they were really watching her father's soul rise to heaven or the hereafter or whatever.

Later he would fall back down to hell where he belonged.

14

GEOFFREY AND MEREDITH HAD OFFICIALLY TAKEN HER FATHER'S vitals—or rather his lack of them—and recorded the time. They'd washed and prepared him as if for some sacrament. When they were done, Geoffrey had pulled the covers over his chest and tucked them around him as if he were a father putting his son to bed. He hadn't covered her father's face. He'd left him as if he were sleeping.

Bree had watched the whole ritual as if it would somehow confirm his death.

After she let them out, Bree stood in the doorway of her mother's bedroom—because it wasn't her parents' room anymore; it belonged only to her mom—and watched the dead man on the hospital bed as if he might rise again. Because really, how could the old fuck be dead? Her mother's voice drifted eerily down the hallway from the den as she phoned the funeral home to come get him, like he was a package they had to send out.

He was gone. It was strange. Bree didn't know what to do now.

She couldn't walk in and look more closely; she could only stand there on the threshold and watch as sunlight streamed across the bed in which his body lay.

"I'll make some coffee, Bree," her mother called as if there wasn't a dead man in her bedroom.

Bree couldn't feel her arms, couldn't feel her legs, her lips. He was gone; he was *really* gone. She wanted to feel free. She felt only . . . numb. Unreal.

"Bree?"

Her mother's voice, suddenly so close, startled her. Bree's pulse raced.

"Coffee?" her mom asked again.

"Yes. Please. Thank you."

Were you supposed to drink coffee after your father died? Maybe you were supposed to cry. Coffee seemed too . . . routine.

She must have stood there a while staring at his unmoving body because finally there was the whistle of the kettle bleating down the long hallway. Her mom was making instant. Bree tore herself from the threshold, backing toward the kitchen as if she were afraid he might come after her.

"Would you like a chocolate chip cookie with your coffee?" Her mother held out the bear-shaped cookie jar Bree had given her a Christmas ago. Her mom loved cookie jars in fun and distinctive shapes. Bree's father, however, would let her put out only one at a time because, he said, the kitchen looked cluttered and messy with them all. Then he'd groused about how much room her collection took up in the cupboards.

Instead of grabbing a cookie, Bree planned what jar shape she'd buy for her mother's birthday.

Is *this* what people did after a death? Act like nothing had happened, even planning the next birthday gift. Really, what *did* they do? Hug and cry in each other's arms? Share all the wonderful memories they had? Make breakfast? Have coffee and a cookie and pretend there were wonderful memories to be had?

"I'd rather have a piece of toast with marmalade," Bree said.

Her mother tapped her forehead. "Silly me, of course. We haven't eaten breakfast yet. I'll make toast."

"Can I have juice as well?"

"Of course, dear."

Bree poured them both a glass as her mother put two pieces of wheat bread in the toaster.

"They said it'll be a couple of hours," her mother said.

Bree froze. Two *hours* with just his body in the house? It was weird. It was creepy. She couldn't stand it.

"I was wondering if you'd go out and get a few things," her mom added conversationally. "We're almost out of milk. And oatmeal. I'll make a list."

Bree's voice seemed to come from far away, totally out of her own body. "Sure. I'll do it this afternoon."

"Oh, no, you can go as soon as we've had our toast and coffee." Her mother smiled the oddest beatific smile as she retrieved the marmalade from the fridge.

Bree stared at her. Were there fewer lines around her eyes, as if she'd suddenly been released from a terrible strain? Were her shoulders less rounded? "Don't you want me to stay at least until . . ."

She didn't know how to finish the sentence. *Until they cart away the dead body?* Or maybe it should be *until they haul the old fuck out of the house?* She couldn't figure out what was appropriate. Except that leaving her mother alone didn't feel like the right thing to do. After all, her mom hadn't wanted to be alone when he died, so how could it be okay to stay in the house all alone with a dead body?

"You go. I'll be fine."

It was wrong. It was bad. It was freaking weird. But after their toast, juice, and coffee were consumed, Bree left her mother alone with her dead husband.

She couldn't think properly. She actually had a grocery list in her purse. Though her mother hadn't said it in words, Bree knew she wasn't supposed to come back until the house was empty.

Her hands shook on the steering wheel even as she turned the heater on full blast. The sun on the concrete was blinding after the days of rain. She couldn't go to the grocery store. She couldn't do her shopping on a Sunday morning with all the mothers and children and families running around. In days of old, they would all be at church, but these days, the grocery stores were equally as busy no matter the weekend day. She couldn't pick out broccoli or bananas or apples or oatmeal with all those people around as if today was a normal day.

Please don't make me do it.

Funny, she'd thought that little-girl voice inside her head would go away once he was dead. Her flesh chilled suddenly, goose bumps rising along her arms beneath her jacket, and she was terrified the voice would never go away. Never, never, ever. Panic started to rise, choking her. She accidentally ran through a yellow light that had already turned to red before she'd entered the intersection, and a furious driver honked.

Let me go, get me out of here.

If she skipped the grocery store, there was only one other place she could go. The place she *had* to go. The person she needed to run to more than anything.

LUKE WAS REVIEWING THE BOARD MEETING MINUTES, BUT HE couldn't keep his mind on the subject. Not after last night with Bree. He'd wanted perfection, and he'd sure as hell gotten it. He'd tried saying that the pieces of herself she gave him up to that point were enough, but now he knew they would never be enough. Last night made him thirst for more, her brilliant smile, the multiple personality that lurked beneath the facade. She was such an odd mixture of creatures, submissive yet demanding, willing to do anything he told her yet controlling every moment of the experience.

He'd called her cell phone both last night and this morning, but she'd turned it off.

She hadn't been answering his calls since Thursday. Yet she hadn't cancelled the date. He wondered how her father was doing this morning. Her mom. If she'd been okay without Bree last evening. What was happening at that house now? He needed to know, needed to make sure he was there for Bree the moment she needed him.

He was about to reach for the phone again when his doorbell chimed. It was probably Redfield from next door wanting to borrow the hedge trimmer or leaf blower or any other number of yard tools Redfield didn't feel he needed to buy because Luke had them all. When he and Beth divorced, Luke kept the house and almost everything in it since she'd wanted a small condo she could manage more easily. But he went over there to fix things for her, a leaky faucet, a blocked drain. He had all the indoor tools required. Redfield borrowed those, too.

He spoke before he'd fully opened the door. "Which one do you want this time, Redfield?"

Bree stood on the front stoop. The circles under her eyes were darker than normal, accentuating the paleness of her skin. She wore the same clothes she'd had on last night, the blazer creased.

"Bree, what the hell's wrong?" He pulled her inside. She had never shown up at his house without calling first. "Is your father okay?" Idiotic question, the man was dying.

"Everything's fine," she said without meeting his gaze, her eyes fixed on the tile floor of his entryway.

He took her chin, forced her gaze up, but all she did was

lower her lids slightly to shut him out. "The fuck it is. Something's wrong. Tell me," he insisted.

His mind whirled. He was helpless. She was here, yet he had no idea what to do for her.

"I was a very bad girl, Master."

Screw the goddamn games for now. "Tell me what the fuck happened, Bree. I can't do anything for you if you don't tell me."

"After you left me last night, I went to a sex club and let two men have me."

Her words slammed his chest so hard, he had to step back.

She kept her eyes downcast like a penitent. "I need to be punished, Master. Please punish me."

What the fuck? She couldn't have. Not after that perfect night together. "Goddamn you," he whispered, the words harsh in his aching throat.

"I know how disappointed you must be in me, Master." She went to her knees on the cold, hard tile, hands behind her back, and lifted her face to him, yet still without actually meeting his gaze. "However you need to punish me, Master, you must."

"Did you fuck them?" Christ, even the question burned in his chest. How could she do that?

"Would that be the worst I could do, Master?" she said so softly he had to strain.

The worst? Letting another man touch her made him fucking crazy. But the worst? "Did you let them make you come?"

She raised her head, and for the briefest of moments, her gaze locked with his. Then she dropped her head in supplication. "Yes, Master. Over and over."

Christ, she wanted to drive fucking nails into him. He gritted his teeth.

"They forced me down and made me do it. I couldn't help

it, Master. I know how angry you must be, how disappointed. That's why I need to be punished."

She was forcing him to it, making him nuts. "Get in the fucking living room." Christ, she'd ripped a hole right through him, but he still wouldn't let her knees bruise on the tile floor. She scrambled to her feet, almost ran to the living room, which was to the right of the hall, taking the two steps down to the plush carpeting.

"On your knees. Don't look at me. Face away."

She did his bidding almost eagerly, going down before the teak coffee table as if it were an altar.

Too eagerly. Through his haze of anger, he began to see, to think. The back of her blazer was a mass of wrinkles, the fine strands of her hair tangled. As if she'd slept in her clothes.

Something had happened. He'd seen that clearly in the wildness of her eyes during that brief look they'd shared.

But was it what she'd told him?

Her father's imminent death was pushing her to the breaking point. Maybe she'd walked in on something in that house—a seizure, coughing up phlegm or blood from his lungs—and it had pushed her over the edge, sent her running to her old way of life before Luke found her.

Or maybe the whole ordeal had sent her running *here* with a story designed to make him crazy, to force him to punish her.

He stared at her back, her muscles rigid with tension. Yes, she would lie to him, incite him to get what she needed. She would think long and hard about what would set him off. If her need was great, she was so very capable of using his emotions against him. If something was very, very wrong.

Luke closed his eyes, ratcheted back his anger. She wouldn't accept what he thought she needed. So he would provide what she wanted, no gentleness, no comfort, just the solace of submission. He couldn't deny her that.

"Do not move. Do not turn," he ordered.

He had toys in the bedroom, vibrators, plugs, scarves, cuffs, ropes, blindfolds. She required something more elemental.

He found the perfect implement in a bottom kitchen drawer. Back in the living room, he stood behind her. "Cross your wrists. I'm going to restrain you with an extension cord."

She let out a long breath that held a shudder of excitement as she crossed her wrists, holding her arms away from her spine to give him better access. Squatting behind her, he wrapped the plain brown cord, lashing her hands together, then looped the end back through itself to secure it.

Rounding the coffee table, he stood between it and the sofa to survey her, crossing his arms over his chest. "Don't look at me, you cheating bitch," he snapped. "Look down."

"Yes, Master." The words came out with a breathless quality as she quickly dropped her gaze, which had been centered on his crotch, his hard cock, and the thing she needed most, his desire for her.

"Do not look at me until I allow you that pleasure. You are to be punished for the ultimate insult you have dealt me."

"I'm so sorry, Master."

A tear trickled from the outer corner of her eye, dribbling along the outside of her cheek until it dropped off her chin to land on her jacket.

"Don't try to gain my sympathy with tears," he said, though he ached to gather her into his embrace. "It's not going to work." He stroked his chin, considering. She wasn't looking directly at him, but she would sense his perusal. "How best to make you pay, slut?" he pondered softly.

She parted her lips.

"Do not," he snapped, "say a word. No suggestions."

She slapped her mouth shut.

He had the overwhelming urge to push past her lips, to shove his cock deep into the recesses and fuck her mouth. He wanted her warmth and wetness. He wanted to give her the thing she always seemed to want most, his climax. Yet the moment required something far more intense.

"Before I decide your punishment, you will make a full confession. I want to hear exactly what you did, from the moment I left you last night. The truth, every word of it. Or I will know."

He would make her say it. In there somewhere, he hoped to discover what had driven her here. And driven her to lie.

15

HE STOOD ABOVE HER, ARMS CROSSED, POWERFUL, HER JUDGE. Bree allowed herself a brief glance up at him through her lashes. His blue and white striped rugby shirt stretched over his muscles, and his jeans cupped the massive bulge of his hard cock.

That was all she needed, his hardness. He wanted her. No matter the lies she told him, he wanted her. It was what she craved, his need and desire for her. Nothing else mattered.

From the moment she'd watched him drive away last night, what had she supposedly done? "You wouldn't let me suck you. I needed relief." She wasn't above making it his fault. *You didn't give me the mindlessness I craved, Master, so I punished you.*

"I couldn't go inside that house," she told him. So very true, but she'd gone inside anyway. Would it have been different if the taste of Luke's come had been lingering in her mouth, washing away fear with the memory of his desire? No, of course not. Her mother would have said the same things; her father would have died in the morning. But perhaps she would have felt differently. Perhaps she could have taken it calmly.

"Go on," he demanded.

She realized she'd gotten lost in her pain, lost in her need, her anger, her desire to blame him for not saving her.

"I got in my car and drove to the city to the place you found me." It felt so right to punish him by taking him back to that night.

"What did you do once you got there?" he said without inflection, but she felt his fuming in the tightness of his tone.

"I went to the slave room."

"You bitch," he said on barely a breath.

Not his usual *sweet bitch* or even a *dirty bitch*. Just *you bitch*. She thrilled to his anger. He was always too gentle with her, even when he was punishing her. When she rang his doorbell, she'd had no idea what she needed. Just him, his touch, his breath on her, his cock, his come. Like a narcotic. She hadn't intended to lie, to make up a story that would enflame him. It just spilled out all over him, because she hadn't wanted his gentleness. She'd wanted to push him.

She tucked her chin, lowered her eyes. And pressed his buttons. "There were two masters. They ripped my clothes off and tied me to the wall with manacles. They fingered and probed me, everywhere. I could hide nothing from them."

She watched his legs as he skirted the coffee table, then felt the rush of air currents as he came down beside her. Fisting his hand in her hair, he pulled her head back, her scalp stinging.

"Did they make you come?" he snapped, his voice as hard and implacable as diamonds. This close, his face blurred in her vision, and his breath fanned her cheek, sweet and harsh, his skin ruddy with anger.

She could hardly drag in a breath. Her blood hummed with excitement and need. "They put their fingers in me," she whispered. "They played my clit. And I came. They licked me and sucked me, and I came. They took turns with me, making me scream."

"Fuck." He growled like an enraged beast.

Her scalp began to sizzle with the delicious ache of his fingers in her hair. "When I thought I couldn't stand any more, they pulled me down off the wall and took turns fucking me."

"Cunt," he whispered, teeth clenched.

Perfect. That word. He hadn't called her the names she needed, not the really bad ones, as if he'd been withholding from her, but now, that word touched her like an endearment. She gave him more. "They took me in every hole. Over and over. I couldn't stop coming for them, and I didn't even know who was making me come. One of them licked me while the other fucked me." She became seduced by her own lie. "They traded off, taking me, using me, pounding into me until my throat hurt so badly I couldn't even scream anymore when I came."

He grabbed her chin, slammed his mouth down on hers, whether to shut her up or because she'd driven him to the edge, she couldn't tell. His wildness entered her, filled her, but she wanted more. With her hands tied, she couldn't push him away, could only revel in the taste of his fury, the crush of his lips. Until he pulled away.

"Did you like it?" He let her look at him now, holding her in that position, his face above her, his breath puffing hard across her cheeks, his fist gripping her hair just short of the agony she craved, and his cock molded against her.

What did he want from her? What did she need from him and how best to drive him to it?

"I loved it," she whispered, watching his amber eyes darken to the color of deep rich earth. "I begged them to take more, to force everything on me."

"Fuck you." His gaze blazed down on her.

"And I took it. I loved it. I begged for more. I told them to hurt me, to use me. And I screamed because it was all so good. They were young and hard and they kept at it for hours, torturing me until I cried with how good and hot it was. I wanted it again, over and over."

Suddenly he hauled her back from the table, wedging himself in front of it. She was wet, creamy, close to the edge with only her lies and his raging touch. He tore apart the fastenings of her blazer.

"Did they do this to you?" He pinched her nipple hard.

She arched, moaned, the pain and the brutal lines of his face making her soar. "No. I wanted them to, but they didn't."

Bending down, he sucked her nipple into his mouth, bit her the way she loved, harder than he normally allowed her. *Yes, yes, yes.*

He straightened, tore at the buttons of his jeans until his beautiful cock sprang free. Hard, the skin stretched, the vein pulsing, the crown purple. "Did they force their cocks down your throat?"

She was down on her knees before him in supplication, arms behind her back, head tipped to gaze upon the full breadth of him. His cock beckoned. She needed it. But he had to force it on her. "No. They only took me and made me come."

"Open your mouth," he demanded.

She did. He shoved himself to the back of her throat, forced her to suck all of him, hard and fast. It was so good, she wanted to weep.

As if he could hear her beg, he made her take him full-throated, driving into her, fucking her mouth. He called her all the dirty, filthy names she needed, the words she craved: slut, bitch, cocksucker, cunt.

They weren't gentle, and he didn't soften them with needless adjectives. In his deep voice, they drove her mad. They thrust her up and out of herself, until she seemed to be floating above them, watching this beautiful, perfect man take the dirty, bad girl that she was.

She creamed without him even getting inside her jeans.

BREE SUCKED HIM HARDER, TOOK HIM DEEPER, ALMOST DRAGGED an orgasm from him. A lesser man would have given in, but he wasn't one of the young, hard cocks she claimed to have had in the slave room. He held himself in check, even as she shuddered and he felt the ripple of her body in orgasm.

She'd lost her control. The climax was no fake. In letting his anger go, unleashing his rage at her lie, her story, her fantasy, her betrayal, he'd given her the release she needed without even touching her pussy.

Christ, now he wanted his own orgasm. But not this way. He wanted it inside her. Pulling free of her succulent mouth, he fastened his jeans. She stared up at him, eyes glazed.

He'd gone wild with the name-calling, giving her what she wanted, loving it as much as she did. "Come on, you fucking slut." He yanked her to feet, steadied her, then bent down and hauled her over his shoulder in a fireman's carry, her arms still secured behind her with the extension cord. "Your punishment for what you've done has only just begun."

She needed power and dominance. He wanted it just as badly.

"Please, Master, don't hurt me," she begged as her body thumped against his back.

He would never hurt her beyond what she could bear. But he would give her more than he ever had before. Letting her slide to the bedroom carpet, he shoved her facedown onto the bed. Leaning over her, he growled in her ear. "Don't you turn. Don't you look at me. You just lay there and take what you deserve, you cocksucking whore." He pulled her head back by the hair until she winced, then let go. "Do you understand?"

"Yes, Master." He felt the sob of pain, fear, and excitement in her voice.

He thrived on the sound, and need forced him to a rougher touch. Reaching beneath her, he yanked the snap of her jeans, tugged down her zipper, then pulled everything off, panties, jeans, shoes, tossing it all aside in a heap.

"Take your punishment, slut." He slapped her ass harder than last week in her condo, harder than he'd ever done. She moaned, cried out, and her cream covered the palm of his hand when he slid down over the exposed pout of her pussy.

"Fucking bitch, you like this too much. You want me to make you come. You're full of lies about how much you hate it."

"No, Master. I'm bad. I know I'm bad and this is my terrible punishment."

"Lying cunt," he said low, forceful, even as he caressed the crease of her pussy, delving into the heat to find her clit. The button was hard, tight, burgeoning against his fingers. He rubbed; she moaned.

"Liar." He slapped her butt again. She writhed.

"I'm going to fuck you now. Facedown. Without touching anything but your hips to hold you while I pound into your dirty snatch. Don't you dare come."

"No, Master."

He tugged open the bedside drawer where he kept his stash of condoms for her protection. He glanced back at her; she'd turned her face away just as he'd instructed. "I'm not even taking my pants off, you slut. I'm fucking you as if you aren't worth more than a quickie."

"Yes, Master." Still facing away from him, she squirmed on

the bed, perhaps massaging herself or maybe she was unable to keep still in her excitement.

"Cunt," he said for effect.

She groaned.

The words were a part of her ritual. Maybe they freed her, allowed her to accept what she thought she was, to take what she deserved and to find her own pleasure in it.

Finally behind her again, the condom covering his aching cock, he stroked her ass, tested her pussy's readiness with his fingers, one, two. She soaked him with her desire. "Look how badly you want this, you whoring slut."

She bucked against his touch, taking his fingers deeper. "Master. Oh God, Master."

With no further preliminaries, he slammed home, sliding deep into her. His eyes ached with the sweetness of her pussy.

Arms still tied behind her, she clenched her fingers.

He felt himself drowning in her depths, in the warmth, the scent of arousal rising off her. He wanted to lose his mind as he took her, but he saved enough to give her what she needed. "Panting bitch. You're in heat. You'll take any man who wants to fuck you."

She did pant, then turned into the comforter face first as if she were trying to suffocate herself.

Still he pounded, sank deep, withdrew. She was tight, so sweet, so warm. Rolling down to cover her, he reached between their bodies and put his fingers to her clit, rubbing her own moisture over her. She moaned, her clit throbbing beneath his touch, then she sobbed and cried and went wild under him. He climbed higher, higher, until there was just the feel of her perfect pussy clenching around him, her pants of "Master, Master, Master" punctuated by the filthy names he called her. As he buried himself in her sweetness, he shot his essence deep inside her.

16

SHE COULDN'T REMEMBER EVERYTHING CLEARLY. SHE KNEW ONLY that she'd reached some orgasmic pinnacle, that now she lay in the comfort of his embrace, and for the briefest moment between sleeping and waking, she wasn't afraid and she wasn't bad. She simply existed, and it was good. She did not have a past, there was no today, no last night, no tomorrow. There was only now.

Slowly she became aware of her chafed wrists, her aching muscles, the rawness of her throat from her cries, and the tenderness of her pussy where he'd taken her hard. There'd been no gentleness. When she came, he'd wrenched it from her.

It felt good to be forced, her climax guiltless.

His chin was scratchy against her forehead, his chest hair soft against her cheek. He smelled of clean male sweat.

Then she smelled herself. She needed a shower. After what he'd done, after she'd accepted her punishment, and with a shower, she would be clean again for a little while.

She moved, but Luke slept on.

She crawled off the bed, and he simply shifted on the comforter without waking. His breaths were deep and even. In the big tiled shower, she turned the controls to scalding. Then she stepped beneath the spray. She stood it as long as she could, but she was weak and had to add a little cold water to mute the burn.

She startled as she felt his body, suddenly there, hard and cool against her blazing flesh. She hadn't heard the door. He soaped between her legs, her armpits, reached for shampoo for her hair. His touch was so sweet and gentle, she wanted to cry.

When they were done, he put on his robe, then wrapped her in a huge bath towel, and carried her to the screened-in sun porch at the back of the house, settling onto a chaise lounge with her in his arms.

Her head pillowed on his chest, she was almost asleep again. Until his voice rumbled against her ear.

"Tell me now. I order you to," he added as if he thought she wouldn't say anything at all if he didn't make it a demand.

She knew what he wanted. "He's dead," she murmured, feeling almost as if she were in a trance. "I watched him die. They said he floated away, and I think I saw it, but I'm not really sure."

He was silent a long time, her head rising and falling on his breastbone with every deep breath. "When?" he asked, offering no sympathy words.

She didn't want them. "This morning."

"Why didn't you stay with your mother?"

"She told me to get out. She didn't need me anymore. She didn't care. So I left."

Luke heard the pain lacing her words, felt the vibration of it through her body. She didn't cry. She'd moved beyond crying. All he could do was take her pain into himself, absorb it for her like the portrait of Dorian Gray absorbed his evil.

He didn't offer meager condolences. He didn't question why she'd needed hard sex rather than comfort. He didn't even ask why, rather than tell him about her father, she'd lied about the two doms at the club. He had the sense to realize that she knew she'd get a harder fuck out of him with that story, that he'd never have been able to give it to her the way she wanted it if she'd told him about her dad first. She knew him so well, knew that giving two doms climax after climax would make him totally crazy. He couldn't even be angry about it. How she'd handled him defined her. He either had to accept or walk. He accepted. He wanted her any way he could have her. Now, he gave her his lap to lay in, his arms around her, and his permission to talk if she wanted to.

He went on with the gentle questioning. "Do you need help with the funeral arrangements?"

"My parents already did that together," she murmured softly, as if she were under hypnosis. "Before. When the doctors said he should think about hospice, they went out and made all the arrangements."

When they'd told the patient there wasn't any hope left. "So the service is planned. That's good." At least there was less to worry about, he supposed.

"My mom's cremating him. No urn." She sighed, then softly added, "Just dust and ash."

She had no inflection as she said it; he couldn't tell how she felt. A hole grew inside him. Isn't that what they were all destined for, dust and ash? It made it that much more important to take what you could now.

"I assume he has a will."

"Everything tied in a neat little bow, all carefully controlled," she whispered.

She had to be suppressing her grief and pain, her sense of loss. First with the sex, now with this almost childlike tone.

"If you need anything—"

"I don't," she cut him off. "I'm fine. We're all fine now. Everything's fine." Her words lingered, then ended on a puff of breath. She tipped her head back to look at him. Her eyes were clear and all-knowing. She knew he heard the lies; she knew he couldn't say anything about it, that he had to accept, that this was the one thing he couldn't push.

"I'm glad it's all fine." He knew it wasn't. He understood the ache of loss that death brought, the complete and total end of everything, no chance to correct mistakes, or to say *I love you* one last time. Inside, he died a little to be so incapable of easing her pain. The most he could do was sit here, his arms around her. And listen when she needed to say something.

"With him gone," she whispered, "maybe I can finally be normal."

He stroked her cheek. Even as true as it was, people didn't want to hear that time healed the loss. Instead he said, "Remember we said we didn't need normal."

She worried her lower lip between her teeth a moment, but "Right" was all she said when she spoke.

In the ensuing silence, he put his lips to her temple, kissed her.

"It's time for me to go," she said after long minutes.

There was one last thing he needed before he could let her go. Cupping her cheek, he forced her to meet his gaze. "What we did was fucking hot. Tell me it was good for you."

He wasn't asking for affirmation of his prowess. He just needed to know that he'd read her correctly, that she'd wanted it hard and angry and had instigated what happened with her story about the slave room. If he knew exactly how to read her, he could duplicate the experience every time.

Her eyes were a murky blue, like a cloudy sky. "You made me stop thinking," she said, and at least that was said with complete honesty.

"Is that what you need from me?" Was that enough for him, to give her the most powerful orgasm he could so that she could stop thinking?

"Yes," she said.

He felt the rightness of it. Yes, it was enough for now, for this moment. The *more* he wanted from her would come later, when she'd dealt with her loss, her grief, her mother, her life after death.

She climbed off his lap, stood, the towel wrapped tightly around her torso. "It's more than anyone else has ever given me. It's more than I've ever taken."

He actually reveled in that bit of knowledge and the fact that she offered it to him freely.

"I have to go now," she repeated. She had to return to her mother.

"Will you be okay?"

"Yes."

He hadn't expected her to say anything less. Rising, he put a hand to her throat, stroked her smooth skin with his thumb. "I'm here. Call."

"I always do."

It was his one constant, that she would always call again. She needed him.

It was not until he stood in the front window watching her car disappear around the corner that he heard her words again in his mind. *With him gone, maybe I can finally be normal.* Not *I can be normal again*, or even *things can return to normal*. She'd never said there was a time when she'd felt normal.

He didn't want to think it. Yet he'd always sensed the shadows in her past. His gut had told him she'd been in some bad relationships, not just Derek, but before. Bad relationships that had skewed her thinking. But did it go deeper? Her need for punishment, that she *deserved* it, the derisive names she had to have. Then that little snippet she told him about the driving lesson. And finally, her response to her father's death, running here for punishment, *needing* it. The reaction was extreme; it wasn't normal. *She* wasn't normal.

Jesus, no. His gut was screaming at him. No, he had to be wrong. Her father couldn't have done anything to her. Luke couldn't conceive of a father doing bad things to his own child.

Yet fathers did, all the time.

IT WAS AFTER LUNCH BY THE TIME BREE WAS ON HER WAY BACK, having purchased the milk, bread, oats, and other things on her mother's list.

The guilt unsettled her stomach. She'd left her mom alone too long. But she couldn't have survived another moment in that house without seeing Luke.

A curious warmth had spread through her as he held her. She'd gone a little crazy, goading him with the most hateful story she could think of, begging him to heap on the abuse. He'd given his all, yet in the moments afterward, it was like a different man touching her, comforting her. In most ways, he was so normal and centered. Even the sex thing wasn't *that* kinky. He called it abnormal, but an unattached male going to a sex club once in a while or playing with a bit of bondage wasn't that far out of the norm. She was the one far out on the edge of the spectrum. But he didn't mind. He gave her what she needed.

Pulling into her parents' driveway, Bree held tight to the steering wheel. There was Luke's house. And then there was this place with its dark walls and its dark halls. Climbing from her car, she realized she'd lost the delicious content Luke had given her in those moments on his bed, in his shower, in his arms. Now, there was only ennui.

All she had to do was get through the scattering of her father's ashes. Then she could go back home. Couldn't she? Suddenly she had visions of her mother needing her for weeks, even months. Her mom had no friends; she was completely alone. Bree's father had never allowed her any friends. He'd claimed he didn't like being alone when she went out, but it was just a way of controlling her and keeping her dependent.

She opened the door and called. "Mom." Her voice seemed to echo in all the silence.

She prayed her father was gone. Not just his spirit, but his body, too.

"I'm back here, Bree." Her mother's voice, oddly cheery, drifted down the hall to her.

She followed the sound. In the bedroom, her mom had pushed the hospital bed flush up against the window frame, giving herself more room. Thank God it was empty. Bree didn't realize she'd been holding her breath until she let it out with a whoosh of relief. Then she saw the dollhouse through the window, sweet and harmless in the afternoon light. She moved until it was out of sight.

Her mom now sat on a low stool beside the bureau. A big black garbage bag at her feet, she was stuffing it with T-shirts, underwear, and socks.

"What are you doing, Mom?"

"I thought I'd make a Goodwill run with these clothes."

"They don't take underwear."

A frown creasing her mouth, her mom stared at the bag a moment. Then suddenly she smiled. "You're right. Get me a kitchen trash bag for all that stuff, would you?"

Her father wasn't even burned and scattered. Bree wasn't sure his body was completely cold and stiff yet.

Die, you old fuck, die.

Her mother had been waiting.

Suddenly, her mom cocked her head. "How do you dispose of medications. Aren't they a hazardous waste?"

"Probably. I can look it up on the Internet."

"Oh, I'm sure hospice can tell us. I called them to come get the bed."

"You don't have to do this now, Mom." It was frightening.

"What else are we going to do? Sit here and mope?" Her mother flapped a hand at her. "Now go on and get the trash bag so we can dump it all."

Oh yeah, this was scary.

17

FOR TWO HOURS, BREE AND HER MOM SORTED THROUGH THINGS that were usable and stuff that needed to be tossed. Like all her father's work pants and gardening clothes. Some of his shirts were threadbare; she remembered seeing them year after year.

It was crazy. Bree held up a button-down she could have sworn he'd had even back when she was in college. "This one has been worn out for ten years."

"You know your father." Her mom smiled, and it was oddly fond, as if now that he was gone, she could pretend there was something to miss.

In the bureau, there was a slew of new shirts, still with the tags on them. "He didn't want to use them until the others were worn out," her mother explained.

Bree excavated another drawer. Her heart simply stopped beating. She hadn't seen that particular shirt in a long time. It was far older than the others, from her middle school days, maybe even elementary school. Later, he'd started wearing khaki shirts because he'd gotten a great deal on a dozen, but this was a blue chambray workshirt, his name stenciled across the breast pocket, and faint grease stains her mother had never been able to wash out. It still smelled like him, motor oil mixed with a cheap drugstore aftershave. She didn't want to close her eyes. If she did, she'd see him wearing it. If she did, she'd see him standing over her. She'd smell him.

She shoved it down into the trash bag.

"Bree, that one's still got some life left in it."

There was *something* still living in it, but not what her mother thought. "It's covered with grease. No one wants that."

"It would be good for a working man."

She looked at her mother, steeling her features. "It's going in the trash, Mom." She stood, marched down the hall, and out the back door by the garage where the trash bins were kept. Throwing the bag inside, she slammed the lid down again. If her mother wanted to dig in the garbage for the shirt, fine.

Back in the bedroom, afraid of the memories, she simply could not paw through one more drawer. "I'll do the bathroom."

Bree threw out his toothbrush, his razors, that damn aftershave, and the male deodorant. She tossed the leftover medications into a baggie, then added the ones off the bedside table. Looking it up on the Internet, she found they could be dropped off at any pharmacy for disposal. She'd take them tomorrow.

Her mom had moved on to the closet where her father kept his better clothes, the polo shirts and Dockers, his shoes. Every bag her mom filled, Bree carried out to the garage and slung it into the trunk of the family car. When that was full, she started tossing them in her own trunk. They could take them to the Goodwill tomorrow.

With each new bag, they seemed to work faster, harder, barely talking, except for Bree asking if her mom wanted to keep this or that. She wondered what a psychiatrist would make of their mania.

In the den, they got rid of his reading glasses, the sportsmen's magazines, *Popular Mechanics*, detective novels.

"I'll get someone to take that chair." Her father's chair. "It's disgusting and dirty." Her mom wrinkled her nose at the age-old stains, mustard, whiskey, the things he'd spilled. She grabbed a flowered flat sheet from the hall linen closet, threw it over the chair and tucked it down until it didn't look like *his* chair anymore. "There, at least it's covered up."

Eyes vividly alive, her mom said, "Let's do the kitchen." She led the way. "I hate whiskey." She dumped the bottle's contents down the drain. Then the Southern Comfort and the tequila. But she waved her hand at the bourbon and the rum. "I'll keep those for bread pudding sauce." She also made a mean rum cake.

They tossed out his sugary cereals. Her mom liked Raisin Bran, Corn Flakes, plain oats. "I hate blue cheese dressing." Almost with a sense of glee, she added that to the full kitchen trash. "And anything with curry." She made a face. She'd cooked curried beef with apples and raisins every Thursday night for the last forty years, but out went the curry powder, too.

It was as if they were purging the house of every trace of him.

"The sheets," her mom said. So they traipsed back to the bedroom to tear the bed apart. His pajamas were still under his pillow. They didn't wash anything, just threw it all in the trash, as if his scent would never come out of the cotton and her mother couldn't bear having the sheets on her bed again. She hadn't even mentioned putting them in the Goodwill bags versus the rubbish bin.

"They smell like death," she whispered.

They smelled like old man and bad memories, Bree agreed.

When the trash cans were full and so were the trunks and backseats of both their cars, all that remained of Bree's father was the oxygen tank and the hospital bed he'd died in. Once hospice picked it all up, he'd be gone completely, no reminders.

"We need a cup of coffee after all that work," her mom said, as if they'd been spring cleaning instead of erasing every scrap of her dead husband's existence.

Minutes later, sitting at the kitchen table over a freshly brewed mug, her mom beamed suddenly. "Let's have tacos for dinner."

Bree's father had hated Mexican food. He'd liked standard American fair, meat, potatoes, and a vegetable, that was it.

"I'll go out and get some taco shells," Bree offered.

"Sour cream and salsa, too," her mom added. "And one of those taco seasoning mixes."

He was dead, he was gone. They were doing things he hadn't allowed, like having Mexican food for dinner. Then her mother was up again, as if she had ants in her pants and couldn't sit still. She pulled the stepstool out of the broom closet.

"What are you doing?" Bree asked as her mom set the stool beneath a bank of high kitchen cabinets.

"I want my cookie jars." The jars Bree's father hadn't allowed on the counter all at the same time.

When they'd emptied the cupboards, the countertop was a jumbled mess, cookie jars in the shapes of Cinderella and Popeye between the toaster and coffeemaker, a snowman next to the flour and sugar canisters. A fat chef with a black mustache, Mother Goose, a bright red fire hydrant, a gingerbread house. And Dumbo the elephant. Her father had hated that one, saying it was a stupid shape because all the cookie crumbs fell down into Dumbo's legs. Which was true, but Dumbo was brightly colored and had the kindest painted eyes.

Together, she and her mother stared at the crowded counter. "Maybe you can put your flour and sugar in the cookie jars, to give you more room," Bree suggested.

"I'll think about it." Yet her mother wore a sneaky smile, as if she was calculating how many more cookie jars she could buy now that her husband was dead.

Later, by the time they were eating tacos with salsa and sour cream on TV trays in the den and watching *Antiques Roadshow* on PBS, even the hospital bed was gone, having seemingly disappeared into thin air while Bree drove to and from the grocery store for the second time that day.

Yet, as Sunday evening wore on, the essence of her father lingered, his aftershave in the bathroom though she'd trashed the bottle, his body odor on the chair despite its new covering, his ghostly shadow flickering on the TV screen, but gone when she turned her head. There was even the odd echo of his demanding voice in the single heartbeat as a show faded to black before the commercials started.

Unlike her mother, she didn't feel free of him.

She wondered if she ever would.

"HOW YOU DOING, BABY?"

"Fine." Over the phone, Bree's voice was distant, flat.

Or maybe it was the darkness outside. It was after ten on Sunday night, a lonely hour. This morning had been a lifetime ago. Luke wondered what had happened during the hours since she'd left him. "Have you and your mom set a date for the service?"

"I told you, we're cremating him, so there's no service."

"You can still have a memorial."

"He didn't know anyone that would want to come."

That was harsh, but it was the reaction he would have expected if the suspicions he'd considered this morning were correct. "The memorial is for you and your mom." It was for the living, not the dead. Maybe it would help Bree let go emotionally.

"My mom doesn't have anyone, either."

Everyone had someone. Didn't they? But he figured pressing

would only push Bree further away. He'd met her mother once, that was all. He didn't know what her reaction would be to anything. If something had happened to Bree when she was younger, wouldn't the mother have known? Who could say for sure?

"How's your mom?" he asked.

"She's fine." Then she laughed, a rough sound before she cut it off. "We cleaned out all his things."

"Today?" They hadn't even scattered the ashes yet. No service, now cleaning his things out the day he'd died. Bizarre. Then again, it could be a catharsis, what they'd needed to do together. Who was he to judge the right or wrong of it?

"She needed it," was all Bree said.

"What about you?"

She took forever to answer. He counted the long seconds with each heartbeat.

"I want to go home," she whispered. "Do you believe in ghosts?"

"No." He believed in things he could touch, see, and feel.

"I'm afraid to turn out the light."

"He's not there, Bree," he murmured for comfort.

"There's a place he might be."

"Where?"

Again, she didn't answer for a long time. "Just somewhere."

His stomach sank. Jesus. It was true. Yet he still prayed his suspicion was wrong despite the fact that it supplied an answer to so many questions about her. "Then don't go there." He waited.

"You're right," she finally said. "I don't have to go there anymore."

"No, you don't. I'll come by and see you tomorrow after work."

He expected her to fight him, but she simply said, "Okay."

By the time she'd hung up, he still hadn't figured out how to reach her, not emotionally at least. Except for a few brief glimpses inside her mind, there was still only the sexual way. He was starting to wonder if that was actually the worst way for her.

ON MONDAY MORNING, BREE CLACKED AWAY ON HER KEYBOARD IN her office. Coffee mug in her hand, Rachel watched from across the roundhouse. Beside her, Yvonne stirred extra creamer into her own cup.

"She looks sick," Yvonne whispered too loudly. Yvonne always whispered too loudly, but Bree didn't look up.

"She's just pale." Rachel differed in her assessment. "She looks like she hasn't slept, but I don't think she's sick."

Bree had arrived at eleven, an hour later than normal, the new normal versus the old normal. She'd said she had to drop off some things on her way to work.

"She's acting kinda weird," Yvonne said.

"Weird how?"

"Too quiet."

"Yvonne," Rachel said, exasperated, "she's *always* quiet."

"But this is a *weird* quiet."

"Her father's dying. That would make anyone act weird."

"Did she say how he's doing?"

"No." Bree hadn't said much of anything, except to explain why she was an hour late. Although *dropping stuff off* wasn't much of an explanation.

"I mean, most people would tell you the situation and everything. I think Erin should ask her if everything's okay."

It wasn't like Yvonne not to do her own asking. She was a tall woman, at least six feet, and big-boned would be the best word to describe her. Her caramel skin was unlined despite the fact that she was somewhere in her fifties—exactly how old, Rachel couldn't say, but she'd be a grandmother come July. Yvonne didn't so much love to gossip as she worried about everyone in the office as if they were her chicks. But today, for whatever reason, she didn't know how to approach Bree.

"I'll talk to her," Rachel finally said.

"Yeah, you have rapport."

Before Christmas, Yvonne had gotten bent out of shape over that supposed rapport. After all, Rachel had worked at DKG only a few months and Yvonne had been there forever. In the last couple of weeks, though, Yvonne had gotten over the jealousy. Maybe it was the grandchild. She had other things to occupy her mind.

Bree looked up at Rachel's tap on the doorframe. She blinked, as if she needed a moment to refocus.

"I finished all the invoicing and everything you gave me on Friday," Rachel told her.

"Yes. Thanks. I was just checking it all. You did a good job." Bree's voice was totally without inflection.

Rachel ventured a few steps inside the office. "Thank you. I can do more, whatever you need." Then she decided it was silly to make small talk and avoid what she really wanted to say. "How did the weekend go at home? Is everything okay? Are *you* okay?"

Bree was already so fair-skinned that it was hard to say she could actually lose any more color. Maybe it was her bloodless lips that gave the impression, and the fact that she wasn't wearing lipstick. She seemed to take a long time to decide what to say, then finally, "I'm fine. The weekend was"—she paused for a slow, thoughtful blink—"difficult."

"I'm sorry," Rachel empathized. "I know how hard it must be." Not really. Her parents were both still living. She'd never lost anyone close. She'd certainly never had to watch anyone die. But she only had to *think* of losing someone to get a queasy feeling. It was the same way she'd felt about Erin losing her son; all she had to do was imagine it and she felt sick to the very pit of her stomach.

"Thank you," Bree said, her fingers poised over her keyboard as if she couldn't wait for Rachel to get out.

"If you need to talk, we can go out for lunch."

"I appreciate the offer," Bree said slowly as if she were carefully picking her words, "but I have to get this stuff done since I was late."

"Oh yeah, sure." Rachel's feelings weren't hurt. She had a thicker skin than Yvonne did. She just wished she could do something for Bree, be her friend, but the girl didn't share much. Rachel had never met anyone quite so closed down.

Then Bree, almost as a concession, pushed some invoices across the desk. "These were in the mail if you want to enter them."

"Sure." At least it was something Rachel could do to help.

Yvonne accosted her almost the moment she was out of sight of Bree's door. "What'd she say?"

"She said she's fine."

"She lying. I can tell. We need to do something."

"There's only so much pushing we can do, Yvonne. We offer, then we have to wait." It was sort of like putting out food for a feral cat. You set down the bowl, then you backed off and let it come to you when it was ready. If it was ever ready. Funny, she figured Bree for the kind that would never be ready.

18

BREE DIDN'T KNOW WHY SHE'D LIED. OKAY, SHE HADN'T *LIED*. ON
the face of it, everything *was* fine. She'd left her mom making
arrangements about the death certificate and claiming the ashes.
So practical, as if she wasn't talking about burning up his body. A
man's body. All that was left of him but the memories. Bree
wished she could burn those up right along with him.

On her way to work, she'd dropped off the used medications
at the pharmacy, then taken all the bags in her car to the Goodwill donation station. This afternoon her mom was going to drop
off the detritus they'd stuffed in her car. Then he'd be thoroughly
gone.

Bree didn't feel anything. Except a little peculiar that it was so
easy to give away his possessions. And guilt that she *should* have
felt something, but didn't. Her mother seemed to have no such guilt.

As she stared unseeing at her computer monitor for long moments after Rachel left, her fingers poised over the keyboard, it
came to her why she hadn't said her father was dead. Because she
didn't want to go home. Her mother's attitude creeped her out. It
was Monday, the day after he'd died, and this wasn't normal, yet
Bree felt herself getting sucked into it. Like, what else can we
throw out that's *him?*

The dollhouse. She could tear it down board by board. Except that she didn't want to go near it. Not yet. Maybe never. Could she lob a Molotov cocktail into it? Or maybe if she left it long enough, it would disintegrate under the harsh elements. Whatever, she didn't want to go home, at least not to her mother's house.

But if they knew her father had died, that's exactly where Erin and Dominic would send her. When they'd lost Jay last year, neither of them had come in for two weeks. And when they finally did, they were hollow-eyed. They were still different now, too, maybe not grieving every moment like in the beginning, sometimes almost joyful for long minutes, especially over the last couple of weeks since the new year had started. But the lines of grief that had grown at Erin's mouth would never go away, and Bree had seen a look in her eye when she caught sight of Jay's photo on her desk, fond, loving, yet tinged with a sadness that would never end.

Bree didn't feel like that. And they'd think her heartless. Or whacked. If she told them about her mom cleaning everything out? Good God, she wouldn't even contemplate it.

If she could go anywhere, she'd have gone to Luke's. She'd have rolled around in his bed, steeped herself in his scent. Even if he wasn't there. At least she'd see him tonight. He'd said he'd come by. She could face her mom and that house if Luke was in it.

The phone rang. She almost shrieked at the unexpected intrusion. Her heart was racing as she picked up the receiver.

"Ah, Bree," Denton Marbury said with his usual boom. She held the phone away so it didn't hurt her eardrums. "I've left several messages for you, Bree. You haven't returned my calls."

Yeah, well, I was busy with my dying father. She didn't say it, though she would have liked the shock value. With Denton

Marbury, a man with a hide as armored as an armadillo, it probably wouldn't have had any effect. "I've been busy, Mr. Marbury, but you were on my list to call first thing this afternoon," she lied. She'd *forgotten* to set up that meeting time he'd requested when she saw him last week. And she didn't feel the least bit bad about that.

"I've been through your files," he said.

She quelled the sense of violation. He was *supposed* to go through her files, but she still disliked having him put his grubby mitts on anything that was hers. "Did you have any questions?" Of course, he did. He never failed to have questions or find fault or offer suggestions on how she should improve.

"I must say, we need to have some serious discussion about your methodology before we can even begin to handle this audit."

She rolled her eyes, then rubbed her temple. "I can answer any questions you might have right now."

"Oh no, no, no," he blustered. "This requires face-to-face. You forgot I mentioned that last week. I'll need you here for several hours."

Several *hours*? That was so much bullshit. She didn't call him on it. She never did. But some little demon raised its head inside her. "I'm afraid that with year-end, Erin can't spare me. But I could arrange for a bit of time over here." Hah. She amazed herself with her audacity.

"Well, if Erin *really* can't spare the time . . ." He trailed off meaningfully.

"She *can't*," Bree emphasized. "Would you like me to call her in here to talk to you?"

"No-no-no," he said almost as one word. "I understand her needs completely."

Right. He understood *Erin's* needs, but Bree's be damned.

Why did she put up with this man's crap? Why didn't she tell him off the way Erin would? She was such a coward.

"Let's schedule our meeting this week."

"Thursday," she said. She probably wouldn't be at work because by then she would have told Erin about her father's death. Erin would insist she have time off. Then again, skipping out on a meeting with Marbury was putting off the inevitable. Obviously ignoring him for the past few days hadn't done any good.

"Thursday at nine is good for me," he said.

"Fine. Good-bye." She could still hear him talking at her as she let the receiver fall back in place. He could bluster all he wanted now. On Thursday, she'd answer his silly niggling questions, which would turn out to be nothing, and she'd be here on *her* turf. She didn't like being alone in his office with him. He always closed the door, and though he never touched her, she felt slimed by his proximity.

At two-thirty, Erin came in to shoo her out. She couldn't very well say that her mother didn't need her anymore because her father was already dead. Dead, dead, dead.

So she left. She thought about going to the town square in Los Gatos and sitting on the grass to soak up the sun on this perfect, cloudless day. Instead she drove home because God only knew what her mother had been doing while she was out.

But it wasn't her mom she had to worry about. It was Luke. In suit pants, with the sleeves of his white dress shirt rolled up, he was mowing the front lawn.

"What are you doing?" she shouted. He'd left work early, and he hadn't even called her. Her mother had taken advantage, putting him to work. And he was going to ruin his clothes.

He simply cupped his ear, indicating he couldn't hear and continued on merrily.

"You've got him mowing the lawn." In the house, she let her exasperation flow over her mom.

Her mother let it roll right off. "He offered."

"You must have said something."

"I said I couldn't start the lawn mower." Flour dusting her apron, she cut Christmas shapes into the sugar-cookie dough she'd rolled out.

"Mom." Bree bet she hadn't even tried starting the mower.

"I'm making him cookies. They'll be ready by the time he's done. It's a fair exchange."

And Bree could give him sex. Gee, then they'd be all paid up. She wanted to scream. "Mom, please."

"I like him. He's a good man, I can tell." Yeah, like her mom was such a great judge of a man's character. "And he's good for you. A woman needs a man to take care of her."

They'd already had this argument. "I don't need him to take care of me." She didn't want any man taking care of her. If you depended on them monetarily, you could never get away when you needed to. Just like her mother had said; she couldn't leave because she was afraid she'd run into something worse. Bree wasn't going to let that happen to her.

Not that Luke was a bad guy. He wasn't like Mr. Asshole Marbury. But she still didn't want to depend on Luke for her finances.

It did occur to her, however, that she depended on him for other things that at times—like when she was feeling totally stressed and crazy—were just as important as money.

"Let's make his favorite meal," her mother said, eagerness animating her voice as she laid the cookies on a baking sheet. "They say the way to a man's heart is through his stomach."

Uh, not. A man's stomach had nothing to do with it. "I don't know what his favorite meal is."

Her mom gave her a dramatic, jaw-dropping look. "How could you not know?"

Okay, what had Luke said about how long they'd known each other? Bree couldn't remember what the lie was. She had a problem keeping all the lies straight, keeping all the secrets she needed to keep. "That *was* our first date, Mom." She hadn't told her mom it was bowling. Maybe if she did, that would put Luke a score down. "We had pizza."

Her mother closed her eyes and smiled dreamily. "Your father hated pizza." She opened her eyes again. "Combination?"

"Yes."

"Oh my." Then she grinned, her teeth yellowed with years of coffee drinking. "I bet he loves lasagna then." She put the two cookie sheets into the oven and set the timer.

Instead of lowering her mother's opinion, Bree had somehow raised it. "I have no idea." God, her mother was in matchmaking heaven. "We should really talk about arrangements. Father's life insurance, the bank accounts, all that stuff."

"He left a list of everything I had to do." At least he'd done that much. "I'm working through it."

"I can help."

"You have other things to occupy you. Honestly, your father set everything up so that it's all very easy. A trust."

"Oh." Bree hadn't asked about any of that. She should have during those excruciating Sunday dinners, especially after he got sick.

Opening the fridge, her mother poured a glass of lemonade. "Luke will be thirsty. Why don't you take this to him?"

It was impossible to have a truly rational conversation with her mother. Though maybe her mom wasn't as incapable as her father had always made out.

Luke was rolling the lawn mower back into the garage.

"Did you do the backyard, too?" she asked.

"I'll wait for the weekend to do that. It's a lot bigger."

Not wanting to tackle it herself, she was grateful. Sweat stained his shirt under the arms, but she liked his scent, clean, not sour. "Mom sent me out with lemonade, and she wants to know if you like lasagna."

"I love both."

"Homemade, too."

"Even better."

"Why are you mowing my mother's lawn on a Monday afternoon? Don't you have staff meetings or board meetings or something CEOish to do?"

He trailed a finger down her nose, then caressed her lips with his fingertip. "You were coming home early. I wanted to be here."

There was something in his touch that made her tremble. A tenderness. She thought of Marbury and his gruff voice, how the sound of it grated on her nerves. And how different Luke's was, deep, resonant. When it strummed her nerves, it made them sing.

Then she thought of the ways a woman could depend on a man that didn't include money. He had it all. She craved his touch even though she knew craving was bad. She loved the taste of his come even as she knew swallowing was supposed to be revolting. She needed to hear him whisper those naughty words in a voice that drowned out the other times, bad times, when men had called her a slut and worse. There were so many things about sex without marriage that were bad and immoral and wrong, and yet Luke made her want all of them. He even made her want an orgasm. It was the whole wanting-what-was-bad-for-you thing.

She didn't say any of that. Instead she told him that her Mom's lasagna was to-die-for. Her father had actually liked it even if it wasn't plain old meat and potatoes.

* * *

"WHY DON'T YOU TWO YOUNG PEOPLE GO OUT FOR ICE CREAM? IT feels lovely and warm outside now after all the rain we've had."

Young people? Mrs. Mason was an anachronism. She couldn't be much more than sixty-five, but she talked as if she were twenty years older, and she acted as if she'd been born into that generation, too. Over lasagna, Luke learned she'd never worked outside the home, she'd never gone to college, and she'd married Bree's father right after her high school graduation. They'd been dating for three years, but he was five years older. Which meant he'd been a twenty-year-old man dating a fifteen-year-old girl. Yeah, Luke could do the math.

If—the big *if*—Bree's father had been doing anything to his daughter, he didn't think the mother could have known. She seemed too . . . motherly.

He learned other things about the Masons, too, that Bree had been their miracle child, coming after almost ten years of marriage when they thought there would never be any children, et cetera, et cetera. Yet he heard nothing that gave him greater insight into Bree.

Of course, he could have just asked Bree about her father. Maybe another man would have. But Bree had to be willing to talk; it had to be in *her* time, not his.

Mrs. Mason rose from the table and began clearing the dirty plates.

"I can get it, sweetheart," she said, waving away her daughter as Bree stood to help. "Go change into something nicer. Luke is waiting for you."

Bree flashed an uncertain glance between him and her mom. "I only brought work clothes."

He wanted the date her mother was setting up. He didn't care what Bree was wearing. For his part, the white shirt was dirty after mowing the lawn, and he'd covered the stains with his suit jacket. He might take Bree to his house first. Yeah, good idea. "She looks beautiful wearing what she's got on."

Mrs. Mason smiled, a happy *gotcha* smile she shot at Bree as if to say *see, he likes you in anything*. She was an odd duck. He'd expressed his condolences when he arrived, and she'd accepted, then blown them off as if she hadn't lost her husband only yesterday. He wasn't quite sure how he'd ended up mowing the lawn for her. Not that it mattered, he was glad to help. But if she was grieving, it was buried so deep not an ounce of emotion showed.

She waved a hand, shooing them away. "Off you go then. Have fun. I won't wait up."

"I'll get Bree home safe and sound." He didn't say he'd get her home early. He had plans.

Out in the car, Bree whispered, as if her mother might somehow overhear. "What's up with that?"

"Maybe she thought you needed some fun." He started the engine and backed out of the driveway.

"She's pushing me at you."

"She elicited an invitation, not the same thing." In other circumstances, it would have been fine, but it was a little freaky now. Her husband had just died. You'd have thought she'd want the company rather than sending them off.

"Did you put her up to this date before I got home?"

He glanced at her. Her nostrils actually flared like an angry animal.

"I didn't arrange anything." He pulled out onto the main road heading toward the freeway. It was still early enough that commuter traffic lingered. "Is she all right?"

"She's fine."

"I mean about your dad."

"I told you she cleaned out all his stuff. She can't wait to get rid of him."

Yeah, Bree was angry, but he couldn't tell whether it was with him or her mother. Or her dad. "She needs grief counseling," he said. Bree should consider going with her.

She gave him a look. He was supposed to be the dom and she the submissive, but there wasn't an ounce of submission in that gaze. "Why don't *you* tell her that?"

This was a side of Bree he'd never seen before. She didn't usually show anger so openly. In a strange way, it was almost comforting. To show anger meant she actually trusted him a little. "I'll talk to her if you want," he offered, though he knew her answer.

"She doesn't talk to anyone. Not even to me." Like mother, like daughter. "Aren't you taking me to your house to fuck?" she snapped before he had a chance to add anything.

Whoa. Something he'd said obviously set her off. "Is that what you want?"

She glared at him, and that spunky look got him going. He was inexplicably hard and ready. Because this was how he wanted her to be. In charge. Demanding. Fearless.

"I think you should follow through on all those promises you made," she said, pulling into her corner of the car.

He merged into freeway traffic before addressing her. "What promises?"

"All that phone sex, the stories, how you were going to take me to a sex club, how much you want to see how badly other men want me. Those promises."

They weren't promises; they were fantasies. After the rage he'd experienced over her story about the two doms, he wasn't so eager to turn fantasy into reality. "I rescued you from the *real* thing when I took you away from Derek."

"Maybe I liked what Derek did to me."

He wanted to yank the wheel, pull over to the side of the highway and go at it with her. She excited him even as she pissed him off. Where was all this coming from? Did she really want another man?

Then he got it like a smack to the head. She was doing exactly the same thing she'd done yesterday morning when she ran to him after her father died. She wanted to goad him into action.

Maybe she needed a taste of what she was asking for to remind her how bad it had really been with Derek. How much better it was with him. "Fine. You ask for it, you'll get it."

He'd give her a lesson she wouldn't forget. And neither would he. He was already hard contemplating it.

19

SHE'D PISSED HIM OFF. LUKE DIDN'T GET PISSED; HE ONLY FAKED IT. Usually. But this time Bree had pushed. Just like her mother had pushed. And yeah, Bree was pissed, too.

Her mom was foisting her off on Luke to assuage her own guilt and to keep herself safe. *Yeah, go ahead and take care of Bree. So I don't have to.*

She was pissed at them both.

Then she'd gotten Luke's back up as well. They'd driven in stony silence to his house. He'd actually made her wait in the car as if he didn't want her inside. Or maybe he'd been afraid of what he'd do to her. The thought had sent an electric shock through her. He wasn't faking; his anger was real. It both excited and terrified her. These were the sensations she craved, fear as important as thrill.

He'd returned to the car wearing a tux. "I'm not one of your biker boy freaks," he'd said when he caught her looking him up and down. "I have more class."

He most certainly did. He was gorgeous in black and white against his dark hair and amber eyes. He hadn't shaved, and a sexy shadow of beard darkened his face.

He drove them across the Dumbarton Bridge to the East Bay

and her small condo. He watched with an eagle eye as she watered her plants, and in her bedroom, he pawed through her closet. Pulling out a hanger, he held it up. "This."

He'd chosen a black lace bustier with an underlayer of burgundy satin. Tossing it at her, he continued his rummaging. She undressed without him even looking. Her chest was nothing to speak of, but when she'd done the fastenings all the way to the top, her breasts plumped above the lace edge, her nipples almost peeping over.

He stroked a skirt in the closet, turned to her, stopped. "You look like the slut you are," he said. "Ripe for fucking. Are you ready to be given to any man who takes my fancy?"

Against the bustier, her nipples peaked. She shivered with need. "You're my master. I have to do what you say."

He stepped close, took her chin between his thumb and forefinger. "And you'll like it as much as you liked it with Derek," he whispered ominously.

She hadn't liked Derek in the end. He abused with no desire or feeling, given her nothing in return except smelly men. She'd wanted the fantasy; Derek had given her brutal reality.

Luke was different. As her anger ebbed, she prayed he'd give her the fantasy she needed. Not that she really knew exactly what that was. He was her master, however, and he would read her mind, finding it for her, she was sure.

"I have to do whatever you say, Master," she repeated.

His gaze captured her totally. "I might make you suck a big cock until you gag on it."

She swallowed. Her heart hammered.

"I might tie you down and have a man force you."

Her skin pebbled though the room wasn't cold.

"Then I'll have you myself in front of the crowd," he whispered his final threat.

She thought of gorging on a beautiful cock that tasted like honey, of being tied down while Luke watched a handsome, gray-haired older man take her, force her. Then she could give herself over to her master for her ultimate punishment. It sounded like the things Derek had tried to force her to do, yet it was all made completely exhilarating with Luke. "Yes, Master." Her voice was almost a whisper.

His face so close to hers she almost couldn't make out his features, he said, "Put this on, whore."

She quivered beneath his words, his caress, then found it was a skirt when she touched the material. Black, pleated, flared. She held it a moment.

"No panties. That way I can simply lift the pleats and show you off as I wish."

Bree's heart thumped hard with her need, her thoughts, her fantasies.

In her lingerie drawer, he unearthed her fishnet thigh-highs as she pulled on the skirt and tossed aside her panties. Moments later, she stood barefoot in the stockings, skirt, and bustier as he circled her.

"Slut-wear. Perfect. Now we need shoes."

He snagged a pair of high heels from the bottom of her closet, which, when she donned them, put her at more than an inch taller than him.

He stood back to survey her, stroking his chin, then suddenly found her wanting. "Makeup. Lots of it. Whore makeup."

He observed from the bathroom doorway as she used dark colors, thick mascara, heavy rouge, and a deep plum-colored lipstick.

When she turned, he didn't compliment her. "You'll do. But it needs one more touch." He held out a black leather collar studded with brightly colored fake jewels. "Ownership," he said.

Derek had bought her the collar. A silver ring dangled from the center of it.

She fastened it around her neck. "Do you need the leash, Master?"

She hadn't minded the collar or the leash when Derek used them on her. She'd only hated his attitude when he yanked on it, pulling her off her feet, or forcing her to her knees to suck something disgusting. He'd only started giving her away when he'd tired of her.

Had Luke tired? She felt the first frisson of real fear. No. Not yet. He was simply toying with her, because she'd pissed him off.

"I don't need a leash," he said, his voice harsh. "Some dogs are so well trained, all their master has to do is snap his fingers for obedience."

The cruel words slammed her. *Be careful what you wish for.* But she'd asked for this, pushed him to it, and she would see it through.

That was the problem with Derek. She'd lost control of him. He took her places she didn't want to go. Until Luke rescued her. Did the rescuer eventually become the abuser?

In the car, he punished her with silence. A million times in the hour-long drive, she wanted to say, *"I changed my mind. This isn't what I wanted."*

But she didn't speak.

In the six months she'd been with him, Luke had only made their sessions better. He had always surpassed himself. Until finally, in her condo and again on Sunday morning, he'd given her exactly, perfectly, magnificently what she needed. She would trust him to give it to her now. He had a plan. He would make it good. He would wipe out the hours she'd crouched in her mother's bedroom, touching her father's things, smelling his cloy-

ing scent, filling bag after endless bag with the used-up remains
of his life.

Luke found a spot in a parking garage a few blocks from the
seedy club in which he'd first discovered her with Derek. Her
hand tucked securely in his, they walked the darkened streets
relatively slowly because of her high heels. Still, he didn't speak
beyond the necessities. In the lobby, after he'd paid their couple's
entry fee, he yanked down on the bustier, her nipples popping
above the lace edge.

"They should see something of what they're going to get."
Surveying her critically, he pinched both buds at once, hard. Electricity buzzed straight to her clitoris. What would make most
women cry set her blood singing.

"There, now they're tasty and red." He cocked his head. "Perhaps I should sell you." He raised his eyes to hers. "How much
do you think you're worth?"

Her mouth went dry. Derek had tried to sell her. "I don't
know."

He merely shrugged, captured her hand in his, opened the
lobby's interior door and climbed the stairs to a place where the
only rule was no rules.

SHE WAS MAGNIFICENT, HER BREASTS SMALL YET PERT, HER NIPPLES
red, succulent, inviting. She was worth her weight in gold, more
than any man could pay. And she was his.

Luke had chosen the sleazy club in which he'd first seen her.
He had witnessed her debauchery, seen the tear trickling from the
corner of her eye. Then Derek the bruiser had slapped it away,
and Luke had seen red. When he won the fight, he'd tossed away
her collar and leash. Only to find she still wanted to wear both.

The dog comment had been beneath him, going too far. Yet the depth of his emotion overcame him. He didn't want normal. He just didn't want to share. Tonight, she would learn *his* limits, how far she could push him before he pushed back.

He abhorred violence against women, even if it was consensual, so he passed the rooms where the walls hung with floggers, paddles, and even hairbrushes. He enjoyed a good hand spanking, but those instruments caused real damage to the skin. Though the fare down here was mild compared to the fourth floor of the club, which catered to hardcore BDSM, with cages and rooms that looked like dungeons where submissives were chained to the walls or medieval-style torture contraptions. The third level provided primarily same-sex activity, so he'd chosen the second floor for tonight, mostly hetero sex, but even this level was known for getting wild.

Relatively early on a Monday night, the hallways were by no means packed. The floor was hardwood, crown molding around the ceilings, the doorjambs ornately carved. Once upon a time, the Victorian had seen a better class of people. Despite his tuxedo, he included himself in that current lesser category, which consisted of men in jeans or leather, ripped T-shirts or bare-chested, and women with collars, leashes, and very little in the way of clothing. Bree was actually more fully dressed than most.

A young man with spiked pink hair and a nose ring brushed past them. Bree stared wide-eyed at the spectacle as if she hadn't been here many times before.

There were, of course, higher quality clientele littered about, men in suits or even elaborate costumes that reminded him of something from the sixties or *Austin Powers*, and women in formal wear, but those couplings were few. Monday night was not for the regulars who were part of the BDSM lifestyle, and in fact, this club didn't attract that crowd. It was too low on the ladder for most serious lifestylers. Upscale had not been his intent. He wanted to give Bree another shot of the seedy side, a lesson in what her life *could* have been but for him.

He pulled her to a doorway. Inside, several couples engaged in oral sex, the women servicing, the men receiving, sometimes switching partners. He knew, of course, that many men preferred the submissive position, but you couldn't judge that by tonight's activities.

He watched Bree. Her throat worked as she swallowed.

"Do you want me to drag you in there and force you to your knees for him?" He pointed to a pimply faced kid barely over the age limit for entry, his eyes glassy as a large woman worked her mouth around him.

Most clubs didn't allow single men. You either had to have a date or an invitation. It kept out trollers and reduced the potential for trouble. But here, if you had enough cash, they looked the other way. He'd never brought his lady friend here. Part of the allure for him originally had been the raunchiness of it all. Sometimes, that's what a man wanted. He'd wanted it that night. Instead he'd found Bree. He'd rescued her and changed his life, changed hers.

For the first time tonight, he felt the jolt of bringing her here. Jesus, what had he been thinking? She was better than this, object lesson or not. Her father had just died, her emotions were all over the map, and he'd lost his fucking mind for even contemplating this place. Especially with his dawning suspicions about her past. There were classier clubs where they could watch and be watched.

"Come on." He grabbed her hand then, pushed back into the hallway, almost knocking over a man in his fifties, a heavily painted older woman clinging to his arm. Voyeurs. Perhaps their first time, if the woman's flushed face meant anything.

But even as he marched on, retracing their steps down the long hall, Bree hung back at a doorway.

"What are you doing?" But he succumbed, stopping behind her in the entrance.

Inside, the walls were painted a deep red with a hint of orange for a rich tone that played as a backdrop to a small crowd. The centerpiece of the room was a large bed draped with a thick coverlet that matched the wall color. A naked and blindfolded woman was restrained to the bedposts with fur-lined cuffs. Flat on her back, her long hair had been artfully spread across the pillows, and beneath the eye mask, her features appeared flawless. In the low lighting of the room, he guessed her to be in her early thirties, her body slim, toned, her breasts large and upright, suggesting enhancements.

"Come on in, join the party, pretty lady." A man of the woman's age signaled to Bree. Tall, outfitted completely in black, his longish hair the same shade as his clothes, he slapped a riding crop against his palm. "My disobedient slave here needs to be publicly punished," he said to Bree and to the audience of men and women lining the walls.

"What has she done?" an older man called as if on cue.

"I asked her to give pleasure to a very close friend of mine and she refused."

A low hum of horror exuded from the assembly.

Pointing a remote, the dom hit a switch and the lights fell, then another button brought to life a spotlight over the woman, the luminescence highlighting the curves and valleys of her body. Her legs were spread, though not restrained, and her pussy glistened in the bright light.

When Luke made a move to retreat, Bree remained rooted. Something about the sight attracted her. He found himself wanting to understand what drew her, so he pulled her into an empty space along the wall. Positioning her in front of him with his hands at her hips, he held her close, his cock finding the soft line along the cleft of her ass. She would feel his every reaction. With her high heels, she was slightly taller as he watched over her shoulder, and her aroused scent rose to tantalize his senses.

"Is this what you want?" he whispered, stirring the fine hairs falling across her ear.

She turned her head slightly. "I don't know. I need to see."

But she was intrigued. And, watching her, so was Luke. The room itself was stylish, the dom and his submissive more attractive than the majority of couples he'd seen tonight.

"I need volunteers," the black-haired man said. Hands shot up before he'd even stated his needs, and he smiled at the eagerness. There was something in that smile, a showmanship, the grin and eyes of a man who enjoyed center stage. "Perhaps we'll have to draw straws." He laughed, then raised his voice amid the murmurs that had grown in volume. "She refused the man I chose for her. She will therefore be required to take five men between her legs, sight unseen."

Bree's shudder shimmied through Luke's body. Looking over her shoulder, even in the dim light around the outer edges of the room, he saw the burgeoning peaks of her nipples above the line of the bustier. She was beyond intrigued. Excitement coursed through her body, and he could have sworn he detected a fresh wave of heightened arousal.

Was it for the punishment?

Or the ringmaster?

20

A GAGGLE OF MEN WAVED THEIR ARMS IN THE AIR REGARDLESS OF the women who accompanied them. Luke wasn't one of them. He was there to watch and learn about Bree, not step into the limelight himself. He was even over the punishment part, the lesson he was supposed to teach her. Now, he wanted to discover what fascinated her about the tableau.

The dom was definitely a showman. He paraded the bed's perimeter, scrutinizing each and every man who'd raised his hand. "We need fucking punishment, gentlemen, not namby-pamby lovemaking." He leaned in close as he stalked past the group, lowering his voice for emphasis. "She likes it hard and rough. She loves a big cock. So you'll have to drop your pants first for inspection."

No one put his hand down at the threat.

Bree followed the guy's path, her head moving as if she were watching a match game, her attention rapt. Luke snugged her closer against his cock to remind her he was right there.

Turning, the dom trailed his crop along his submissive's leg, up her thigh, then suddenly swatted the lips of her sex. She moaned and writhed on the bed.

"You see that," he exclaimed to his audience. "If I ask, she doesn't obey. But if I force her, she's dying for it." He turned at that exact moment and captured Bree with his gaze. "Is that how you like it, beautiful lady?"

Bree vibrated with tension along Luke's body. He felt rather than heard her low moan.

"She doesn't speak unless I give her permission." Luke paused for emphasis, holding the younger man's gaze. "And I'm not giving her permission."

"Thanks for the warning, my friend. Perhaps you and I should talk"—he held Bree with his eyes as he licked his lips— "about permission later."

Luke merely gave him a hard look until finally the man smiled and moved on. Message received; Luke wasn't sharing tonight.

"Now who will be first?" the man called out like the ringmaster he was.

A paunchy guy of about fifty shoved through the crowd that was growing with every passing moment. "I'll do it." He hefted his hand against his jeans.

The dom eyed his gut. "Be serious, dude."

The guy puffed up his chest. "Maybe you should check the package first before you make a snap decision."

With that challenge, the dom suddenly shot out his hand and grabbed the guy's crotch, holding his gaze as he felt him up. Then finally, he let out a long breath. "Holy hell, ladies and gentleman, we have a winner here." He backed off and lightly slapped the man's shoulder with his crop. "Let 'em see."

Holy hell was right, Luke thought as the man undid his pants and exposed himself. He was hung like a horse. A *huge* horse.

Luke nuzzled Bree's ear. "Do you want that?"

She shook her head, hair brushing the side of his face. "I don't like him."

"Size isn't everything?"

She turned to rub her cheek against his like a cat. "You're as big as I want."

He was above average, but he certainly didn't have the monster cock the old dude did. "Such a diplomat," he murmured.

The dom climbed onto the bed as if it were his stage and leaned over his slave. His lips next to her ear, he whispered loud enough to fill the room. "He's so big, my sweet, that I'm not sure this will be punishment."

She wriggled on the bed. He traced her body from nipple to nipple with the tip of the riding crop, then headed down to her mound. And finally, dramatically, he murmured, "Fuck her now."

The pot-bellied chosen one didn't hesitate a moment. Crawling onto the bed, he removed neither his shoes nor his jeans, merely shoving them down over his hips. He rolled on the condom the woman's dom threw at him, then, in the next beat, he impaled her.

It was an impressive sight, all that engorged flesh filling her to capacity in one swift thrust. She didn't scream. She was already wet and ready.

He fucked her hard, just as instructed, grunting with exertion. The woman's breasts bobbed and jiggled. Wrapping her hands around the small chain of the cuffs securing her to the bed, she held on, braced herself to take more. Then slowly, she dragged her heels up his calves, spreading herself wide to give him everything. She panted, moaned, sobbed, shouted, and it was all with pure pleasure.

Reaching between the pounding bodies, her dom pinched her nipple. She screamed then as he held on, his knuckles turning white with the pressure, and her body bucked. She was coming, hard, endlessly, taking her punishment, loving it.

Against him, Bree writhed in empathy. He wanted to touch

her, test her. Insinuating a knee between her thighs, he pushed her to a wider stance, then slipped his hand beneath the front hem of her pleated skirt. Her skin was slick with desire, her pussy wet and hot.

As he rubbed her clit, making her body shake, the showman on the bed looked up in that precise moment. Watching Luke's hand work magic beneath the skirt, the subtlety of his action making it even hotter, the man licked his lips as he stared Luke down.

Neither of them paid attention to the grunting orgasm of the man between the submissive's legs until finally the guy heaved himself off her, breathing hard, his dick still semi-erect in the aftermath.

"How about you, sir?" The dom pointed at Luke. "Would you like to give my lady a try?"

Before him, Bree stiffened. Maybe he wasn't the only one who didn't want to share.

He withdrew his hand from her deliciously wet pussy, raised his fingers to his mouth and licked them. Then he smiled. "I'm doing fine right where I am."

"I'm enjoying the view, too." The man grinned with white teeth that seemed to glow in the spotlight. Then he leaned once more over his woman. "Was that enough, my sweet? Or do you need more punishment?"

"I haven't learned my lesson yet, Master. I need more."

He ran a hand down her flank. "I thought you would." Then he rose from the bed, examined the sea of waving hands.

"You," he said, pointing.

A skinny young guy was already unzipping his pants as he stepped from between a couple of much beefier men. His cock sprang free.

"My, my," the ringmaster enthused. "Now that is a sight." He raised his gaze to the kid's eyes. "What's a young whippersnapper doing with a cock like that?"

"I can squirt three feet," the kid said proudly.

"Well, isn't that marvelous. Perhaps we need to have you fuck her, then pull out at the last moment so we can bear witness to that testimony."

The kid nodded eagerly. He took the condom and his position on the bed. Holding out a hell of a lot longer than the older guy, he went at the prone woman for ten minutes with fast steady pumps. Going back on his haunches, he dragged her legs over his thighs and fucked her upright as she writhed, panted, moaned, and tossed her head on the pillow. Tears of pleasure sparkled at her temples. She shuddered twice in what Luke figured were two separate orgasms.

"He made her come like that, without even touching her," Bree whispered, an awed hush in her voice.

She'd never come from fucking alone. She needed the spanking, the filthy words, and his fingers on her. The times he thought she had were more of her fakes. But she was captivated by this, the way the woman moved her body, angling her hips so the kid was riding her G-spot. It was the slow, steady thrust, too, that worked her, and served to hold off the kid's climax at the same time.

Then their ringmaster snapped his fingers. "Come on, boy, we have others waiting here."

"Yes, sir." The kid began a fast, hard pump that made the woman's breasts damn near bob to her chin. "Jesus, I'm gonna come," he shouted.

"Don't hide the come shot, boy," the dom warned.

The kid pulled out, tore off the condom, tossed it into the crowd who hooted and hollered as he stroked his cock three times and exploded in a massive come that splattered the headboard before he directed it down over the woman's face, neck, and breasts. It was a veritable shower.

Her dom crawled close once more, scooped some of the white come from her throat onto his fingers and fed it to her. She licked him clean, greedy for more.

Bree rubbed her ass against Luke, stroking his cock between her cheeks.

"Do you want some of that come?" he murmured, nuzzling her ear, burying his face against her hair. He loved being the voyeur with her, feeling her skin heat, her scent rise, her pulse race, her breathy moans. However the evening had started, it had turned into a sexy little fantasy they were sharing.

The tableau on the bed ended and another began. The ringmaster searched for his next victim.

"I want to do it," a woman's voice called out, and a hush fell over the room. In the relative darkness along the wall beyond the reach of the spotlight, Luke couldn't make out the owner of the seductive voice.

The dom laughed. "Did you bring a strap-on?"

"I don't need one. She'll love what I do to her."

He turned to his lady on the bed. "That's an idea I hadn't thought of," he murmured, interest animating his features. "What do you think, my sweet? Shall I let her have you?"

"Oh, Master, no."

He guffawed. "She has a safe word, and she didn't say it. That means you're in."

The woman who stepped to the center of the room wasn't gorgeous. She was, in fact, rather matronly, at least fifty, with neat auburn hair dyed to cover her roots, and full breasts. She could have been someone's mother. She wore a tailored suit of pale blue that she began unbuttoning as the audience waited with its collective breath held. Though not slender, her muscles were toned. Nude, she climbed gracefully on the bed, then tentatively ran her fingers along the woman's body.

"Her skin feels delicious."

Even the ringmaster seemed overcome, mesmerized by the soft touches accompanied by the gentle moans of his submissive.

"The others didn't kiss you, did they," the matron murmured just before she spread her legs to straddle the other woman's hips. First she licked the kid's come from the slave's cheeks and throat, lapping up every drop. Then she opened her mouth and took her willing victim with a deep tongue kiss that could be heard in the near silence of the room as they shared the taste of come between them.

He'd seen two women play at clubs before. But this was something more. The sheer eroticism of that kiss was hypnotic. Their bodies moved together in a sweet rhythm, breasts touching, mating.

"It's beautiful," Bree said on a breath.

He wrapped an arm tight around her waist and leaned fully against the wall, pulling her with him. "Yes," he agreed.

She put an arm back, wound it around his neck to hold him to her, tipped her head to put her lips to his ear. "They're so gentle with each other."

Men weren't always gentle. And she didn't usually want gentle. Fucking was good when it was hard, but this was different, almost magical.

Even as they seemed lost in their kiss, the older woman reached down between their legs and stroked the other's glistening pussy lips. She was slow, tender, caressing, until finally her fingers dipped inside. A long, deep moan electrified the air. Beneath her, the slave took her punishment with delight, her hips lifting, pressing, begging for more.

Bree's breath quickened, and she moved sinuously against him.

"Do you like this? Do you want a woman?"

On the bed, the two ladies ground their pussies together in imitation fucking, the silence in the room broken only by their mingled breaths and moans.

And Bree's answer. "No. I want you, Master."

"Liar."

He wondered if he could handle watching her with a woman, if it would be different than giving her to a man.

Woman-On-Top broke the delicious kiss and began crawling down her lover's body. She tweaked the pert nipples, eliciting a gasp, licked the kid's come away, then trailed kisses down her abdomen until she lay between the submissive's spread thighs, her breath puffing on the open pussy swollen with need. Then she bent to lick the turgid button of the woman's clitoris.

"Touch me," Bree whispered, her voice low, harsh, needy.

He had a better idea. "Touch yourself. Reach under your skirt and stroke your clit for me." It was halfway to the fantasy he'd conjured for her on the phone, masturbating with an audience, even if they weren't the center of attention.

She did as ordered, and his cock filled the crease of her ass, lengthening, his balls tight, aching, as he saw the ruffle of her hand under her skirt.

Her scent drove him crazy. The moan low in her throat made him dizzy. His chin on her shoulder, he saw her lips part, her eyes close, until only a moment later, they shot open so that she didn't miss a single sight.

Was it the touch of a woman she wanted?

On the bed, the older lady licked, sucked, lapped, her fingers in the woman's pussy working her G-spot.

"Yes, yes, yes," the submissive chanted, her hair flying as she flung her head back and forth. Her hips undulated, tipping high for a deeper penetration. "Oh Master, it's so good."

It was then that Luke keyed on the man. He wasn't watching his slave. He wasn't salivating over the scene on the bed. He was staring at Bree as she touched herself, lost in the moment.

He was so close, his whisper carried to Luke's ears. "Let me touch her."

"Fuck off," Luke said mildly. Yet against him, he felt the rising shudders of Bree's body. Pulling back slightly, he took in her cheeks tinged with pink, her breasts plumped above the lace bustier, her nipples jewel hard and deep red.

He thought of what she wanted and needed, of what he could give, what he could accept.

He wouldn't allow another man to make her come. He'd kill before he allowed that. But there were some limits he was willing to stretch for her pleasure.

21

"PINCH HER NIPPLE," LUKE INSTRUCTED.

The dom stepped closer. Bree laid her head back against Luke's shoulder as the man stroked her breast. She was so tight against him, Luke could feel she was holding her breath. In anticipation, he was sure.

"Such perfect nipples, beautiful lady." The guy's fingers went white with the sharp pinch he gave her.

She gasped, bit her lip, and her knees buckled. Luke clenched his arm beneath her breasts to keep her on her feet.

"Come for us, pretty lady," the dom crooned. Then he turned his gaze to Luke. "Christ, I want to taste her. Just her fingers. I'll pay anything."

Bree moaned. This was what she wanted, needed, a man to pay her homage, to want her so badly he'd give anything. Not the way Derek had tried to sell her, where it had been all about his power and nothing to do with her desirability.

Grabbing her hand with his, Luke dove beneath her skirt. "Let him taste your fingers," he demanded. As soon as she withdrew her hand from between her legs, he took her place, working her hot clit, easing into her channel, then back out.

She was tense and needy in his arms. She wanted, yet she was scared. She needed, yet she feared he would punish her later in ways she wouldn't like. He understood all this after his months with her; he recognized the nonverbal signals. He was her release. He was her boundary. Whatever he said he wanted suddenly became her need.

"Do it, you dirty little cunt, or you'll pay for disobedience."

She put her head back a moment, closed her eyes, sighed. "Yes, Master."

Their ringmaster shifted so that Luke could watch—the movement intentional, he was sure—as Bree raised her fingers to his lips.

The dom sucked, licked, savored, his dark blue eyes never leaving her face. All the way to his bones, Luke felt her tremble with the enormity of it, her delight in it. She was desired, and in so many ways, it was more than any one man alone could ever give her, more than Luke knew he was capable of giving her. It was his acceptance she craved, and the other man's need; his command over her, and the dom's heated gaze on her. For tonight, it didn't have to be fucking or sucking. It was the sights, the sounds, her heightened senses, the hot, needy, unquenchable yearning that drove a man to do crazy things for the woman he had to have above all others. With the other man's mouth on her fingers, and Luke's touch between her legs, she shuddered, made a sound that was half groan, half moan, then her whole body shook with climax, her thighs clamping on his hand, holding him close, inside her, deep, more than just his fingers, a piece of himself that Luke would never get back. It was the fantasy he'd created for her over the phone, but better. Yet in many ways, it confirmed his worst fears.

He was trapped by his own lesson. Even as he held her in the throes of orgasm, he wondered how long before she needed him to give her to another man in order to get the same high?

How long before she wanted to be the woman on that bed?

LUKE DRAGGED HER OUT OF THERE SO FAST, SHE KNEW HE WAS pissed as hell. But at what? Because she'd let the dark-haired man lick her fingers? Luke had told her to do it. But maybe he'd expected her to say she didn't want it. Or was it because of the women? Or because she'd made him go into that room in the first place?

As he hauled her along the sidewalk to the parking garage, she trembled. If she hadn't been so long-legged, she might have stumbled in the high heels, but she managed to keep pace. She loved his he-man act. It made her pulse race and her breath quicken. Yet his silence and the grim set of his jaw frightened her, too, as if nothing had changed since they'd arrived at the club. His eyes were the deep amber of a rampaging lion. What if there was a backlash?

What if he gave her to another man and didn't want her back?

What if there was only her mother to go home to in the house where her father had died?

"Luke."

He turned, his gaze dark. She shut her mouth.

In the parking garage, the spot he'd found was next to the wall in a darkened corner on the other side of a concrete piling. Before she even had a chance to protest, he opened the back door of his car, pushed her face first onto the backseat, and came down on top of her, the door crashing closed behind him.

The interior was dark and suffocating with her face against the seat. Her heart hammered.

"You bitch," he whispered in her ear.

She shivered at the tone, half afraid, half melting with need.

"You wanted him to fuck you, didn't you?"

"No," she whispered. She wasn't sure what she'd wanted back there. She wasn't sure what Luke wanted to hear.

He pulled her head back by the hair. Her scalp tingled, but the pain streaked down to her very center and turned her molten.

"Then tell me what you wanted, and don't lie, slut." His breath was warm and sweet against her nape as he pinned her beneath him, his cock pressed hard against her.

She thrilled to the evidence of his desire. "I loved that he wanted me, but that you wouldn't let him have me."

He laughed harshly. "You manipulated me, you little whore."

"No, no. I did what you wanted, Master." She truly couldn't tell if this was real or an act, and the uncertainty made it that much more exciting. She thrived on desire inextricably linked with fear.

"You liked it too much." He shoved a knee between her legs, spread her, then delved between her thighs, finding her wet pussy and swollen clit. "Tell me the truth. You wanted him to fuck you."

"No, Master. I wanted you to fuck me in front of him."

He was silent and still a long moment. "Why didn't you beg me to do it then?" His voice was rough, skeptical, distrusting.

"Because it's better if you order me to do what you want."

"Why?" He stroked her clit.

She shivered with need. She could admit she had the need. She'd been so worked up in that room, she'd wanted the orgasm. She'd wanted release. He gave it to her the best way possible, with her back to him so she didn't have to see. It could have been her own hand beneath her skirt. "When you make me do it, I don't have to feel bad."

He didn't give her time to even think before he shot another question at her. "Why did the women make you hot?" Pushing her leg with his, he forced her wider and pumped his cock against her, only the pants of his tux separating them.

She could barely think, couldn't remember exactly why. "Because it was dirty and taboo, two women touching and kissing like that."

"You like the taboo."

"I don't like it." She gasped as she felt his hands again, unzipping himself. "It's just horribly erotic. And I hate myself, but I can't help getting wet."

"So you do like the taboo."

No, no, she wanted to say, to deny, but he was right. She sometimes hated herself for it, but yes, taboo spelled excitement.

She heard the tear of a condom, and he held himself aloft to roll it on. "Would two men together do the same thing?" he asked as he put the crown of his cock to her and rubbed her pussy.

She gasped with the contact, how easily he slid over her, how wet and ready she was. "Yes. It would be horrible and yet so exciting."

"Would you like me to fuck you to the sight of it?"

"Yes, yes."

He slammed home inside her, so high and deep, he stole her breath. Then he stilled, his body wrapped around her, inside her, claiming her. "Tell me more," he demanded.

"Yes. I'd want it that way. Watching them. You taking me to the sight of it. As long as you forced me." In her head, she knew there was never any force to what he made her do, but with the words she could pretend and make the guilt melt away.

"I'll always force you. And you'll do everything I order you to. If I tell you to fuck another man, you'll do it. But don't you dare"—he bent and nipped her neck hard like a mating jungle cat—"don't you *dare* want it or like it or need it." He pulled out, thrust hard, then held still with his cock buried deep and his voice a harsh rasp. "I'm your master, you dirty little slut, and I'm the only one you'll ever want."

"Yes, you're my master." She whimpered in fear and pleasure and pain. "I only want you." It was only Luke who could do this for her, tapping into all her varied emotions.

"I'm going to fuck you now. I'm going to take you like the bitch you are. And you will come, because if you don't, I'll hurt you. I'll punish you. I'll make you pay." He shoved one hand beneath her and put his finger to her clit.

She could barely breathe through the terrifying ecstasy.

"Say yes," he demanded.

"Yes."

He fucked her. It was hard. It was fast. It was so incredibly good in a world where everything was supposed to be bad. Bree screamed. She didn't want to come; he forced the climax to roll over her, dragging her down into the depths of his desire with the hot pump of his cock inside her and his shout of ecstasy filling her head. She came for him, no faking, no lying. Hard. Long. Over and over until she felt as if everything had gone black and perfect.

HE CRADLED HER IN HIS ARMS IN THE BACKSEAT. A PARKING garage security truck had driven by twice now, but their clothes were straight, her hair smoothed, everything back in place and G-rated.

He'd rescued her from Derek, tried to offer the tenderness he thought women wanted, but it was force she really desired. Not violence, but the act of a dominant man subjugating her, making her do things she wanted but couldn't admit to. And he'd loved it. His climax had been explosive, tearing through his body, dizzying him with its force.

The distinction between Derek and him was that his desire for her was part of everything, even as they bore witness to bondage and debauchery in a cheesy sex club, as he threatened her with other men, as he fucked her hard without an ounce of tenderness, he still wanted and desired her above all others. That made him completely different from Derek, who'd fallen into the degradation side of the whole thing. He'd forgotten about making her feel special at the same time, stopped caring that she needed to know he got off on her sucking another man's cock *for* him, that no other woman made him feel the way she did.

Tonight was possibly the fucking best sex they'd had. Maybe it was the devil talking to him, but he wanted her the way she was tonight, hot, sexy, needy, crying out for him, and coming so hard that she dragged him right along into bliss with her. The night they'd gone bowling, he'd seen a new side of her, had wanted that personality, yet the woman she was tonight had captured his soul. He wanted both; he just wasn't sure he could have them together.

There were so many damn problems with what they did together. In the aftermath, he could hear her confessing that she needed to be forced so she didn't have to feel bad. Someone long ago had done a number on her. Her father, or another man, someone had taught her wrong things about sex. And Luke was playing right into what had been done to her. Yeah, he was caught between the proverbial rock and a hard place. He didn't know how to stop. He didn't *want* to stop.

Because fuck if she hadn't taken them both to heaven. "I am pleased with you," he said formally. "You have done well tonight."

She sighed her contentment. "Guess we can't tell my mother what we did on *this* date," she murmured, her eyes closed, lips curved slightly.

He smiled for her though she couldn't see. "She might not have a full appreciation for it."

She snuggled deeper into him, then tipped her head back to meet his gaze. "Is that what you'll make me do next time?"

"Which part, the woman on the bed with all the men, or the two women?"

"The dom," she whispered. "Trade me to him."

His heart lurched. He had no intention of letting any other man touch her or have her. He knew now that a part of him would kill if he thought that's truly what she wanted. But he was open to fantasy as long he was the one in control of it. Besides, with her, the threat might very well be better than the reality. It had been tonight. "The next time you piss me off, I'll consider what punishment you deserve, forcing you to fuck or suck. Or masturbating for a crowd." He gathered her hair in his hand and bunched it against her head, holding her. "But part of the punishment will be my pleasure in watching you so I'm going to choose your torture with my needs in mind, not yours."

"Yes, Master," she murmured, a sleepy little sigh whispering out of her.

"If you're a lucky girl, it might be the dom from tonight."

"Then I'll have to be very bad."

"Bitch," he snapped. "Don't make it sound like you want him or you'll piss me off." But he savored the easiness with which she teased him. It was unusual.

She shook her head, serious, smile gone. "Only you, Master. You aren't like the other men I've known."

He'd never asked how many men. He didn't want to know. Usually it was the shoe on the other foot, with the woman not wanting to know her lover's past, but he knew that his experience was mild compared to hers.

They sat together like that, her in his arms, for long minutes as he drank in the feel of her. Until finally she spoke. "I'm afraid to go home to my mother."

He made a noise of attention, waiting for her to go on.

"I don't know how to get away from her. When will she be ready for me to leave? Sometimes she seems fine, but others, she's just . . . strange." Then quickly she put her fingers to his lips. "Don't answer. I don't know why I'm saying all this."

He didn't know what would make her feel better.

"But it's time to go," she said, the moment abruptly over. "I have to be at work in the morning."

There would be other nights. She needed him. Of that he was sure.

But was he good for her?

22

SHE'D HAD TO SNEAK INTO THE HOUSE LAST NIGHT, TERRIFIED HER mother would catch her wearing the bustier, short skirt, and fishnet stockings, and ask her what the hell she'd been up to.

Bree kept remembering what she'd said to Luke in the car. That she didn't know how to get away from her mom. The bizarre thought had come to her in the comfort of his arms, when her defenses were down and her mind had drifted into a bad place. It was funny how they could have that hot interlude in the club, followed by the things he did to her in the backseat, and she still let herself get distracted with bad thoughts.

What she should have concentrated on was that he'd had the opportunity to give her away and he didn't. He'd played his part so perfectly. He'd been so good at it, she'd believed completely that he would follow through on his threats. Yet if he had, it would have ruined it all.

She didn't have time to think about it all now. She had to face the day. She had to tell Erin about her father. She couldn't keep pretending forever.

"Bye, Mom," she called before she headed to work.

Her mother poked her head out of the kitchen door. "I'll see you tonight, sweetheart. Is Luke coming over again?"

There was something irritating about her mother's overly hopeful smile and bright eyes. As if she were pinning all her hopes on Luke. Maybe Bree did need a keeper, but not in the way her mother meant. She had financial security. It was emotional security she was lacking. She'd had it for five seconds after Luke pulled out of her last night. Then poof, it was gone. She just couldn't seem to hold on to a man or security.

"Mom, we can't be dependent on him."

Her mother merely flapped her hand and went back to the breakfast dishes. It was as if she didn't see the correlation between dependency and the relationship she'd had with Bree's father. If you were dependent, you couldn't get away when you wanted to. Her mother should *know* that.

Okay, work. From her mom's house, the drive wasn't far. She girded her loins, so to speak, as she entered the front door. Rachel waved enthusiastically from her closet-size office. Across the roundhouse, Erin was at her desk. Engrossed in something on her computer monitor, she traced her finger across the screen. Santana, Steve's favorite band, drifted in from the manufacturing area. Steve, their quality control manager, looked like a former Hell's Angel, with all the requisite tattoos, and his music reflected it. Bree hurried to her own office, dumped the umbrella by the filing cabinet, then hung her coat on the rack. It wasn't raining, but the sky was dark and foreboding.

Please don't make me do this.

When would that pitiful voice inside her die?

Okay, just breathe. But all sorts of terrors coursed through her, making her skin shrivel and her knees buckle. She sat down heavily in her chair.

She was afraid Erin would think her lacking in emotion. What if Erin asked about a funeral and, God forbid, wanted to attend? How was she supposed to say they weren't even having one? She wouldn't be able to act normal, and Erin would start asking questions. Of course she'd want to know why Bree had come to work the day after her father died without breathing a word of it. Then Erin would know there was something terribly *wrong* about Bree.

She should have told Erin yesterday. She could have passed the test then. Maybe it would be better to wait until Erin came to see her, which she inevitably would. Wimp. Always reacting, never acting.

Do it, do it, do it.

She got up too fast and felt dizzy. Then she almost lost it when Erin wasn't in her office. She'd been there a minute ago, for God's sake. Where could she have gone so quickly?

"You okay, Bree?"

She jumped and almost shrieked, catching herself at the last minute. "Dominic." Where had he come from? She felt her palms start to sweat.

"How's your dad doing?"

"He's dead." The words just fell out of her mouth. *Take them back, take them back.* She hadn't meant to do it like that; she'd intended to lead into it. Now it was too, too late.

"Oh Jesus, Bree. I'm so sorry." Dominic touched her arm. He was tall, over six feet, and his height made her want to curl into him, bury her face against his dark hair. Not in a sexual way. Not even in the way she wanted Luke to comfort her. But because Dominic was a strong man, a kind man. And he didn't want anything from her. He was safe.

His eyes, dark with emotion, traveled her face as if he could read something in her features. "You should have called us. You didn't need to come in."

What did he expect her to do? When he'd lost Jay, it had been so different. A child versus an old man. A sudden tragedy, instead of a cancer the family had known about for months. The beginning of heartbreak instead of the end of a long, bad journey. When Dominic came back to work after Jay, he'd been a ghost you could see through.

It wasn't like that for Bree. She didn't feel sad. She didn't feel anything except relief and guilt. She didn't want Dominic to pick up on those *wrong* emotions.

"I'm just glad he's out of his misery." Like a dog that had to be put down. Oh yeah, she didn't want Dominic to hear *that*.

He nodded, his gaze full of shadows. He was thinking about Jay, she was sure, and she hated to be the reminder.

Yet he touched her shoulder in sympathy and comfort. "You should be with your mom, Bree, not here."

"She had things to do." Her mom didn't need her. Her mom was throwing out more stuff. Today, she planned to tackle the garage where her father had kept all his tools and odds and ends. Bree'd had to tell her not to go hog wild and throw out things they needed for the house and yard maintenance.

But she couldn't reveal all that wackiness to Dominic. Instead she added, "She's managing. Mom's stoic." Even that didn't seem like enough explanation and she rushed on. "She's always got to be doing something. Do-do-do, that's my mom." She tried to smile, but it felt oddly stretched across her face. Then she realized she probably shouldn't be smiling at all. "I think she needs some alone time to assimilate and get herself centered and . . ." She let her voice trail off because she just seemed to be digging a deeper hole with all the meaningless chatter.

If Dominic noticed she was babbling, he didn't mention it. He simply shook his head in empathy. "I know how hard it is. That's why this is a time for family. You go. We'll be fine."

"But I've got the check run to set up."

He gave her a look. "Erin can do that. Go home, Bree."

Suddenly she was glad it was Dominic who'd found her instead of Erin. He didn't ask any particulars, didn't probe for details. He had all the right words and none of the difficult ones, no questions that would show her up.

But God, she was hiding behind nonanswers and idiotic chatter, not facing up and saying what needed to be said. She needed to change, grow a backbone, do *something*. Take charge. Decide what to do instead of letting someone else make her decisions for her.

Only today wasn't her growth day. After a few more pointless words, Bree took the opportunity Dominic gave her and ran. She didn't even stop to grab her umbrella and raincoat. Yeah, a wimp.

DOMINIC FOUND ERIN IN MANUFACTURING BREATHING DOWN Matt's neck. They'd given Matt, one of their techs, responsibility for assembling the transducers in-house. The transducers were the probes that took the readings the ultrasonic gauge measured and were integral to a quality instrument. They'd been outsourcing the production for years with Leon, but Leon was retiring. Matt, a skinny kid in his midtwenties with lank hair and hangdog features, had taken on the transducer assembly with more enthusiasm than they'd gotten out of him in six months. Erin had made the right choice in trusting him, but she couldn't resist a little mother-henning. It was in her nature.

Dominic stood for a moment watching her. His wife took his breath away. She always would. They'd come close to losing each other when they lost Jay. He would ache for his son every minute for the rest of his days, but if he'd lost Erin, too, he wouldn't have survived. Somehow, in the last few weeks, they'd found a way to go on together. Yet it was moments like this that brought home to him once again how fragile life was. When he'd seen the struggle and pain in Bree's face, the way she'd blurted out the news of her father's death, then the horror on her face after she said it.

He'd seen all that. But he'd seen more.

"Got a minute, babe?" he said to Erin.

She looked up, her features a mask of concentration, her focus on the task. Until she blinked. And smiled. God, he loved that smile. In ways, they'd regained that exciting sense of newness in a relationship that would normally be long gone after fifteen years of marriage. God yes, he'd have traded his life for the return of his son, but he had Erin, and this time he'd hang on to every precious minute of their life together, taking nothing for granted.

"What?" Her eyebrows knitted together.

Dominic crooked his finger until they'd moved out of earshot, closer to the inventory shelving. "I just talked with Bree," he started.

"Her father's dead," Erin finished for him, putting a hand to her forehead. "Dammit, I didn't even see her come in. I should have been watching. How's she doing?" It was so like Erin to blame herself.

"Kinda abnormal. She talked."

"What do you expect?"

"I mean she *talked*." Bree usually said as little as possible to him. "She was downright chatty." Sort of, at least for Bree. It was hard to put into words what was bothering him.

"She was like that with me. Almost as if she didn't know how to say whatever it was she wanted to say, and she actually babbled."

"She had this crazy notion she had to take care of the check run," he said. "I sent her home."

"Oh, Jesus, I can do the check run. Is her mom okay?"

"I guess so. She said her mom had things to do, whatever that means."

Erin pursed her lips. "She shouldn't even have come in. When did he die?"

"I don't know. She didn't say."

"So I guess they haven't decided on when they're having the funeral. I'll give her a call later, make sure she's okay, and find out about the service. We should attend, and send some flowers, too."

That was Erin, making sure everyone was okay. Still, he worried about Bree. Never one to wear her feelings on her sleeve, he nevertheless wondered if her father's illness, then his death, had pushed her to a breaking point.

"LUKE, THERE'S A WOMAN OUT HERE, BUT SHE DOESN'T HAVE AN appointment." His secretary's voice was low, wary, unsure. "I don't recognize her name from *any*thing I've ever seen in your calendar. And she doesn't even have a business card," Linda added, low and incredulous.

"Who is it?" he prompted. Linda wasn't usually so reticent. In fact, she sounded almost . . . spooked.

"She says her name is Miss Mason."

Bree? In the middle of the morning? Not once during their entire relationship had she ever come to his office. They'd fantasized about it the other day, having her suck him at work, but he hadn't realized she even knew where his office was located. Not that he'd ever hidden his company's name from her.

"Send her in. And hold all my calls until I'm done."

His secretary was efficient, but she didn't like surprises. She certainly wasn't used to women showing up unannounced, especially without a business card or appointment, *good heavens*.

Bree entered, and Linda closed the door behind her.

Dark circles beneath her eyes, no lipstick, and skin so pale the shadow of her veins showed beneath the surface, Bree, as the old saying went, looked like death warmed over. She'd pulled her hair back in a hasty ponytail but wisps had blown loose, and her black blazer seemed to hang on her frame. His biggest desire in the world was to wrap her in his arms.

"Master," was all she said, and he knew his embrace was nowhere near what she needed from him now.

23

"LOCK THE DOOR," LUKE SAID, HIS VOICE DELIBERATELY HARSH AS he rounded his desk.

She did.

"Come here." He pointed to a spot three feet in front of him. She stood there, awaiting his instructions.

"What the hell do you think you're doing showing up at my office unannounced?" It touched him deep inside that she came to him, that she'd needed him. This was no social call. Bree didn't understand the meaning of that. She was here because she had to have what only he could give her. And it wasn't the time to think about why, to feel guilty because of what had been done to her in the past.

So he pushed. "What do you think my secretary thought of that? Do you realize how you've embarrassed me?" He prepared her for the punishment she required, excited by the prospect, here, in his office, his secretary outside, his notebook open on the conference table for the meeting he had in fifteen minutes.

He strode the two steps to her and stabbed a finger at the carpet. "Get on your knees, you dirty bitch."

She went down with an avid light sparking in her dark eyes.

His heart raced at her eagerness. "Suck me. Do it now, and make it good so that I forget my anger with you."

Her fingers trembled as she unzipped his pants, not even bothering with his belt buckle. She pulled him free, and he was already hard, pulsing for her. She would always do that, flipping an on-switch in him with just a look, a word, a breath.

When she tongued his slit, he growled, fueling her. As her lips slid down over his crown, he tipped his head back and savored her sleek wet mouth. "That's so good, baby."

He didn't know if he wanted to come. Sometimes, just the feel of her around him was enough. He could let it go on forever.

She grabbed his thighs, held on, and took him deep down her throat. His legs quivered with the effort it took to stand. She shot him high so fast, he couldn't think of the right words. "God." No, that wasn't it. "Cunt." She sucked him harder. Yes, dirty, filthy, hot, crazy words. "Cocksucking little slut."

She went wild on his cock, tonguing, sucking, drawing him deep, then sliding back out with a suction that made his eyes feel like they'd pop. His balls ached, but he held off.

"Don't you dare make me come, dirty whore."

She moaned, her mouth still wrapped around him, her tongue working him.

"Your punishment will be not receiving my come the way you want." When he didn't think he could stand it anymore, when his heart was drumming, his pulse pounding, and his breath was a rasp in his chest, he pushed her away.

She fell back on her ass, her hands supporting her, eyes wide, needy.

He could barely breathe as he shoved his cock back in his pants and zipped. His skin was hot beneath his white shirt. "Bitch," he whispered. "Whore." It felt good, as if he could blame someone else for his own denial, and he wondered if that was one of the things a true dom got out of it, a submissive to blame and take your punishment for you.

"Get up," he ordered.

She stood, her skin tinged pink with her exertion.

"Step out of your shoes and bend over my desk."

She kicked off her high heels, pushed his pen holder and stapler aside, then leaned with both forearms on the desk. She hadn't said a word beyond that first one when she entered. He relished her silence, her need.

Moving up behind her, he blanketed her body, reaching beneath her abdomen to unbuckle her belt. "This would have been so much easier if you'd worn a skirt. Don't ever show up here again in slacks. You will always wear a skirt so that I can get at you easily. Do you understand?"

"Yes, Master," she whispered, a needy whimper in her voice.

It fueled him, her compliance, her pliability, her desire to do anything for him. There was so much power in that, and while he liked the equality of sex, a man and woman taking and giving, she'd made him enjoy complete control.

He pulled her zipper down, then slid the pants over the milk-white globes of her pert ass. "Step out of them," he said when they were bunched at her ankles.

She did, and he pushed the pile away with his foot. Then, leaning over her, his lips at her ear and his fingers sliding down the crease of her ass along her thong, he whispered, "From now on, you will wear thigh-high stockings beneath your skirts. And dirty, horny bitches don't wear panties. I will call you at work and tell you to touch yourself for me." Beneath him, she shuddered, her breath coming faster. "I might call you while you're driving," he went on, "and you will spread your legs for me. You will be available twenty-four/seven, at my beck and call to do whatever I tell you. I might need a blow job after a hard meeting, and you will drop whatever you're doing to come here." His cock surged. He didn't know why he hadn't thought of that before. "Do you understand, my sweet little cunt?"

"Yes, Master." Tears of pleasure laced her voice.

He had them both going with his words. The possibilities overwhelmed him, and as he traced her pussy, beckoning him from beneath the black satin of her thong, he wanted to fuck her, strip her down and take her, shove his cock deep. Now. Forever. He had a condom in his suit pocket, planning for tonight, if he got the chance. But not yet, there was more punishment to be meted out before he fucked her.

He didn't even glance at his watch. Beeman would be arriving for their meeting, but he could wait outside. Luke rather liked the idea of making Beeman wait while he had her. He wanted this. Now.

Backing off, he slapped her ass hard. "Don't make a sound, you little cunt."

She didn't scream or cry, but reduced it all to a moan in her throat.

He pulled her panties away, the crotch clinging briefly to her warm, wet pussy. Letting the black thong drop to her ankles, this time he didn't tell her to step out of it, craving the decadence of the satin binding her feet.

"I'm going to spank you now for the impudence of coming to my office uninvited."

He swatted her hard, then, needing the feel of her, he let his fingers slide down the length of her pussy. All that sweetness, all that moisture.

"Spread your legs, my dirty slut."

She moved them as far as the panties would allow.

He delved deeper, finding the button of her clit. She moaned and rocked against him, going prone on the desk and stretching her hands out to hang on to the other side.

The phone buzzed. He held Bree's hair, forcing her face down. "Don't make a sound," he whispered, then punched the intercom button, his hand still between Bree's legs, stroking, caressing. "Yes?"

"Luke, Mr. Beeman is here for your meeting."

Bree shuddered as he filled her with two fingers. But she didn't so much as breathe. A piece of him wished she wasn't so obedient. He almost liked the heat of being overheard.

"Tell Beeman I'll be another half hour at least." Then he clicked off.

And clapped Bree's ass so hard, she squeaked before she managed to cut it off.

"Do you see what you've done, forcing me to cancel meetings? And my secretary has probably guessed what you're making me do to you in here. Whore."

He slapped her again, hard. Her fingers curled white around the edge of the desk, and this time when he delved between her thighs, her pussy drenched his fingers.

He gave her more of what she wanted.

BREE COULDN'T BREATHE, IT WAS SO GOOD. HER BOTTOM ACHED, her pussy was so wet and needy, his fingers inside her filling all the hollow places. And the names he called her, the things he said. She was bad, dirty, terrible. He knew she wanted everything he did to her.

He gave her butt a stinging blow, then slid between her legs to her clit, and she almost screamed with orgasm. Not yet; he hadn't given permission. She couldn't come until he let her. Nor could she scream when he finally allowed her to climax.

She didn't know what she'd needed when she came here. But Luke knew, forcing her to her knees immediately, his cock delicious in her mouth. And now this.

She was nothing but sensation, pain, pleasure, his fingers on her, in her, her cream dripping down her legs, the incessant slap on her butt and the stroke along her pussy making her wild.

"Master, Master, Master, I'm going to come." She wasn't even sure if she said the words aloud or it was just her mind crying out to him.

"Don't come yet, little bitch. I'm not done." He punctuated with a particularly hard slap and followed up with the sweetest of caresses against her pussy, her clit, her G-spot.

She wanted to cry with delight and need, even felt the moisture beneath her eyelids, which she'd screwed tightly shut. But she didn't come, pushed it away.

She couldn't hear all the words, the full sentences, the demands and orders, just the important words, slut, cunt, whore, bitch. They were terms of endearment. They were his special names for her. *His* slut, *his* whore, everything for him.

The moment was so close, she whimpered with the strain of holding off. Only his voice telling her not to come kept her from the peak. She was invaded, taken over, controlled, his touch so perfect, the pain so intense, the pleasure even better.

Then suddenly the blunt tip of his cock pressed against her. She clenched her fingers around the edge of the desk as he rammed home deep inside.

"Take this fucking, you little bitch. You're mine. I can do anything I want with you, anything. You're my little slave."

Reaching beneath her, he played her clit as he stroked deep and hard inside her. The cloth of his pants rubbed the burning skin of her ass, more pain, more pleasure.

"You will come when I say and not before, slut. I will take

mine from you before I let you come." His voice was like a thread winding through her mind, every cell, tying them all together, tethering her to him.

"Bitch," he whispered, and she felt him fill her to capacity.

"Cunt," he murmured, and she clenched around him, dragged him deeper, begging, needing.

She writhed beneath the onslaught of his cock, gasping, tears leaking from her eyes.

"Whore," he muttered.

And she felt her body start to give, to take over, tipping her into orgasm.

"Not without me, slut."

She gazed at the white knuckles of her fingers on the edge of the desk a moment before she closed her eyes.

"Come now," he demanded, and she felt the spurt of him inside her, the pulsing of his cock, his low grunting breaths at her ear, and she let herself tumble into climax. She felt everything, the air currents beating around her, the rasp of his slacks against her backside, his belt buckle slapping her, then finally the weight of him crushing her against the wood desk.

She seemed to be drifting in some place that was far from reality, though she felt him backing off, getting rid of the condom, zipping. Then he lifted her in his arms, her thong wafting to the floor.

The office was large, with a sofa, chair, and coffee table, in addition to the desk and a small conference table. His walls were tastefully decorated with photographs of birds in flight. She thought of flying away with them.

He plopped down on the leather sofa with her in his arms. She was naked below the waist, but her skin was hot, her face flushed.

God, what had she done coming here begging for . . . something? She hadn't been able to go home. She'd driven around aimlessly until she realized she was turning in ever decreasing circles around his office building. And she'd succumbed.

"I just wanted to hear your voice," she whispered. A phone call wasn't enough. She'd needed his voice and his touch.

When she wanted to run away, he'd become the place she could run to. She wrapped her arms around his neck and held on as if he'd try to get free of her if she didn't grip him tightly.

Dominic had told her to go home, but she couldn't face home. She couldn't face her mother, not the clearing out, not the old ghosts, nothing.

"Make me safe," she said, her words barely more than a breath. She'd never been safe. Men always changed, always decided you weren't good enough, always moved on, but before they left, they made you feel as if you were worthless, useless, unloved, unwanted. No longer special or precious.

Only Luke had let her keep coming back. For now. How much longer?

"You're safe," he murmured against her hair.

She held him tighter. "Don't make me go." She clutched so hard, her arms trembled.

"I won't."

Squeezing her eyes shut only served to make her head hurt, and suddenly the tears were so close to the surface, she couldn't stop them leaking through her closed lids. "I'm so scared," she whispered, "I'm so scared." Scared of what, she didn't know, but she kept saying it in the hopes he would make it go away, turn it into a lie. Make her safe.

SHE HAD NEVER CRIED BEFORE, NOT LIKE THIS. NOT EVEN WHEN her father died. She'd cried in the throes of orgasm, though Luke could never have said whether the tears were of pleasure or pain. But after sex, they ended.

He could not have said why it was so profound that she did so for him now.

"Don't be scared," he murmured with every breath against her hair, as if she were a child needing comfort. "I'll take care of you. I'll be here. I'll always be here."

He couldn't imagine ever letting her go. What she asked for now was the intimacy he'd craved, tenderness, comfort, the sweet moments after sex where two souls communed. He *needed* her to need him. He wanted her dependence so that he could provide for her. He held her, absorbed her pain, her tears, and felt as though he were the most important man in the world.

Yet he'd become a part of her ritual, the scene she played out over and over to make herself feel better. While he loved how she needed him, ran to him, there was a wrongness to it he'd never felt before the last few days. Like he'd become the abuser who said he was sorry afterward. He feared what he was doing, no matter how perfect and good it was for him, would prove to be bad for her in the final analysis.

24

GOD, THAT WAS PATHETIC. SHE WAS ASHAMED. SHE'D BAWLED LIKE a baby in his office until his secretary buzzed him for his meeting.

"What's up with that?" Bree asked herself as she drove home. She couldn't quite remember what it was all about except that long spiral down about how he'd leave her eventually, blah, blah, blah. But she'd remembered to drive directly over to her condo and pick up the clothing he'd told her to wear, only dresses or skirts, no pants. Oh yes, she'd jumped to follow those orders.

He'd come to her tonight. She'd cried, so he'd be there. Is that how she wanted to keep a man? With tears and neediness?

In her mother's driveway, she shut off the engine and rubbed away a cramp in her calf. This couldn't go on. She couldn't keep depending on him. He'd get tired of her antics and leave even sooner than he'd already planned.

She shook herself and shoved open the car door. What did it matter? Men always left anyway. They always got tired. She'd survived it before; she would again. It hurt for a little while, then it was over, no big deal.

But the thought of not hearing his voice anymore left an ache around her heart.

"I'm in the kitchen," her mother called cheerily before Bree even closed the front door.

"She's manic," Bree muttered under her breath. Her mother was too happy. She'd always been stoic, not happy. The change was unsettling. What if this was the beginnings of dementia? How would Bree take care of her?

She followed the scent of cookies. Her mother had been baking again. When she wasn't throwing out stuff, she was baking, baking, baking. Who was going to eat all of it? Oh yeah, Luke would eat it.

"Look what we've got." In the kitchen, her mom's eyes were maniacally bright as she pointed at the freshly baked tray of chocolate chip cookies. A small cardboard box sat nearby on the counter.

Ignoring the cookies, Bree pointed to the box. "What's that?"

"Your father's ashes."

Bree swallowed, but her throat hurt, and her breath suddenly seemed to come too fast for her nostrils to handle. That's all they came in, just a plain cardboard box? Probably because her mother wasn't willing to pay for an urn. She opened her mouth, but that was even worse, as if there was ash in the air, getting sucked down with every breath. Her mom had been baking with her dad's ashes on the counter. Oh God.

"I hadn't imagined they'd do it so quickly, but they called, and I just rushed right down," her mother said without the slightest hint of emotion. Even Bree had emotions; she just wasn't sure what they were.

This was totally freaky.

"I thought of the perfect place for him," her mom said as if she were talking about just the right spot to plant amaryllis bulbs. It was then that Bree saw the Dumbo cookie jar next to the box. Her mother pulled on Dumbo's curled tail, the jar's handle, and removed his rear end. "We'll put him in here."

In Dumbo's *ass*? Oh. My. God.

"It never really worked as a cookie jar anyway, because you couldn't reach the front cookies and all the crumbs went down into his legs." Just like Bree's father always said. Her mother sounded like a parrot. "But this is perfect, don't you think?"

"Uhh." That was all the sound Bree could manage.

"Here, you put him in." Her mom shoved the box at her.

Bree almost screamed and jerked her hand away before it touched her. "This is crazy. You can't put him in a cookie jar. Take him out and scatter him over the ocean."

For the first time in the past three days, her mother glared at her. "This is where he deserves to be, Brianna. In a place he hated." She grabbed the box, opened it, and pulled out a plastic bag secured with a nylon cable tie, a metal tag attached to it.

Dear God. Her father was in a baggie with dog tags identifying him.

Her mother cut the cable tie with a pair of kitchen scissors "It's perfectly fitting," she said, then turned the bag upside down and fed the opening into the cookie jar.

Bree expected to hear chinks and clunks against Dumbo's ceramic sides, bone fragments, but there was just a *pfft* of air. Did everything get completely incinerated, pulverized, what? She suddenly felt lightheaded, dizzy, even sick as her mother emptied the bag with a final puff of gray.

Bree couldn't stand it anymore, and she backed away, stumbling over God knew what, maybe her own heels. "This is completely dysfunctional. Are you just going to leave him on the counter?" Bree wanted him gone, his memory expunged, so they could be normal. Or at least pretend they were. God forbid she'd have to come over for Sunday dinner with his freaking ashes on the counter.

"I haven't decided," her mother said. "I might put him in the bathroom on the back of the toilet."

"We should talk about this, Mom." It was dementia. Or maybe a nervous breakdown from all the stress of the last few months. "You've got unresolved feelings." They both did, but neither of them would do more than dance around the subject. *Did you know, Mom?*

Her mother simply stared at her. "It's just ashes. It's not even him. Let me have my petty fun."

"You sound like you hated him." Just as she had the night they stood by his bed waiting for him to die. *Say something now, Mom.*

Her mother snorted. "Of course I didn't hate him. He's your father."

That didn't mean anything at all. As far as conception went, he was just a sperm donor. "We should really talk about this." Bree wasn't sure she even wanted to, but her mother was acting too outlandish to ignore.

"There's nothing to talk about." She crumpled the empty bag, tossed it, the cable tie, and the metal tag back into the box and opened the door beneath the sink to throw the whole lot in the trash. Like garbage. Then she pushed Dumbo back into his place on the counter among the other cookie jars.

Bree would never eat another cookie from one of her mother's jars.

Then, as if nothing totally insane had happened, her mom asked, "Is Luke coming over for dinner?"

Bree felt as if she were spinning off into space. She couldn't think, couldn't deal, and the most she could manage was to go right along with her mother. "He didn't say anything about dinner specifically, just that he'd see me later."

"Well, I'll make something special." Then her mom smiled and pointed her finger at Bree. "He adores you, and he'll be here, don't you worry. You need to hang on to that man, Bree. He's older and wiser and he'll take good care of you."

God, she sounded like that silly song from *The Sound of Music*. They were both completely nuts. "Mom, would you quit with that?"

But her mom didn't quit. "Now go take a shower. You look awful, your makeup's a mess, and your hair is a bunch of tangles."

Gee, thanks a lot, Mom. She didn't say it, didn't want to fight about it. Her mother had always wanted her to put on more makeup, do something more with her hair, and wear more dresses instead of slacks. "Look, Mom, we need to talk about stuff like arranging to see the lawyer."

Her mother flapped a hand. "I'm going to see him on Thursday at nine."

Dammit. Bree was supposed to meet with Marbury at nine on Thursday. "Why didn't you tell me you were making an appointment? I've already got something Thursday that I can't miss."

"Oh, I don't need you, dear. It's just a formality. Your father set up that trust and everything will go as smooth as cream."

"But, Mom—"

Her mother pursed her lips. "You worry too much. I'm not an idiot. I can do things on my own."

"Then what do you need me here for?" She didn't mean to sound so harsh, but her mother simply exasperated her.

Her mom grabbed her arm, her fingers pinching into Bree's flesh even through her jacket. "You can't leave me. I need you here, Brianna. I can't face this house on my own yet." Her eyes were suddenly wide, stark.

"You're alone in it all day."

"But I know you're coming back and that makes it easier."

Bree stared at her mom. Maybe she should get rid of the damn ashes instead of putting them in a cookie jar. That would sure as hell banish the ghosts more quickly.

She knew she wasn't a good daughter, but the least she could do was stay a few more days. A normal person would. It was expected. Sometimes, you just had to suck it up and pretend you were actually normal.

"Okay, Mom. I'll stay." Maybe she could figure out if her mom had developed dementia.

"SO YOU ALREADY HAVE TWO DAUGHTERS. DOES THAT MEAN YOU don't want to have any more children when you remarry?"

Bree almost spat out the homemade minestrone her mom had prepared for dinner. "Mom. Leave him alone."

"I'm just making conversation, Bree."

"That's fine," Luke said, all good-guest and smiles. "I have no plans either way right now, Mrs. Mason."

He was so damn sexy in his dark suit and white shirt, Bree itched to touch him. She had never itched to touch a man before, not like this, where she just wanted to rub up against him like a kitten. It was this weird new phenomenon with Luke. Since her father had died? She couldn't pinpoint it exactly.

But geez, her mom was wearing her out with all the push-push-push, and she was terrified Luke would ask for a cookie out of Dumbo. "It's time to go anyway," Bree said. "We'll be late."

"I didn't know you had definite plans." Her mother let her mouth droop. "You didn't mention that before."

Bree smiled, her face brittle. "Very definite. We should get going."

"But I made dessert," her mother said plaintively.

"You can wrap it up, and Luke can take it home with him."

"It's bread pudding. It has to be hot."

In the meantime, Luke was sitting back, his soup bowl empty, the warm French bread gone. Watching. What did he see? What was he thinking? That she was rude to her mom?

Bree took a breath and wished he'd jump to her rescue with a word of agreement. Why did he have to keep coming over anyway?

"I would love to take a piece home, Mrs. Mason. And I promise to heat it up in the oven, not the microwave."

Oh thank *God* he'd said *something*.

Her mother beamed. "Yes, the oven is much better. I'll dish it out while Bree finishes getting ready."

"She looks lovely the way she is."

God, he was a schmoozer, too. She'd primped for him tonight with makeup and fresh hair, and a skirt, the way he'd ordered her. Stockings, no panties. Just for him.

He excused himself to use the restroom, and Bree helped her mother carry the dishes to the sink.

"Bree, your shoes are too tall again." Her mother practically hissed the comment in her ear. "You need to change them. A girl should never be taller than her beau."

God. "He's not my *beau*. And Luke loves my high heels." Her fuck-me shoes, he called them. "Leave it alone." Then she turned and put her hands together in a prayer. "Please, please, please stop with all the pushy questions. You're embarrassing me."

"I just want to know his prospects."

"Mom, he's forty-five years old, a CEO, divorced with two daughters. He's stable, and his prospects aren't your concern."

Her mother pouted as she filled a plastic tub with bread pudding.

Yet when Luke returned, she beamed, handing over the container and telling him what temperature to set the oven at.

"Thank you. And I'll have her home early," Luke promised.

"Oh, don't you worry about me being alone. I'm fine. You two have fun."

Right, that's why her mom had begged Bree not to leave her. Bree rolled her eyes. She hadn't even talked about going out with Luke, but she couldn't stay in there with her mother pestering him.

"How are you feeling?" Luke asked after he'd climbed in the car. Polite as always, he'd opened her door first.

"I'm fine."

"Everything okay with your mom?"

"You heard her. She's fine." Putting good old Dad's ashes in Dumbo's ass and planning her daughter's freaking wedding, too.

"You seem a little tense."

"I'm not tense," she snapped. God, this wasn't where she wanted to go. She never got all emotional and bitchy with Luke, but she'd done it two evenings in a row now. That wasn't what their relationship was about, but she couldn't seem to help herself when she was around her mother.

"After this morning, you might need to vent some of your feelings," he said as he drove away from the house.

She didn't want to vent. She didn't want to admit she had feelings. They were difficult to quantify and analyze. And she couldn't tell him about Dumbo. "I have nothing to vent."

He sighed audibly as the car came to rest at a stoplight. "All right. Your mom seems to be handling everything great. She's a strong woman."

Why that pissed her off, Bree couldn't say, but she snorted.

"Yeah, right, you should have seen what she was doing this afternoon."

"What was she doing?"

Shit. Why had she said that, for God's sake? He'd pick at it like a bone. "Forget it. I shouldn't have said anything."

But Luke never let *anything* drop.

25

THAT'S JUST WHAT LUKE DID. PICK, PICK, PICK.

He pulled out of the light he'd stopped for and said, "*You* mentioned your mother. Maybe I can help."

"I don't think so," Bree whispered, the words rough in her throat. He'd think they were both nuts if she told him about her father's ashes.

"Tell me. You know you want to or you wouldn't have brought it up."

He said it like he thought he knew women, how their minds worked, and maybe he did after living with two daughters and a wife. But he didn't know *her*. "Look, I didn't *mean* to say it, and it's not your business." The last part came out more sharply than she intended. She was being a bitch when he was only trying to help, yet there was also a part of her that marveled she could speak to him this way. A man. Her master. She was terrified to say no to Marbury, but here she was telling Luke to butt out.

"So. You feel that how you and your mom are doing after a death in the family isn't my business." In the oncoming lights, his jaw tensed and his nostrils flared. "Then why don't you tell me what *is* my business."

"The sex, Luke. That's what we are, sex. You've always liked that. The stuff we did this morning in your office." Though she'd never come to his office before. Yes, yes, she *knew* she'd crossed a line there. But they'd fantasized about a quickie. It *had* been discussed.

"*Which* stuff in my office?" His voice was hard. "When I was spanking and fucking you? Or when you were crying in my arms?"

"That was an aberration." She couldn't tell him what it was really about. Total and complete fear of everything in her life, for God's sake. And that was *before* Dumbo.

"So you're saying we're *just* about sex."

Somehow that didn't sit well either. That wasn't how she meant it. Because they weren't *only* about sex. They were about . . . She was trying to think how to put it, but he didn't give her long enough.

"Fine. Then let's have sex. How would you like a spanking? Or maybe I'll tie you up and fuck you. Or give you to a bunch of men and let them do it because I've had a long workday, and I can't be bothered." He glanced at her, eyes narrowed, gaze shadowed in the darkness of the car. "What would you prefer? Come to think of it, your preferences don't matter, do they, since I'm your master." He was on a roll. She'd once again pissed him off, and now he was blazing. "We'll make this about me and look for someone I can fuck while you watch."

A stone crystallized in her stomach. She didn't want him to touch anyone else. She hated the idea. Derek had done that, made her watch. When he was tired of her. He'd even hit her once when she complained. Luke never hit her. He never would. Some men just couldn't. But Luke wasn't above testing and pushing and goading.

So she tossed it right back at him. "You're the master. You can have whatever you want." If he took her up on it, she'd die.

"You're right, I am the master. I am in control, a fact you

seem to forget when it's convenient. So tonight, my game." He took a freeway ramp heading in the opposite direction from his house. "What are you wearing under that dress?" He waved a heartless hand at her.

"Stockings. No panties."

"Good girl. I can't believe you actually followed a command since you've been so uppity this evening. Now sit there and be quiet until we get where we're going."

Bree sat in the unbearable silence of the car. She knew she'd been a bitch, dumping all her desperation concerning her mother on Luke's head. Her father had been the same way, taking out the worst of his anger on his family, hiding what he was from everyone else who knew him. Yeah, he saved the worst for the people he was supposed to love. Luke wasn't like that.

Sometimes, when she had too much time to think, she imagined meeting his daughters. They would love him, adore him, think he was the greatest. She knew that about him. That's why he was the best master, too. Yet she'd just pissed him off to hell, and now she'd have to pay the price in punishment. There was definitely a horrible little thrill in the prospect.

Maybe she'd actually started to piss him off on purpose just to get him all riled up.

HE DIDN'T LIKE THE PETTINESS IN THE SILENCE, BUT HE'D MADE the threat and he had to carry through. That was how their relationship worked. He could actually smell her in the close confines of his car. With the threats, the orders, she was suddenly excited, tense with desire and fear, her most potent combination. It worked every time. And he hadn't even called her a slut yet.

What he did added to her issues, he was sure, yet he had no idea how to change it. This was now their ritual. Anger, hot sex, then a breakdown. In those brief moments of aftermath, she needed him for more than sex. And he *needed* those moments. It was whacked and getting worse.

But she was his submissive, and she'd been a bitch. That couldn't go unpunished. It would undermine his authority. If they reversed their roles, he could lose her, because this was what she wanted, a firm hand. He had to admit his blood was up, too. She'd gotten him going with all the thoughts she put in his head. He could feel the sting of his hand as he slapped her ass, and his cock hardened. He saw her prone and tied, at his mercy for anything, and his pulse raced. He pictured her tied to a bed with a line of men wanting a piece of her, and him kneeling over her, hand fisted in her hair. *"Do you want them? Or do you want my cock deep inside you while they watch and salivate with how badly they want you?"* He'd take her himself no matter what she begged for; it was just a matter of how he did it. She would love it all.

He glanced over at her huddled on her side of the car, knees pulled up, body turned awkwardly against the constraining seat belt.

Maybe in a true dom–sub relationship, this is exactly how it was supposed to work. She shut him out, pushed him, acted the bitch to incite him. He was supposed to react; that was his role. He felt uneasy that they were once again escalating the play, the anger, beyond what was good for her in view of what he suspected about her father. Yet she responded, she'd opened up afterward, if only briefly. He told himself that was enough.

Christ, he wanted this, too, the game, the heat, the push-pull of angry emotional sex. It was a high. "Don't you want to know where we're going?"

"I'm yours to command, Master," she said softly, the thread of excitement running through her voice.

"You're so fucking easy, slut," he murmured.

"Only for you, Master."

"I'll put that to the test."

Pulling off at a hotel complex near the freeway in the heart of Silicon Valley, he chose one of the more luxurious offerings, which was also reputed to be notorious for business hookups.

"I thought we were going to a club," she said, uncurling her legs and sitting straighter in the seat.

"I never said that."

"But—"

He shot her a look, and she cut herself off. "Don't *but* me," he said. "I'm pissed. You're going to do everything I say with no questions asked. Do you understand?"

"Yes," she whispered.

"And what are you?"

"I'm your dirty slave slut."

"Yes, you are. Now take off that bra. I told you I don't want you wearing anything under your clothes."

"But in front of my mother—"

"She's not here now."

Bree wriggled out of her bra, then tossed it in the backseat. His seat belt already unfastened, he leaned over her in a quick move and slid his hand up her skirt. "Spread your legs, pretty little whore."

She gave him space between her thighs. She was warm, wet, and he savored her wide eyes, the feel of her clit under his finger, and the gasp that fell from her parted lips.

"You want this. You're already wet and hot over it."

"Yes."

He tipped her head back and crushed his mouth to hers. She was sweet, the kiss deep, and it sent his blood pressure soaring. "Dirty bitch," he whispered against her mouth. Then he pulled back and licked her cream from his fingers. Christ, he loved the taste of her.

"I might want to finger you under the table, and you will spread your legs for me immediately," he told her as she smoothed her dress down over her thighs. "We will sit for a while and pick out my victim together. I want you to have to choose the woman you're going to watch me fuck."

She swallowed, a light sparking in her eyes, then she nodded. At what point would she stop him? When would she grab his arm and tell him it would kill her to watch? How far would he have to go before she told him she didn't want him to do it?

There was an exciting rush to the scenario, like a gambler placing a bet too big to pay off if he lost, but he felt Lady Luck beside him and couldn't resist the temptation.

She worried her lip. "How will you pick someone up if you're sitting with me?"

He smiled like a shark. "Ladies love stealing from the competition, don't they? When we find one, you and I will simply part as if we're only business associates. Then I'll charmingly tell her I want my *associate* to watch." He smiled, wide and false, waiting for her reaction.

She didn't reveal anything. He'd given her too much time to steel herself.

He climbed out and let her get her own door. He didn't hold out his arm to escort her as they entered the lobby, which was large and glass-fronted, filled with potted plants, the marble floors teeming with travelers, mostly business dress as if they were wearing uniforms. Registration had a short line as they passed, heading for the bar entrance.

Inside, the ceilings were high, the seats fairly full, and the noise at a low hum. The booths around the perimeter were raised and separated by mirrored planters full of leafy greenery. In the center, candlelight flickered in the shiny surfaces of the black lacquer tables.

He spotted a couple leaving a corner booth and herded Bree toward it. The man gave him the up-and-down as they passed, his gaze skating over Bree, then he smiled as if he figured it was the older man, younger woman pickup scenario. Based on the twenty-something blonde he was leading out, perhaps the guy was seeing his own reflection.

Luke ushered Bree into the empty booth. "Now, pick a victim," he said with a genial tone.

"It's your taste, you need to choose." She gave him an expressionless gaze, then added, "Master." The pause said it all. She wasn't happy. Good.

"How about that one?" He jutted his chin a couple of booths over at a brunette in her midthirties with outstanding breasts.

"Whatever you want, Master." She was much quicker with the *Master* this time.

"No. I'm feeling like a redhead tonight."

She flattened her lips into a straight line and said nothing.

He was having too much fun at her expense. He put his hand on her knee. She didn't move. "Spread your legs," he murmured.

She was her master's submissive and did exactly as she was told. Her skin was warm, the stockings sleek as he slid beneath the skirt. He held her gaze as he reached the top of her thigh, felt bare flesh and the silkiness of her trimmed pubic hair.

Her breath puffed a little faster, and in the candle's light, he saw her pupils dilate.

"You're wet." He stroked lightly. "You're ready to watch. You want to, need to. I'll tie you down, force you to watch, and that will make you even hotter. Maybe I'll make her lick you, too, the way that woman did the other night."

Her chest rose and fell, her skin porcelain above her low-cut neckline, and a pulse beat faster at her throat. Then she licked her lips.

"Thirsty?" He stroked her thigh, soaking up the shudder that ran through her.

"Yes," she said, her voice almost seeming to crack.

The waitress was overextended and harried, rushing between tables, and hadn't noticed them yet. "I'll get you something." Giving Bree a little time alone would be the perfect strategy. She would survey the available women and make herself crazy wondering exactly how far he'd go. "What would you like?"

"You're the master, you should choose for me."

"Hard liquor," he said, sliding out of the booth, then he leaned in, his face down to hers, the scent of her shampoo washing over him like the sweet caress of a flowery Hawaiian breeze, yet spiced with the aroma of her arousal. "You probably need to be drunk for this."

26

BASTARD, BREE THOUGHT AS HE WALKED AWAY. SHE WAS LIGHT-headed and wet between the legs from his touch. He was too good-looking, too sure of himself, too sure of her. Picking a buxom brunette just to point out the flaw of her small breasts to her. Or a redhead. Trying to drive home that he needed someone else. Then putting his hand up her skirt.

He made her wet and needy with fear and excitement.

What if she said what she thought, what she wanted? What if she told him she hated the idea of another woman having him and yet a terrible thrill raced through her at the same time? What if he got mad? Her life was full of scary what-ifs. She was afraid of things that hadn't even happened, always trying to come up with ways of making sure they never would happen, anticipating reactions, plotting, planning, keeping her mouth shut, pretending.

He stood at the end of the long bar, his finger crooked at the bartender who was already running from one end to the other, grabbing bottles, glasses, mixers. Yet Luke was the kind of man people jumped for when he signaled.

Instead of a highball glass, the man pulled down two champagne flutes from the glass shelving along the mirrored wall of the bar. The low lighting flickered in the reflection and the room seemed to narrow down to Luke and the bartender as he poured champagne. Champagne made her more tipsy than a hard drink, the bubbles going to her head faster.

Then Luke was laughing, his smile deep, wide, head slightly turned. A woman about Bree's age sat on a stool next to him. A redhead. She was pretty, her hair short and sassy. Was that why he'd gone to get the drinks rather than waiting for a server to come to the table? Bree drummed her fingers. He turned fully toward the redhead, holding only one flute of champagne, the other one still on the bar. They laughed together this time.

Bree's skin flushed hot. She never said what she wanted or what she didn't want. It was always *yes, Master, whatever you want*, sometimes with passive-aggressive sarcasm, but she always said yes. She didn't care what men did to her, as long as they wanted her, made her feel special, desirable. If Luke had given her to the dom at the club on Friday, she wouldn't have minded as long as he'd stayed with her and told her how excited it made him, how hot and hard, how it was all about her.

Yet right now, she was miles across a crowded room, and he was laughing with another woman. It was terrifying. She wanted to crawl across the floor and beg, debase and humiliate herself, anything to get him to stop, to notice her.

The bartender brought his change, Luke waggled his fingers at the two champagnes, and suddenly there were three. Luke and the woman tipped glasses together, and she drank deeply, her eyes steady on him. Then she ran a finger down the sleeve of his suit jacket.

Bree flinched as if she felt the arc of electricity between them.

Please don't make me do it.

She didn't want to watch him. And yet, as he gazed down at the big-breasted redhead, Bree could feel the wetness between her legs, every breath in and out of her lungs, her skin sensitized, her heart pounding. There was a certain excitement in being a voyeur, especially remembering what he'd said he'd do to her, tie her down, make her watch, make her do things. Yet at the same time, jealousy fueled her blood. God, he could probably see mountains of the woman's cleavage from that angle.

Bree didn't have cleavage.

He didn't look at her across the tables, didn't turn. But she felt him. He knew she couldn't take her eyes off him, knew her thoughts. *Do bad things to me. Anything you want. Everything you want.* She knew he was totally and completely aware of her.

He leaned on the bar and let the woman touch him, just his arm, but still an invasion of his personal space. She flipped her hair back, probably thinking it was sexy, and even over the distance, Bree thought she heard an annoying tinkle of laughter.

Would he bring her to the table? He'd bought her a drink. It was the start of something.

"You're just too damn pretty to be sitting all by yourself without even a cocktail."

Bree jumped, knocking her knee on the underside of the table. The man slid a glass of white wine to her and slipped into the booth. "Mind if I join you?"

Forty or so, short dark hair, suit and tie, handsome, with a nice smile and a wedding ring he didn't bother to hide. Her gaze shot to Luke.

He was otherwise occupied.

"You looked so thirsty. Waiting for some girlfriends?"

She shook her head and didn't touch the wine.

"A man then." He raised a brow and looked even more attractive. "Is he late?"

A normal person would have used the opportunity to give Luke a little payback. Bree was suddenly terrified and not in a good way. She didn't know how to talk to men, how to flirt. She didn't know how to pay Luke back, and she didn't even want to. She wanted Luke to direct everything, not have to take charge herself.

Go away. She tried to say it with her eyes, yet all she could manage was another headshake.

"So you arrived early." He smiled, and it was nice. "Is he going to be jealous if he sees you drinking wine with another man?" His eyes sparkled in the waver of candlelight. "Maybe that will be a good thing." He waved the backs of his fingers at the wine. "Go on, taste. I got you something sweet because you look so sweet."

Man, he was bold. And sure of himself. Just like Luke. She chanced a glance at Luke. He'd turned and he saw, picking up on her every move like radar.

She was suddenly parched under his penetrating gaze and grabbed the wine to slake her thirst. It was far too sweet, more to her mother's tastes, but the man . . .

She looked at him, his handsome face and more than decent body. Why was he hitting on *her*? She wasn't the USDA choice piece of meat here tonight. The woman with Luke offered more cleavage. So did the brunette Luke had pointed out.

"Name's Frank." When she didn't say anything, he added, "And you are?"

"Her name's Bree." Luke's low voice didn't even startle Frank, nor did the menace in Luke's tone as he went on. "She's taken. Buzz off."

Frank kept on smiling. "So I was right. Jealous lover in the wings."

Luke pushed the wine away from her fingertips and back at Frank, then replaced the glass with a champagne flute. "Jealousy would imply I have something to worry about." Luke shark-smiled the guy. "I just prefer that Bree isn't bothered by lounge lizards."

Frank laughed out loud, turning a few heads. "I haven't heard that term since I watched the old fifties movies when I was a kid."

"Yeah. But it fits." Luke's lips thinned. "Do I have to bodily remove you?"

She thrilled to his voice, casual yet brittle, charming yet hard. Like the night he'd taken her from Derek. He meant what he said; he would not back down. And all for her.

"Maybe we should ask the lovely lady." Frank indicated her with an arch of his brow.

Were they fighting over her? It was awful, the antics of a self-absorbed woman, but it excited her. She was wet and wanting more, needing the affirmation. "What if I said you should both sit down, and I'd share." She waited a beat, letting an image settle in their minds. "The drinks, I mean," she clarified after her point was already made.

Luke's eyes glittered, promising retribution. He sat in the round booth, moving in on her, lowering his voice so it could only just be heard above the din of conversation. "I'm the one who decides when to share, not you, my sweet." He raised his gaze to Frank. "Tonight, I'm not in a sharing mood."

She opened her eyes, going for the wide and innocent look. "But just a few minutes ago," she said, not knowing where the temerity came from, but loving it, "you wanted to share that woman over there." She jutted her chin at the bar. The redhead was still sipping her champagne and gazing wistfully at Luke.

He chucked her under the chin. "Different kind of sharing, baby."

Frank's face was fairly glowing, his cheeks ruddy with either amazement or desire, maybe both. "Guess I found the right party, didn't I."

Luke stared at him for long seconds. "Right party, wrong time." Then he grabbed Bree's hand and practically dragged her out of the booth.

"YOU DO REALIZE THIS MEANS PUNISHMENT."

Luke hadn't dropped her hand since the moment he'd yanked her out of the bar. "I leave you alone for five minutes, and you're already trolling for other men."

"I wasn't," she whispered weakly.

"You were." He punctuated with a growl rising up from his chest. He couldn't say how he'd felt when he lifted his gaze to the table and found her flirting with another man. It was a heady brew of astonishment, anger, jealousy, fear, and desire. He was well aware Bree hadn't started it, but she sure as hell hadn't ended it either. Promptly forgetting the redhead named Liza, he'd waded in to do the ending for Bree.

Only to have her make that suggestive remark.

Emotion and desire were inextricably connected; the higher the emotion, the bigger the kick of desire. In that moment, he'd wanted to haul her up out of the booth, force her face first onto the table and take her that way. All very macho.

That's what she did to him and for him, pushed his emotions higher until his desire simply burst out of him.

At the car, he whirled her around, shoved her up against the driver's side door and plastered his body to hers. "You were trolling. And you will be punished."

"Honestly," she started.

He stopped her with a hand beneath her skirt, a finger in her pussy, and suddenly she was gasping for air.

"See how wet you are," he whispered against her ear. "See how much you wanted him."

"I—I—" She wasn't capable of more as he played her clit.

"You test me, push me. You want me to punish you. You ask for it, beg for it because you're a dirty, horny little slut."

She quivered and moaned against him.

He wanted her this way. When he threatened, she melted, and this was what he wanted, needed. Most women didn't need the threat; she did. He just needed to shut down the naysaying voice in his head whispering that it wasn't good for her.

He pulled away, let her straighten her skirt. "Get in the car." He didn't play the gentleman and follow her around to open the door. Instead, he climbed in and started the engine, then, once she was beside him, he couldn't resist a taste of his fingers as she watched, the remnants of her desire coating them.

She opened her mouth. He pointed a finger. "Don't say a word. I'm so pissed I can't talk to you without hurting you."

He pulled out of the lot, making his plans. "Fast hot sex," he muttered to himself. "Lots of it. With you tied. You won't be able to stop me." He entered the freeway and headed home. "I'll show you what it means to push me to the limit."

The silence beside him was electric. Her hot sexual aroma perfumed the car. Like the scent a feline gave off when she was in heat, attracting every male.

"You did this on purpose to incite me. To force me to punish you."

She squirmed in her seat, and he knew she loved this theme.

"You better be afraid of what you've unleashed, slut," he warned, his voice harsh enough to rasp in his throat. He was into it, playing her game, giving her what she wanted. As if he were truly *forcing* her to do it, that it wasn't her desire.

The sexual tension in the car rose until it was so thick around them he could damn near touch it. By the time he pulled into his driveway, he was as hard as marble.

Still in silence, he rounded the hood, opened her door, and yanked her out of the car. She stumbled; he acted as if he didn't care. She tripped on the step; he let her catch herself.

The house was dark, cold, and smelled faintly of Italian seasonings. "Where to punish you . . ." he mused to the empty hall.

Then he had it. "Brilliant," he muttered to himself. "In the dining room. Stand in the corner next to the sideboard." She followed his direction, facing the wall. "Not that way. Turn around. Face me, whore." The name calling and abuse was becoming so easy, second nature; it fueled them both.

She gulped, but did as he said without a word.

Over her head, he took down a hanging plant. Beth had loved the greenery. He didn't know why he kept up the habit. Now, he laid bare the hook in the ceiling.

Leaning in, he pointed his finger right between Bree's eyes. "Don't you move; don't you run."

"No, Master," she whispered, her first words since getting into the car.

He left her there in the dark, standing in the corner like a naughty child.

SHE HEARD HIM MOVING IN THE HOUSE, SLAMMING DOORS, DRAW-ers, muttering, and her excitement grew exponentially with every sound permeating the darkness. She could feel her pulse beating fast at her throat and wrists, her heart thumping in her chest.

She wanted this, whatever it was. And oh, she'd had such an idea from the moment he took the plant down from the ceiling and she saw that hook. She couldn't catch her breath, and without her panties, her thighs were coated with her desire. She dripped with it. He'd ordered her not to run, but she couldn't anyway. She wouldn't. She had to have whatever he planned to do to her.

27

LUKE WENT IN SEARCH OF IMPLEMENTS. IN THE BEDROOM, HE gathered scarves and a blindfold. Perfect. He slammed the bureau drawer for effect, then the bedroom door on his way out. As he passed back down the hall, he flipped the light switch. Illumination streamed into the dining room, stretching across the hardwood floor, enough for him to see but still leaving her in the dark, so to speak.

"Hold your hands out, slut, wrists together."

She trembled, a fresh wave of her scent wafting up to cloud his mind. He wrapped one scarf around her wrists, binding them together in front. The second scarf he slid between her tied hands, knotted the ends, then raised her arms high enough to slip the loop over the hook in the ceiling.

Then he stood two inches from her, his face right up in hers. "You are *my* whore, no one else's. Do you understand?"

"Yes, Master."

She was the perfect height for fucking while standing up. Reaching behind, he unbuttoned and unzipped her skirt. With her slender figure, it simply fell to the floor at her feet.

He went down on his haunches to lift one foot then the other and whisk the skirt away. "Your cunt is mine, isn't it?" He blew a warm breath on her pretty sweet pussy, neatly trimmed, fragrant with need.

"Yes, Master," she said with a hitch of desire in her voice.

He rose once more. "You don't deserve to look upon your master while he fucks you, whore. Do you?"

She agreed with everything. "No, Master, I don't," she said on an exhale of breath.

He slid the elastic band of the blindfold over her head and patted the padded material in place across her eyes. With no light in the dining room, she would now be in complete darkness, nothing seeping through the edges. Her senses would be heightened, expectant.

He stepped back, said nothing, let her stew a moment. Christ, she was gorgeous. Long, long legs in black stockings, the trimmed triangle of hair against her milk-white thighs, her belly button beneath the tight top begging for his tongue to tease it.

"A true slut needs to be fucked while half dressed. Because she's such a whore, she can't wait to get her clothes off before she has to have a cock in her." He tugged up the Lycra of her shirt and let it rest above the swell of her breasts. In the coolness of the house, her nipples pearled.

She shivered. He thought about turning the heat up. Instead, he gathered both nipples between his thumbs and forefingers and pinched hard until she cried out.

He leaned close, breathed in the hot spice of her arousal. "Sluts like pain, don't they."

"Yes, Master. When you hurt me, it washes away all my unworthiness." Like a sinner giving confession and receiving absolution.

"You have to pay for what you did tonight with Frank."

She murmured her assent.

Still pinching one nipple, lighter this time, he slid his fingers down her belly to her drenched pussy. He strummed her clit until her whole body trembled. Pain, punishment, and pleasure, she needed it all.

"Don't you come yet, bitch. Not until I say."

"No, no, Master, I won't." She ended on a gasp, then clenched her muscles, a move intended to stave off the orgasm that threatened.

"Spread your legs wide," he ordered, kicking her feet apart. Then he grabbed her chin, held her when she might have stumbled off her heels. "Don't you dare come while I lick you."

She shook her head almost wildly.

She was tied. She was spread. She was his. He went to his knees before her, oblivious to the hardness of the floor. It wasn't any harder than his cock, and it kept his senses keen. He smelled her perspiration born of desire and need, the sweetness of her juice. Then he tasted her. God, he could never get enough of her. She was so clean, soft, pink, gorgeous. She made him *feel* the sex between them. With her, it wasn't a physical act, it was an experience. When he told himself he needed more from her, he hadn't realized how much he already had if he only knew how to use it. She was a woman with a wealth of sensations and emotions, and there was so much more to discover with her.

She gushed against his mouth as he licked her, sucked her, took the swell of her clit between his lips and worried it until she was crying and trembling above him, her legs shaking.

Putting his hands to her thighs, he held her wide and took her with long sweeps of his tongue.

She panted and moaned. "Please, please, please," she chanted.

She was close. He backed off. "Don't you do it, slut. Don't you come. Your punishment will be worse if you disobey."

She was born to disobey and be punished for it, and as he took her once more with his mouth, he pushed two fingers inside to stroke her G-spot. Her cries filled the room that was suddenly no longer cold, but hot, hot, hot. She quaked, her thigh muscles bunching, tensing, and her body swayed against the scarves binding her to the ceiling hook. The climax was magnificent, a flood of sweetness. Her cream covered his lips, filled his mouth, and he held on, licking her, drinking her.

When he finally rose to his feet, her cheeks were wet with tears that had leaked from beneath the blindfold. The moisture sparkled like diamonds in the dim light from the hall.

"Bitch," he whispered, pretending it was a sweet nothing. "Whore."

Her chest heaved with need. "I'm so sorry, Master, I didn't mean to come."

"Shut. Up." Two words, two sentences. "I don't want to hear any more out of you, you disobedient little slut." Then he grabbed one of the smaller scarves he'd left on the table and wound it around her face, filling her mouth as he tied it off in back. "Not one more word. Not a moan. Not a plea. I'm going to fuck you, and you will remain silent and take it, you dirty little whore bitch." He pulled her head back by her hair, bared her throat, her skin fragrant, delicious. He bit her. She made a noise, though her lips closed around it. "Now you can't deny you wanted Frank to fuck you."

She shook her head at him. Hand fisted in her hair, he held her still. "Liar," he whispered. "You wanted him down between your legs like the slut you are. You're so bad. You need so much punishment. I've been lax with you."

Her breath puffed. She was slick with need, her skin, her pussy.

"I'm going to fuck you like a whore, restrained, blindfolded, and gagged." He wasn't sure the moment he'd started *needing* this, too, getting off completely on it. When had it stopped being about her? He was changing, too. Yet again, he ignored the warning voice in his head. This was what they both wanted, stepping fully into the bondage and humiliation game.

"I will have you," he growled. The omnipresent condom in his pocket, he was ready, donning it with expert fingers. Then he lifted her, wrapped her legs around his waist. She wasn't anchored, and her body swayed as if she were on a swing. He backed her up against the wall.

He couldn't kiss her through the gag. She couldn't see him through the blindfold. He could only fuck her. It was almost impersonal. Until he thrust deep inside her, and *everything* became so fucking personal, it stole his breath. Her body gloved him, sucked him in. She tightened her legs at his waist. The fit was snug, delicious, her inner muscles working him. She dragged him closer to the edge despite the fact that he hadn't moved in her yet. Lost in the feel of her, he had to stop a moment to remember to breathe.

"Bitch," he whispered, and slammed home once more, shoving her into the wall. A small part of his mind thought of the bruises she'd have on her spine, but he pounded into her again and again. So much emotion, he didn't know what was real, what was faked for her sake, the anger, the need, the rush of desire.

I want you, I need you, I have to have you. You're mine. Words over and over in his mind until there was nothing but them and her body around him, milking him with her climax, and the sharp rise of his own orgasm crashing over him.

BREE CLUNG TO HIM, TOOK HIM DEEPER, LET HIM FILL HER, NEED her, want her. She soared. It wasn't climax, it was something more, something so much better. She didn't feel the unforgiving wall, the ache in her spine, the tightening of the scarves around her wrists, or the dryness of the cloth in her mouth. In the darkness behind the blindfold, there was only the feel of his body and the words he kept saying. *I want you, I need you, I have to have you. You're mine.*

She'd driven him to the admission; he couldn't help himself. *This* was what she'd always needed from a man, to know *she* was the special one, the precious one, the *only* one.

Now he leaned heavily against her, squishing her between the wall and his body. Deprived of sight, there was only sensation, his raspy breath shooting against her throat, his shirt clammy with perspiration that was already cooling in the dark, the roughness of his clothing against her inner thighs as she clung to him, the beat of his heart against her chest, the thrum of her own blood through her veins.

"Christ," he muttered into her hair. The guttural, needy quality of his voice made her tremble all over again. "You drive me to it. It's your fault. You force me to punish you."

He gave her the words she craved. She'd never wanted to analyze why she needed them, why they made everything all right. She wanted only to wrap her arms around him, feel his skin, taste his lips, whisper to him, feast her eyes on him. All she could do was let him hold her.

Until finally he puffed out a rough breath. "Shit. Didn't mean to leave you hanging." He laughed at the joke, but his speech was slow, drowsy, as if he were still lingering in some orgasmic never-never land. Pushing away from the wall, he disentangled, until there was no contact at all, and she stood awkwardly with her arms over her head and her heels wobbling on the floor. There was only his scent left marking her body.

He fumbled with the scarves at her wrists, then the knot above her head that held her bound to the ceiling hook.

"Dammit, they've tightened. I'll have to cut them off. I'll get a knife from the kitchen."

His footsteps receded. The room was suddenly cold, her heartbeat loud in her ears. He'd taken off neither the gag nor the blindfold, and the darkness was suddenly disorienting. She felt naked and exposed, her nipples stiffening uncomfortably in the cool air. Her wrists throbbed where the knots had constricted and were starting to cut off her circulation. Her knees felt as if they'd buckle without the scarves holding her up. God, she wasn't going to accidentally pull the hook out of the ceiling?

Then his hands were on her again, sliding up her arms, slicing through the scarves tethering her to the hook. She was suddenly free, though her wrists were still bound together, but as he went for the blindfold, the darkness dizzied her, her knees weakened, and she stumbled. She went down too fast for him to catch her, and without sight or the full use of her arms she couldn't break the fall. She couldn't see it coming when her forehead whacked into something hard.

Stars, pain shooting across her scalp, inside her skull, then she was flat on her ass on the floor.

"Fuck," he spat out. "Jesus Christ." Luke yanked off the blindfold, tugged off the scarf he'd used to gag her, then sliced through the ones securing her wrists. "You okay, baby? What the hell was I thinking?" He put his lovely cool fingers to her forehead, through her hair, then looked at his hand. "Thank God you're not bleeding."

Picking her up, he cradled her in his arms as he carried her out of the dining room and down the hall. Her shirt was still a tight band above her breasts, her nipples bared, her pussy exposed. The feeling returned to her hands and fingers in painful pins and needles. Her mouth was dry.

It had been beautiful and perfect while he was doing it. She hadn't noticed the aches and pains. Or rather she'd reveled in them. But now, not so much.

In the bathroom, he flipped on the light, and she closed her eyes against its onslaught. After setting her on the toilet lid, he pulled her shirt down, covering her breasts with a careful, gentle touch. Then he was opening and closing doors and drawers. She slitted her eyes and held a hand up in front of them to block the light until her pupils adjusted. Hunkering down before her, Luke upended a bottle of hydrogen peroxide onto a cotton ball, then dabbed at her forehead.

"Ow."

"I'm sorry, baby." His eyes were dark, stricken. "The edge of the sideboard didn't cut you open enough to bleed, but there's an ugly gash that needs to be cleaned." He dabbed the wound. She tried not to whimper, but it stung like a son of a bitch. "I should have been more careful," he murmured, his voice raspy with guilt. "I should have realized your legs would be weak."

"It's not your fault."

He didn't look at her. "You need to go to the hospital and get examined to make sure you don't have a concussion."

She snorted. "I don't have a concussion. And I'm not going to the emergency room. That's ridiculous." The wound throbbed slightly, but she didn't have a headache. "It was a bump, no big deal."

He gently smoothed her hair back, dabbed again at the gash as if that would change everything. "I'm sorry," he whispered. "I'm an idiot."

Derek had hurt her far worse, and he'd meant to do it. Other men had as well. They never said they were sorry. *You drive me to it. It's all your fault. You force me to punish you.* Luke had said that, too, and she liked it. Yet those other men had said it when they did bad things to her, when they hurt her on purpose.

Things she accepted because she had to. Because she deserved them.

I don't know what that means, she wanted to say. *I don't know what's wrong with me.* There was a terrifying pathology to it all. Why did she have to have sex the way she did? Why was it okay to come only if she was being punished?

She didn't want to think about it, *couldn't* let herself think about it. If she did . . . *Everything* would come tumbling down around her.

"I need to go," she said, pushing at him. She didn't want to think about that stuff, not here, not now. Not with him. Awful, terrible things might spill out and drive him away.

"I'm sorry."

Quit apologizing. Bree wanted to shout at him. But then he'd think something was wrong, and he'd nag at her until he forced her to say something she'd regret. Keeping her voice calm and steady was a strain. "It wasn't your fault. I stumbled. It was all good. I liked what we did. But it's late and my mom will expect me home soon."

He backed off as she stood, and damn if she wasn't overly conscious of being nearly naked with too much light shining down on her. "Where's my skirt?"

"On the floor in the dining room. I'll get it."

While he was gone, she took the opportunity to stare at herself in the mirror. He was right, the skin wasn't actually broken, but there was a thick, bloodred, inch-long line that was already turning a sickening shade of purple. She must have hit the edge of the sideboard. The skin around it was puffy and reddened. She should ask for some ice to cut down the bruising and swelling, but she didn't want to stay long enough for that.

Get out, get out, get out. The night was ruined. It had been so good. Kinky and exciting. The woman he'd bought a drink for.

Frank hitting on her. Luke dragging her out and punishing her so very well.

But she'd screwed it all up, and now she just needed to run away from all the aftermath.

She wished she had her own car.

"Here you go." He actually held out the skirt to her as if he wanted to help her step into it.

She grabbed it from his hand. "I need a moment." Then she pushed him out and practically slammed the door in his face.

Why did she always ruin a perfectly good thing?

28

FUCK, FUCK, FUCK.

He'd called her a bitch, a slut, a whore, and a cunt, tied her up, blindfolded her, gagged her, fucked her against a wall, and had the best damn climax of his life. Then he'd let her fall into the sideboard. As he was dropping her off at her mother's house, the bruise was already unsightly.

What they did was supposed to be fun. He wasn't supposed to hurt her, not even inadvertently. Over the last two weeks, he'd been escalating, pushing her for more, doing more to her. And fucking loving it. All while her father lay dying. Or dead. Their relationship was whacked, and things were out of control. His fault, he *knew* better.

"Bree."

Hand on the passenger door, she stopped. "Don't apologize again," she said, her hair falling across her face to hide the damage. "It was an accident."

"Accidents like that shouldn't happen." The roughness, the punishment, though it was playacting, couldn't be good for her, not with unresolved conflicts made worse by her father's death.

She reached out, touched his hand, angling just enough to show him a smile. "It wasn't your fault. I'm to blame."

The words exemplified her issues. *She* deserved it; *she* was to blame.

She was out of the car without giving him a chance to refute that. As he watched the front door close behind her, he wondered how much longer they could do this before she broke.

IT WAS AFTER TEN, AND THE HOUSE WAS DARK. SHE TIPTOED DOWN the hall.

"Bree?"

Shit. "Yes, Mom?" She stepped into the shadows of her room and didn't turn on the light.

Instead her mom turned it on for her as she followed Bree inside. "Oh my God, Brianna, what happened?"

Luke was fucking me into the wall and I lost my balance. Rough sex really takes it out of you, doesn't it, Mom.

Okay, no, she wouldn't say that. "Stupid me, it was raining and I yanked open the car door and hit myself on the corner of it." It hadn't rained all night, and the car door would have hit her body, not her forehead, but whatever.

"You silly girl." Her mom put out a hand, but stopped short of touching Bree. "You should be more careful."

Her mother believed. Her mother had always believed whatever she was told when Bree was growing up. She was too old to start seeing the truth now.

"I'll get you some frozen peas. They'll help stop the bruising."

Bree didn't tell her mother it was already too late. The wounds she had would never heal.

Later, as she lay in her bed, her mother in hers, Bree held the peas to her forehead until they started to melt, and ice water trickled into her hair, down her throat, and soaked the pillow.

Or maybe that was just her foolish tears.

* * *

LUKE WAS CALLING HER PHONE. SHE KNEW IF SHE DIDN'T ANSWER it, he'd never call again. He would be lost to her forever. Yet she couldn't move, couldn't see, couldn't speak. As if she were still knotted to the hook in his ceiling.

Don't go. Don't leave me. What did I do wrong? Why don't you love me anymore?

"Bree, wake up."

Someone was shaking her. But she couldn't see. Where was Luke?

"Bree, your cell phone's ringing. Wake up."

Bree cracked one eyelid. The sun streaming across the bed was so bright it hurt. It wasn't Tuesday night anymore, but Wednesday morning. Her cell phone rang shrilly in her mother's hand. Bree had never used musical tones, just that annoyingly incessant ring.

"It's the second time she's called, Bree. Your boss."

"Oh." Bree grabbed the phone, her head swimming with the sudden movement. "Sorry. Thanks." She pushed the button. "Hello?"

"Hi, Bree, it's Erin. I just wanted to check how you're doing today."

Bree gingerly touched her forehead. It throbbed. "I'm fine." Then she remembered to add, "Thanks."

Her mother still stood in the doorway, but as Bree finally sat up in the bed, she disappeared down the hall toward the front of the house.

"Did you need me to come in to work?" She hadn't set the alarm, and she figured Erin and Dominic would think it was weird if she came to work the day after she'd said her father died.

"No, no, we don't need you. It was just that Dominic told me about your dad, and I wanted to say how sorry I am."

"Thanks. He isn't suffering anymore." At least not on earth, though maybe somewhere down below, where it was very, very hot.

"Dominic and I would like to attend the service."

Shit. This was it. "We're not having a service."

"Oh," was all Erin said.

"We don't have any relatives in the area, and Mom didn't want to put herself through all that. We're having him cremated." And his urn was the ass-end of Dumbo the elephant. *Really* couldn't have a memorial service with Dumbo on the altar.

"Of course, I understand." Erin's tone said she didn't understand at all, but she was too gracious to say anything. "Perhaps we can send flowers."

"Thanks, but that's really not necessary." She felt her face heating with embarrassment.

"Oh. Well." Erin was used to the niceties of normal families, not a dysfunctional one like Bree's. "If there's anything we can do . . ."

"Thanks a lot. My mom will appreciate your concern."

"You take all the time you need to help your mother through."

Bree grimaced and was glad Erin couldn't see it. "I'll be in tomorrow for that meeting with Mr. Marbury."

Erin gasped. "Oh, Bree, that can wait. I'll call him and cancel."

"No," she said too sharply, then backed off a bit. "He's just got a few questions so he can get ready for the audit. I don't want to hold that up."

"For that matter, I'm sure we can move the audit out, too, to give you more time to prepare."

"No." This time she managed not to sound as harsh. *She* was prepared. It was Marbury who wasn't. She didn't want him coming back at her and saying any issues were her fault because she hadn't explained it properly to him. "I need to get this done, Erin. I'm fine, I can handle it."

"Bree, I really feel you're rushing things. You need time."

Time for what? Almost all evidence of her father's existence had been wiped clean from the house. Her mother had sold his car a couple of months ago because they knew he'd never be driving again. There was only one thing left. Out at the back of the garden. The dollhouse.

"Please, Erin, let me do this. I'll take time afterward." She felt her voice rising, her pulse gathering speed. "Please don't call Marbury."

"All right. It's okay. I'm sorry. I know you need to do it your way." Just like Erin had to do it her way after Jay died. "What time is the meeting?"

"Nine. But I don't need you to be there with me." She wanted to handle this herself, and she didn't want Erin to see Marbury in action. Although with the meeting being at DKG, he probably would be better than his usual asshole self.

"Whatever you need to do, Bree."

"Was everything fine with the check run?"

"Yes. Between Rachel and I, we got it all loaded, approved, and printed."

With Rachel doing AP and AR input, now the check run, maybe they didn't need Bree at all. It was another reason she needed to get back there. To prove her worth.

"We'll see you tomorrow, then," Erin said. "Unless you change your mind later and want me to cancel Marbury."

"I won't."

After she said good-bye, she realized her hands were shaking.

"You're still wearing the same clothes you went out in last night." Her mother was in the doorway again, as if she'd been just outside listening.

God. She wasn't even wearing her bra. It was in the backseat of Luke's car. Still in bed, she tugged the blanket up. "I was tired."

"That bruise is bad."

Damn. What would everyone say at work? She'd have to come up with something better than saying she'd whacked herself with a car door.

"I guess the peas didn't work." Her mother stared at the package puddled on the carpet.

"Makeup will cover it," Bree said confidently. "Could you hand me my robe, please?" Despite being in her clothes, she covered up, but once she'd sidled by her mother and closed the bathroom door to shower, the mirror told a totally different story. Her forehead was several shades of purple in a four-inch circle above her eyebrow, with a crimson slash in the center where she'd connected with the edge of the sideboard.

Uh, no. Makeup wasn't going to cover that.

"JESUS H. CHRIST." THAT EVENING, LUKE WAS DISGUSTED. EVEN IN the relative darkness of his car, he could see the bruise on her forehead, a deep purple and already turning color. He'd done that to her. "You told your mother you ran into a door?"

"She accosted me the moment I walked in last night. I couldn't come up with anything else on the spur of the moment."

He literally felt sickened. The explanation sounded like something an abused wife told her friends and coworkers. But Mrs. Mason hadn't batted an eyelash, even calling Bree a silly girl, and let the man responsible for the injury leave with her daughter on his arm.

Yeah, he was sick to the pit of his fucking stomach. There was something wrong. Because the mother displayed signs of being totally oblivious to warning signals. She could have ignored them when Bree was too young to take care of herself.

"Where are we going?" Bree said as if she sensed they needed an immediate topic change.

"My place. I'm going to make you dinner." He'd never thought of it before, but he needed something that didn't require their usual roles. He stabbed a very ungentle finger in her direction. "And we're not fucking later. If we do anything, we'll make love." He couldn't take the chance of hurting her again.

"Yes, Master."

With the title, she put them squarely back in the dom–sub standing. It was where she was comfortable despite what had happened last night. Curling her legs beneath her, she turned against the seat belt and leaned into him, her breath sweet, her heat arcing across the console between them. "But you do need to fuck me, Master. You know I get all uppity and obstreperous and you have to put me in my place."

"I am not hurting you tonight," he insisted.

"You never hurt me, Master." She stroked his arm. "Punishment isn't hurting, because I deserve it." Then she lowered her voice to barely a whisper. "I want it that way. I need it that way. And you love giving it to me that way."

Fuck. Last night was too good. Until she'd lost her balance. He'd lost his equilibrium, too. He wanted it back. He wanted the woman she was the night they went bowling. But that woman wasn't Bree Mason; she was only a figment. He almost wished he'd never started wanting more intimacy from her, when what they did was just hot sex, when it was uncomplicated, when he knew her next phone call would lead to a deliciously kinky encounter the memory of which he could whack off to in his morning shower. He believed she'd been happier then.

The lights were blazing in his house when he pulled into his driveway. He hadn't remembered leaving them on when he left this morning, that's how dazed and fucked-up he'd been.

Bree was out of the car and clinging to his arm before he could get to her door to open it. "Take me out tonight, Master. I'm not wearing panties. You can fuck me anywhere you want."

His blood heated in his veins with images of pushing her down on a table in front of fifteen men, lifting her skirt, and claiming her with a hot fuck while they watched.

That's what she did to him. Made him want crazy things until he couldn't see straight and he just did them. And loved them. She was right about that. Yet there was an edge of desperation in her words, her voice. *That's* what was wrong with all this now. She wasn't supposed to be desperate. It was supposed to fun, but she was using kinky sex to mask the bad things in her life.

"I'm not fucking you tonight," he repeated sternly as they climbed the front steps. "Making love is all you get." But would that make a fucking bit of difference now? He fit the key in the lock, but the deadbolt was already open. What the hell?

The door burst inward. "Dad, I need to talk to you about Stephie and doing some sort of intervention." Keira clapped her mouth shut the moment her eyes lighted on Bree. She wore a letter jacket in the green and gold school colors, and her hair, as dark as his, was pulled back in a ponytail high on her head. Her lips parted and stayed that way as she stared at Bree. More specifically, at the bruise on Bree's forehead.

Fuck. He closed his eyes a moment. Had he hung the plant back on the hook, thrown out the ruined scarves, and put the blindfold back in his bedroom? Fuck, fuck. He couldn't remember. "You didn't tell me you were coming home, honey."

Keira didn't make a snide rejoinder. "Sorry. I should have. But I was just so pissed about Stephie."

"Let's go inside and you can tell me." He still had hold of Bree's arm, but she was cemented like a block of stone to the front stoop. "Bree, I want to introduce you to my daughter. This is Keira."

It would have happened sometime, but he'd have preferred the first meeting to come without the bruise. Now, after the initial shock, he remembered getting rid of the scarves and blindfold, though the plant was still on the floor. Whatever.

"It's nice to meet you I should go home," Bree said, her voice a thin whisper, the two sentences running together without a pause, as if they were one.

"Don't be silly. I'm the one butting into my dad's party." Keira had never been one to begrudge him a new life after the divorce. She wasn't clingy, resenting the women he dated. He just hadn't brought many home for her to meet.

"No," Bree said more strongly. "I really do need to get home. My mother isn't feeling well."

"But . . ." Keira trailed off. Obviously Bree's mother had been well enough for her to come in the first place, so good old mom was just an excuse.

Bree stood there, her face whiter than normal, drained of color, the bruise stark.

Okay, she didn't want to meet his daughter. It wasn't great timing. She wasn't wearing underwear, which was definitely an uncomfortable feeling in front of Keira. "I'll take you home, Bree."

"You don't have to rush, Dad. We can talk about Stephie when you get back. Or in the morning."

Stephie. Intervention. He remembered what Keira had said when she opened the door. He could also hear the urgency in her voice, if not in her words.

"I won't keep him," Bree said, her voice breathy and rushed. "In fact, I can take a cab."

"You're not taking a cab." He felt rough inside. "I'll be back," he told Keira. Then he took Bree's hand in his and headed back to the car.

She tried to pull away. They didn't generally hold hands except as a show of ownership at a club.

Maybe that's what it was in front of his daughter. A show, a statement. *I'm your father, but I'm a man, too, and this woman is mine. You'll have to accept it.*

Bree would have to accept it, too.

29

BREE CURLED IN ON HERSELF IN THE FRONT SEAT AS LUKE DROVE, and they sat in silence most of the way back to her mother's house. His daughter. She knew both his kids were at college, so she thought she'd never have to meet them. How utterly, horribly embarrassing. The girl probably heard them talking about sex, for God's sake.

She was so young, fresh, and innocent, so pretty. So normal. Bree didn't think the girl had ever been afraid of anything in her life. And the way she'd examined Bree, as if she was looking at gum—or worse—on the bottom of her father's shoe.

"I'm good with you meeting Keira," Luke finally said, as if they hadn't been sitting there without saying a word for such a long time. "We didn't have to rush off."

"I don't do father-daughter meet-and-greets." She sounded bitchy and mean.

Luke's lips stretched in a thin line at her comment.

Why did it bother her anyway? She could have faked courtesy. She faked it at work all the time. She faked everything.

"What I meant," she said, trying to appease him, "was that you just don't introduce the woman you're fucking to your daughter."

His jaw rippled and tensed. "I'm not *just* fucking you."

"I saw that look on your face, Luke. You wanted to crawl away into a hole when she saw us."

"I was surprised. I couldn't remember if I'd cleaned up after last night. It wasn't about you."

"That's exactly what it was about. You were thinking 'holy shit, I have to introduce my daughter to my fuck buddy.'" Not that she'd ever thought of him that way. He was . . . her master. "And I'm not even wearing panties."

He winced, and she knew he'd had the same thought, but he didn't allow anything into his voice. "Whether you admit it or not, we have a relationship."

"Yes, we do," she said rationally. "I'm the slave and you're the master. And masters don't introduce their submissives to their daughters."

He shot her a glare. "You always remember you're my slave when it's a convenient tool. I should have ordered you to go into the fucking house and make nice."

She might have felt better if he had. He was a good father. She knew that with the way he talked about his daughters, his tone softening, his eyes lighting, a gentle smile creasing his lips. And the way Keira had addressed him. *Dad, I need your help.*

He'd called her *honey.* Bree's father used to call her *honey* when he told her to go play in the dollhouse.

Dammit, Luke was nothing like her father. She wondered how it would have been to have a father like Luke.

Please don't make me, Daddy.

She never would have had to say those words.

She swallowed hard, painfully. "I'm sorry," she whispered, though she didn't know exactly which thing she was apologizing for. Or even if it was to Luke.

Just as moments before she could feel the tension squeezing her into the corner of the car, something gentled in the air around him. "The timing wasn't right, but I'll arrange for you to meet both my daughters. I *want* you to meet them." He reached for her hand. "Don't make me order you to do it."

He let go to turn the corner onto her mother's street. The house was on the left, and the lights were on. Her mother was going to wonder why she was back so soon.

"Bree, look at me."

She hadn't realized she'd been staring at the house.

"Kiss me goodnight," he said.

"What?" The words seemed totally foreign.

"Kiss me. And don't make me order you to do that either."

"I kiss you all the time."

"I want one now."

"Okay. Sure." She didn't understand the disquieting light in his eyes. But she thought about his kiss in the car after they'd been bowling, how good it had been. How she'd wanted to be the kind of woman who deserved a kiss like that.

Putting a hand to his cheek, she leaned in slowly. She started with just a caress of her lips against his. Then her tongue along the seam. He parted for her, and she tasted him, minty, his breath sweet. She leaned harder against his chest, opened her mouth, and took him with a long, deep sweep of her tongue. Her breath ratcheted up. His heart beat solidly against her. She wrapped her arms around him, plastered her chest to his, and kissed him with everything she had. Like the night after bowling. Like in her fantasies. Like she'd never kissed before. Not with anyone. Men didn't want kisses from a woman like her. They wanted other things.

"Christ," he said, finally coming up for air. "I needed that. Jesus."

She'd needed it, too. She'd never realized how badly she needed it.

She needed *him*. Oh God. She *really* did.

AS LUKE PULLED HIS CAR INTO THE GARAGE, BREE'S TASTE WAS still on his lips and her scent continued to cloud his mind. That kiss. It was electric. So much more than he'd expected from her. If only he hadn't had to leave.

"I'm home," he called as he entered the kitchen through the garage door.

Keira swept in blanketed by a fog of lavender. In fact, the whole house smelled like lavender. She'd taken a bath while he was gone.

He'd missed the perfume of women in the house. He thought of Bree, of having her sleep over, of watching her luxuriate in the tub in a haze of sweetly scented steam.

"She was very pretty." Keira opened the fridge. "But really, you shouldn't hit her where people can see the bruises."

Something welled up inside him. Guilt. Hard-edged. He lashed out against it. "I would *never* hit a woman. You should know me better than that."

Keira closed the fridge without retrieving anything, her gaze stricken. "I'm sorry, Dad. I was joking. I know you'd never do anything like that."

He immediately felt like crap. He'd lashed out at Keira because the truth was he did a lot of things to Bree most people wouldn't approve of. He'd liked it all. If he could just believe that what they did together wasn't bad for her. "Sorry I went off on you. It's just not something you should laugh about."

"You're right." Keira pressed her lips together. "Especially with what I came home to talk to you about."

"You could have called, honey."

"No. This needs one-on-one." She smiled, forgetting his harshness of moments before. "We need a chai for this."

"Guess it's going to be a long talk then." They'd often gone to the local coffeehouse for a chai and a talk, he and Keira and Kyla. Beth had been jealous of those father–daughter chats, yet she'd never made her own kind of tradition with the girls.

Ten minutes later, they were ensconced in the coffee bar with large steaming cups. The place was packed, students with notebooks and laptops, couples, teenagers, everyone with coats and umbrellas just in case. The scent of freshly ground coffee had seeped into the wooden surfaces, the floor by the counter was shiny with a million scuffmarks, and the roar of the steam valve was like music amid the voices and laughter.

"Okay, what gives with Stephie?" he asked, then sipped the spicy brew.

"Her boyfriend beats her, he's got her hooked on drugs, and he makes her have sex with other guys to pay for his habit." That was Keira. She didn't pull any punches.

And it was a punch right to his gut. "Jesus." Okay, that wasn't him; that was Derek. But it was still too close to home.

"You see why I had to drive home for a face-to-face?"

Yeah, he did. "Have you talked to her parents?"

"I left messages. But they never called back."

"Did you leave *that* on a message?"

She clucked her tongue. "Right. Even *I* wouldn't leave that to a message. I drove by their house, but there weren't any lights on." Then she touched his hand. "Dad, I don't think I can do this one on my own."

"That's really why you came home." He softened inside.

"Yeah." She gave him a pleading look. Kids, they always got to you at the strangest times, suddenly making you feel needed and important and big. "You know how to handle this kind of stuff, Dad."

Right. With Bree, he'd almost broken Derek's nose. He'd do the same for Keira or Kyla. He'd do it for Stephie. "Of course I'll go with you, honey. Where is she now?"

"I tried to get her to come here, but she's with that *freak*"— her lips twisted as she said the word—"and it's like he's got some insane hold over her. I just want to get her parents to come down and take her home or something, anything."

He'd raised a kind, caring woman, and he was proud of her.

Then she grimaced, plucking at the letter jacket. "You know what I'm most afraid of, Dad?" she said in an almost childlike voice.

"What?"

"That her parents won't do anything."

He covered her hand. He'd met Stephie's parents, and they were indeed a disinterested lot. He'd wondered why they'd bothered to have a child. Once she'd turned thirteen, they'd thought nothing of leaving Stephie alone while they went on vacation. Keira usually brought Stephie over to stay.

It made him think of Bree. Her mom seemed normal enough on the face of it, maybe a little manic, perhaps, but normal. Until you looked beneath the facade, like when she hadn't said a thing about that bruise. Something had happened in that house, something had gone wrong, something that made Bree the woman she was, a woman who needed punishment for some imagined crime she'd committed long ago.

"Let's deal with her parents flaking out when the time comes, honey, *if* it comes, okay. They might surprise you so don't start thinking with a negative attitude yet." He picked up his chai. "Let's do it."

She squeezed his hand. "Thanks, Dad. You're the best."

For her, maybe he was. He was no longer sure if he was the best for Bree.

AS A CHILD, WHENEVER HER PARENTS TOOK HER TO A RESTAURANT, Bree whispered her order. As if her voice wouldn't work. She couldn't remember what she'd been afraid of, why she could only whisper. Maybe she'd been scared she'd order something too expensive and her father would get mad. Or that she'd spill her milk or break a glass. Whatever it was, she'd been so frightened, she couldn't manage more than a whisper. The waitress would ask her to repeat herself, and, like a self-fulfilling prophecy, her father would get mad. The angrier he became, the harder it was for Bree to talk, like a merry-go-round she couldn't get off. In the end, her mother started ordering for her. But then there were other things she had to be afraid of.

Marbury was one of those things. She couldn't sleep on Wednesday night after Luke dropped her off. Thursday morning, her skin had the pallor of porridge that had been warmed up in the microwave too many times, and the smudges beneath her eyes were so dark, she looked like a football player.

On the way to work, she almost hit a car at a stoplight. When she walked into her office, she couldn't breathe, as if all the air had been sucked out of the room and the walls had closed in on her.

When Rachel ran over to offer her condolences, Bree put a finger to her lips and shook her head. That was the cool thing about Rachel, she knew exactly when to back off.

I can do this. I'll be fine.

Denton Marbury would have to behave himself with other people around. She knew her numbers inside and out. She was thirty-five years old, not eight, and this was her office, not a dollhouse. She could do this.

Erin stuck her head around the doorjamb, leaning out of her office next door. "You okay?"

Bree gave her the thumbs up. If she tried to speak, she was afraid it might be nothing more than a whisper.

Erin stared at her harder. "What did you do to your head?"

Damn, she'd forgotten. Bree put her fingertips to the bruise. Obviously makeup did *not* work. It was a wonder Rachel hadn't said something. "I was rushing and my mom opened the kitchen door. And I ran right into it." Thank God it didn't come out as an embarrassing whisper. And blaming the bruise on an accident with her mom sounded better than saying she ran into a door on her own.

"Oh Jesus." Erin puffed out a breath. "That's all you two need right now."

"I'm fine," Bree said. "I had an X-ray." Lies upon lies.

"You sure you're good to go with Marbury today?"

"Piece of cake." Yeah right.

"Okay." Erin backed up a couple of steps as if she was still unsure. "Call me if you need me. I'll be right next door."

Bree smiled widely, then toned it down, afraid her face would crack, and mouthed, "Thank you."

Five to nine. She could hear every tick of the wall clock in her office. The wait was interminable.

When her computer finished booting up, Bree opened the files she'd need on the desktop and angled the monitor so it could also be viewed from the chair she'd placed on the other side of her desk, just in case Marbury wanted to see the actual calculations. She spread the hard copies in their folders out on the desk, too, all neatly organized, everything at her fingertips.

Then Denton Marbury opened the lobby door.

30

DENTON MARBURY LUMBERED THROUGH THE FRONT DOOR, HIS feet angled out like a duck's. Her heart raced. He was just a man, Bree told herself. He wasn't even all that smart. She was faster at understanding things than he was.

He stopped outside Erin's office first, his voice thunderous as if he were talking to a stadium crowd. "Erin, so good to see you."

"You, too, Denton," Erin's voice carried around the doorjamb separating her office from Bree's. "Thanks for coming over here. It makes everything easier for Bree."

"Yes, yes," he boomed. "We want to make everything easy for Bree." But he slid Bree a narrowed look.

"I'll be right next door if you and Bree need me."

He fluttered pudgy fingers at her, then turned to Bree in her office.

"Good morning," she said. "I've got everything ready." She was proud of the fact that she didn't speak in a whisper and her voice didn't shake. In college, she'd had to take a speech class, and her legs had wobbled so badly, she could actually hear a resulting quaver in her words. But not so today.

"You're so efficient, Bree."

She was sure he wanted Erin to hear how polite he was.

Then he shut the office door. She suddenly felt sick.

Please don't make me do it.

"You don't mind if I close the door, do you, Bree?" He smiled at her with fleshy lips. "We don't want to be disturbed or disturb anyone else with our discussions."

"That's fine." But she couldn't help licking her dry lips.

He looked at her forehead, but didn't mention the bruise as if he didn't want to be drawn into her drama. Then he pulled the chair around from the front of the desk and sat beside her. "There, that's much better. I can't crane over the desk like that to see your monitor."

He was a big man, and he overflowed the seat like a soufflé rising over the sides of the pan as it baked in the oven. His rumpled brown suit smelled of onions, and his breath was sickly sweet with cherry throat lozenges.

But she *could* do this. "What would you like to go over first?" she said, once again pleased with how steady her voice sounded.

He didn't have a briefcase, hadn't brought a notepad, not even the IRS audit notification. Still, he said, "There are some questionable items in the expense category."

She breathed deeply. There was nothing questionable. But he'd make her prove it. She opened the file folder rather than reference the spreadsheet on the computer because she didn't want him to lean over her to see the monitor. "Which items in particular?" she asked.

"Let's start with the laptop. It should be depreciated rather than expensed."

She pursed her lips. "It's a Section 179 asset. Which means we can choose to expense it rather than depreciate it." Which he *should* know. "With the way technology changes and how often we have to update our computers, it makes more sense to expense."

He smiled without any nicety to it. "Just checking that you know these things, Bree."

He was the tax accountant. She didn't *have* to know. It was *his* job. But she was such a good little girl, she didn't say anything. "Next issue."

They spent half an hour going through the expenses, and her head was starting to ache with the roar of his voice next to her ear. He had a comment and an argument for everything.

In the end, though, she didn't change a single line item.

"Fine, whatever, leave it," Marbury snapped when she proved him wrong again by looking up the tax law on the Internet.

She was pleased, even if she was subjected to three minutes of Marbury leaning over her to read the three sentences that backed up her position and negated his. One full minute a sentence, a freaking eternity. "Anything else on the expenses?" she asked sweetly.

"No. Let's move on to inventory valuation."

He made her show him the bills of material and the process and routing system they used for calculating the labor involved in making the products. She and Erin had given him a demo when they first purchased the enterprise system a couple of years ago, so this was another of his intimidation tactics, trying to show her up.

He grunted. "All right, let's go over the labor and overhead rates."

Okay, this one she needed the spreadsheets for. So he could see her calculations in each cell. She'd written good footnotes, of course, but the actual calcs would make it easier. She slid her chair as far to the right as she could so that he could see the monitor without having him practically in her lap.

"I use the average hourly rate of the three techs and benefits," she explained. "Plus Steve in QC."

"He doesn't add value," Marbury said, his tone derisive. "He's overhead."

"Yes. But his cost can be more accurately applied on labor units. For every hour the tech spends assembling, he spends ten minutes testing."

He leaned back in his chair, the seat bottom creaking beneath his weight, crossed his arms over his chest, and glared at her. "There's no way you can quantify it that way."

"I've done time studies on it," she insisted.

They argued about it for five minutes and finally Bree said, "We've done it this way for the last five years." This was the first time Marbury had even asked about the rate calculations. "Changing now," she said flatly, though her palms were sweating beneath the desk, "would constitute inconsistency."

"What-ever," he snapped in almost two separate words. "Move on."

Her stomach was churning, the air in the office was too close and muggy with his heavy breathing. *How much longer?* she wanted to shout at him.

"Overhead rates, then." She opened the file, went over every detail with precision until her throat was raspy with talking. He just didn't seem to get it. "Let me explain again, so you understand," she said ever so politely.

He looked at her, his eyes suddenly beady and venomous. "I understand perfectly." He stabbed a finger at the screen, his arm brushing her breast.

She almost screamed.

"This"—one stab—"is the most ridiculous"—stab, stab—"calculation I have ever seen." His voice rose with every jab at the screen.

"It's pretty simple—" she started.

"Don't"—he stabbed at her face this time, just missing her nose—"ever interrupt me when I'm talking."

Her legs started to shake uncontrollably, and she wasn't even standing.

"Your tone has been patronizing during this entire discussion." His spittle sprayed her cheek.

She didn't know what had set him off. She hadn't been snippy or mean or even condescending. "I wasn't," she said in the tiniest of whispers.

"You little bitch."

She recoiled, grabbed the arms of her chair, tried to roll it back, but she was already too close to the wall.

"Don't you try to make me look stupid." His eyes seemed to bulge.

"I wasn't," she said again, but this time she couldn't manage more than mouthing the words. You could never know, never predict what would set them off. And when they got angry, there was no stopping them, no stopping the punishment. She was trying to be strong—

The office door suddenly swung open, and Erin came in, her red hair flying behind her.

With a push of his toes, Marbury flung his chair back from Bree. He smiled. The only telltale sign of agitation was his florid complexion. "Erin." Then he stopped as if he couldn't think of another thing to add.

After the abrupt entry, Erin suddenly changed her style and sauntered into the office, her smile wide yet lacking in good cheer. Perching on the edge of the desk, she rummaged among the papers littering the surface without really looking at anything. "We have very thin walls at DKG," she said, then picked up a folder and began slapping it against her palm.

Marbury cleared his throat. "I'm so sorry, Erin. Bree and I will keep it down. We were just having a lively debate about overhead rates, weren't we, Bree?" He didn't even look at her, just expected her to back him up.

Oh no, he would never do anything bad.

"Lively debate," Erin enunciated sharply, "is one thing." Then she leaned down, putting her face on level with Marbury's, and added steel to her voice. "But don't *ever* call one of my employees a bitch."

He blustered, then finally stammered out, "Well—well, it was a slip of the tongue."

Erin stood, ignoring his *slip of the tongue.* "You've got all your answers and all the documents you need to complete the audit. That's *your* job, not Bree's." She folded her arms beneath her breasts. "The fact that you had *any* questions at this late date makes me wonder if you even understand our taxes."

She was mighty before him. Marbury's fleshy jowls wobbled. "It was just an update, to make sure we're on the same page." He stood and the chair shot back against the filing cabinet. "But we're all set, so I'll be off." He looked around as if he thought he'd had a briefcase. "Thank you, Bree, for your time and effort." Then he sucked in his gut and sidled past Erin.

"I'm sorry about that," Erin said as they both watched the door hit him in the ass when he duck-walked out the front entrance. She turned back to Bree. "You don't have to take that kind of crap from him."

"I'm sorry."

"What are *you* sorry for?" Erin pulled over the desk chair Marbury had vacated and sat. She crossed her legs and clasped her hands, resting her forearms on her thigh as she leaned forward.

"That you had to come in here." Bree's stomach still felt

queasy, and she was totally demoralized that her boss had to run to her defense.

Erin touched her hand. "I know things are really bad for you right now, but you don't have to take that kind of abuse from people, Bree." She sat back. "Maybe I overreacted, barging in here, but I've been worried about you. And you and I are going to start looking for a new accountant right now."

"We need him to finish the audit. It won't look good to the IRS if we change right in the middle."

Erin regarded her a long moment. "Whatever you think is best, Bree. You're my accountant, and I trust you to make that judgment."

Her eyes suddenly ached as if she were about to cry. She should have been able to handle it herself. She should have told Marbury to fuck off. Instead, she just sat there and took it.

"Bree," Erin said softly. "Tell me what to do for you. I'm helpless here."

Jesus, she was actually going to cry. Swiping a finger at her eyes, she grabbed a tissue from the box in the bottom of her drawer. "I just need to work. I don't want to be at home." The only other place she wanted to run to was Luke's office, but she'd done that on Tuesday. She couldn't keep running to him. Or to anyone else.

God, it was freaking *pathetic*. Only wimps cried in front of their boss. You'd never see a *man* doing it.

"All right," Erin said while all the thoughts whirled around in Bree's head, "you work as long as you want. I won't bug you anymore about going home. And forget Marbury. If he fails on the audit, I'll sue his ass or something."

"Thanks, Erin." It was all Bree could manage. She started cleaning up the folders.

She was aware that Erin stood for another long moment

watching her, but she pretended to be engrossed in her papers until finally Erin left. She didn't go to her own office; she went to engineering where Dominic had his lab. They were going to talk about her, Bree knew it. Maybe they thought she was having a nervous breakdown.

"But I'm not," she whispered, squeezing her eyes shut. More than anything, she wanted to call Luke. But he had his daughter here. She'd probably stay through the weekend. Of course she would. It wouldn't make sense to drive back to school until Monday.

You little bitch.

When Luke said it, she got wet. From Marbury, it was terrifying. It meant bad things were going to happen.

Oh God. Bree couldn't catch her breath for a moment. She couldn't call Luke, couldn't see him. Her palms felt clammy, and her upper lip started to sweat. What would she do? She'd go crazy without something to blot out the morning with Marbury. Work would be fine, but tonight, God, what about tonight? She'd gotten so used to Luke being there, to seeing him when she got home, sitting across the table, eating dinner, making conversation.

Then taking her somewhere to make her forget everything but the feel of him.

Okay, calm down. It'll be fine.

She thought about Luke, his touch, his voice. And tried to relax. Stretching out her fingers, she flexed them like a cat. Then she did what she always did, what she was so good at. She pretended everything was all right and she was perfectly normal. She'd done it so many times before. She could do it now.

31

STEPHIE'S PARENTS HAD FOLLOWED KEIRA BACK TO SCHOOL THIS morning. Luke couldn't believe they'd waited instead of rushing to her aid last night, but at least they were going down to the university.

After the pep talk over their chai lattes, Keira had handled last night's discussion with Stephie's parents herself, keeping at them until they understood the gravity of the situation. Luke had simply been there as moral support.

Keira had called him in the afternoon, and Stephie was returning home with her parents. "She didn't even put up a fight, Dad," she told him.

Christ, he was proud of his daughter, his heart swelling in his chest.

Now all Luke could think about was getting home to Bree. He'd gone to her mother's house so many nights in a row, it was starting to feel natural.

It was later than usual for him, close to six-thirty, but the driveway was empty as he pulled in. Bree wasn't home from work yet. She'd had an important meeting, he recalled her saying last night. Perhaps it ran longer than she'd anticipated. He rang the bell.

Mrs. Mason answered wearing an apron over her flower-print

dress. "Oh, Luke. Bree said you were with your daughter tonight, and that you wouldn't be able to come over."

"She drove back to school this morning." He didn't mention the reason for her trip.

"Oh, how nice. Come in. I'm not making anything special for dinner since I thought you wouldn't be here."

"You never have to make anything special for me."

She flapped a hand at him. "I love having a man to cook for." She wore the smile of a content woman without a care in the world. He didn't understand her. It was as if sometimes she'd forgotten her husband had existed. She rarely mentioned him. She refused to have a service. She didn't appear to be grieving in any way. It was pretty damn strange.

Unless she was happy he was gone.

"Whatever you cook is great," he said, betraying none of his inner thoughts.

"Grilled ham and cheese. I haven't had one in ages, and I thought I'd treat myself."

"Sounds good. Especially since I'm inviting myself." Maybe, over dinner, without Bree, he could finally learn a few things. He didn't intend to ask any point-blank questions that were better left for a psychiatrist's office, but maybe he'd find *something* to help him understand what Bree truly needed.

Mrs. Mason led him into the kitchen as she *tutted* away at him. "Don't be silly. You've got a standing invitation."

Everything was out-of-date, flat-cornered Formica counter-tops, brown appliances, brick-colored linoleum. As if everyone in this house had stopped moving forward, something holding them all captive in the past.

He spoke even as he observed her. "You've been baking cookies." A rack of oatmeal raisin cookies were cooling, and the sink was filled with soap suds, a big bowl, and the tips of two beaters.

"I have to fill all my cookie jars," she said as she pulled a frying pan from the drawer at the bottom of the stove.

Based on the proliferation of jars on the counter, that would be one hell of a lot of cookies. "They smell good."

"Dessert," she said. "Milk and cookies. Now go wash up while I fix the grilled cheese."

He felt like a small boy as she shooed him away. She was an odd bird, and he was fast coming around to agreeing that Bree had good reason for being worried about her.

In the half bath off the laundry room, there was another cookie jar on the back of the toilet, this one in the shape of Dumbo the elephant. Cookies in the bathroom? Curiouser and curiouser. He took care of business and washed up. Then, with his hand on the doorknob, he realized he couldn't resist. Retreating the few steps to the toilet, he lifted Dumbo's tail.

He stopped. Stared. Okay, not possible. The contents looked like . . . ashes. Jesus God.

Luke carefully put the lid back. All right, he did *not* see that. Bree's father's ashes could not be in a cookie jar on the back of the toilet. No way. Maybe it was bath salts. Yeah, bath salts. That looked like ashes.

When he returned to the kitchen, Mrs. Mason was humming as two sandwiches sizzled in the frying pan.

"When's Bree going to be home?" he asked. "We can wait for her, if you'd like."

"Oh, she's going out for dinner up in the city."

His spine tensed. "What?"

She glanced up at the sharpness of his tone. "In fact, I thought she was with you. But then you showed up."

"Why didn't you say something when I first arrived?"

"I thought it would be nice if it was just you and me." Then she totally contradicted herself. "She's with girlfriends from work.

They wanted to take her out and show her a good time with all this unhappy business lately."

Unhappy business? This was just plain wrong. And after finding Dumbo in the bathroom, he had to call her on it. "That's an odd way of putting it. Her father just died. That's more than *unhappy business*."

She flipped the sandwiches in the pan. "I know what everyone thinks. That I should be mourning and sad. But he was sick for a year and a half." She shrugged. "I do feel a bit of relief. I'm not going to pretend I don't." She tamped the bread down with her spatula until cheese oozed out the sides.

In a way, he understood. After a long illness, there had to be some relief that the misery was over. But as he looked at her, his gut shouted that there was more to it, a lot more.

"Do you forgive me, Luke?" Though her hair was white, her eyebrows were still dark, with springy little hairs sticking out. They looked like slashes across her forehead as she raised one brow at him.

He tried to sound comforting. "Everyone deals with death and grief differently." But he kept seeing Dumbo on the back of the toilet. They *were* ashes.

"Yes, they do," Mrs. Mason agreed. "I cried for months after my mother died. I was eighteen. It was before my husband and I were married. She went in for a hysterectomy, and she died on the table. It was all so unexpected. My father never recovered."

"I'm sorry."

"But with my husband, it was different."

"Yes. The length of his illness. Watching him go downhill." But the ashes in the bathroom. That defied the pat explanation. "And Dumbo?"

She laughed, waving her hands, the spatula dripping grease. "Oh, that's what this is all about. It's just a little private joke. My husband always said he wanted to be one of my cookies in the jar so I could gobble him all up. I know it seems morbid, but . . ." She shrugged.

"To each his own," he finished for her. But it felt . . . *wrong*. She wasn't stable.

She plopped the grilled sandwiches onto two plates, cut them in half, then carried both to the table in the nook. She'd already poured two glasses of milk.

"Which friends did Bree go to the city with?" The first bite of grilled cheese sat heavy in his stomach, but he ate because right now, he needed to figure out where Bree had gone, and this woman had the answer.

"She didn't say." Did that sound cagey?

Bree didn't have girlfriends. That's what bothered him. Even if the girls at the office—whom she'd never mentioned as being friends—had taken her out to cheer her up, they wouldn't have gone all the way to the city. An evening in San Francisco was something you planned for and did on a weekend.

Unless you were going to a club. And if she was, she wasn't with any girlfriends.

The sandwich congealed in his stomach.

"Is something wrong with the cheese, Luke?"

"No. It's good," he said automatically, but he was thinking. Bree wouldn't do that. She would not go to a sex club without him. Not alone. That was stupid, and she was way past that kind of behavior. Wasn't she? He reached for his phone, pulling it from his suit jacket pocket. "I'll just call her and see how she's doing."

"That's a good idea. I'm worried about her. She didn't wake up easily this morning."

The phone rang and rang, so at least he knew it was on. But her voicemail answered. He didn't leave a message; she would see the missed call. "Are you sure she said she was going up to the city?"

"Yes." But now she sounded uncertain, her forehead creased in extra lines.

"What exactly did she say?" His gut went rigid.

Mrs. Mason put a fingertip to her temple. "I can't remember her exact words, just something about a club she knew up there."

Goddammit. His pulse was suddenly racing, and his head began to pound with an ache behind the eyes. "What time did she call?"

"Just before you got here." She gave him a wide-eyed look.

He no longer believed it was innocent at all. "And you didn't see fit to tell me then?"

"Like I said, I wanted you and I to get to know each other better. She'll be home soon, I'm sure."

"Mrs. Mason, her dad—*your* husband—just died. She's emotionally vulnerable right now. She shouldn't be running up to the city where neither of us can get hold of her."

Suddenly, the woman smiled. It gave him chills. "You're right," she said. "You'd better go find her. I should have thought of that myself."

Find her? It was just past seven. The club didn't open until nine. Where the hell would she go in the meantime?

Of course. Home. Her place. To change into something sexy.

When her father died, she'd spun him a tale about going to the club, about the two doms. She'd done it to incite him to action. Is that what she was doing now? She thought he was with his daughter so suddenly she needed to reel him back in?

Goddammit. He didn't know what the hell she was up to. But he was sure as hell going to find out.

* * *

SHE WAS SHAKING; THE DAY HAD ONLY GOTTEN WORSE. NOTHING in particular, just an increasing tension that gave her the jitters, and, by the end of the day, had scrambled her brains.

Bree could not face her mother. She could not face the house in which her father had died in the back bedroom. She couldn't face the window beyond which lay the dollhouse of her youth. Maybe when it was completely dark out back, when she couldn't see even its shadow. Maybe then she could go back. Late. After her mom was asleep.

So instead, after work she went home. Her *own* home. She'd called her mom and told her she'd be late, clubbing in San Francisco, she'd said. Isn't that what normal single women did every once in a while, go up to the city with girlfriends for fun? It *sounded* normal. Oh God, she so wanted to *be* normal.

But her condo was cold. Unwelcoming. Of course, she couldn't call Luke, not with his daughter there. Besides, what was she going to tell him, that she'd freaked out because Marbury yelled at her? It was too humiliating. She found herself in front of the open closet door. Black and crimson lace called to her. A dress with a tight bustier bodice attached to a slim black skirt. She'd never worn it, but in the shop when she'd tried it on—over a year ago—the bustier had pushed up her breasts, the laced front fastenings had tightened around her waist, and she'd suddenly grown the perfect hourglass figure.

She held it against her body and stared at herself in the full-length mirror on the closet door. With black fishnet stockings and four-inch heels, she'd be totally desirable, eminently fuckable.

She put on the dress and admired her reflection. She slipped on the stockings and shoes and became a sexy, seductive lady of the night. Not Bree the boring accountant. Not the wimpy woman who let Marbury terrify her. With those shoes, the woman in the mirror could have walked all over him. And left marks.

As she climbed behind the wheel of her car, a tiny voice told her she was too stupid to live for even considering going to the city by herself. But the woman from the mirror put her phone on vibrate and shoved it into her clutch along with her license, forty bucks, and a tube of lipstick.

Luke was busy. Luke was with his daughter. He had a family, a whole and complete life that didn't include Bree, and it was only a matter of time before he realized he would never want a woman like her, a slut, around his kids. Hell, why not admit it? She didn't *want* to run to Luke. She didn't want to depend on him because he'd be gone soon, and it would be so much worse the deeper she got with him. For just tonight, she wanted to lick her wounds the old way, cruising a club where no one knew her. And she didn't care if she was too stupid to live.

The traffic was horrendous, and it took her over an hour and fifteen minutes to get across the Bay Bridge into the city.

Her blood was high, her skin buzzing. Long ago, she used to do this, not often, just a few times when she couldn't breathe shut up in her apartment. She'd sneak out, like a serial killer whose blood lust had suddenly raged out of control. A couple of different occasions, she'd even met men who looked after her for a few weeks or months.

And really, what bad thing could happen to her tonight that hadn't already been done long ago?

She rather liked the idea of simply disappearing, her car found a week later with a parking boot on it, and no one would ever know what happened to her. Not that she had a death wish. But sometimes there was a certain relief in making up a story like that.

The garage she and Luke had parked in last time was too far away, so she drove round and round, biting her lip till it hurt. She'd finally found a spot a couple of blocks from the club. She was too early, so she sat in her car with the doors locked and the radio on, tapping her fingers on her thighs until finally the dashboard clock turned over to nine-fifteen. She pulled out once again to circle. After fifteen minutes of that, she found an open meter two doors from the club's entrance. She'd chewed her lipstick off, but her lips were as red as berries when she checked her makeup in the review mirror.

She was ready. Her blood was humming.

Yet she had the disquieting thought that without Luke, she would never find the relief she needed.

32

BREE FED THE HUNGRY PARKING METER WITH QUARTERS SHE stored in a change bin below the car's cup holders. The city was sharply cold on the January night, but she left her jacket on the front seat. She didn't want to spoil the dress's effect. Since it was early evening for the club scene, the patrons were arriving in a trickle. Bree waited a couple of minutes at the bottom of the steps leading up to the Victorian-style facade, then chose a couple to follow inside. Being a single woman, she got in for free, but there was safety in numbers.

As they paid their couple's entry fee, she hung back in the lobby. It wasn't the same without Luke; nothing was the same anymore without him.

Then the man opened the inside door, holding it politely for his partner and Bree. The music from upstairs drifted down the stairwell, and she followed the woman into the interior.

"You shouldn't be alone," the lady said. She was older, perhaps Luke's age, forty-five or so, but her skin had the soft, unlined quality of a woman who'd used moisturizers religiously since she was a teen and never ventured into the sun.

"I'm meeting someone," Bree offered up the lie, wishing it were true.

"Stay with us until you find him," the woman said.

Bree saw the wisdom of it. "Thank you."

"Your dress is gorgeous. I wish I could wear something like that."

"Darling, you'd look perfect in that dress," the man said as he flourished an arm to allow the ladies to precede him up the stairs.

"You're so sweet, baby," the woman answered, touching his shoulder.

Bree took in the matching wedding rings. Married. Wow. Not that she wasn't well aware married couples visited the clubs and swapped and all that stuff. She'd just never heard them be so nice to each other.

They weren't the most attractive. The woman had a few extra pounds and a horsy face, and her husband, well, portly was a diplomatic description. Yet they looked at one another with kindness and affection. People who looked at each other that way didn't generally go to sex clubs. Maybe they were voyeurs.

Then she wondered how she and Luke appeared to others.

At the top of the second flight of stairs, the man once again opened the door with that chivalrous flourish.

"Thank you," she told him and followed them in. It was the same level Luke had brought her to last time.

"Margie and Ron," the lady supplied.

Such normal names. "Bree."

"Were you headed to any room in particular?" Margie wanted to know.

"I'm just going to wander the milder rooms until my friend arrives."

The entrance opened onto a large area for dancing, a few tables, and a bar on one end. The dance floor was empty despite the disco music playing, and only a couple of tables were occupied. There were hallways to the left and right and another at one side of the bar. This level provided a variety of entertainment; themed rooms, a movie theater with bean bag chairs and big screen TVs playing all manner of porn. Bree had never figured out why someone would come here to watch porn, first because you could watch that at home, and second because when the place got jumping, you could see all that stuff for real. The next floor offered same-gender activities, though voyeurism by straights was welcomed, and on the floor above that, hardcore BDSM. Which wasn't to say that bi and bondage activities didn't occur on this floor, the other night being an example, when the master gave away his submissive and allowed that woman to take her.

"Why don't we wander with you?" Margie said. When Bree nodded her assent, Margie tucked her arm through Bree's, and they walked like girlfriends. "Since I'm assuming you've been here before, tell me what your favorite room is." Margie steered them into one of the hallways, which was uncrowded at this early hour. Ron followed a couple of paces behind.

"I just like to watch," Bree said.

Margie laughed, a lusty sound. "We all like to watch, darling. It's a question of *what* we like to watch. I must admit I'm partial to two men going at it, but Ron's a bit homophobic."

"I am not," he denied.

A couple of punk rockers in black clothing, black fingernails, black eye makeup, and spiked hair passed them heading the other way. The only thing that clued Bree in on male versus female were the small breasts beneath the black T-shirt one of them wore.

"Have you ever watched two men?" Margie probed as they neared the DVD room.

At one time or another, Bree had seen just about everything, but the best had been the other night with Luke. "Yes, I've seen it. But I think I prefer something with a bit more bondage."

Margie slapped at her arm. "Bad girl."

They stopped at the door of the theater and peeked inside. Big-screens played on each of the four walls with various scenarios of man–woman sex, but the bean bag chairs were empty.

"Dear," Margie said over her shoulder, "we got here too early. There's nothing to see."

"I told you so," Ron commented in typical marital fashion.

"I have an early breakfast meeting tomorrow, but I did so want something naughty tonight," Margie confided. "I suppose you felt the same." She led Bree to the next door.

"Yes." They could have been talking about going out for a mocha or a shopping spree. Except that inside this room, which was festooned with painted palm trees and ferns and monkeys flying between the branches, a woman was going down on a man with the biggest cock Bree had ever seen.

Margie let out a low whistle. "Goodness, I could suck that."

Ron was suddenly close behind them. "Shall I ask him if you can have a go, sweetheart?"

"I need a bit of a look-see first, babykins."

Babykins?

"She always likes to check out everything that's available before she chooses," Ron explained.

With Margie on her arm and Ron trailing them, Bree's tension melted away. Her insides were no longer quaking. There was something soothing about Margie's easy attitude. She was so accepting, so normal. Even as she said she'd love to suck the big cock.

Maybe Bree wasn't so incredibly abnormal after all. Maybe she was just *different*, with varied needs. *Different* wasn't such a bad word.

They inspected more rooms as the hallway began to fill up with more partiers. They laughed and giggled like girlfriends, swapping ribald comments. It was actually fun.

"I'd love to watch Ron fuck you, dear. What do you think of that?"

Bree almost laughed at Margie's exceptionally mild tone. "I don't think so."

"Sorry, sweetheart, I think you struck out," Ron said with a hint of laughter in his voice.

"It was worth a shot," Margie quipped, then lowered her voice for Bree. "You're very attractive."

There was nothing to it really, but as they walked her down the hall, she felt Ron breathing down her neck, and Margie's hand on her arm began to tighten like a claw. She was suddenly trapped between them, especially as the clientele cruising the rooms had multiplied and begun to swarm around them. Would they drag her into a room and force her? Where rape fantasies were the norm, no one would pay much attention if she screamed.

Isn't this what you wanted? a voice whispered. *Debasement, humiliation, punishment. Isn't that why you're here?*

She didn't know why she was here, except that Marbury made her feel out of control and terrified. And bad sex made her . . . made her what? Feel like she'd atoned?

Then, dear God, she'd atoned over and over and over. And she hated herself for needing it that way.

"I should go now," she said softly. Coming here had been a bad idea. It was a reaction to Marbury, seeing Luke with his daughter, knowing it was only a matter of time before he was gone, feeling she had no place to turn. The fun she'd experienced with Margie was just a disguise for darker things. This place and these people didn't make any of it better. Only Luke had made things better the night he rescued her from Derek.

Margie's hand was a vise on her arm. "Not yet, dear."

"No, no, I really have to go." She needed Luke. She was so good at pretending, she could pretend he'd be there forever. Until he wasn't. Why not? She tried to tug her arm out of Margie's grip.

"Well, well, if it isn't my favorite little submissive."

She knew that voice. Suddenly those darker things were closing in on her.

The master from Monday night blocked the middle of the hall, clubbers flowing around him. Where had all the people come from? How long had they been wandering?

He reached out a long finger and traced the bruise on her forehead. She'd forgotten about it. Margie and Ron hadn't said a word.

Her flesh chilled beneath the master's touch. "I ran into a door," she said because the lie seemed to be the only thing she could remember.

He gave her a long look with dark, penetrating eyes. "I would never mark you."

"It was an accident," she said, feeling almost desperate. She yanked her arm away from Margie and backed up, only to find Ron right behind her.

"That's what they all say," the master whispered.

Ron cupped her ass, squeezed.

"I want to watch you fuck her," Margie said, and Bree couldn't tell whether she meant Ron or the master. Or both.

Music and voices and laughter and moans, the sounds of sex, the slap of a paddle, the slip-slide of lips on flesh, the smell of come, the sweat of men. She couldn't breathe. "I want Luke," she whispered, but no one heard her, no one paid attention.

Behind her, Ron massaged her waist, pushing and pulling the material of her dress, rubbing his cock along her ass.

The master, gaze holding hers, spearing her straight through to her soul, moved his lips. "I'm going to fuck you. You're going to love it. You've never had better. You'll forget all about *him* and you'll be mine."

"I—" she started.

He put his finger to her lips. "You'll do what I say. Because you have to. Because you came here looking for me. He's not right for you. He'll leave you when you need him most. Only I can give you what you deserve."

How did he know all that? As if he'd plucked the thoughts right out of her head.

"You dirty, filthy, cocksucking whore. *I* will give you the punishment you deserve." He spoke as if he knew her innermost being, but his words did nothing for her. He wasn't Luke; Luke's voice had become the only way in which the words worked for her.

With Ron pushing and pulling at her waist, her nipple had somehow worked its way above the bustier, and the master darted a hand out to pinch her hard.

She wanted to scream. Yet with all the weakness inside her, she rolled her head back on her neck so that all she saw was the dirty ceiling tiles, and let him do what he wanted. The way she always had since she was a little girl. Maybe the way she always would.

LUKE HAD GONE TO HER CONDO FIRST. IT WAS DARK, LOCKED UP, empty. His only other choice was the club. On the drive, he'd morphed from pissed to terrified. She was alone. Anything could happen without him there to protect her. She could be raped. Or kidnapped. Or worse. He had visions of the cops finding her body in some isolated warehouse.

When he reached the city, he'd hoofed it from a parking spot a couple of blocks from the club. He'd bribed the attendant to let him in despite the fact that he was a single male. If you had money, you could get anything you wanted.

Luke had prowled the rooms, his gut tense. He'd spotted her sometime before ten. With a couple. His instinct was to drag her out of there. Instead, now that he could breathe and his terror had receded, he hung back to watch. She was smiling, laughing, having a great time.

He didn't get it. She absolutely confounded him. Why, after everything they'd done, everything they were to each other, he the master, she the slave, lovers, whatever you wanted to call it—why had she suddenly thrown it all back in his face and run out to a club alone? Simply to incite him? Or because of Keira, because, instead of inviting Bree inside, he'd taken her home as if he were ashamed of her?

He'd told her mother Bree was emotionally vulnerable, but it didn't explain anything. Not after that kiss she'd given him last night. That was a fucking communion. He should have called her today. But he'd been running late because of Keira. And he didn't expect *this*.

So he fell back into the slowly expanding crowd and watched. He hated how fucking hot she was in the bustier dress. A dress she'd never worn for him.

The couple—middle-aged, unpretentious, average looks, a little on the heavy side—seemed harmless as they led Bree from room to room, sometimes going in to observe for a bit, sometimes peaking inside only to move on again. He couldn't discern if they had intentions toward her.

The crowd grew thicker around him, and he became separated from her by far too many bodies. The woman stopped in the middle of the hall, the man all at once way too close to Bree.

Luke dodged a couple who'd suddenly decided sucking cock in the middle of the hall was totally appropriate.

Then he froze, his blood rushing through veins that had suddenly shrunk to the size of a pinhead. That fucking dom. He touched Bree's forehead. She didn't move. She took it; she accepted. She even let the fat man hold her hips and grind his cock against her backside as the dom stroked her skin and the woman watched with avid, glowing eyes.

Then the bastard pinched her nipple, and Bree's head fell back, her hair flowing like silk over her shoulders.

Fuck, fuck, fuck. Luke's brain went into countdown to an explosion. The shock of betrayal was physical, a clenching of his teeth, the contraction of his heart. His feet rooted to the floor, he wanted to turn around and leave her to her own debauchery.

Fuck her.

Yet he could hear his own breath rough through his nostrils, and he knew he wouldn't leave her. He could hate her for doing this, but he would never leave her defenseless.

33

"TAKE YOUR FUCKING HANDS OFF HER." LUKE HAD NOT EVEN BEEN aware of his legs moving, but he was there, right beside Bree, the scent of her perspiration perfuming the hall.

"Ah, so now the knight in shining armor deigns to show up," the black-haired dom mocked.

"Yeah," he said. "She's mine. You know it. Back off."

The man curled a lip at him. "Let's ask her what she wants."

The couple had taken a step back, better to behold the brawl. Bree simply stood there, her arm out as if the woman was still holding it, her nipples pert above the bustier. Head down now, she stared at the floor as if the patterns in the hardwood were fascinating.

Her lack of acknowledgment only pissed him off more. "She doesn't get a choice. I'm her master."

"Right," the guy scoffed, the small mob in the hall no longer moving, but stopping to observe the fun. Then he stabbed a finger dramatically at Bree's forehead. "That's why you need to beat her to make her comply." Luke winced inwardly at the man's words. "Because you're *such* a good master."

Oh yeah, the guy was a showman, his eyes passing over the

crowd, directing them with a resonant voice that wasn't loud but carried just the same. "Isn't that right, everyone? A good master has to beat compliance into his submissive."

There were murmurs through the hall, some of them growing ugly. Luke resisted the urge to explain, took a step closer to the man, and lowered his voice to a growl. "She is mine. Back your ass off."

"Shall we fight over the lady's honor? Have a duel?" The dom brandished an invisible sword.

Luke was uncomfortably aware that he was on the opposite end of the spectrum now, Derek's end, the villain's end, the man who had abused his submissive. *This* dom was now her defender, the way Luke had once been.

There was only one way to regain the upper hand. He'd dislike himself for it later, yet he turned on his heel and faced Bree. "You've been feeding your new friends the wrong impression."

She raised her head, met his eyes. "I told them the truth, Master. They wouldn't believe me."

"How are you going to make it up to me?"

Her eyes flashed across his face, trying to read his mind, to figure out how to please him, how to give him what he needed, how to appease him. "Suck your cock?" she asked.

The crowd hooted. The woman who'd been hanging on Bree's arm clapped her hands.

"That's not good enough," Luke said. "You need to show them that you'll do anything for me."

She searched his face. She wouldn't find the answer. He was a mass of emotions that included anger, guilt, incomprehension, shame, and beneath it all, desire. A deep desire to have her here and now, to prove to them all that he was the only one she wanted.

Yet in the core of his soul, he wanted her to take his hand and lead him out, away, to a place all their own, without all the posturing.

Tell the bozo to fuck off.

"Tell him you'd rather have a real man fuck you in front of *him*," the dom said. "A man who doesn't have to beat you to get what he wants." The crowd punctuated with more hoots and a chant of "fuck him, fuck him."

If she touched the guy, Luke would have to do bodily harm. But he stood tall, fists clenched, jaw aching with the strain of waiting for an answer. The crowd waited breathlessly with him, and for long, long moments, the hallway was so silent, he could almost hear her heartbeat echoing off the walls.

Finally she spoke, so softly that even he had to strain for her words. "Fuck me while he watches."

Damn her. He'd wanted her to beg him to take her away.

"Hah," the dom barked a laugh, and Luke wanted to smack the smile off his face. "We both should fuck you and you can choose between us." The asshole pumped a fist in the air. "We know who'll win, don't we, my friends." The crowd cheered him on.

Luke stepped so close that her sexual perfume clouded his mind. She was aroused. Before, her scent had been tinged with fear, now it was pure sex. "I'll fuck you for them," he murmured for her alone. "I'll make you come for them. I'll make you scream." He waited two beats. "Then I'm leaving. With or without you."

BREE SHUDDERED WITH HIS INTENSITY. HIS EYES WERE SO DARK, angry, forbidding, so terrifying, she couldn't take in enough air to breathe.

Yet he'd come for her, and her body was on fire for him.

She had no doubt he'd walk out on her and expect her to run to catch up. Or he'd leave her behind. That was her punishment. She wanted to know why he was here, how he'd found her, why he'd left his happy little home. But those things were all secondary. What mattered was his closeness. The heat of his body, the hardness of his cock, the angry tick in his jaw muscle.

He was here. He'd left everything at home to rescue her, had *known* she needed rescuing. It didn't matter how; it just was.

"Whatever you want, Master."

With her words, he grabbed her hand and dragged her away from them all, Margie, Ron, the dark master. The throng parted like it did for John Wayne dragging Maureen O'Hara in *The Quiet Man*. His limit reached, his patience ended, where all that was left was brute force. She damn near had her orgasm right there.

But Luke was just starting. Yanking her through the first doorway he came to, she was greeted by the sight of a bare-assed man taking a woman on a swing. Behind them, the wall was a huge screen projecting a poppy-filled field to create the feeling of sex in the outdoors. Luke hit a switch on the wall, and the projection changed to an aerial scene from a plane as if the couple was now skydiving.

"Out," Luke commanded. Hearing the masterful tone, the guy pulled out, tugged his pants up, and toddled off with his lady.

"Screw the swing," Luke's dark-haired taunter said, and punched another button on the wall as he entered. The swing retracted, the projector turned off, and the room was suddenly lit by unrelenting overhead lights. "You don't need props. Do her on the floor."

Luke smiled acidly and reached beyond the man for yet another button. A bed came down out of the wall. "Screw the floor. I don't want to hurt her backside."

They were fighting over her. It was the oddest battle, but it *was* a battle. A sexual duel. She was the prize.

Then Luke picked her up bodily and tossed her onto the bed. She bounced. He straddled her body, then began deftly popping the front fastenings of the bustier. Beyond his shoulder, she could see the room filling up with spectators, Margie and Ron right up front for the show.

Her breasts bared, Luke pinched her nipple. She didn't scream. She could only moan.

"That's what you like, isn't it. Pain. Fast and hard." He tweaked the other nipple.

She felt her moisture coating the insides of her thighs. "Yes, Master."

Then he slid back on his knees and shoved the bottom half of her dress to her waist.

A breath shot from his nostrils. "You little bitch. You aren't wearing panties."

You little bitch. Oh yes, it was so different when Luke said it. Nothing like Marbury.

Her body flushed with need. "You told me I was to wear only dresses, Master, and never any panties."

Looming over her, he bracketed her throat with his hand, held her still, put his face right down to hers. "Only for *me*, slut. Not some salivating crowd and a hotshot asshole who *thinks* he's a man." She quivered with the rage roughening his voice. "You will be punished. Not just tonight. It will go on and on."

The spectators cheered, though she didn't know how they could have heard his soft and deadly voice.

He put his hand between her legs. "Look how wet you are, my filthy little whore."

He stroked her, delved between the lips of her pussy and caressed her clit until she quaked with his anger and the need to come.

"Let me taste her," someone said. She thought it was Ron.

"Fuck off." He didn't even turn his head, just kept his fingers against her, his eyes on her. Her body rose to meet him, wordlessly begging him to go deeper.

"Do you need a little help there? Looks like you're having trouble getting it up," the dom jeered.

Luke ignored him as if he were a fly not even worth a swat and braced an arm by her head as he played her clit. "You like this, don't you, all the attention, all the men wanting you."

She parted her lips but the words wouldn't come.

He worked her faster, his fingers covered with her juice. "You love driving me to crazy things. You love the power." Then he pushed a finger inside and found her G-spot.

"Master." She gasped out his title.

"You piss me off, then sit back and wait for me to go wild on you."

"No, Master." She couldn't explain what she'd needed tonight, couldn't tell him about Marbury, and the horror of letting the horrible man say those things to her, only to find she wanted exactly *this*, for Luke to find her and go wild for her, just as he said. "I needed you." She cried out with the words. It wasn't climax, it was more, a need so great it couldn't be assuaged. "And you weren't there."

"I'm here now," he said, his voice grating.

Her heart literally sang. He *was* here. For her. "Fuck me, Master. Fuck me for them. Show them you want me. Please."

She wanted him to show *her*. Every time, she needed him to prove it all over again.

"If I fuck you, I have to stop long enough to put on a condom." He'd have to stop touching her, stroking her, turning her into a crazy thing. "You'll need to touch yourself while I get ready."

He pulled her hand down and laid it between her legs. "Rub yourself for him," he whispered in her ear. "It's what you want anyway. To give him a show. To make him see how hot you are. Give them all a show."

Just like the fantasy. "No, it's only for you."

"Liar," he muttered harshly. "Stroke yourself for them."

He pulled back and away, leaving her with legs spread and pussy exposed.

"Do it," he ordered.

She started the play, fingers round and round her pussy, her clit, until she closed her eyes and tipped her head back into the mattress.

He grabbed her chin. "Look at them. I want you to see them watching you."

The dom stood at the side of the bed, arms crossed over his chest, a massive bulge in his jeans. Margie stroked Ron through his open zipper. Men. Women. Leering. It was terrifying, exhilarating. She wanted them to watch her, to want her, to caress themselves for her. She was so wet, so hungry for it. *Want me, need me, desire me.*

On his knees between her legs, Luke drew a condom from his pocket, unzipped, pulled out his thick cock and stroked himself as he watched her with eyes as avid and greedy as the rest of the crowd.

"This is what you want, isn't it. To see me hard for you. To know I want you, that I'm the one who'll do anything to fuck you, to have you. That I'm wild for you."

"Yes, Master, yes." With his words, his cock, his touch, all the eyes on her, she was so close to the edge, she could fly off into nothingness.

Then the condom was on, and he covered her, hiding her from the throng, his cock at her entrance. "Put me inside you," he whispered, eyes blazing.

She covered him with her own moisture, wetting him, preparing him, then arched slightly to take half an inch.

Arms straight, he braced himself above her, lasered her with an angry gaze, then plunged into her. So deep, so good. The crowd roared, and she thought the sound might be coming from inside her. He rotated his hips against her, caressing her clit with the movement.

A moment later, he shifted, pulling back on his haunches to drape her legs over his thighs. His cock in her was now visible to the crowd, the deep penetration.

"I need a cushion under her ass."

It was Luke's rival who reacted, pulling a pillow from the head of the bed, then sliding it beneath her as she lifted her hips.

"Perfect," Luke purred. "I can feel your G-spot." He pumped slowly. "Do you feel me?"

"Yes, Master, exquisitely." It was a measured, relentless torture that thrust her to the edge.

"Touch your clit. Caress it." He kept the pace slow, mind-altering. "Filthy whore," he muttered. "This is what you wanted all along. You incited me to make me punish you. To make me hurt you."

She no longer heard the people around them. The faces blurred and receded. Until there was only Luke, her master, his body taking her, forcing her, his words washing over her.

"You're what I've wanted all along," she told him, then started to come in a long white explosion of light. He drove harder. She screamed soundlessly, lips parted, eyes squeezed shut. There was only his cock in her, his body pounding her, his touch, his scent, his voice, the pulse of his climax inside her.

Finally, in his arms, she found the relief she'd been seeking.

34

BREE WAS DAZED, AND LUKE SHOULD HAVE BEEN FLOATING IN that space right along with her, lying in her arms, basking in her warmth. It was what he craved. Those sweet moments after sex where his body was replete, his head filled with her scent, and her skin caressing his. But he'd just allowed himself to be goaded into fucking her to show his prowess.

There was the crowd around them, too, seething with tension. And that fucking dom. Luke pulled out, backed away, tossed the condom without giving a damn where it landed, and zipped his pants. Then he pulled down Bree's skirt. She could barely help him.

"Well, that was some show," the ringmaster called. "But we still haven't proven who's better."

The fastenings of her bodice were almost too much for Luke in his current state, but he managed. He helped her to a sitting position. "She's not fucking you," he said. "She neither wants nor needs you."

As he pulled Bree to her feet, the dom blocked his way to the door. "You still haven't let her speak." The man stood with legs parted, hands on his waist.

"Did you let your submissive speak?" Luke challenged, tucking Bree close to his side, helping her stand.

The man smiled. "Touché."

"You gave her away to other men. And to a woman. And right in front of her, you begged to touch another woman."

"That I did. It's my right to punish. But I don't raise a hand to her." His eyes flashed. Luke almost believed the guy bought into his own rhetoric, that he truly was fighting on Bree's behalf for the right not to be beaten, that within all the bluster, the man didn't like to see a woman brutalized.

It was that insight only that made Luke explain. "She fell," he said with excessive quietness. "I don't hit women or children." Then he smiled with teeth bared. "Now fuck off."

The man stared him down for a full thirty seconds. Luke met him eye to eye.

Finally, the guy took one step to the side. "I believe you." Then he turned, spread his hand out like a courtier, and the crowd swept aside.

Luke got her the hell out of there.

"You know where to come back to if he starts mistreating you," the dom called as his parting shot. Luke didn't allow Bree to turn around or even acknowledge the man.

"My car," she said a couple of minutes later as he herded her along the sidewalk outside. "It's back there."

He held her tighter. "I'm not letting you drive alone. I don't trust you to go home."

"But I need my car."

"We'll take BART up tomorrow and get it." He would drive them to the station, then they'd ride the rapid transit together.

"But my car might get towed, and I have to go to work tomorrow."

He stopped and gave her a look that should have reduced her to a quivering puddle. "Then get in your car, and I will follow you to your mother's house. If you deviate from that route, I will run you off the road."

She swallowed.

"Is that understood?"

"Maybe you should take me to my place instead," she whispered, staring at the concrete.

A group of four couples headed up the club steps, laughing, the women giggling. He stared after them a moment. What did she want? What did she need? Could he ever actually give it to her? Or would she forever be running off somewhere, scaring the crap out of him, just to incite him to acts of debauchery?

"*Not* your place," he said. "And not mine. You don't deserve any one-on-one time after what you did."

She raised her head. "Didn't I do exactly what you wanted me to, Master?" Her eyes were still slightly dazed and puzzled. She really didn't get it.

"What if I can't rescue you?"

"I didn't need rescuing, Master."

He grabbed her chin, held her so she couldn't look away. "Anything could have happened to you." More than what had already been done to her, but she refused to see that. "Now don't piss me off any more than I already am. Get in your car and go to your mother's."

"Or what?" she said so softly he had to read her lips when a raucous bout of laughter floated across the night.

He knew what she was trying to do. To provoke him into taking her home for punishment. If she'd said she needed him to make love to her, he'd have done it in a heartbeat. He didn't ask why she'd come to the club tonight. He didn't ask what she'd needed that he couldn't provide. It couldn't be explained. He didn't think she even knew herself.

"You really don't want to test me right now, slave," he said so very quietly.

Slowly, she shook her head.

"Then get in your fucking car and drive to your mother's."

As she headed back down the street in her too sexy dress, his heart beat fast and hard against the walls of his chest. He'd been *that* close to issuing an ultimatum. But when you did, you could never back down.

He wanted her to offer her body and soul without all the hidden meanings, without forcing him to be the heavy. He had sympathy for what had been done to her in the past, but playing the bad man all the time was draining him dry.

HE'D MADE HER TREMBLE DELICIOUSLY. IT HAD BEEN SO GOOD, the way he talked to the dom, how he took her so forcefully. His headlights shone in her rearview mirror. He was *there* in so many ways.

He was right, he'd rescued her. He hadn't asked why she was there. She didn't want to talk about Marbury or tell Luke she was jealous of his daughter. She didn't want to admit she'd been frightened of Margie and Ron and the dom. She didn't used to be frightened. Or rather the fear was part of the turn-on. She'd thrived on it. But somehow, in the hallway, sandwiched between the three of them, she'd gone queasy. Then Luke was there. Right when she needed him.

She didn't want to be sent off to her mother's like a naughty child. She'd make him see that wasn't what he wanted either.

By the time she got home to her mom's, her eyes smarted from his headlights in the mirror. It was cold as she stepped out of the car, and she pulled the jacket she'd brought from the passenger seat and wrapped it around her, suddenly shivering in its warmth.

He made a slow circle at the end of the cul-de-sac, then stopped in the front of the house, but didn't get out. She was forced to walk out into the street to talk to him.

The night was quiet with only the hum of faraway cars on the main road. He rolled down his window. "Go in, it's cold."

"Let me get in the car with you."

"I already fucked you tonight."

It wasn't enough. She needed more. "Why'd you leave your daughter?"

"She went back this morning."

God. She could have called him. All along, she could have gone to him. But would she have? She didn't mean for the heavy sigh to leave her lips.

His brow furrowed. "Were you pissed about my daughter interrupting us last night?"

"No, not pissed."

"Then what?"

I had such a bad day, and I needed you, and you weren't there. I'm afraid someday you won't be there at all. Her fears were pitiful. "I thought you were busy."

"So you went to a club?" He said it mildly, but she sensed the iron in his voice.

"I didn't want to come here to my mother's."

"So you went to a club?" he repeated. This time, she thought she heard his teeth grinding.

"I just—" *Tell him the truth.* The whisper echoed in her head. *Tell him about Marbury.*

She'd wanted to cry in her office when Marbury yelled at her. She'd felt like weeping when Erin had to rescue her. She was thirty-five years old, and she'd damn near burst into tears at work because a man, an *asshole*, yelled at her and called her names. Could anyone have a clue how humiliating that was?

Luke wouldn't understand. She begged *him* to call her names. She invited his fury. How could she explain about Marbury? How could she explain that when her *Master* said those things, did those things, it was wonderful. But Marbury was different.

He opened the door and climbed out slowly. "You just what?"

With her high heels, they were of a height, and yet he seemed so much taller, so much bigger.

"I needed something," she whispered, ashamed she couldn't tell him the truth.

"You needed something, and you chose to go elsewhere. One night, and you couldn't wait for me."

"I'm sorry." What she'd done sounded churlish. Yet even if she told him about Marbury, he wouldn't understand. Men didn't cry at work. They got angry. They didn't melt into messy puddles of goo.

He'd never understand that she was terrified he'd leave her. So she'd left him.

With the streetlight shining down on his dark head, his eyes were in shadow as he stared at her for long, excruciating moments before he spoke. "As I drove up there, I was terrified something really bad was going to happen to you."

She swallowed. She should have thought of that. "I'm sorry," she whispered.

She felt his eyes on her for an interminably silent minute. "I can't give you what you need," he finally said.

Something inside her screamed. *No, please don't go.*

"I didn't like some of the things I had to do tonight." He paused. Her ears roared in the wait. "The things we do aren't good for you, either. You have to see that."

She wanted to wrap her body around him, hold him, never let him go. "You're not leaving," she said so softly that she knew he had to read her lips.

"We can't do it your way anymore. It's eating at us."

"But I only went there because I had a bad day at work and there was this meeting with a man and it didn't go well, and I couldn't call you, and I just had to do something."

He cupped her face, stilled her. "That's the problem. You *could* have called me. You should have known it didn't matter who I was with or what I was doing."

He'd seen through her lies, but still she tried. "But your daughter—"

He squeezed her cheeks between his palms. "You don't trust me. I'm like every other man to you. You would have let that guy in the club fuck you to get whatever it was you needed instead of coming to me no matter what."

It was true. She hadn't wanted it in the same way she needed Luke, but she wouldn't have stopped the dom. She never stopped them. She never stood up and told them they couldn't do it to her. She never told them she didn't want it even when she truly didn't. She never had.

"You can't even deny it," he said so quietly she heard the death knell in his voice.

"No," she whispered.

"I'm not good for you anymore. I'm becoming like the rest of them."

"You are good." She'd had so many men, and he was the one good one. But even for him, she couldn't stop needing things the way she needed them. She couldn't be a different woman. She'd been this way too long. Yet she couldn't go on making him do what demeaned him. "I'm sorry I can't change."

After all, this was only what she deserved, what she'd always deserved, since she was child.

Bree backed away. Luke's hands fell from her face, and she was cold, so horribly cold. As if she'd been buried in the grave her father should have occupied.

BREE DIDN'T TURN AS SHE CLOSED THE DOOR OF HER PARENTS' home. She didn't fight for him. He knew her well enough to know she wouldn't anyway. She was not a fighter.

The hole in his chest was the size of Calcutta, the ache ceaseless, the regret boundless. Yet he couldn't continue contributing to her issues. Punishing her, calling her names, spanking her, it was all part of her ritual, her symptoms. If she had him to run to, she wouldn't face her problems, she'd get help.

For a moment there, he'd thought she might have some sort of revelation. That she would tell him something that suddenly made it all clear, that provided the key to fixing what was wrong with her. About her father. Her life. Something he could fucking *fix*.

Yet all it had been was a bad day at work, a difficult meeting. And she'd gone to the club. He knew it was so much more than what she said. Yet she still could not tell him. He couldn't live with the fact that she didn't trust him. She would *never* trust him.

35

THE BEDSIDE CLOCK POUNDED THE BRIGHT RED NUMBERS OF eight forty-three a.m. into her head. She hadn't told Erin she wouldn't be in to work on Friday morning, but she could call now, and Erin wouldn't care. Erin would gush with understanding.

She and Dominic were so fucking understanding.

Bree put her legs over the edge of the bed and sat up slowly. Her head ached as if she'd gone on a drinking binge. She was naked, the dress, stockings, and high heels in a crumpled pile on the carpet next to the bed.

Her mother knocked softly on the closed door. "Bree, I made you breakfast."

She realized it was the scent of coffee that had woken her.

"I'm coming, Mom." She pulled on her robe and shoved her feet into a pair of old slippers she'd borrowed from her mother, then shuffled like an old woman to the door. The hall was empty, but the rich aroma of coffee led her to the kitchen like the pied piper.

"You slept late, dear," her mother said, all cheery. Even her apron, patterned with bright red roses, was cheery.

"Ugh," was all Bree said.

"I made eggs and fried tomatoes."

Bree loved fried tomatoes, the tangy taste. Her stomach growled. She'd forgotten to eat dinner, and she was lightheaded from hunger.

"Did Luke find you last night?"

Bree slid down into a chair at the table. "Yes." God, she wanted to get out of here, go home, stay in her bed for days. But she was trapped.

"Did you have a nice time?"

"Depends on what you consider nice," Bree answered softly. If she hadn't gone to the club without him, would he still be in her life? Maybe. For a few weeks or months. But she wasn't worth more than that. Better to take the pain and get over it.

"You know what I mean, dear. Luke adores you."

"Right." Bree sighed, suddenly unable to touch the tomatoes and eggs on her plate. God, when would her mother stop with the whole Luke-is-a-gift thing? "That's why he left me last night."

"Dear, he didn't leave you." Her mother *tutted*. "He came here. He thought *you* were going to be here. He didn't realize you were going up to the city on your own."

She looked at her mother, the gay apron, the bright smile. "So you told him where I'd gone?"

"Of course I did." Her mother flapped her napkin and laid it across her lap. "He's a good man. He'll take care of you."

Something started rising in her. She couldn't call it rage. Yet it was black and seething, and in a way, it was better than the despair in which she'd awoken. "He isn't going to take care of me, Mom. He left me. Not just for last night, but forever. He's gone. He's not coming back. He doesn't want me anymore." Instead of the pain she'd expected when she said the words aloud, she experienced a blaze of satisfaction at the look of horror dawning on her mother's face.

Slack-jawed, her mom stared. "How could you let him go?"

"I didn't have a choice in the matter." She wasn't so sure about that. He'd certainly wanted *something* from her when he climbed out of the car. She hadn't been able to figure it out, though. But this was about her mother's attitude, not what happened last night. "He didn't ask for my opinion on the matter."

Then her mom's face turned mean. It was the only word for it. "What did you do, Brianna?" she snarled.

Bree sat back, dropping her knife and fork on the plate. "Me?" She stabbed a finger at her chest. "*I* didn't do anything. *He* left."

Her mother stood, threw her cloth napkin in the middle of her plate of food. "You're lying."

"I am not lying."

But her mother didn't listen. "I had it all planned, how he was going to take care of you, make sure you were okay."

"I don't need that, Mom." But a little voice said she did. Last night proved it. If Luke hadn't arrived, what would those people have done to her?

"You can't take care of yourself. You never have." Her mother put her hands to her waist. "Look at your job, just a bookkeeper after your father paid all that money for college. He had to loan you the down payment on the condo, too. And don't think I don't know about all those men. Luke was the one that would have made all the difference."

Bree felt a rumble welling up from her gut to her chest. "You mean Luke was the one who would have taken me off your hands so you didn't have to feel guilty about me anymore."

"I don't feel guilty. I've always taken care of you."

Don't say it, don't say it.

She ignored the irritating whisper. There were too many goddamn irritating whispers in her head saying she was bad and wrong and to blame for everything. Rising to her feet, she faced off with her mother. Bree was taller, she was younger.

And she was fucking angrier. "Have you forgotten the night your *husband* died? How sorry you said you were for letting me down?"

Her mother backed up a step. "We were both upset that night. We both said things."

"We were speaking the *truth*." Her eyes started to ache in their sockets. "And I am *not* the one to blame. *You* should have taken care of me."

Don't say it, don't say it. Never tell, never say it aloud.

But she would say it. "You *never* listened to me. You *never* wanted to hear."

This time, her mother backed straight into the wall. "Brianna."

"You never wanted to see." Her eyes burned, and fire raged through her blood. "Why didn't you come out and look?" The words scratched deep lines inside her throat. She couldn't breathe past them.

"I don't know what you mean." Her mother put a hand over her mouth.

"You're such a liar. You've been lying for years. You didn't even make him tear it down when I was gone. You just left it there."

"Left what?" Her mother's voice, so quiet, so timid all of a sudden. She knew exactly *what*.

"That fucking dollhouse." Bree's lips trembled and her teeth ached where she clenched them against the tears. She would not cry.

"The dollhouse?"

"Don't tell me you don't know what I mean," she shouted. Then she grabbed her mother's hand in a brutal grip and dragged her to the back door. "Don't you fucking deny it."

"I don't know what you're talking about, Brianna."

But Bree heard the truth in the weak tone with which her mother said her name.

She threw open the door, and together, they took the back steps and rounded the corner of the house, Bree pulling her mother all the way. The sun shone down on the pink shingles, the gay yellow siding, the latticed windows with their pretty lace curtains her mother had made, and the brightly painted flowers that hadn't faded with all the years of weather and abuse.

"What did he build it for? Why was it tall enough for him?" She threw open the door. "Why did he put that chair in there?" His old lounge chair, still with the imprint of his ass after all these years. "Why do you think he didn't get rid of it when he bought the one that's still sitting in *your* den?"

Her mother clasped her hands tightly together in front of her. "You were just a little girl. You misunderstood whatever he did."

"I didn't fucking misunderstand a thing about what he did to me. And I told you I didn't like the man in the dollhouse. I *told* you I didn't like him."

Then she was screaming, and she couldn't seem to stop. Yelling and yelling at her mother who stood crying. She couldn't even hear her own words anymore, didn't know what she was saying.

Until she saw the woodpile. And the ax, still buried in the chopping block and rusted with disuse after sitting out in the rain all winter.

Her mother cringed when Bree yanked it out of the block as if she thought her daughter might actually use the ax on her. But Bree threw it into the side of the dollhouse with all her might.

The glass shattered and flew, the flowers bled their red paint, the shingles trembled with the onslaught. She chopped and she chopped until the damn house resembled kindling. The only thing that remained standing was the chair, the one he used to sit in like a king. With her on her knees before him.

She was still on her knees, chest heaving, her cheeks wet, her eyes blind with moisture.

"I'm sorry," her mother said from so very far away.

Bree blinked. For a moment, she could see, but could do nothing more than stare at the face of the woman who had carried her in her womb and was supposed to take care of her.

"You didn't tell me details. I didn't understand." Her mother stopped. "Don't look at me like that," she whispered.

Bree said nothing. But she looked. Like *that*.

Her mother shifted, sunlight shining through the wisps of her hair. "I didn't want it to be true."

And still Bree stared at this woman who was supposed to have been a mother to her. Silhouetted by sunshine, the shadows fell across her face creating the illusion of great fissures in her skin. Or maybe the cracks were all too real.

"He told me he'd never touch you in a bad way," her mother said.

Bree closed her eyes. So her mother *had* asked him. "And you believed him over me," she finally said, her throat aching with all the things she'd screamed.

"I *needed* to believe him."

"We both believed him about everything." Bree was surprised she couldn't hear the wail of sirens in the distance, that the neighbors hadn't called the cops with all the shouting, screaming, and hacking. She stared at the ruined remains of her childhood dollhouse, her childhood prison. She'd believed him when he told her she was to blame, that she was bad, that he was forced to punish her for all the mistakes she made. That he did those things to her and made her do things to him because he loved her, because she was special, because it was his duty to train her to be good. "And oh, I was good, Mom, I was really, really good."

"You've always hated me, haven't you?"

Bree looked up, blinked, cleared the tears. Her mother was presumably the sane one. It was her father who'd been mentally deranged or whatever the hell was wrong with a man like that. Didn't that make her the guiltier of the two?

Her mother shook her head very slowly. "I know I deserve the way you feel about me. But I always loved you."

Bree believed that. "You were so weak, it didn't matter whether you loved me or not."

Closing her eyes, her mom absorbed the words like blows, holding her belly against the pain. "I deserve that," she whispered.

Bree hadn't said them to hurt. She wasn't vicious anymore, not like she'd been in the moment she'd picked up the ax; she was simply drained of all feeling. "I'm sorry, but right this moment I don't feel anything about you at all. You're not even worth hating."

She longed to go to Luke, wrap herself in his warm jacket covered in the scent of him. But she'd screwed that up. She'd lost him.

And if she didn't get to work, she'd lose her job, too. She sure as hell couldn't stay here. She pushed to her feet, her knees wobbling, and tossed the ax back into the wood pile.

"Will you ever forgive me?"

Wrapping the ratty robe tighter around herself, she turned to her mother and said the only thing she knew to be absolutely true. "I'm not sure. But I do know I'll never love you."

* * *

"ARE YOU OKAY?" RACHEL WHISPERED THE WORDS LOUDLY AS BREE pushed through DKG's front door.

"I'm fine." She was always fine. Isn't that what she told everyone?

Rachel came to the door of her office. "I mean after that thing with Denton Marbury?"

"Why didn't you ask me about it yesterday?" Bree had kept her head down, working in her office the rest of the day, but Rachel could have come in. She usually did. Bree didn't mean the question rudely. She just needed to know.

"I figured you needed time to process. I know you don't like to talk a whole lot."

Rachel was so nice. Like a mother fish flitting all around the edges of her school of baby fish, keeping them safe, checking on them, circling them to keep them close.

She was a born mother. No one would ever hurt Rachel's children. Especially not their father.

"Oh, well," Bree said. "I'm fine. Thanks for asking." It was her stock answer. She crossed the roundhouse to her office. She remembered that day last year, just before Christmas, when Rachel had walked in to find her crying. Bree had tried to say she was fine then, too. Rachel wouldn't let her alone. Suddenly all the stuff about her father dying and her mom wanting her to come home had simply spilled out. All those things that she'd kept bottled up inside. Just as they had this morning with her mother.

She kept everything inside until it spewed. Until she couldn't control what came out of her mouth. Because *nothing* had ever been fine, and she'd *always* lied about it.

What would happen if she talked?

What if she'd told Luke last night? What if she'd told him about Marbury and how he yelled at her and suddenly she felt like a little girl again, unable to defend herself, unable to stop it, the same way she'd felt in the dollhouse with her father? What if she told Luke that when her father decided she was too old to punish her any longer, she actually felt abandoned, rejected, no longer wanted or loved or special? That when she grew up, she found men who would treat her the same way and make her feel special again, even when they were hurting her? *Especially* when they were hurting her.

What if she'd told him *everything*? Would that have made him stay? Or driven him away forever?

Bree made it to her office before her limbs collapsed under her. In desperation, so she didn't have to think, she grabbed her watering can. There was still a bit left in the bottom of it. She moistened the earth in the philodendron's pot; it didn't need much. Breaking off a couple of yellowing leaves, she threw them out, then wiped off the dust dulling the shininess of the new leaves. Nurturing the plant had given her such solace in the past. It was so healthy. Because of her. Because she cared for it, babied it. Like a child.

"How are you doing, Bree?"

Erin stood in the office door, her smile too bright as if she, too, were nervous about what might come spewing out of Bree's mouth.

"I'm fine," Bree answered. *I just told my mother that my father molested me as a child and I hate her for not stopping him. So everything's peachy-keen.* She clenched her fists so the words didn't escape.

But Bree wondered what her life would have been like if her mother had nurtured her daughter the way Bree nurtured her philodendron.

Then, very rationally, very thoughtfully, no spewing involved,

Bree said, "You know, on second thought, I don't really think I'm fine at all."

The world didn't fall apart. Erin didn't yell at her or tell her she was stupid or call the men with the white coats. She simply said, "Do you want to talk?"

Bree was never honest. She never told people what she thought. She never revealed her secrets or her fears. Not to anyone. Not even to Luke.

Jesus, forget about her mother's nurturing, Bree didn't even nurture herself as well as she took care of her plant. She just took what everyone dished out. As if she deserved it. *Did* she deserve Marbury?

Maybe it was time to be honest. To say enough was enough. She would never grow if she didn't. "Marbury makes me feel uncomfortable."

Erin closed the door and took the chair across the desk. "I'm sorry about letting him get out of hand yesterday. Sit down. Let's talk."

Bree sat as ordered as if it weren't her own office. "It wasn't just yesterday. I always feel that way." She felt otherworldly, as if she were having an out-of-body experience, her soul hovering near the ceiling and watching the two women below.

"You should have told me, Bree. You can always tell me anything. We'd have gotten someone new long ago."

Bree wanted to open her mouth and say all the things she'd thought since coming to work at DKG. But she was scared. She was *always* scared. She could have been a controller if she wasn't so scared. Or a partner at an accounting firm. Or a CFO.

Instead, she was a bookkeeper who had to borrow the down payment on her condo. She would always be a bookkeeper. She would always run out to a club when she felt bad and find the first man who wanted her, let him do anything he wanted, and she'd still feel bad in the morning.

Luke was the only one who hadn't tried to make her feel bad.

"It's okay, Bree, you can say whatever's on your mind. This is closed-door here." Erin sounded like a therapist.

"I could do a better job at it than Marbury," Bree said and waited for the sky to fall on her head.

It didn't.

Erin didn't call her crazy or snort out loud with sarcasm or incredulity. She didn't even laugh. "I believe you. Shall we give it a try?"

No, no, no. She was scared. What if she failed? What if she screwed everything up and they had to pay thousands and thousands of dollars in back taxes and penalties? All those forms. All those governmental agencies.

But dammit, she had to grow up. "I could take more classes and do online research."

Erin leaned forward. "Tell me, honestly, how much of the work do you already do that Marbury simply transfers to a form?"

"All of it." The truth. Bree almost sagged with the relief of saying it. "I know I should have said something before and saved the money on Marbury's fees."

"Maybe you didn't know you could do it until just this moment," Erin answered.

Bree realized how smart Erin was. Because Bree still didn't know for sure that she could do it. She simply knew that she didn't want to be merely *fine* for the rest of her life. She didn't want to keep on living like a frightened mouse. She'd taken a lot of risks, but never the *right* risks. She had never stepped beyond her fears. She had only lived within them.

She'd moved in her father's shadow for thirty-five years, always afraid, wanting to be special but knowing she wasn't.

But he was dead. She'd held her mother's hand and watched him die. It was time to forget. It was even time to forgive. It was time to become DKG's accountant instead of just a bookkeeper.

"I think you can do the audit, too, better than Marbury ever could." Erin smiled. "How about I call him and say we've found another accountant?"

"No," Bree said, then took a deep breath. "I'll tell him."

It was time to be strong. It was time to start living outside her fears.

36

SHE WAS SEATED ON HIS FRONT STOOP, THE PORCH LIGHT HE'D left on shining against the blackness of her hair, and shimmering in a halo around her head.

Luke couldn't analyze the emotions that coursed through his body. Relief, joy, fear, hope, remorse, all of that, sure. But the only thing that mattered was that she was here.

Usually, he would have parked his car in the garage, but he left it on the driveway and walked up the path to her. He stopped a foot from where she sat on the step above him.

"You're a caretaker," she said softly.

"Yes." His heart contracted in his chest. Having no way to help her had been eating at him, but he thought of the years ahead without her, and that emptiness would eat at him even worse, until he was a shell of a man. "Tell me how to do this so we can both get what we need. Because I'm not willing to lose you."

She rose to stand several inches above him because of her shoes and the steps. "Maybe you should take me inside and make love to me the way you want to. The way you've always wanted to and I wouldn't let you."

He closed in on her, cupped her face in his palms. "It isn't the way we had sex. It's the things we did outside of that. The things we couldn't say to each other."

She laid a hand over his, holding his palm to her cheek. "You mean the things *I* couldn't say. Will you give me another chance to try?"

"Yes," he whispered. "We both deserve another chance to get it right." Then Luke took her inside and let her feed his soul.

In his bedroom, he undressed her with a tenderness she'd never before allowed him, slipping the buttons of her blouse from the holes. "God, you're beautiful."

"Tell me more," she whispered to him. After he'd pushed the blouse from her shoulders and unhooked the front clasp of her bra, she put his hands to her breasts, held her palms over them. "Are they too small?"

"They're perfect." He pinched her nipple. "Does that feel good?"

She hummed her satisfaction. "I like the pleasure and the pain. Do it harder."

He pinched the nub more tightly. She put her head back, moaned, and the scent of her arousal rose to swirl in the air around them.

"Tell me how it feels," he begged.

She dropped her head, held his gaze. "It makes my flesh burn and my body wet."

Her skin bore a rosy hue in the bedside lamp he'd turned on. He trailed a finger down to the waistband of her skirt, noting that she'd followed his order, wearing a skirt instead of slacks.

Gathering the material in his fingers, he tugged it up, slowly, revealing her thighs, then the tops of her stockings, and finally the neatly trimmed thatch of hair between her legs. "No panties." He smiled.

"I was hoping you'd call me at work and ask me to touch myself for you. You told me one day you would."

He would. He wanted it, calling her up, ordering her to the restroom to touch herself while he could hear her.

She seduced with the erotic lilt of her voice. "It made me feel all wet and sexy thinking about it, especially when someone walked into my office. Like I had this special secret."

He loved that she'd dropped another barrier, telling him what she wanted and how it made her feel. "Put my hand on you," he said.

She guided him down, cupped him against her warm, wet center. He rubbed her with the heel of his hand.

She leaned in close, lips to his ear. "I want to masturbate for you. I've always loved doing it."

Christ, she'd made him wild when she spread her legs for his pleasure. "Take everything off first."

"Except the stockings," she said. "I like the stockings. They're naughty."

He luxuriated in her desire to do these things for him. As he shucked his clothes, she dropped the skirt and crawled onto the bed, flopping back against the pillow. The stockings, sheer black against the pale skin of her thighs, were a heady sight. His cock was already hard, a vein beating in time to the rapid pulse of his heart.

He stood in front of her, stroking himself, the ache growing in his balls. "Do it for me now." He liked the pleading quality of his voice, a man desperate for a woman.

She trailed her fingers up her thighs, pulling her feet together as she did and spreading herself like a feast before him.

"Your pussy is gorgeous," he said with awe, the way he'd always felt when he first saw her naked each time she was in his bed, when he got his first glimpse of her lush sweetness.

She caressed herself from vagina to clit. Then she raised her fingers to her lips and licked the juice from them. "Do you like the way I taste?" she murmured.

"I'd fucking die for the taste of you on my tongue." The head of his cock purpled with need. "I want to watch you do this for a room full of men."

"You do?" she asked, not losing her rhythm.

"Yes. I want them all to see how sweet you are. And know that you're mine." He didn't want to give up some of the kinky things they'd done or dreamed of. He simply wanted her emotions to be different about it. "Would you like doing that?"

She rolled her hips, rubbing herself at the same time. "I liked the way you fucked me at the club. I like to be watched. I'd like all of that. But only with you doing the touching." Then she laughed. "Or me."

He climbed onto the bed, going back on his haunches, still stroking himself slow and steady. "I want to lick you to orgasm for a crowd." Finally, he leaned over her, between her legs, close but not touching. "My sweet dirty filthy little slut, I'll fuck you in front of them until you scream my name."

She raised her gaze to his as he poised above her. "You can spank me and tie me up, too."

"Damn right I will." He'd even tie her to the hook in his ceiling, but this time he'd make sure she didn't fall. It all felt different now. *She* felt different to him. She'd changed since last night.

"It feels good when you slap my bottom, then slide down to touch my pussy. You do it so perfectly."

His balls filled to bursting with the light of excitement in her eyes, the breathiness of her words. He'd loved her moans when he did those things to her.

"And I like it when you call me late at night and talk me into an orgasm." She touched his cheek. "There are no limits to how much fun we can have."

Something shifted inside him. "Why is it suddenly fun? It never was before."

Her eyes deepened to midnight blue. "I want to make it fun for you. I want to change," she whispered. "For you."

He held still above her. "You can't do it only for me."

She put a hand to his face. "You made me see that I want to. You made me see that I don't want to lose you." She rose on one elbow and put her lips to his. "I want to be different for *me*," she whispered against his mouth, "as well as for you. I might get scared and fall down again. I might hurt you when I don't mean to. But I'd rather run that risk than not have you at all." She let herself fall back down against the pillow. "You have to help me, Luke. I need you to help me. I was always asking for your help, even if I never said so in words."

For the briefest of moments, he wondered if she was simply repeating the thoughts he'd telegraphed to her. But in the next moment, he felt the truth deep inside. She trusted him. Before the night was over, he knew she'd tell him everything.

He put a hand to her pussy, touched the sweet, wet flesh. "I'll always help you, baby." Slipping a finger inside her, he worked her G-spot until she writhed beneath him. "Do you like this?" He knew before she answered that she did, but he wanted her say it.

"It's good, Luke." She rolled and pumped to match his rhythm, then gasped. "Make me come with your mouth."

He didn't wait for another invitation. It had always been about what he wanted. *Master, do you want this? Master, do you want that? Master, make me do it. Master, whatever you say.* "Tell me how badly you want it."

She cupped his cheek with her hand, closed her eyes and bit

her lip a moment with a sudden wave of pleasure, then whispered for him, "I love your tongue on me. The way you find the right spot and don't let up until I want to scream. You never miss, as if you know my body by taste and touch. As if you know *me*."

After all these months, she was finally saying what he'd always wanted to hear. It wasn't about his prowess or his ability to stimulate her body, but because he knew *her* inside and out.

"I've been dying to taste you." He crawled down her body, trailing kisses over her breasts, her abdomen, the pubic ridge, and finally the sweet, succulent lips of her pussy. "Christ, this is the prettiest pussy I've ever seen."

She laughed. "Yes, it is."

The flesh was plump and pink with arousal. He parted her and blew warm air on the burgeoning button of her clit. She wriggled and murmured nonsense. Testing with the tip of his tongue, he gave her the tiniest amount of what she'd asked for, flicking back and forth.

"Harder," she whispered. "Lick me and suck me hard."

She would always want things hard, the pinches, the licking, the fucking. It would always be an element of her desire. But now it no longer had the desperate feel to it, a way to blot out the past or give in to a ritual.

He worried her clit with his tongue, then sucked the nub into his mouth. She flooded him with moisture, the sweet, hot taste of desire.

"Oh, oh, oh," she chanted, letting herself go in a way she never had for him without being punished first.

She twisted her fingers in his hair and pulled him closer. "Yes, please, yes." She pushed against his mouth, forced him to take her harder. Her body rose and fell, then, with a cry, she crushed her legs to his head and came.

He'd never felt power in quite the same way, not when she was tied or blindfolded or he spanked her ass or called her names or fucked her in front of that crowd.

She came until he heard his name on her lips, tears leaking into her voice. "Luke, Luke."

Her taste had never been so sweet. He climbed her body and cradled her face in his palms. "Kiss me," he begged.

She offered him everything, her lips, her tongue, her soul. Pulling him tight, she gave him the taste of her mouth salted with her tears.

"Fuck me, baby." He didn't call it *making love*. *Fucking* was hotter, sexier, needier. Yet without the love, there was nothing in it.

"Fuck me," she whispered, and he felt all the love he needed. Her arms around him, she spread her legs to take him.

"No," Luke said. "Not like that. I want you on top."

He had always been the one on top, the one with the control, the power, the one doing the taking.

Men had taken control, told her what to do, forced her. He was giving back all the power that had ever been taken from her.

37

LUKE ROLLED THEM TOGETHER UNTIL HE WAS ON HIS BACK, BREE sprawled on top of him. She put her lips to his once more, her hair falling like a curtain around them. She tasted herself, but his sweetness was stronger, more potent. She'd said all the right words for him, come for him. They were things she'd done for him before, but the feeling was different. Now it tasted of freedom.

She had never ridden a man. The men she'd known didn't want a woman that way.

"I'm yours. Take me any way you want me," he murmured, his eyes dark in the single lamp he'd lit. His cock was hard, jutting up toward his belly.

"You're the only man I've been with in the last six months," she said.

"I know."

"I'm on the pill, and everything was clean on my last doctor's appointment." She always had herself tested. Stroking his cock, she kept her eyes down, focused on the flat circles of his nipples. "I want to feel you inside me."

A man had not taken her without a condom in years. They

always had them. As if before they touched her, they knew she was unclean. That it was written on her face, on her body.

Luke had made her clean again.

"There's only been you." He stroked her cheek with one finger. "But I always wanted to protect you anyway. Above all else. Now I want you to take me with nothing between us. Flesh to flesh."

It was like a vow.

Pulling back, she bent down to caress his cock with her tongue, licking away the drop of pre-come, savoring it. He was salty-sweet against her tongue. She'd always loved doing this to him, for him, despite what other men had done to her in the past. She'd loved the power of it with him, even as the power frightened her. Now she could enjoy it simply for the taste of him and that perfect groan that fell from his lips as she sucked him hard and deep.

She rose once again, leaving the glisten of her saliva on his cock. She could do this. She could be normal. She could have everything. "I want you." There was no shame, no fear. Yes, those emotions would rear their heads again. But not in this moment. And when they did, he would be there.

Lifting slightly on her knees, she laid his cock to her center, rubbed him against her, the heat of his naked flesh branding her his forever. Lowering slowly, she eased him inside, the broad tip of his cock piercing, then filling her all the way to her heart. She closed her eyes, tipping her head back to savor the feeling, so different than when she lay prone beneath him. This was her doing the taking, her staking the claim.

He cupped her breasts, feathered his fingers over her nipples. "Christ, you are so fucking gorgeous."

Yes. She was. She wasn't the ugly thing that had knelt at

her father's feet begging forgiveness. She would always have those thoughts and memories, always have to fight them. But it was all right. Luke would help her. For him, she *was* beautiful.

"Fuck me. Take me. Make me yours," he pleaded.

She rose and fell on him, a steady rhythm that stoked her fire and stroked her G-spot. He put his hands to her hips, but didn't force the pace. He let her have it the way she wanted it.

And it was so damn good. His hips were firm between her thighs, the hair of his legs soft against her calves. Then he put his thumb to her clit and rubbed her as she rode him.

"Oh my God." The touch shot her higher. She took him faster, bracing her hands on the bed beside him so she could slam down on his cock. "Yes, yes, yes," she chanted.

Then he pinched her nipple. Bree cried aloud. She liked the pain, as if there were a direct line between her nipple and her clit. When he pinched both, she felt everything cut loose with a burst of heat that shot out to her extremities, then flashed back, inward, and exploded in shards of light. She felt his throb, then the pulse of his climax. He wrapped her tight against him, thrusting up to drive deep as the heat of his come filled her, perfect and pure with nothing between them.

"Christ," he muttered into her hair.

She slid her legs down luxuriously against him, then rolled them both to the side so his cock could remain inside her.

She wanted him inside forever. "That was good," she said, her lips muffled against his chest. She suddenly felt oddly shy.

"Yeah."

She tipped her head back to look at him. His gaze was on her, eyes seeming to see straight into her head. "Did it feel like I've changed?"

He curled his finger beneath her chin. "That was perfect. And the only change I wanted was for you to let me in."

"I will."

"I won't get pissed if sometimes you pull back." He said it as if he had no doubt she would at some point.

Of course, she would. She'd get frightened, maybe a bad day at work, or a man like Marbury, a man who reminded her too much of her father. "But I'll tell you, I promise."

"Tell me now," he murmured. "Tell me what happened Thursday. Tell me why you really went to the club."

She could try to explain that Marbury had frightened her. But Luke couldn't understand that without knowing everything else, and she'd never told a soul all the details, never said them aloud. Not even this morning with her mother. Even then, she hadn't said it *all*. Her mother hadn't needed to hear it. Living in denial, she'd still known the truth deep inside.

Her mother. Sometimes, if you were to move forward, you had to put everything else behind you. You had to forgive so you could forget what needed to be forgotten.

"Tomorrow I have to go talk to my mom, and I want you to come with me." She twirled a finger in the hair on his chest. "And on Monday I have to see a man who makes me nervous and tell him he's fired. So I need to practice that confrontation with you." She would face Marbury, but it didn't mean she wasn't still scared. She would always be scared. That just made it all the more important when she confronted what she feared. It would be that much more of a triumph.

Luke tipped her chin, his gaze tender on her. "I'll help you with anything you need."

She'd never asked anyone for help. She'd never trusted anyone to help her. She'd never trusted anyone with her fears. Or her terrible secrets. Not since the day her mother had chosen to believe her father rather than her. But now, she would give Luke her trust. "I have a lot of secrets I need to tell you," she whispered. "And some of them are not so nice."

She knew without a doubt that Luke would accept her, believe her, stand by her, and never leave her.

In his arms, she was saved. With him, she could face anything, where alone, she'd been lost. She wasn't lost anymore.

Keep reading for a preview of the next
steamy DeKnight novel by Jasmine Haynes

THE PRINCIPAL'S OFFICE

Available soon from Heat Books.

HE WAS RELATIVELY NEW TO THE AREA, HAVING MOVED THERE TO start a job last fall, only five months ago. But even so, he didn't make a habit of prowling grocery stores early in the morning looking for a partner. He'd needed a couple of items, and he didn't like waiting in line, so he'd stopped in after his run along the canal. That's when he saw the woman staring at the refriger-ated juice section, like a child in front of a candy store window seeing the very thing she wanted and knew she couldn't have.

She was perfect: blonde hair just past her shoulders, a pretty profile that showcased full ruby lips, tight white T-shirt outlining mouthwatering breasts that were more than even his big hands could hold, and jeans that hugged the delectable curve of her ass. She wasn't too thin, yet seemed well taken care of. Best of all, there was no ring on her finger. He never played with married women. He came from a long line of attached players with no limits, and he wasn't about to be like any of them. He'd even gone so far as to avoid marriage for the same reason.

She was no sweet young thing, but closer to his age, forty, or possibly a couple of years younger. He wasn't into sweet young things, preferring his partners to be older, seasoned, more sure of themselves, of who they were and what they wanted. Women who were old enough to want to try something new, something daring.

He was as staid as they come during work hours, with a position that required a quiet, unwavering authority, steadfast diplomacy, and a lot of psychology. But after hours, his life was his own business. After hours, anything goes.

He smiled as she finally made up her mind and reached for the fridge door. Her breasts plumped with the movement.

Oh yeah, he'd like to try something daring with her.

RACHEL STARED AT THE ROWS AND ROWS OF JUICE BOTTLES. SHE was a frugal shopper, buying only what was on sale, because in her mind, the sale price was the real price, and anything else meant you were overpaying. She lived for coupons. Penny-pinching was the only way she could make ends meet. Sure, her ex paid half the boys' expenses since they had dual custody, but the cost of living in the San Francisco Bay area was high; gas prices were astronomical; and cable TV and high-speed Internet, not to mention the boys' cell phones, just might bankrupt her. She had a full-time job she enjoyed with excellent medical benefits, but she was a receptionist. Her salary barely covered standard monthly expenses. Her ex was the real breadwinner. Their house was underwater so they hadn't been able to unload it during the divorce settlement, and they were still waiting for the market to recover. In the meantime, she lived in it. The boys were with her every other week; teenage boys could eat you out of house and home. For the most part, she made healthy, home-cooked meals and only occasionally brought home fast food. It would have been cheaper to buy soda for the boys to drink, but she did her damndest to make sure they learned healthy habits.

So she wanted that damn juice, which was on sale at half off, plus she had a coupon. Wouldn't you know, though, the last bottle had twisted on the rollers, stuck fast, and there wasn't a grocery clerk in sight to help her out. Well, she was *not* going to be bested by a damn juice bottle. Yanking open the refrigerator door, she put a foot up on the rubberized track, grabbed the edge of the shelf, hauled herself up, and stretched until her fingers just brushed the plastic bottle. If she could just knock it a little, dislodge it . . .

"Let me help."

The male voice was deep enough and close enough to send a delicious shiver down her spine. She would have gotten out of his way, but she felt him along her side as he leaned into the fridge door with her. His hand to the small of her back set a flame burning low in her belly. She couldn't have moved if her life depended on it. Oh no, this was just too good to miss. With barely a stretch, he straightened the bottle and set it rolling down the tracks to her waiting hand.

She was breathless when she turned to look up, and up some more. He was close enough to make her eyes cross, and she could focus only enough to take in short blond hair, piercing blue eyes, and a square, smooth-shaven chin.

"Thank you," was all she could manage. She didn't want him to move. It had been so long since she'd felt a man this close, breathed in his pure male scent, musky with testosterone and clean workout sweat.

He stepped back out of the fridge slowly, his body caressing the length of hers for what seemed like eternal moments, until his heat was replaced by the cool blast of refrigerated air.

"My pleasure," he said in a deep voice that sent her blood rushing through her veins.

She was so used to her ex's average height that this man, though she was five foot five, made her feel petite. Tall and broad, he was a Viking who'd just stepped off his ship. Except for the running outfit. All in black, tight jogging pants outlined his muscled thighs, and the Lycra shirt framed his powerful chest. She was staring, probably even drooling. In days of old, yeah, he'd have been a Viking or a knight. These days, a cop or a fireman. Or a corporate raider.

The man made her remember how long it had been since she'd had sex. With the divorce and all the crap that went before, it had been two years. Two *years*. She'd been so busy and worried, she'd hardly noticed. Until *this* man had stood so close to her, awakening her.

She realized she must have been staring at him like he was an ice cream cone she was dying to lick. And suck. And swallow.

Too bad she couldn't afford a relationship right now.

"Well, thanks again." With great effort, she tore her eyes away and grabbed her shopping cart. A man was the *last* thing she needed in her life. She had enough trouble managing her sons— teenage boys were murder—not to mention her ex. No siree bob, she did not need a man.

Yet she allowed herself one last glance over her shoulder as she wheeled her cart down the meat aisle. He was watching her. His gaze turned her hot inside and out.

No, she didn't need another man in her life. But she sure wouldn't mind a little casual sex. At the very least, the Viking was something to fantasize about.

HE WAS A BELIEVER IN THE LAW OF ATTRACTION. IF YOU WANTED IT badly enough, it would come to you, whatever it was. Like attracts like. He'd felt the sizzle of her body against him. He'd felt her scrutiny, sensed her desire in the quickening of her breath, the perfume of her hormones. So when he started his engine just as she was exiting the grocery store, her full cart and a young clerk trailing in her wake to help load the haul into her minivan, he didn't feel any need to rush her, get her phone number, give her his. Law of attraction, he'd knew he'd find her again.

Or she'd find him.

ABOUT THE AUTHOR

With a bachelor's degree in accounting from Cal Poly San Luis Obispo, **Jasmine Haynes** has worked in the high-tech Silicon Valley for the last twenty years and hasn't met a boring accountant yet! Okay, maybe a few. She and her husband live with numerous wild cats (one of whom has now moved into the house of her own accord). Jasmine's pastimes, when not writing, are speed-walking in the Redwoods, watching classic movies, and hanging out with writer friends in coffee shops. Visit her at jasminehaynes.com and jasminehaynes.blogspot.com.